I0634715

HIGH SKIES
and FAT HORSES

"THERE'S A LITTLE OF THE APPO KID IN ALL OF US."

HIGH SKIES and FAT HORSES

A Novel of War and Human Imperfection

William J. Wallisch

"THERE'S A LITTLE OF THE APPO KID IN ALL OF US."

SUNSTONE
PRESS

SANTA FE

© 2015 by William J. Wallisch
All Rights Reserved.

No part of this book may be reproduced in any form or by any electronic or mechanical means including information storage and retrieval systems without permission in writing from the publisher, except by a reviewer who may quote brief passages in a review.

Sunstone books may be purchased for educational, business, or sales promotional use. For information please write: Special Markets Department, Sunstone Press, P.O. Box 2321, Santa Fe, New Mexico 87504-2321.

Book and cover design › Vicki Ahl
Body typeface › Sylfaen
Printed on acid-free paper
⊗
eBook 978-1-61139-319-4

Library of Congress Cataloging-in-Publication Data

Wallisch, William J., 1940-
 High skies and fat horses : the Story of the Appo Kid : a novel / by
William J. Wallisch.
     pages cm
Includes bibliographical references and index.
 ISBN 978-1-63293-022-4 (softcover : alk. paper)
 1. United States--Air Force--Airman--Fiction. 2. Vietnam War, 1961-1975--Fiction. 3. Alcoholics--Fiction. I. Title. II. Title: Story of the Appo Kid.
 PS3623.A36433H54 2014
 813'.6--dc23
                        2014034582

Sunstone Press is committed to minimizing our environmental impact on the planet. The paper used in this book is from responsibly managed forests. Our printer has received Chain of Custody (CoC) certification from: The Forest Stewardship Council™ (FSC®), Programme for the Endorsement of Forest Certification™ (PEFC™), and The Sustainable Forestry Initiative® (SFI®).

The FSC® Council is a non-profit organization, promoting the environmentally appropriate, socially beneficial and economically viable management of the world's forests. FSC® certification is recognized internationally as a rigorous environmental and social standard for responsible forest management.

WWW.SUNSTONEPRESS.COM
SUNSTONE PRESS / POST OFFICE BOX 2321 / SANTA FE, NM 87504-2321 /USA
(505) 988-4418 / ORDERS ONLY (800) 243-5644 / FAX (505) 988-1025

To Pat, with all of my love and thanks for insisting that I publish this book.

Thank you Rick Herrick, Donald Anderson, Alfred Kern, and James Dickey for your keen editors' eyes and literary advice. Pat, for resurrecting this manuscript and Sunstone Press for taking a chance on this tale of war and human imperfection.

Arirang

(Mountain of Happiness)

Lonely is the wind,
A restless song over the mountainside
A gentle sigh,
That breaks the silence of a golden memory of you.
Yesterday is gone,
It took my heart far from the world we knew
To build a dream
Among the ancient Pines beyond horizons of blue.
Arirang, Arirang, Mount of happiness
My heart will sing in warm contentment
When my days of wandering are through.
Arirang, Arirang, Mount of happiness
The wandering wind through ancient Pines
Recalls the golden memory of you.

  —Traditional Korean folk song

Author's Note

Among the farmers of Korea there is no better blessing than to have high skies and fat horses. To wish this for your neighbor is to bid him the promise of all things good. Those who work with the land know that a good harvest is all that a man and his family can hope to have. To wish an outsider high skies and fat horses is to care for him deeply.

1

Tolsan-Do

I first saw Tolsan-Do from the window of a weary old C-47 that finally slugged its way through some bad weather between the Korean mainland and the island. The old bird tried to make it for two days, but each time it had to turn around. Such was often the case with these choggy flights that brought personnel and supplies back and forth between Osan Air Base and the remote island-based squadrons. Once we even lost an engine for a while. I couldn't have taken another try. I had managed to get drunk on the eve of each flight. So I was perpetually riding with a magnificent hangover.

Up front were the two grubbiest pilots I'd ever seen. I don't think they felt any better than I did because they had been part of the endless party I had attended at Osan Air Base Officers' Club.

I was jammed in the cargo hold among all of the mailbags, truck parts, and supplies headed for my new island assignment. The door to the cockpit wouldn't fasten, and I could see the pilots clearly each time the plane's bucking caused the door to slam all the way open. I felt more like I was on board ship.

And the airplane was cold. I could see my breath. The GI issue winter field parka I wore felt good, with its fur-lined hood. I literally tried to wrap myself in it, with the hood pushed well forward so I'd get maximum warmth for my face. My hands pulled back into the husky sleeves, I was shivering from both the cold and the hangover. What a ride!

The left engine of the old crate was knocking and blowing. It sounded like a backfire. Every once in a while it would shoot out a cloud of smoke and crap that would go trailing off to the side and behind us, leaving a dirty black streak alongside the fuselage. I knew we weren't going to fall out of the sky, but if we did, at least it would end the cold, the bucking, and the hangover.

That went on for hours, until the pilot known as Mad Dog Murawski stuck his head out in time with the opening door and yelled, "Whitman, your island's coming up, out the window on your side."

We banked to the right, and there was a large land mass, sitting there in the East China Sea. Right away I could clearly make out the imposing mountain that lay smack in the center. Called Mount Tolsan, I already knew from the maps I'd studied that it was six thousand and some odd feet high. The island itself, Tolsan-Do, was sixty miles by forty miles, population roughly one hundred thousand South Korean souls.

We came in from the northeast and dropped very low. So low, in fact, that I could see huts, roads, and all sorts of landmarks. There were little patches of farms everywhere, and even though it was late fall a few teams of great Asian oxen were hitched and doing work in the fields. I liked the look of things. The trees on the mountainside looked like green moss covering the volcanic rock. We even flew over several good-sized towns.

Fishing villages lined the shore. I saw one after another as we flew the coastline. It wasn't long before I saw a smaller mountain, really a hill, that had the golf-ball radar domes that were the hallmark of my trade. They were really huge inflated rubber domes, kept under pressure and supported by a skeletal system of hollow tubed ribs. Inside were the radar dishes that were surely tracking our flight path.

There were several buildings by the domes. That would be radar ops, where I'd be spending a lot of time. Below the hill, I could see a large compound. That would be the radar squadron itself.

We started in. No real runway to land on, these island sites sported grass strips. I could see a group of trucks, jeeps, and vans waiting by the strip. There were also a couple of fire engines and an ambulance. The dots standing near them would be my new buddies, I thought. For one year I'd be here, working as a military advisor to the Korean Air Force. Captain Norm Whitman, screwed again.

The landing was surprisingly smooth. Coming in from the sea that way was downright spectacular. Looking out the window I could see the waves right under us, and then there was the sudden rush of grass, jeeps, trucks, people, and landing strip buildings whooshing by. It was like a blur. Then we stopped for just a moment. The engines revved again, we turned about, and taxied up the strip, led by a covered jeep with a flashing red light.

The trucks and people outside were on us as soon as we came to a stop. Before I could even stand up, the cargo door was open and the smell of fall on Tolsan came rushing in, along with five or six airmen from the American compound. Nobody even noticed me. Eager hands grabbed the mailbags and satchels as I gingerly got out of their way, edging myself through the hold to the threshold of the plane.

I stood there for just an instant. Somebody said, "Watch out, huh," and that made me step on the flatbed that was parked right outside the door. I got off that fast, too, because I could hear things hitting it. These guys really couldn't wait to unload their treasures.

A major was standing in front of the jeep that had done the leading honors, and I guessed he was going to be the new boss. I was just hung over enough to not care about how I'd handle the first encounter, so I merely set a direct course for him. As I did that I took in his face. In what was surely just a second or two, whole volumes of past history went off in my brain. Thing was, I'd seen him before. And as I started to put two and two together, I felt like I might lose control over either my ass or my stomach.

I'll bet the people at headquarters had told me a dozen times that my boss on Tolsan would be a Major Dubbs. I grimaced at how many times I'd heard that. But it hadn't sunk in; I didn't make the connection. Now the circuits lined up and I put in all of the patches. This was the same Major Harold Dubbs that I had as an ROTC instructor my freshman and sophomore years in college.

He was going to be my boss—here on this Korean island—for a whole year.

The problem was that he hated me. He had even sworn to kill me if he ever saw me again. I had made life so miserable for him—on purpose—that he even requested an early transfer from our college.

I had been a pre-med student at Maynard College. I was going to be a big surgeon. I was going to be the Surgeon General of the United States, for chrissakes. What the hell did I need with ROTC? But they made us—all of us—take the first two years, regardless of major or anything.

So, I had made up my mind that I'd do everything I could to make life miserable for these Air Force bastards who were making me—soon to be a gifted healer of mankind—take their lousy course. And Dubbs, the first and second year instructor, was the target of all of my frustration. I taunted him in class, marched out of step on the drill pad, and dreamed up scores of ways to wear the uniform incorrectly.

But the thing that I did to foul up his precious President's Review was the last straw. This review was *the* big event in the world of ROTC at Maynard. That was when the whole cadet corps was turned out for a special

Friday afternoon parade expressly to salute the president of the college. It was a big event. They filled the bleachers at the parade ground. Mostly the gung-ho guys got their girls to come out for it, but it drew a lot of others, too. I think the faculty felt obligated to attend.

What I did to kind of screw it up was to spiff up my uniform, shoes, and hat real good, but I also wore one of those glasses, fake nose, and mustache deals. I was on the outside, nearest the reviewing stand, one of those who saluted the brass when we passed. When I did, the stands gave a double-take, especially the colonel who was the commander of ROTC. Most of the crowd in the stands loved it. I mean, it was so subtle, so quiet. But boy did it get a reaction. People afterward said it was great.

Anyway, this same Major Dubbs tried to have me thrown out of ROTC so I couldn't complete the requirement. It didn't happen, but he told us in the last class that we were the biggest bunch of "snobby little rich boys" that he'd ever seen. "And, as for Mr. Whitman here," he had said, "I'll just tell you that the Air Force is permitted to take neurotics, say, but psychopaths are thrown out as soon as they're identified."

After that class, he stopped me at the door for just one more word in private. He put out his arm to stop me and whispered, "Whitman, if I didn't want to throw away fourteen years, I'd show you how a man handles these things."

I just walked under his arm and said, "Someday, maybe, after you become one," and walked off. That's when he yelled after me his promise to never forget, or something like that.

And now here he was, the same guy, standing in front of a jeep in Korea, my commander. Incredible! And there I was, walking toward him, my face still buried in the hood of my parka, hoping he wouldn't remember. Incredible! I just couldn't believe the way life worked out.

But I had found out something about myself. I always assumed things like this were really a lot bigger than they were. It had been four years since I had graduated from that school, so it was six years since he'd had me in class. One cadet, out of hundreds, and he'd been back into the hassle of the Air Force all this time, too.

"Major Dubbs?" I said.

"Yes," he said in that same dumb voice.

"I'm Captain Whitman, sir."

"Yes, I know. I think you were one of my ROTC boys at Maynard, weren't you?"

Incredible!

That initial meeting between me and Dubbs was softened a little bit by the interruptions of the men unloading the plane. They had questions about where to take what and there didn't seem to be any movies on board. "Let's hold on to what we got, sir, until the fuckers send us our movies," this staff sergeant said.

"Yeah," said Dubbs. "I'd like to see that James Bond one over again."

"Fuck 'em," yelled the sarge to the flatbed. "Hold on to the movies."

And then somebody else came up and asked about what to do about something and then the two pilots came over, and that gave me a chance to back away and look over the scene.

"Are you the new captain?" said a voice behind me.

I turned around and there was one of the oldest captains I'd ever seen, though he wasn't in that bad shape. He was just a lot older than we usually were.

"I'm Paul Fisher, sometime spiritual advisor here," he said, then put out his hand.

With the parkas on, you couldn't see badges or anything on the uniform that told you who was who, who did what. The rank on the hat was the only thing you had to go on. He might be joking about the spiritual thing. Well, I'd have lots of time to check everyone out; that was for sure.

"I'm glad to know you, Paul. I'm Norm Whitman."

He seemed a good guy, hands in his pockets, standing with me and looking around at the activity.

"Most of us come down to meet the choggies. It breaks up the routine."

"Yeah," I said. "I guess you start looking for things to do around here after a while."

"It's your mind or your liver. That's what our medic says, anyway," this Fisher guy said. I got a signal from that. Maybe there were some good parties here, at least.

By this time the trucks were pulling back and moving off the strip. Dubbs was saying goodbye to the pilots. The pilot I had done some serious drinking with came over to me.

"Whitman, take care of yourself. We'll keep bringing you beer as long as the weather holds."

"After last night, Mad Dog, I've decided to give it up."

"Yeah, sure," he said.

"We'll probably talk on frequency next time," I said, because I knew I'd be working on the hill, flight following the choggies on radar and radio when they came in.

"Right," he said and caught up with his buddy.

They soon had the old bird cranked up and taxiing down the runway. All the trucks stayed for the takeoff. Then off they went, dipping a wing as they turned to follow the coast around for a northern heading back to Osan. I was really here now, I thought.

"Whitman." It was Dubbs. "Come on and I'll haul you up to the squadron area. Your stuff's on the trucks somewhere."

I had forgotten about my gear.

"I'll see you later, Norm," Paul said. "I'm riding back with the ambulance."

"Oh, Okay. Right, Paul." I said.

"Father, if you don't mind, your Jewish chauffeur is waiting to take you back to the Vatican," said this bespectacled enlisted guy.

"Norm, this is our medic, Sergeant Goldman."

"Not another officer! I thought we were getting rid of them. But as long as you're here, Captain, sick call is every morning in the dispensary, or in the club every night."

"It'll take you several months to get used to this character, Norm," said Paul, grabbing the medic by the arm and giving him a few mock punches.

"Just don't pull rank on me, sir," said the medic.

"Let's go, Whitman," shouted Dubbs, already swinging his jeep around.

So this Paul Fisher was a chaplain, a priest. He looked like a good guy. The medic was a smart ass, but the kind that I liked. Two good guys, one bad guy, so far. But it was going to take a lot of good guys to make up for one Dubbs.

He pulled the jeep up alongside me, and I got in. There was a grubby dog in the back seat.

All of the other vehicles were winding their way around the flight line toward the dusty road beyond. Dubbs followed and we were soon riding along a Tolsan road.

This was farming country. There were fields on either side of the road. It was evident that the powerful Asian ox was the primary source of farm power, though there were also some strange looking trucks out in the fields, too.

The farmers lined their fields with rock fences that stood about five feet high. You could see those things running everywhere, carefully and sturdily built from the volcanic rock of the island.

Dubbs was telling me that there was a steam bath in the BOQ, but I was more interested in the countryside. We passed through a small village every once in a while, filled with thatch-roofed Korean huts. Mostly you saw Korean women around them, working on the ground. Outside of one large village there was a large, muddy pond. I'll bet there were fifty women strung out around its shore, banging away at their day's washing with a wooden club.

"They call that a Tolsan washing machine," Dubbs said. "How'd you like your old lady to sit out on a shit pond like that and beat on your shirts?" he added, laughing,

By keeping my attention on the scene, I avoided answering him. And then we were in the town I had spotted from the air, just about two miles from the squadron.

"What's the population?" I asked.

"Oh, I guess this'd be around five thousand or so. I get down here once in a while, but it smells like any other place in Korea."

It had a wonderful, strange smell, I thought. The stores and houses were built right next to each other. Most shared common walls. There were sidewalks of a fashion, with a ditch running between them and the street. Gray and brown were the colors that hit your eye, and the impression you got was that of a very busy place. The street was fairly broad and held a fantastic mixture of jeeps, trucks, oxen drawn carts, and—everywhere—bicycles.

There were people on the sidewalks, and people on the streets. They were walking at a pretty good clip, preoccupied with direction. A lot of women had children strapped on their backs. Many carried large bundles on their heads. The bikes were loaded with goods. It was incredible how much a Korean could put on a bike. They were a primary source of transportation, piled high with things like sticks, old soft drink cans, or straw mats.

All of this activity had a certain noise about it. It was like a clanging, like two pieces of metal banging together. And you could hear hucksters yelling their wares and goods above the din. I liked the feel of it, and I wished they knew it.

Dubbs was swearing and maneuvering the jeep around the slower moving traffic. There were a number of carts being pulled by Koreans. These had long handles. The guys just got in front of them, picked up the handles, and pulled.

"Goddamn bastards! They just keep walking in front of ya," he yelled. Then he beeped the horn over and over as he swung around a man pulling a cart loaded with old bicycle tires. As we passed, Dubbs yelled out my side

"Yeah, you dumb bastard, you better look at me." He did look at us, but his face was passive and showed only the concentration of his pull. "I'd love to run his ass right over," he said.

I gave the man a smile. But he looked away. That made me feel awkward.

Then we were out of the town and took a hard left turn. More rock fence lined fields and then a curved arch that announced in both Korean and English that you were entering the 771st ROKAF Aircraft Control and Warning Squadron. A pretty spiffy looking Korean guard, complete with white gloves and silver helmet, waved us through.

Up until this time it really hadn't been essential to talk. But now we were going to stop the jeep and get out, and Dubbs and I would have to converse. Yet I supposed this all wasn't really so bad because he'd been fairly civil on the way up. Oh, he was still a clod. He had made asses of us both driving through the town. But he was trying to communicate with me.

"Here she is," he said. We pulled up in front of a neat little cluster of Quonset huts, painted white and blue. They reminded me of a YMCA camp I'd once been to. "This here's the Q."

"Looks great," I said, trying to sound enthusiastic about it, him, life, everything.

"Well, it's not great," he said.

We stood in front of the jeep, and he pointed out the American headquarters building, our dining hall, the supply hut, the firehouse, motor pool, and NCO Club. They were built on either side of the street that ran through the American compound. On a small ridge above it we also had a small BX, the medical hut, enlisted dorms, something called the hunting lodge, and the civil engineer's building. It was all neat as a pin, clean, and painted white and blue.

The trucks were being unloaded. Things were being carried into the supply area, dining hall, BX, club, and headquarters. The enlisted guys were dressed in fatigues and parkas. They all looked like green clad delivery men, bringing an order.

"I'll show you the inside of the Q," Dubbs said. We went through the door, into a long hallway. One side of the place was hallway and the rooms were partitioned off on the other. "We got lots of rooms, but I want you to take this one down here," he said, swinging open a bare little room with a bed, dresser, table and chair. It was okay. "You can really have a good time fixing these up like home."

"This'll be fine," I said.

We walked down the hall and pushed open a swinging door. "This is your shithouse, here." We walked into a large, neat bathroom. It had three stalls, a couple of showers and sinks, and tile flooring. It was really large. He pushed open another door, and there was a little Korean woman putting clothes into a washing machine.

"This is Mrs. Kim. She's our house girl and her husband's our houseboy." Mrs. Kim pushed her hair in order and bowed several times in a smiling, embarrassed sort of way. "Mrs. Kim, this is Captain Whitman." She looked very nice.

"I am so happy to meet you," I said.

"Well, let's keep going. You'll see plenty of her. She'll keep your duds and your room clean. Her old man's part of the deal, but he ain't as good as her."

"Nice meeting you, Mrs. Kim," I said again as we backed out of the room.

Dubbs stood just outside the john, in the hallway, and held up his finger. "Now, I got most everyone on this end of the Q. I'm on the other end, and that's pretty much my shithouse down there. Now the steamer's in my end, so you can use it like from three in the afternoon to about five. Otherwise, I want everyone down here. I like quiet."

"Sure, this'll be fine," I said, trying to get along with the asshole. I'd never had a steam bath in my life, anyway.

"As I remember, you're a little bit of a smart ass, so I'm just tell'n you I don't want a lot of horseplay in the Q."

So he remembered me. I just looked at him. And then I put my eyes on the floor. I'm a funny guy. I just can't seem to get those kinds of orders right. For some reason I just have to do what I'm not supposed to, even though I know better. Dubbs was going to have trouble. I fully intended to take my first shit in his "shithouse."

Two sergeants came down the hallway and broke the silence. "Major Dubbs, the Captain's stuff is in the living room," one said, and added a "Hi, Captain Whitman."

"Hi," I said. "Thanks for bringing my stuff, gents."

"Okay, well you might as well get settled in," Dubbs said.

"Yes, sir."

Dubbs turned on his heel and nearly pushed the two sergeants out the door. I waved to them. One said over his shoulder, "Come over to the club, Captain. You can meet the rest of the troops. We're all there every night."

"I'll do that for sure." And then I was alone in the BOQ, thinking that it was going to be a long year.

I carried my bags into the room, and it only took me about ten minutes to put everything away. You brought only bare essentials. All the rest was shipped. That was called hold baggage. You shipped that months ahead of your departure. I had, of course, waited till the last minute, so it didn't even get off until I had left Bedford Air Force Station. My situation left me with couple of sets of fatigues, a change or two of civvies, essential shoes, a bathrobe, and a picture of Angie and the kids.

That all put away, I just sat in the chair and looked around. The room had a curved ceiling. It was plywood walls, painted white, blue trim. There was a window, but it looked out on the side of a steep hill that was only about three feet away from the wall of the hut. I had a view of the side of a grassy hill.

The bed was a single, GI bed. Iron. The dresser was a GI dresser, some kind of stained wood. Then there was a long closet, with a sliding door. It had a light that burned in it to keep out mildew. Mirror above dresser, shiny linoleum floor, light on ceiling, desk lamp, desk, chair, and door. That was my room. Fix it up like home, hell. I knew I'd never change it beyond where it was right then.

There was no one in the Q, outside of the Kims. It was very quiet. I thought I'd maybe take a walk outside, but I felt hesitant, shy. I didn't want to see Dubbs again. When, I wondered, do you eat? Maybe I'd just sit in this room, away from what was ahead.

I knew how and why I had gotten into this mess, but it was still incredible. Even after being in for three years, I was still amazed that I was in the Air Force! Doing a job called Weapons Controller! Weapons Controller. I had first thought it was some guy who sat in a big warehouse. People might come in and say, "Give me two tanks, an airplane, and six handguns." It wasn't that. It was radar.

What we did was to sit in a dark room and peer into a yellow radarscope that had a turning sweep line that "painted" flying objects yellow. We identified the bad yellow dots and ran good yellow dots—that could shoot missiles—against them. That was how the nation carried out air defense, protecting itself against a bomber invasion. And you could win something called air superiority that way, too, if you were fighting a war on some other guy's territory.

I was sitting in this Quonset hut, in Korea, because I'd been sent to teach the Koreans how to run those yellow "blips" at each other. And even though I could say all of that, it seemed incredible that I ended up doing this job. I, who graduated from one of the best liberal arts schools in America. Talk about fate. Career planning. I had about as much imagination as a whore standing on a street corner on payday.

What I decided I needed was a drink. Waltzing down the hall, I soon discovered a rather nice, well-stocked corner bar in the living room of the Q. I resolved to take a crap in Dubbs' shithouse, and then have my first drink on Tolsan.

I tramped down the Q hall on the linoleum floor with my field boots, enjoying the sound they made. I picked up the pace. I marched by the bar in the living room, saluted and said to the booze, "I'll be right back." Then I marched down the hall to find that shithouse. The boots sounded great, so I picked up my cadence and laid those boots down so hard I thought I'd be able to shake the place down if I had about eleven more miles of hallway.

I came through that swinging door with a bang. It even made a cracking sound on the wall when it hit. I damn near drove it off its hinges and on through the wall. I arrived in Dubbs' shithouse in a sound of glory. But I didn't expect to see a Korean woman standing there by the sinks, towel hastily wrapped around her, cringing in fear of whatever she imagined was coming through the door. She must have just come out of a shower. God! I didn't think we had a ladies' bathroom.

I even looked around, just for an instant. There were urinals everywhere. This had to be the right place. She looked at me, and then ran around the corner, probably back to where the showers were. I said, "Excuse me," and backed out. Was that Mrs. Lee? No. This lady was much taller, and really a hell of a lot better looking. Was she somebody's woman? A moose?

I decided I'd leave her be, and go for the real business of getting that drink. Maybe she was somebody who snuck a shower once in a while. Or maybe . . . she belonged to Dubbs?

I went back to the bar and soon I happily poured myself a double scotch on the rocks.

"I see you found the watering hole, Norm." It was the guy from the flight line. He was coming in from outside and still had his parka on.

"I can always find it," I said, toasting my drink. "I'm sorry . . . ah . . . are you a priest, or a chaplain or something?"

"I am," he said.

"Priest? Catholic?"

"Yes."

"Well, Father, I'm really glad you're here," I said, and I meant it.

"Call me Paul, or Father Paul. Whatever feels right," he said taking off his parka. Sure enough, there was a silver and blue cross sewn on his fatigues. It made me feel just a little less homesick.

"Can I get you something?" I was firmly in place in the bartender's position.

"What are you having?"

"A healthy belt of scotch," I said.

"That'll do just fine, Norm."

I poured him one, and I was just about to say something when Dubbs came into the room from his end of the Q.

"Listen, I thought I told you about staying the hell outta this end of the building, period. You scared the hell outta my . . . my friend." He looked at the father. "He walked in on Sue down there."

"Well, Harold, it's his first day. There's a lot to take in."

"Yeah, well, I don't want him down there like that. I told you that, Whitman."

He was really steamed. What a jackass!

"Sir, I'm sorry, I thought I heard you walking around down there and I was going to invite you for a drink."

"Well . . . thanks . . . but don't look for me down there."

I could see a figure behind him, leaning halfway out of a room, taking all of this in. That must be the friend I barged in on. It hadn't taken her long to send out an SOS.

"My interpreter takes a shower down there sometimes . . . and you shouldn't be down there like that."

I just stood there. This was just too much. I had this guy up tight already. There I was catching hell, only on the island a couple of hours. I didn't say anything more. The dumb ass just kept on standing there and she just kept on leaning out to hear. Then he turned and left. He went into that room.

"Ah, well, Norm, you've met Sue now. That's the spirit. Get around. Don't be a stranger." He patted me on the shoulder.

"Is Sue what I think she is?" I asked.

The priest raised his glass and downed the rest of his drink.

"What a start I've made." I poured us each a full glass of scotch.

"Ah, don't worry about that," he said. "Dubbs should be the last of your worries."

"Geez, Father," I said, feeling the effect of the second drink, "I was screwed with this assignment before it even started." And I went on to tell him about my previous encounters with Harold Dubbs, Major, USAF. He got quite a kick out of the whole thing. I could tell it well, complete with voice impressions.

"Can he hear this? I just happened to think. They're right next door," I said with a lowered voice.

"Hell, Norm, I've always wondered if he could. I've kind of left it up to the angels. If he can't hear you, then you're okay. And if he can hear you, then you're keeping everything above board. Either way, you're in good shape." He said all of that in a magnified hoarse whisper.

"Dubbs said I shouldn't be down here like this." I said in a whisper driven by the fourth scotch. "Down here like what . . . in my fatigues, right? How should you, I mean, one be down here? I should go and get some kind of crazy outfit on, bang on his door, and say 'Can I be down here like this?' And then keep on trying on outfits, until he says, 'Yes, you can be down here like that. That's more like it.'"

That seemed very funny, and we made up descriptions of outfits. Doctor, gorilla suit, Batman, Cupid, and him dressed for high mass. One thing was for sure, this was one damn good chaplain.

After about an hour of belting it down hard, he finally said, "Shall we go eat?"

And we headed for the dining hall. I had a friend. Angie would be so pleased. It was a priest.

The two of us set out for the dining hall, another Quonset hut just up the street, but Father Paul altered the plan with a great suggestion.

"Norm, let's go to the NCO Club for one drink with the troops before dinner. You can meet them all right away."

"Great idea," I said.

And we did it. As soon as we walked through the door, Sergeant Goldman, the medic, spotted us.

"Here they come, slumming again. Here come our leaders. Get the Father a glass of wine. He's practicing for Sunday. Can't seem to get the wine to blood part down, can you, Father?"

"Ah, Norm, if you didn't already feel just a little insane here, Goldman will fix that. He's also good for reminding you of your sins. He keeps you humble and contrite, don't you Goldman?"

Goldman looked a lot like Groucho Marx, though he was just a skinny little guy. He seemed very bright, and it was obvious that he really liked the priest.

"Captain Whitman, welcome to the NCO Club. We can always use your money, sir. Mr. Kwak here can mix anything, and we have a hell of a lot more to offer than that little hole in the wall you have over in the BOQ. A place, I might add, that I'm not worthy of being invited to."

"Goldman, you know Major Dubbs would love to have you over there with him every night," the priest said, patting the medic on the shoulder.

"Actually," Goldman said, "at this moment, I quote Groucho Marx when he said, '*I don't want to belong to any club that would accept me as a member.*'"

Paul turned toward the bar. "Mr. Kwak, this is Captain Whitman," said the priest to the tall Korean behind the bar.

"I happy to meet you, sore." He was a dapper looking fellow, very proud of his position. Little wonder, this was a good job. Any Korean lucky enough to work on an American installation was doing very well indeed.

We ordered more scotches and talked with Goldman. He was a street-wise New Yorker who taught in the medic training center before this remote assignment to the island. I'd guessed he was a pretty good medic. It turned out that he was also the manager of the NCO Club. He didn't really like officers; but if he approved of you, he was the kind of NCO you'd be damned glad to have on your side.

"So, if you always had this dream to be a doctor, how the hell did you end up a radar officer in the East China Sea?"

"I flunked organic chemistry," I said, already drunk enough to be pouring out my life story to them.

"Well, you don't want to be a doctor anyway. They're the officers. They don't know a damn thing about medicine."

"Marty's a hell of a doctor himself," the priest said, finishing off what must have been our fifteenth drink.

"Look, Captain Whitman. We have an additional duty here called medical officer. When they kicked Captain Wakin off this rock, I was left without a medical officer. I'll think it over and maybe you'll get the job. Just keep your nose clean, sir."

"Norm, that'd be quite an honor. Goldman is pretty fussy about who gets to supervise him." The priest handed me another scotch. The jukebox was playing, and I was feeling no pain. I liked the NCO club.

"Supervise! Nobody would dare supervise me, Father! The last officer that tried to supervise me is in Leavenworth."

One by one, the rest of the troops came in for a drink. They had come from the enlisted dining hall. Father Paul and I still had not eaten, but that was the farthest thing from our minds. I met the motor pool sergeant, the supply sergeant, and the fellows who kept the electronic gear going. There were even two who kept the navigational aids in shape. In all there were twelve. Their club was really something for such a small number.

Goldman and Father Paul were pretty much the center of attention. One tried to outdo the other. They either threw jabs at each other, or tried to outdo each other with stories. The stories were good.

The priest was older. As a matter of fact, he had been an enlisted man in World War Two. He had gone all through the war before getting his education and ordination. He was forty-six, which seemed utterly ancient to me at twenty-eight. We were the same rank.

"The only reason why I allow the chaplain in here every night is the fact that he was an enlisted man. I'm still putting you on probation, Captain Whitman, until I have enough to make a decision, one way or the other."

"He's Catholic, Goldman. I need parishioners."

"Not good enough." Goldman pretended to examine me carefully.

From that point on, the night turned into a haze. I drank a lot more and talked my head off. We never did eat, but I did demonstrate my raw-egg-in-beer routine. The Chaplain could do it, too. Goldman told me—after I had put three eggs down—that you could get salmonella from them, but I told him I had enough alcohol in my stomach to kill the plague. He agreed.

A lot of the enlisted guys had Korean girlfriends, and that whole group sat at the tables near the end of the club. There was a rather cozy fireplace down there. They all sort of sat there, girls silent, their boyfriends chatting away about whatever. When the guys came up for drinks, I'd meet them and we'd say a few words. But they were caught up in the girls, the whole scene of it. It almost seemed kind of melancholy to me. Especially when I'd see a girl stare away at nothing while her beau talked with a buddy.

The Father, Goldman and I ended up playing the slot machines that abounded in the club's game room. I must have poured ten bucks into them. It was the first time I'd ever played one. The combination of two cherries would keep me up for a while, but the one-armed bandits would eventually take my pile of coins. I could see how these slots bandits could hook you.

Booze always brought me into a new group quickly. If I found the party—wherever it was—I had found my kind of people. And these two guys were really the best on the site. Especially since there weren't a lot of officers around, I would have been hard pressed if the chaplain hadn't been there. Most of the enlisted types were tied up with the live downtown routine. One thing for sure, I wouldn't be messing around with the whores. All I needed was a good case of syphilis.

Dubbs did stick his silly face in the game room at one point, and the chaplain and I had said something like "come on in."

He just shrugged, and said, "I wondered who was making all the noise."

"He sure hates noise, Chaplain," I said, pulling down the arm on the twenty-five-cent machine.

"He sure hates us," said Father Paul, getting two cherries.

By the time the club closed I had seen about all of the Americans. There was a Lieutenant Andy Packer who was also a controller, but I missed him. Father Paul told me Andy had been on the hill when I came in, but had said he was going downtown after his tour in the darkroom was over. Father Paul also said we had a civil engineer, but that he was always downtown with his girl, or *yobo*.

At around one in the morning Goldman closed down the club. The GIs had taken their girls downtown to their hooches for the night. It was just the three of us, plus the cook and bartender.

"Now we'll teach Norm the language by way of song," announced the priest. "This one, Norm, is sung to the tune of *Frére Jacques*. It's a round."

He stood up on a barstool, putting his hands up, like Leonard Bernstein.

"*Yobo sayo, yobo sayo, e-dee-wah, e-dee-wah. On-ya-ha-shaw-meka, on-ya-ha-shaw-meka, kimchi* pot, very hot."

We got pretty good at singing that, or at least it seemed so.

"Norm, this is a grand way to learn the language," said Father Paul, still standing atop his bandstand.

"I feel like I'm in some kind of Donald O'Connor musical," I slurred.

"*Yobo-sayo* means 'hello.'"

"*Yobo-sayo*," I said.

"And *e-dee-wah* means 'come here.'"

"*E-dee-wah*," I answered, playing the part of Donald O'Connor.

"*On-ya-ha-shaw-meka* means 'How are you?'"

"I'm fine, but I need a refill," I said.

"And '*kimchi*,' Norm, you've eaten '*kimchi*,' haven't you?"

"No, I only eat scotch on the rocks."

"*Kimchi*'s hot, and it's made in a big clay pot. If you've got stuffed up sinuses, it'll help a lot," said Goldman, clapping his hands together.

And then we sang the song again, my pronunciation getting better all the time.

"Okay, now, since this is Norm's first night on the island, we all have to go downtown and eat *kimchi*."

"Father, his first night's over and we're working like hell on the first morning," Goldman protested.

"The *kimchi* pot's very hot and we need for him to have some a very lot."

"Okay, okay, I'll lock up and we'll go get some *kimchi*."

I sort of staggered along with them as the lights went out and things clicked shut. Then we were out in a beautiful, quiet Korean night. There wasn't any overcast at all, and the stars were so bright that you were almost lighted by them. They were so dramatic they almost made noise. More rightly, it was like an organ was playing some heavy Bach piece.

While I stood and looked at the stars, the priest and the medic shouted at each other, the upshot being that Goldman would bring around our transportation. I just stood there watching that sky.

"Norm, my boy, you're going to make a happy addition to our Tolsan family. Goldman approves of you, so there's smooth sailing from here on in."

"How wonderful. Would you please have him talk to Dubbs? Look at that sky," I said, changing the subject. "Did you ever see anything like that?"

"It's truly the mind of God," he said, working hard to maintain his balance. But he was serious.

"There's always a sky out here like this. Everywhere in this part of the world, Norm. The eastern family of oceans and waters does it. It looks like this in Hawaii, and out on the islands of the Pacific. I watched these stars in better days, younger days. I watched them before, during, and after the war." This sounded more like a preacher.

Two headlights and the loud roar of a big vehicle interrupted the peace and the sermon. It was Goldman in the site ambulance.

"Hop in," he commanded from the cab, and we did. The cook and bartender jumped in the back.

"*Yobo-sayo, yobo-sayo*," we sang together, riding through the dark compound, the security gate, and out onto the town-ward road. I was having a ball.

"Goldman," I shouted over the engine and the priest's singing, "do you always travel around in an ambulance?"

"Only when I'm going to make a house call," he said, holding the wheel against the bumps and pulls of the rutted dirt road.

When we came into the town, it was pretty well closed down. Goldman took each of the employees to their houses. What a good guy. He didn't just drop them off on a corner.

It must have been two in the morning. But he pulled the big ambulance purposely and deliberately in front of a rather dark section, just as if we had business there.

"Let's go," he said. The three of us piled out. The stars were here, too, though the quiet was not as deep. I could hear dogs barking off in the next block. The town gave off a hum, a strange sort of noise that said there were people here at rest.

Goldman was banging on a door, and sure enough the lights went on inside the place. It looked like a garage. A face appeared at one of the garage-like windows, a Korean face, of course.

"Mista Goldie, you comma right in here," the Korean said, smiling.

"Mister Min, we have *maekchu* and *kimchi* now, okay?"

"Yessa," he said and turned his face toward the back. He yelled out some loud words in Korean and got back a melodic answer, spoken by a woman.

"She come with it soon. You sit down now."

"What is this? The local snack bar?" I said.

"This is Mr. Min the proprietor of the icehouse. You can always get a cold beer here."

Goldman sat down on the floor, on a mat that could easily accommodate the three of us.

"Sit down, Padre," he said. "Captain, you sit down, too. We're going to eat the national dish of Korea."

Our host, Mr. Min, passed out these huge cold bottles of Korean beer. It was called OB. I couldn't believe the size of the bottles. After all of the scotch, the beer just slid down my throat. I was thirsty for liquid that didn't burn. Swig, swig. It was great. I made bubbles run up through the liquid as I chugged.

Then I looked around the icehouse. It was a very clean, neat place. I turned, and sure enough, there was a large ice room in back of us. Stacked up in rows were huge blocks of crystal clear ice, very much like the stuff I saw delivered to neighborhood houses when I was a kid. The big thing then was to ask the iceman for chips to suck on.

"Mr. Min."

"Yessa."

"Do you give little kids ice chips to suck on?"

"Yessa."

"So did the iceman on my block," I said, trying to focus my eyes on him.

"Smalla world, Captain," he said.

He handed me a fistful of ice chips. I drank my OB beer and ate the ice chips with relish. It all tasted wonderful.

Then through the door came this grubby looking GI. He was a first lieutenant in fatigues, no hat, mud caked up to his knees. He was holding a dirty hanky to his bleeding nose. It was the first time I saw Packer.

"Oyster, my man, you're just in time to meet the new senior radar controller," said the priest.

"Geez, I'm really glad I found you guys. You'll never know how happy I was to see that ambulance, Doc."

This guy was the original *Sad Sack*. He had a slow way of talking that sort of rolled out of his mouth. The accent was somewhat southern. He was as pale as the ice, and the bare bulb hanging from the ceiling made him seem ghostly.

"Norm, meet Andy Packer. We all call him Oyster."

He smiled a rather nice smile for the time of night and the circumstances, changed hanky hands, and shook mine with a clammy bloody hand.

"I knew you were coming down today 'cause the choggy pilot told me you were on board. Geez, I'm sorry I didn't stick around. I had to get downtown. Turns out I shudda stayed where I was."

He slumped down, leaning against the wall. The nosebleed had stopped, meantime, and he put the hanky back in his pocket. Some of it still stuck out. One leg was stretched out, the other he somehow tucked under his butt. What a sight. They gave him a beer.

"Lieutenant Oyster, sir, what the hell have you done now?" said Goldman, feigning a glare of grave disapproval.

"Well, I went down to see if I could catch Adja backdooring me, and she wasn't even in the hooch. But I did find every whore, old man, mother, derelict, and bum in this part of Korea in there eating my food, playing my tapes, and sit'n their asses on my goddamn bed."

"Well," said the Priest, "did you stand up, assert yourself, and kick them all the hell out of there?"

"Gosh Padre, I couldn't do that. It wasn't their fault. She's the one who lets 'em in. I can't create a big thing downtown."

"Well, what the hell *did* you do, Lieutenant, sir?" said Goldman.

"I guess I walked around town for an hour or so looking for her, kinda giving all of them a chance to clear out, anyway. And when I did get back, the place was all locked up."

"There's more?"

"Yeah, I went over to the teahouse and got something to eat, along with a beer or two."

"And now you're here?"

"Naw. That bitch. I went back over. When I did, I saw the lights go out inside just as I turned the corner. So I banged like hell on the doors. She didn't let me in. So I went out back, broke the window out with a stick, and went on in."

"Good, Oyster! That's the stuff!" said the priest.

"Yeah and somebody was in there with her. When I got in, he hit me in the face and made it out of the door."

"Jesus Christ," said the priest.

"Yeah, I know, she's no damn good. I told her this was it. I moved out."

"You moved out? Hell, you own the place. Why didn't you kick her the hell out of there?" barked the medic. "Honest to God, Andy, you're such a wimp."

"Well, Doc, you don't throw women out in the middle of the night. She'll go. She'll go."

Then the *kimchi* came. Mr. Min seemed oblivious to the hour. He and this cute little Korean woman placed big bowls of it in front of us as if they were serving royalty. They were all smiles.

"Hot," said the woman with the most wonderful smile as she put it in front of me. She put her hand in front of her big grin so I'd not see it. That was the polite custom.

Now the *kimchi* itself looked like a big wilted salad, covered with pink spices. Packer was mumbling about something, but I turned my attention to the treat ahead. This was an event. My first taste of *kimchi*!

God, it was hot. I couldn't believe it. The stuff was pure fire. So hot, in fact, that I felt real pain in my gut. I must have been very animated because I suddenly realized that I was the center of attention. Everyone was laughing at my reaction to the food. I immediately grabbed for the rest of the beer and drank the bottle dry.

"Wow: That's hot . . ." I managed to get out. But then I couldn't say anything else. I was gagging. I was actually short of breath. My eyes and nose were running.

"They put this all in a big crock, Norm, and bury it underground for a couple of months so that it'll ferment. Winter *kimchi's* the best kind."

"Best kinda winter *kimchi* you got there," said Mr. Min.

"Well, I like it," I gagged. "And I'm going to get used to eating it, because I want to be a good Korean while I'm here."

That brought some silence to the group.

"You like the taste ah, sore?" said Mr. Min.

"I do, but I'll have to get over the heat, that's all."

"I fix."

He said something to the woman. She left.

"Mr. Min likes your attitude, sir," said Goldman. "I'm marking down 'good attitude' in my book. Good attitude, Captain Whitman, first night on station. Looks good for medical officer."

She returned with another bowl. I took it, bowed from my sitting position, and ate a forkful.

"Mild. Good," I said, chewing.

"Mild," she said and laughed. "Mild."

"These guys zapped me with a hot bowl when I got here, too," said Packer. "That's part of being a green bean newbie."

"Well, I like this bowl and before I'm gone I'm going to have an eat off with Mr. Min here. With a little practice, I'll be saying, 'bring me giants.'"

The lieutenant blew his nose absent-mindedly, and it started to bleed again.

"Pinch it, Oyster," Goldman said.

"I am. I know."

"You don't know shit," Goldman said.

The priest had been sitting straight as an arrow, but all of a sudden I noticed that he was now curled up and sleeping like a log.

"Well, folks," said Goldman, "it's beddie-bye time for the padre. He's going into his last act for the evening. Let's go. Sir, if you can control your nose, we'll carry him to the ambulance."

A couple of bows, and we bid the Mins goodnight. Goldman gave them some money. We staggered outside with our load. The doors opened, and he was deposited on a padded bench that ran along the inside wall of the ambulance.

"You guys keep sleeping beauty from falling and breaking his ass or something, and I'll get us back. Can you do that, Lieutenant?"

"I've done it a hundred times, with or without a bloody nose," he slurred.

And we were off. We were shut inside, so I couldn't see anything. It was just constant motion and motor noise.

"I guess you met Dubbs?"

"Yeah, and how."

"Geez, I hate to cut up the boss, but he's a real shit."

"And how."

"It's going to be strange sleeping in the Q tonight. I usually sleep with Adja."

I couldn't see him at all, but I could tell he was wishing he were with his *yobo*.

"Why don't you then?" I asked.

"Do you think I'd be dumb?" he said eagerly.

I banged on the wall, near the driver's side. Nothing. Then I banged again and yelled Goldman's name several time. The ambulance stopped. In a minute he was opening the doors.

"I know. Don't tell me. He wants out. He wants to walk back downtown, right?"

"Well, Doc, she can't help screwing up once in a while. Geez anyway."

"Okay, okay, get out. Captain, sir, hold the Father, sir." As he slammed the door shut again he said, "Officers! God, why do I bother?"

When the brakes screeched one last time, I guessed we were back at the compound.

"Okay, Captain," whispered Goldman. "Let's carefully, quietly, get him to bed. I don't want that fucker Dubbs to see him this way."

"Right," I said.

The chaplain was really more out cold than he was asleep. He really zapped out when he went, but up until that time he had been wondrously coherent. While I was thinking that, I accidentally hit the ambulance door with my butt. It slammed shut. We had put the father on a stretcher. Goldman looked over my shoulder.

"Sir, pardon me, but you're a klutz. No shit."

I said quietly, "Dammit! "

The birds were starting to sing in the trees. It was almost dawn. I was glad it would be Saturday. We could all sleep in and I didn't have to worry about showing up for work.

We got the stretcher into the Q and deposited the father on top of his bunk. I didn't even know which room was his, but Goldman had known just where to find it in the dark Quonset.

"Let's take off his shoes, and then we'll just throw this spread over him."

"Okay, Sarge. Look, doesn't he look as peaceful as a sleeping angel," I said giggling.

"Yeah, he's an angel all right."

The room had a nice overstuffed chair in it and the usual, predictable crucifix on the wall. Black bound books were scattered on the desk and dresser. I guessed his chalice was in the black box on the desk. Just for the heck of it I opened up his closet, and there were the trappings of the church, hanging neatly. A Roman collar was lying on the closet floor. I could tell Mrs. Kim was doing a great job on his linens.

"Do you want to go through his drawers now, sir, or after breakfast?" said Goldman, pulling down the single blind in the room.

"Naw, the chalice will bring enough by itself. I can't get much for the rest of the stuff."

"Come on, let's go. I'll make us some eggs over in the club kitchen."

We carefully closed the door. Down the hall, and almost out the door, my escape was halted by a familiar voice.

"Whitman . . . wait outside, Sergeant."

It was Dubbs, in his bathrobe and slippers.

"You get that drunk in?" he said, putting his fat face into mine.

"Ah, who, sir?"

"The missionary drunk. Fisher. Who else?"

"Well, we all just got in, yes. But he wasn't drunk."

"I saw you two carry him in. He was stoned."

We just stood there looking at each other. Then he leaned up against the wall.

"Whitman, you managed to pretty well establish your style first day here. Let me tell you something. This chaplain's here because he's a fuck'n drunk. He's farmed out so's he won't be crawling around, fuck'n up on the mainland. General Perry kicked his ass out of Osan and down here to this shit hole where he'll be outta the way. So, you really picked out a great pal. And Goldman's always just an inch away from being court-martialed for his fuck'n attitude. Yeah, you've picked out good friends."

"Guilt by association, sir?"

"Fuck'n up by association."

"I'm not going to fuck up, sir. But I figure my free time's my own, and we didn't do anything wrong, I assure you."

"You went downtown first night on station. I got a local operating procedure that says you have to wait one week before you leave the compound."

"You didn't tell me that, sir."

"I don't have to. You're supposed to go over to the headquarters and read the OI file."

"I'll do that tomorrow."

"Yeah, you better."

Then he turned and walked away. Goldman was standing outside. Dubbs stopped at the screened window and looked out at him.

"When you take the employees home you're supposed to get that vehicle back ASAP, Sergeant Goldman."

"Sir, we were late closing up tonight. I had to make a coin count on the machines and pull a spot inventory. We got out late. Sorry, sir."

"Goldman, you always have the wrong answer for me. Do you understand what I'm say'n?"

"Sir, I know it's late, but I wonder, sir, if those pills worked okay with Sue, sir?"

Dubbs looked out through the screen at the medic for a long moment.

"You just keep in mind what I'm say'n." Then he looked around at me. "Loafing around with enlisted men ain't any better down here than it is anywhere. We have to share a club 'n all, but it still makes you less effective."

Then he walked back down the hall.

"Goodnight, sir," I yelled after him. I walked outside where Goldman was. "Hey, I'd better not do anything more. I'm just going to get you in hot water. I'd better rack it."

"You afraid he'll write you down for associating with enlisted scum?"

"Let's go get the eggs," I said, grabbing him by the arm. "That's the least of my worries."

We walked along in now what was the dawning morning. It was a beautiful one, too. Korea was known as the Land of the Morning Calm. At least out here it was.

When we got inside the club we sat at the little snack bar in the club's rather nice dining area. Goldman fixed great eggs, and hamburger was the meat.

It was really a good session for me because he took off his mantle of jabs and cynicism for the most part and really filled me in on the site and what was going on. It came as no surprise that everyone hated Dubbs. But the thing I really wanted to know about was the chaplain's status.

"Look, the chaplain's got problems. He's a great guy, but he's trying to work something out right now. I think I'm going to like you, Captain, but I'd be breaking a confidence if I told you what's bothering him."

"Is he in trouble or something, or what?" I said, scooping eggs and pressing a little more.

"Naw, he's okay. The big shits up in Osan just found it convenient to ship him down here. I think they were looking for an excuse. He did battle on behalf of a couple of enlisted guys as it was. So, when his problems grew a little, they put him on the choggy."

"Man, I'll tell you one thing, it's unusual for a site this small to have its own chaplain."

"Yeah, I know. I know. And that makes him feel silly, too. Hell, you and Packer and maybe three more are the only GI micks on station. But he has his service every Sunday. And a lot of guys go, just to make him feel useful."

"That's too bad."

Well, I thought, I wasn't the only one down here that felt a little uncomfortable. At least I was here because there was a genuine job.

"How does Dubbs treat him?"

"What do you think?"

"Yeah, I guess. Dubbs chewed on me a little back at the Q. He insinuated that I'd be keeping bad company with him."

"Well, Dubbs is the biggest asshole on the station. Hell, he keeps his whore right in the Q!"

"Yeah, I think I met her. I was clowning around, and I walked in on her as she was coming out of the shower."

"We always have that on Dubbs. He isn't going to go too far with me, anyway, I'll tell you that."

The medic was easy to talk to. His New York accent sharpened his features.

After we finished our eggs, I began to feel the need to seriously think about sleep. Sun was streaming in the club windows. It wasn't anything new for me to stay up all night long. It was just nice that I wouldn't get hell from Angie for doing it.

"Hey listen," said Goldman, "you'll be good for the Father. And for chrissakes, watch out for that damn Packer. He's unbelievable."

"Boy, he sure must love that girl."

"Yup, yup," Goldman said, imitating Packer's voice and gestures. "My name's Andy Packer. I'm from Oyster, Virginia, you know. That's where they pack the oysters in the cans ya buy. Geez, ma girl Adja's the sweetest little thing you've ever seen, you know. She shits on me, but I'm too goddamn dumb to care, you know."

"Yeah, he jumped when I asked him if he wouldn't feel better getting out and going back downtown."

"Hell, he does that kinda shit all the time. God, just try to keep him straight half of the time, will ya?"

"He likes the Koreans, doesn't he?"

"Christ, he likes everybody. He's a pushover."

"I thought it was nice of him not to want to throw all of those people out of his hooch. He didn't want to start any trouble," I said. That was about the only other subject I hadn't discussed with my early morning companion.

"Yeah. That makes up for what Dubbs does to 'em. One of these days Colonel Lee's going to put out a contract on Dubbs, I'll tell you."

"Okay, Colonel Lee. Is he the ROKAF commander?" I said, wanting more in spite of my yearning for bed.

"Lee's the commander. He's a good guy. But he has to take a lot from Dubbs because that's where the money comes from."

"So Dubbs rubs his nose in it, huh?"

"You bet. Calls Koreans 'slopes' to their faces when he's drunk."

"I'll tell you, Goldman, I left a beautiful family to come over here. I'm determined to do some good as long as I'm here. I really think I'm going to like the Koreans. You can bet I'm going to give them my best."

He smiled.

"I'm serious, dammit!" I said.

"Well, that's good, because they haven't had a hell of a lot of luck with their advisors in the past. Yeah, that's good. I like Korea, too."

We both kind of stared into space for a while. Morning, without a night's sleep, was really starting to put both of us out of touch.

"I'm gonna have to call it quits. Thanks for the great breakfast," I said.

I struggled off my stool and stuck out my hand. Goldman liked that and shook it very strongly.

"Sir, on behalf of our people, I'm happy to offer you the position of Medical Officer. We can talk about a salary later."

"Sounds like I'm chief babysitter, too."

"That, too," he said.

"I accept both." We walked out of the club together. I turned left for the BOQ. He went up over the ridge to the enlisted quarters. It was quite a first day, night, and early morning on station. I felt happy.

2

House Call

The Q was quiet when I finally got there. I hit the bed, clothes and all, and slept countless hours. I'd awaken once in a while, and then go back into a deep sleep.

When I finally woke up, I felt bad. I had a headache, and my entire digestive system was churning. The gas pains were incredible.

I realized I had to get to a toilet as soon as I could. And when I did it was horrible. Everything I had ever eaten in my whole life was running out of me. I sat there for quite a while. I didn't dare move.

Eventually, I crawled back to my room. Nobody was around. I hadn't set my little clock, so I had no idea of the time. But I needed something for all this hangover pain.

"Norm?" It was the priest.

"Hi, Father."

"What's wrong. Hung over?"

"Yeah, but worse. I've caught something, I think. Don't get too close to me."

"Stay there, I'll call Goldman," he said. I guessed he'd just gotten up himself. I felt like a jerk. I was embarrassed.

"He was at the club and he said you were right on time. What did he mean?"

"I don't know," I said, feeling like I could only last a bit longer until I'd be sitting on my throne again.

When Goldman came through the door, he did so with loud yells.

"House call, make way for the doctor. Where is he? Where is he? Show me . . . ah, there he is. What a fine looking young captain. A real credit to his corps."

I was lying on the bunk.

"Sarge, I'm embarrassed to tell you but I've . . ."

"You've been shitting and shitting, haven't you, sir."

"Yes.

"Well, that's just what you had programmed for yourself. You ate Mr. Min's ice last night, telling him all about your wonderful childhood. And kindly old Mr. Min gave you a bunch of ice chips loaded with amoebic dysentery. You and Mr. Min haven't broken one single law of nature."

"Well, why didn't you stop me?" I said.

"Because I didn't know if I liked you or not then," he said.

"Oh, brother!"

"Well, I do now and, besides, you're my supervisor. I'll give you this to take, and you'll be just fine by Monday."

He took two bottles from his black bag, one pills and one a white liquid.

"Just follow directions. It's good for you to have a case of dysentery. You'll be careful now, even when you're drunk."

I took my bottles down to the bathroom for the next session. When I returned to the room, Goldman and the priest were still there, sipping on beer cans.

"Norm, do you want a beer?"

"No," I said, easing onto the bunk.

"You should just drink water and don't eat anything for a while." Goldman patted me on the foot. "You'll be fine."

"But we're going over for chow," he added.

"Yeah," said the priest. "I'm going to eat tons of the chicken dinner tonight, ha, ha."

They stood and beamed at me. And the Father pulled down my blind.

"Wouldn't want Dubbs or anybody to see you so miserable."

"Before you guys go, do you want some ice?" I said.

"No, we know better, Captain. Take your medicine."

The door closed. Then it opened. Goldman stuck his head in.

"It was too late. You were sucking away. I thought, 'let him enjoy. Fifty-fifty chance he's taking on getting sick. I'll be there if he does. Enjoy.'"

"Just you wait, Goldman," I said with a mock fist waving.

"See you later. The medicine'll work. It's really harmless, that bug, and it'll pass quickly."

The door shut again.

I had gulped down the liquid with the pill. My gut was feeling better already, but my rear end was sore. The combination of the bug and the *kimchi* was unbeatable. Yeah, I thought, I'll be damn careful the next time.

Being hung over, no food for ten hours or so, and that god awful bug combined to make me shaky. With the door shut, a kind of depression came over me. I was very alone. Hangovers could sometimes put me into what I could almost describe as a feeling of terror, or panic, of being set apart from reality. At the least I was edgy. I felt like I had to grab onto something, just to hang on to life itself. If I didn't, I got the feeling I might even fall off and die.

Lying there in the Q with the door closed brought it on. Everything was terribly quiet. Evening was coming. I had literally lost Saturday. I had the feeling I was losing more.

Guilt sets in with that, the feeling that I'd done something unforgivable, terrible, that people were waiting just outside the door. At any moment I felt like there might be some group at the door to take me away. I was sure I was being talked about, by even the medic and the priest. And Dubbs, Dubbs was sure to be after me. I needed a beer.

At least a drink would bring me back out of the depression. If I could down one beer, and even a shot or two, then I could eat. But I was afraid to leave the room. I was afraid to even sneak down to the bar for that other medicine I so desired. I knew I'd have to wait the evening and the night through so I could try a new day, one that would begin with a good breakfast. I had screwed myself up again.

I did lie there for endless hours, thinking about myself, and a million crazy things. It was a weird state, brought on by physical misery and compounded by the utter remoteness I felt in my room, on a surrealistic Korean island, thousands of miles from home. Sometimes I guess I was dreaming. I'd come in and out of wakefulness, punctuated by that horrible terror I felt, that intangible fear of something I couldn't quite put my finger on.

I thought about Angie, and I was glad she wasn't a part of this nightmare. In a strange way I was glad to be gone from her so I could work this out by myself. I could lie on my bunk, squirm and toss, and not have to answer her questions or judgments about my irresponsible behavior. She and the children wouldn't have to witness any of this. I wouldn't have to control my nausea and my fear and force myself to play daddy and husband. I was so terribly distant from those responsibilities, and morning was so far away that I might not even see the dawn. I might just die, right here, I thought. Part of me wished I would.

I'd go from worry over what would happen to me here on Tolsan to dreamy, sweaty fantasies of the past and what my future could have been. In my haze I'd go back to the Pennsylvania summers of my childhood. Specific events appeared, like the picnic my father's company held every July for its employees and their families. I saw myself running from my father's car to that big pavilion at South Park where I'd reach into a full tub of icy soda pop for my favorite cream soda and then run to join in the three-legged and burlap races that made this picnic so much fun.

I redid college in these dreams, graduated Phi Beta Kappa, went to Harvard Medical School, served as a Navy doctor. Never once did I have to go to a shitty island in the South China Sea or sit in front of a radarscope or drink pissy rice drinks in icehouses where amoebae live in the ice chips.

After my distinguished Navy service, I went into private practice. I saw one patient after another, giving them long explanations of their illnesses, and then I'd be performing great surgical feats before astounded medical students, nurses, colleagues, and scientific reporters. They'd applaud my work as I'd snatch a soul back from sure death, and the wives of my patients would kiss my hands in gratitude. Everyone would stand aside while I, a lonely figure, would walk out into the darkness of the night, down the steep hospital steps, my shoulders bending under the weight of the vast responsibility given to me by my Creator--beautiful nurses longing to go with me, but knowing that I could not give myself to them, for science demanded my constant and faithful attention. And my mom and dad were so proud.

These dreams and makeovers went on with such intensity that they were controlling themselves. I was shaking. I felt my skin crawl. I was itchy. And then there were thousands of black roaches racing back and forth on the walls and ceiling of the room. You have the DTs, I said to myself. Hold on Norm. I gathered up the covers, closed my eyes, and held on with all my might. Christ, I had been fearing the morning. Now I couldn't wait for it to come!

I promised God and myself that if I lived through the night, I wouldn't drink a thing tomorrow and that I'd make myself strong for Monday. I'd eat breakfast and walk in the fresh air. I thanked God that I had a Sunday to do that. I knew I'd still be sick on Sunday. Tomorrow's hangover was sure to be a record breaker.

3

Sabbath

Sunday was that shaky day. I was weak and had a sunken feeling. I had one hell of a headache and my nose was stuffed up. But I did wake up at the crack of dawn, and I had not died. The dreams were gone. The roaches were gone.

First thing I did was to find out what time it was. Seven. Wonderfully early. I got that reading from the electric clock on the Q bar. I looked at the bottles behind it and said to them, with my mind's voice, no, no, no, you're not going to have another go at me, evil stuff.

I took a long shower. I vomited twice. I put on a nice pair of fatigues, clean and starched by the lady in the Osan Visiting Officers Quarters. Crisp. I even put some polish on my brogans. Shaved, clean, pressed, and shined, I set out for the dining hall. It was seven forty-five, and I was feeling hungry.

The dining Quonset was divided in two. There was an officer's side and an enlisted side. The officer's door was on the street. You had to go around to get to the enlisted entrance. I was a bit apprehensive about going inside. I hoped Dubbs wouldn't be eating breakfast. I didn't want heads to turn. I still had a little of the terror, the depression.

Merciful. The tables were set. Someone had already had breakfast at one of them. The place smelled good, but it also made me feel just a little sick. It was like going out and playing too much ball after a layoff. You can only take a little. Food was good. I needed it. But just a few innings. The odor suggested too much breakfast.

I felt queasy. How did you eat here? I thought. I've always hated getting started at new routines, new places. New school, new base, new job, new friends, you always had that awkward break-in period that found you doing something dumb, everyone watching you fuck up. This was a new dining hall.

"Godda morning, sore." It was a little Korean guy, dressed in white, wearing a cute little cook's hat.

"Hi. Could I get something, some breakfast?"

"Yes, sore, you sign in," he said, motioning me to a little stand by the kitchen entrance.

"Oh yes. Sign in. Sure."

I saw that each meal of each day was logged. You signed your name, rank, and filled in the spaces where you selected how much you were to pay. I paid officer basic meal, plus surcharge. Breakfast totaled sixty cents. Cheap.

Dubbs was the only other name recorded. He had been up bright and early. Thank God I didn't have to worry about seeing him.

I sat down. The little man had taken the sixty cents and had put it very officially into a tin fishing box. Change was divided up in the tackle sections. It was painted Air Force Blue and said DINING CHARGE.

"Now, watch you hava, sore?"

"Ah, some orange juice, a poached egg, some toast, and coffee. Is that okay?"

He smiled at me like I was a little kid.

"Okay." He said and he shuffled out on American shoes that had the backs cut out of them. He had converted black GI shoes into Asian clogs.

The door banged. It was a blond-headed guy in his late fifties I guessed.

"Gut morning, sir," he said very crisply. "May I sit vis you?"

"Yes, please do. I'm afraid we haven't met. I'm Norm Whitman."

"Ja, I heard you vas here. I'm Klas Von Kluen. 'Dutch' to everyone zo."

"And you're a civilian here?" I said, impressed with his neat, orderly manner.

"Ja, I'm civil engineer. My boys and I keep zis place running, clean, and freshly painted."

He went over and signed in. He also ordered a large breakfast. Four eggs. Wow, I was going to have to work some to match that.

He asked me about my flight down and how I liked things so far. Our food came. The talk and eating calmed me and put me in a good frame of mind. The shakes were all but gone, under control at last.

"No, I *am* Dutch," he said in answer to my question. "Actually zo I was born in Holland, ve lived in the Indonesia since I vas a very small boy."

So he was an Air Force contract civilian on the Tolsan compound. I really like accents and I got a kick out of listening to him. And I liked him. He seemed like he was probably a hell of a good engineer.

"You go to mass?" he finally said at about our third coffee fill.

"Is it soon? Yes, I'd like to, but I didn't know where or when."

"Ja, Fazer has it in the little theater yust down our street. I always go, bud I am not a Katholic. He needs people there."

So we got up and went down the street. It started at nine. I was so far having the kind of day Angie would be proud of. If she could look in on me, this would be the time I'd hope the cameras were running. I was glad to be off beer and scotch. I shivered at the thoughts of the drinking bout I'd started in Osan days ago. The bug was gone, too. I had crapped so much, it would probably be Wednesday before I'd have to go near a stall. Just as well. Give it a rest, along with my stomach, brain, and liver.

The theater was a nice little place. It had a projection booth and rows of real show seats. There were even movie posters in real lobby glass cases. Candy counter and all, it sported a wide screen in front. There was a potbellied stove off to one side.

The seats were pretty well filled. I was surprised. I saw Goldman down front, along with a good number of other enlisted types. There were even some Korean civilians and a few ROKAF people. Dutch and I took seats in the middle row. A portable altar, with burning candles, was set up in front. I was Catholic, so I got a good feeling from all of it.

While I was checking out the theater, the priest came from somewhere and said, "Norm, you'll be altar boy today."

"Look, Father, I've never really done that before. I've been a commentator, but the altar boy thing passed me by." I really didn't want any part of that. I was enjoying my rehabilitation, but lying low. I wanted to be a spectator, a face in the crowd for the next couple of days or so.

"It's easy. You don't do much."

He took my arm and up I stood, always the guy who gave in easily. I envied my friends who just had the ability to somehow say no. That was it. Good enough. NO. But not Norm Whitman. You just grabbed him by the arm.

I followed him down front and into a little room to the right of the screen. It was filled with movie stuff, extra chairs, odds and ends. His surplice was hanging there, ready to go over the cassock top and the standard issue Air Force pants he was wearing.

"If you've been a commentator, we'll combine both jobs and make it all very easy. You go out first and take one of these folding chairs with you. Say, 'please stand'; I'll come in and begin the mass; you will read the epistle—this one on page 536—when I tell you; and the only other thing you do is pass the plate and bring up the wine and water when I tell you to."

"Okay. I can do all of that," I said. It was simple enough. I took the chair and went out.

"Give me a count of 25," he whispered behind me, bringing green robes over his head.

I set up the chair, conscious that everyone was looking at me. Yet it was a feeling of being home in a way because I had been commentator for Father Bob Rush for three years until I stepped on the first plane to Tolsan. I counted twenty-five or more.

"Please stand," I said as I had so many times before, with Angie, Mikie, and Shelley just a little distance away. But now it was an odd mixture of GIs and Koreans, very few of whom it seemed were really Catholic.

The Father came in and began the mass.

"In the name of the Father, and of the Son, and of the Holy Spirit."

"Amen," we answered.

And it went the same as it always had, ever since I was a child.

"And also with you," I said automatically, along with those in the theater seats. Through the Penitential Rite, the Kyrie, and all of the prayers we went, until I found myself responding to his nod by reading *The Epistle of Saint Paul to the Ephesians, Chapter 5, Verses 15 to 21*. As I did I couldn't believe the words I was reading aloud. "Brethren: See to it that you walk with care: not as unwise but as wise, making the most of your time, because the days are evil. Therefore, do not become foolish, but understand what the will of the Lord is. And do not be drunk with wine, for in that is debauchery; but be filled with the Spirit, speaking to one another in psalms and hymns and spiritual songs, singing and making melody in your hearts to the Lord, giving thanks always for all things in the name of our Lord Jesus Christ to God the Father. Be subject to one another in the fear of Christ."

The response to that was, "Thanks be to God." My own response was to marvel at the coincidence that would bring me to read that epistle to that group on that Sunday. Well, I thought, we had sung songs to each other at least. "Thanks be to God."

By comparison the Gospel was uneventful: Jesus healed the son of a royal official in Capharnaum. Paul's sermon followed that. It was about keeping the old chin up, even though you fell once in a while.

It wasn't long before I started out the plate among the crowd. Goldman winked at me as I did. Dutch nodded approval. The Koreans were very serious and looked past me. It came back with a respectful amount in it. Military payment certificates and Korean coins.

"Father, all powerful and ever-living God, we do well always and everywhere to give you thanks . . ." Never changing. He did well. I stopped listening and began to examine him. For forty-six, he had a good head of blondish red hair and a broad, strong face. He was very careful to say his mass slowly, and he spoke each word, every phrase with deliberation. He had large hands, matching a frame that stood about six-one or so, one heavy load to carry into the Q. He liked the sauce, the slot machine, and Mr. Min's icehouse. He loved saying mass.

"On the night He was betrayed, He took bread and gave you thanks and praise . . ."

As I poured a little wine and a little water for him in the Chalice, I felt his strength and commitment. He was an outcast, saying his mass on a tiny spot in the South China Sea. He could have been anywhere. His priestly brothers had now said, or were now saying, or were going to say their masses in thousands of other places, but all in the same traditional way.

"Lord, I am not worthy to receive you, but only say the word and I shall be healed."

With firm deliberation he held up the host and said, "The Body of Christ," and put it into my mouth.

"Amen," I said.

And most everyone else joined me at the communion table. I noticed Dutch and Goldman did not. But they did come up and shake his hand. That was a nice touch. As they did he said, "May the spirit of Christ be with you."

Finally, he said, "The mass is ended. Go in peace."

Dutch and Goldman and I helped Paul fold the altar cloth and pack up the portable altar. Everything fit into a rather slick GI mess kit, courtesy of the chaplain service and Uncle Sam. He put his robes in a plastic bag.

"Now for a good breakfast," he said.

"Ja, I'd like the more coffee, too," said Dutch.

We closed up the theater and walked up to the dining hall. What an oddball group. What a Sunday service.

I did the rest of Sunday like a model guy. We all did. The Father ate a huge breakfast; Dutch and I must've put down a gallon of coffee while he ate. Goldman didn't hesitate to stride right into the officer's side of the mess hall with us. He said coffee was very bad for you, but managed to wash down a large breakfast with the stuff.

Even Packer wandered in, looking like a vampire who had forgotten to go to sleep in his coffin. He had coffee.

We sat around, talking. The priest said there was at least one day in the week when he knew who he was, and Goldman remarked as how he was lucky he wasn't a Rabbi. "You'd mess up your Saturday nights because you'd have to be in the synagogue."

Packer told us he'd forgiven Adja. Goldman, Dutch, and the priest all made booing sounds at that, along with "Pussy Whipped Bastard" and other appropriate titles.

"Aw, geez, she's the only thing that keeps me sane here, Doc," he slurred out, hands shaking so much he could hardly hold his coffee cup.

Goldman blurted out, "Sane? Christ, you're always a nervous wreck over her, or getting yourself drunk, or beat up over her. Sane? Christ!"

"Ja, you need to sleep in the koo, you need to. Den you can see how krazy you are for going dere to her all da time. She makes a fool from you."

Packer just sort of looked down in his coffee with a silly smile while all of that was being said. He was very good-natured about it, but I knew he was eager for the subject to change.

And it did. I was filled in on a number of things: when the movies were, what you could buy at the BX, where you bought stamps, which meals in the dining hall were special, what you could do on the island, and other loosely connected items that brought us to almost noon. In just about an hour we'd be in time for the big Sunday noon meal.

The priest said he'd be going to visit one of the Catholic rectories up island. "We won't see him till Tuesday," put in Goldman.

"I'll take you on one of those trips sometime, Norm," the priest said, pretending not to pay attention to Goldman. "We've got a number of churches here."

"Don't invite me, ever again," said Goldman, pushing away from the table. "Thank God he's got a Catholic to travel with him now."

We broke up, but I did return with Dutch to eat the Sunday meal. As manager, Goldman put in his entire day working at the NCO Club. That was one place I wanted to stay away from for a while.

Packer said he'd be going back to get Adja. He told Dutch and me he'd meet us at the theater. "There's going to be a James Bond again, you guys." That sounded pretty good to me.

On impulse, I stopped at the door of the headquarters Quonset on my way back from lunch. The door was open. A sergeant was typing at one of the desks. His name was Mountain, Master Sergeant Mountain. The nametag, "Mountain," sewn to his fatigues, amused me.

"Catching up, Sarge?" I said, walking toward the group of desks.

"No, sir, typing a letter to my folks."

"Oh, well, that's even better."

I had met Mountain at the club on Friday night. He was the First Sergeant for the Air Defense Operations Team, called ADOT. He was the top sergeant, or *First Shirt* in military speak.

"Sarge, could I have our Operating Instructions and anything else that's not classified to read? I thought I might get a head start before movie time."

"Yeah, sure, sir, just a minute. And, by the way, that desk will be yours."

"Okay," I said, getting the feel of the chair and view of the rest of the Quonset. I amused myself by going through the drawers until Mountain brought me several typical black three-ring government binders and a couple of headquarters-produced pamphlets. I settled back to read unexciting procedures for the next couple of hours. Mountain told me to leave them on the desk when I was through.

I read about the radars and how ADOT's job was to provide liaison between the USAF and the ROKAF. There were procedures for following the choggy supply flights on radar, complete with frequencies and things having to do with the Tolsan landing strip. The whole job was so damn easy I knew I could turn off the mental lights for the next thirteen months.

Dutch came by and asked me if I was still going to the movie.

I said, "Hell, yes," and placed all of the books on my new desk. We locked up and headed for the theater. The morning had been God's time. The afternoon ADOT's. The evening was James Bond's.

Bond got a packed house. The movies were free. The seats were filled with all sorts of humanity. All of the enlisted men were there with their girls, and there were lots of Korean Air Force people as well.

"Dey love dese moovees, even if dey can't speak English too gut. It make gut lessons."

I spied Dubbs in about the third row, along with his little honey. And I'll be damned if Packer and Adja weren't sitting right with them. So that was Adja. Dubbs and Packer sat on either side of the girls, separated and looking dully ahead. But their girls were chattering away in Korean. They seemed very tight with each other.

In contrast, the other GIs with dates were talking with each other, while their girls sat in that same tired dreamy state. They reminded me of salesgirls at their registers, waiting for customers. They were, in fact, at work. They were *yobos*, working girls, moose, whores. Some of them were quite good looking.

"My girl visits her parents," said Dutch.

"Where do they live?" I asked. It almost sounded like a normal thing, yet the whole idea of this old Dutchman having a girl was bizarre.

"She vent to Seoul by da plane out of Tolsan City. I brought her from dere, so I pay for it each time a year."

"Oh, I see," I said, then was rescued by the lowered lights and the playing of the national anthem. There in the flicker of the movie we all stood. I saw Dubbs standing and thought about the national anthem playing for the President's Review.

The cartoon was Donald Duck, who also was thrown in this place. I had seen him a thousand times, but always in a familiar setting. I prayed that he could take me back to where we both belonged, in an American theater. But we were still in Korea when that ended and *Goldfinger* made his appearance. I shut out everything around me and escaped into the film.

When the movie was over, the reality of where I was switched back on with the lights. Everyone stood, the magic abruptly ended. They all had that post-fantasy look about them, that embarrassed look you had because you sensed others might suspect you were still a character in the film. I, James Bond, stood without embarrassment and walked back to the Q with Dutch and Goldfinger.

We joined a crowd of strollers, mostly sergeants and their girls, walking towards town. I spotted Oyster and Adja. "What time tomorrow, Andy?" I said, catching up with him.

"I'm on the hill. You'll be with Major Dubbs, I guess, getting yourself cleared in. Works at 0700."

"Okay."

"Norm," he said with his slow sloppy smile, "I'd like you to meet Adja."

She was a bright looking girl, rather tall, I thought. She peeked a big smile at me, put her hand over it, and looked down, giggling.

"Hello, Adja," I said, bowing an awkward bow.

She pulled herself close to Packer like a little child, putting her face into his shoulder and giggling.

"She said you look like a butterfly when she saw you in the movie theatre."

With that, Adja punched him a couple of times with that familiar going-steady, senior-prom punch we've all seen.

"I don't know about that," I said, laughing.

"You butterfly I bet," she said and pulled Packer off ahead, trying to get the two of them to run away from me.

"Ja, day all look you over pretty gut in dere. There is only one girl who doesn't have a *yobo* now. When word spreads, Miss Chun show up some night all dressed up like crazy for you."

"Well I'm sorry to disappoint everyone, but I'm not in the market . . . for that just yet."

Dese girls like vat dey call 'long-time' vis a GI. No butterfly. Short time iss not gut. Dey like you pay rice bill, und den you get the pussy," he said, lighting up a beautifully carved pipe.

"Well I have a big rice bill to pay in the States, and two kids to feed," I said, getting off the walk at the door to the Q.

"You vill get horns soon enough for Pussy. Bill iss only tirty dollars American a month. Vorth it," he said behind me, moving toward the next Q door.

"I can pound off cheaper than that," I yelled through the screen.

He laughed.

Shakes over, stomach good, I threw off my clothes and went right to bed. Didn't even bother to wash. The hell with it. I was tired, the right kind of tired. Not a drop of alcohol all day and I'd eaten three meals. I knew I'd be able to wake up at six, steady as a rock, ready to put in a good first duty day. I wished I always felt like this. I fell asleep within ten minutes or so, dreaming about making love to Angie.

4

Benjamin 12

When the alarm went off, I jumped out of bed, showered and shaved like a champ. I really felt alive. It was still dark outside. When I wasn't hung over, I enjoyed a morning like that. Being in a barracks again, up before the sun, reminded me of Officer Training School at Lackland Air Force Base in Texas, where mornings were warm. I always felt good then. You couldn't really afford a hangover there ever.

I showed up at the mess hall at six-thirty. Dubbs was at the table, making slurping sounds over an ugly dish of eggs and grits all smashed together. I told myself he was eating caterpillar guts. That was fine, but now I'd have to eat cereal.

"Morning, sir," I said after I signed in.

"We can spend the morning breaking you in," he said without looking up.

Bless Dutch for showing up just as the little waiter, Mr. Moon, was delivering my toast, cereal, and cup of cream.

"Vell, gentlemen, another Monday comes." He was dressed in a shirt and bow tie under a rather nice winter windbreaker. He looked the part of the site civil engineer.

"You know Colonel Lee wants to borrow your cement mixer to do some patch work on his sidewalks?" said Dubbs, wiping his fat mouth and lips with a nice napkin.

"Ja, iss okay vis me, Major . . . I vorry about it sitting in dis kolt vetter anyway."

"Yeah, well give me an excuse to tell him no. Fuck 'em. They broke their own."

"Sir, vee do not use it now. It's really okay."

"Fuck 'em. I'm worried they'll break ours, and then where the hell will we be."

"My boys vill only tell someone over dere, Ja. Anyvay. Let dem have it."

"Yeah, well that's fine. You better fix it though. Them slopes can't take care of a fucking thing." He stood up. "You ready to go over?" he said to me.

"Yes, sir." I really wanted more coffee, but if asshole was ready to move, I was ready. "See you later, Dutch," I said, getting up.

"Ja, you come over, and I show you engineers."

Dubbs walked with his face pointed forward like I wasn't even with him. I walked with him on my right, giving him the traditional place of military respect. I was determined to do well, in spite of the big jerk. One thing for sure, though, I was bothered by his attitude toward the Koreans. Goldman had said Lee was a good guy. And we were supposed to give them cement mixers, or anything else they needed. That was the whole idea.

"Go on in," said Dubbs in front of headquarters. "I wanna check on something in the Q."

"Sure," I nodded, thinking he'd probably go over for one more fuck, or maybe even a blowjob. God, the gall of keeping her right in the Q. That had to be against some kind of regulation. Shit, Angie wouldn't be allowed to stay there. Dubbs' whore, yes.

Sergeant Mountain was already there, typing away. "Letter home?" I asked, kidding.

"Yeah, one more before the next choggy."

I went over to the potbellied stove that was a familiar sight in all buildings in Korea. They ran on liquid propane. I warmed my hands. The door banged.

"You read anything yet?" It was Dubbs, hanging his parka up on a hook.

"Yes, sir, as a matter of fact I read all of this unclassified here." The books were still on my desk.

"Okay, then Mountain'll give you some stuff to fill out, and there's a control test you're required to take. You have'ta make a hundred on it before you're certified. Mountain?"

"Yes, sir, I've got all that laid out for the captain. I'll give him the classified to read, too."

"I gotta go downtown for a while. I'll be back to take you around on the hill after lunch. Packer's up there now. If you get the test outta the way, you can pull tour tomorrow." Back on went the coat. I don't know why he didn't just keep it on.

"Okay, sir," I said, giving it an honest-to-goodness smile that said, Boss I'm gonna do a good job for ya.

Mountain was very efficient. I studied a three-page sheet that told you about approaches and procedures, navigational hazards, and everything else you needed to flight follow a C-47 into the area. The goal was to memorize the frequencies and emergency procedures. The high peak, Mount Tolsan, was 6,397 feet above sea level. You had to keep that in mind.

I passed the first time around because Mountain changed three of my answers. I then was qualified to go on to the classified, which I read. The big thing there was that if we went to war, the Air Force guy assumed control of the radar squadron. That meant a major, Dubbs, would take command over the commander, a Korean full colonel. I wondered about that one.

That all done, Mountain ceremoniously announced to me that I was now Benjamin 12, my code name over the air. The site was Benjamin; I was controller 12. Yet, Dubbs, Packer, and I were really the only three. I guess if I had only three tanks I'd number them 565, 566, and 567, too. What the hell, military strategy.

All of a sudden it was eleven-thirty. "Sir, let's get some chop, huh?"

"Sure," I said.

"Why don't you eat over with us today?"

"Great, yeah, yeah, I'd like to talk to the people who really make this place tick."

"I don't know about that, sir."

Goldman was at the first table as you walked into the enlisted side of the mess hall. "Attention, everyone. *Achtung!* It's an officer coming in the door, attention. Oh, never mind, it's only Captain Whitman."

"Goldman," I said, "you make a person feel so wanted."

"Now you'll probably rate me down on my APR because I got too familiar, won't you, sir?"

"I'm going to write it here, in big letters, right here in the lunch book. Goldman is a S-M-A-R-T A-S-S. There. It'll be noted by the accountants up in Osan. It's a message to them, at least."

We sat at a big table and that was good because I met a lot of the NCOs, this time without their *yobos*. There was Mountain and, of course, Goldman, who was the center of attention. He was telling of his boyhood days on the streets of New York. Letting him run his mouth gave me a chance to look at the faces and review the names. They all seemed glad enough to have me sit with them.

I read the nametags and looked at the faces. Staff Sergeant Camp, a black, was the motor pool NCO. Airman First Class Biggs worked for him. Airmen First Class Snider and Kelly, who had gone to communion on Sunday, were the Air Force Communications Service people who maintained the TACAN and other nav aids the planes used to find the island. Staff Sergeant Clayton was the supply NCO; Airman Second Class Hillsome worked for him. I think there were two of them because it took two guys to carry the boxes they got from the planes. Staff Sergeant Ellis, out in the kitchen, ran the mess hall. Quite an operation when you considered that they were all there so three controllers could sit on the hill and advise the Koreans. We had our own movie, dispensary, BX, mess hall, motor pool, fire department, living quarters, assorted buildings, and big NCO club. You'd think the three controllers could just as easily have roughed it with the ROKAF. It was a good bit of money to keep three radar guys there.

Now to complicate things even more, there was something called the hunting lodge. Tolsan had these great pheasants running all over the place, and VIPs came from everywhere in the Asian theatre to hunt them. We even had a couple of trucks for the hunters to get around in. They were called bird wagons. Season was over, but when the hunting was in full swing, Special Services from Japan sent more sergeants down to us, along with a bunch of bird dogs. They hired local guides. The NCO club boomed with business, and we'd be up to our ears in generals, admirals, and embassy people. Now I knew why we needed all of this. I was assigned to a hunting lodge. I'd flight follow hunting inbounds and outbounds.

"You know," I said, "it's only smart to eat lunch with the NCOs if you want to know the story. I think I've really had the briefing on the site now. I'm ready for Major Dubbs' tour."

"And tell him you're the new medical officer, sir." Goldman said.

"As well as the hunting OIC, sir," said Mountain with a smile.

When I got back to headquarters, Dubbs was waiting in front. He had donned a baseball cap with a major's leaf sewn on it. It was blue and said "Tolsan" on one side and "Thirteen Months in Hell" on the other. "Harold" was sewn in white letters on the back. Cute. Nice souvenir, I thought. His ugly wife and kids will love it.

Dubbs started my tour by pointing at the vehicles parked outside the Q.

"Now, I got my own jeep because that's the AFAG jeep. I wear three hats here," he said, standing beside the jeep with the red light on top. I remembered he led the planes with that, parked them. "I'm site commander, ADOT Team

Chief, and Air Force Advisory Group. AFAG's the money. That's why Colonel Lee has to pay attention. Radar job's nothing. I let you and Packer sit the hill. First Shirt runs the site. A controller doubles as hunt OIC. I watch the AFAG stuff. I keep 'em outta Uncle's pocketbook."

I liked the three hats part. I guessed he must have had two other baseball hats somewhere. Maybe one said "asshole" on the back.

"You get your driver's license in Osan okay?" he said, opening the jeep door.

"I didn't know I was supposed to, sir," I said, genuinely surprised.

"Shit, yes, you're supposed to. On your clear-in sheet it tells you to do that at the Osan motor pool." He was sticking his fat face close.

"I guess I missed that."

"Ah, well, nobody's gonna know. What the hell. Let me see you drive up the hill, and we'll call it okay."

I looked at the jeep and the thing coming up from the floor. The thing with the black knob. There were also some extra pedals on the floor.

"You know what, sir? I've only driven a stick shift once."

"Huh?"

"Isn't that something for an American?" I said with a big smile. "We just always had automatics at our house. I've only driven a stick shift one time."

He looked at me like I was a dunce. I felt so awkward. Why did this stick shift thing have to raise its ugly head again? I had been doing fairly well only an hour ago.

"You're gonna have to learn, that's for sure, Whitman. I can't be taking you up and down and neither can Packer. That'd fuck us up all the damn time," he said, getting in the driver's side. "Shit, get in now. I'll drive. Watch how I do it. We gotta get up to see the place. You get Packer to teach you right away."

"Yes, sir," I said getting in. "I'm really sorry about this, believe me. I feel like a dumb shit."

"Well, you should," he said, starting the fucking thing and backing it up.

Soon we were out the gate again, but this time it was a left turn and up a steep climb. The road crisscrossed its way up what was called the hill. On top was radar operations, Benjamin Control. Benjamin 12, who could not drive up himself, was on his way. Next to him was Asshole One, who didn't say one word.

We passed a lot of Korean airmen, walking up, walking down. I guessed there was a crew change going on. Dubbs drove by them the same ignorant way he'd done in town. He kept his speed down, however, because this was steep and the road was really close to the edge. But ignorant nonetheless.

The road was red clay, on the side of the hill. I guessed it would be hell if it were wet. That frightened me when I thought about doing this with a stick shift. Jesus Christ, it was always something.

When we finally got to the top, the view was spectacular. Above us were the radar bubbles, seeming even more imposing against this high blue Korean sky. Down below you could see out and across this part of the island and well out to sea. The sun's reflection on the calm water was silvery. The villages and farmlands spread out between the bottom of the hill and the water made a beautiful sight. People, vehicles, and animals in the fields were miniatures. It was lovely.

A bunch of Koreans was going in the cement ops building.

"They carry their food in little shit cans. Shit food in shit cans," he said, with the ROKAF guys looking at us as they passed. "Don't worry, the slopes can't hear that," he said, almost as if he had read my mind. "All they know is their little shit sandwiches and shit cookies and shit tea. Let's go."

Inside, Benjamin Control looked like a hundred other radar operations rooms I'd been in. All dark, radarscopes sitting on raised rows, the front of the room was dominated by a big plastic board that went from floor to ceiling, wall to wall. Behind it the plotters were drawing backwards so the rest of the crew in front could see the tracks of airplanes in the area. Each row of scopes had another above it. They rose up, like the steps in a football stadium. I could see Packer's outline, in a parka, sprawling over a dais on the top row. Face to one side, resting on his parka covered arms, he was fast asleep.

We walked up the aisle. There was a lot of chatter in the room. The radar sweeps were yellowish. I knew how to run this place.

Packer was really sleeping soundly. He was so out that his lips were pressing hard against the back of his hand, with spit running out over it.

Dubbs just kept walking up the aisle steps toward him.

"Boy, they sure did a good job on him at the Academy," he said as much to the room in general as to me.

The Academy? The Air Force Academy? I thought. It couldn't be. I couldn't believe what I had heard Dubbs say. I'd never met an Academy grad, but surely Packer wasn't one of them. Hell, that was the top place to go. He was a nice guy, but he wasn't what I'd imagined an Academy grad would be.

"Hey, hey, Packer." Dubbs shook him, grabbing the fur on his parka hood.

"Huh?" he said, sitting up. When he did, a spit string formed, running from his hand to the corner of his mouth. It was a miracle the thing didn't break. He just looked at us, dull eyed, with this silly spit string running from his mouth to the back of his hand.

"You know they used to shoot guys for sleeping on duty? You know that?" said Dubbs.

"Yes, sir, geez, I guess I don't have any excuse. It's been so cold in here I really just started out trying to get warm by pulling myself into my parka." He was operating now, wiping away the slobber. "Geez," he said, wiping the spit from his face with his hand and then further wiping it all over his parka front.

"Yeah, they can't heat this place worth a damn. I'da said something if it'ahd been me. Don't sleep though, you'll look as dumb as these bastards."

And I guess that was it. Dubbs really didn't seem that bothered. I thought this would be a big deal. Nothing. I just stood there, taking it all in.

"I'm leaving Whitman up here with you for the rest of the shift. Show him the ropes, and then show him how to drive a jeep, will ya?"

"Sir?"

"We always had an automatic . . ."

"Yeah, okay," Dubbs said, interrupting me while Packer studied me, to see what there was in my appearance that kept me from knowing how to drive a jeep. For just a minute there I didn't like him. At least I knew how to keep from slobbering all over myself.

"Anybody been up?" said Dubbs, leafing through the standard logbook resting on top of the table.

"Lee for about a half of an hour. He made a call. We were supposed to get fighters, but they crumped."

"Okay, I'll see you guys later."

"Yes, sir," we both said.

Dubbs bobbed back down the aisle, not really looking at anything. Then he was out.

"Man, I thought he'd really get on you for sleeping."

"Naw, he doesn't give a shit about anything you do up here just as long as you get the choggy in. Most of the time it's just cold, dark, and boring."

My short spurt of dislike for him passed. It was a mixture of the Academy thing, his sleeping, the spit string, and my announced ineptitude with a stick shift. And I guess I saw just a tad of deference in Dubbs' treatment of him, even though he'd seemed miffed when we first saw Packer asleep.

Packer showed me the logbook and how we made entries. The radar sets, known as UPA-35s, were the same as I'd worked with in the states. The surveillance reporting system UPA-10s was standard too. There really wasn't anything different about the place at all. It was a typical Ground Control and Intercept operation, short name, GCI.

The only thing I'd have to learn was the communications system and the area of responsibility, the airspace we protected from air attack. Packer showed me that, by pointing to the outlines drawn on the big plastic board, the entire Korean peninsula was outlined, along with the coast of China to its left and the islands of Japan on the right. Lots of sea in between, Tolsan was in the very center. We had radar coverage about three hundred to three hundred fifty miles out, though our sister sites could give us an entire air picture by reporting positions over surveillance lines that were always open. Likewise, Benjamin would tell, as it was called, tracks to sister Korean and Japanese sites where there were boards just like ours.

At Benjamin we were the center of the board, but Osan would be the center of its board and so would Osaka be the center of its. And all of the tellers could keep tracks straight by plotting on a grid system called GEOREF. It was a latitude-longitude deal that compensated for your position. So, there was always a lot of chatter over the lines as the plotters were told by the surveillance tellers the positions of other moving aircraft outside their coverage.

You needed a UPA-35 to control fighters and the GI position had one for itself. The Korean controllers had them, too. You also needed air-to-ground communication. The surveillance guys, the tellers, had a simpler scope. It was all really simple, kind of crude.

Packer knew his stuff. He had me read in pretty well in just about an hour. We made a comm check with Osan and it worked out fine. There were these old-fashioned World War Two switches you used to ring up adjacent sites. You talked on black field phones with push-to-talk buttons built into their handles. It was all old stuff.

This was the first time I'd seen the Koreans at work. They wore a different kind of blue uniform from ours, with smaller enlisted patches that looked more like Boy Scout insignia. They were all very busy and serious about what they were doing.

"Any of the officers on duty now, Oyster?"

"It's break time for them, I think. They have a little room out back where they have meetings and drink tea. It's fun to get invited there, as a matter of fact. Man, I really zonked out this afternoon."

He stretched his arms out. He looked better in the dark, with only the glow of low lights and radar on his sunken face. "Adja and I stayed up late after we got home." He stretched again. He yawned. "She thinks you otta meet Miss Chun."

"Who's that?" I asked, playing the role of the innocent.

"She's a girl, a *yobo*. Pretty nice. She was with an Army sarge who was with us for a while. When he rotated back to the states, she couldn't find a steady long-time GI, 'cause everyone was taken. So, she left for a while."

"And now she's back?"

"Yeah. She'd make a good *yobo*, man. You get to *testo-testo* first time. You ought to try her out."

"You mean I could fuck her on kind of a trial basis to see if she'd be worth moving in with? Is that how it works?" I said, looking at him in a kind of wonder.

"Yeah. There's no hard feelings, either, Norm. But that's about the only short-time you're going to get here. Osan's all different. They've got clubs everywhere."

"Yeah, I know. I got down to Chicol Village while I was processing in."

"Man, it's great when you go TDY back to Osan. I hit the ville first chance I get. Variety." Then he looked down. "Well, I used to, before I met Adja. I wouldn't do that now. I wouldn't want to bring anything back."

"Well, listen, where the hell would this Miss Chun go if she didn't get a long-time when the Army guy left? What would a girl like that do down here?"

"*Kisaeng* house."

"Like a geisha, right?"

"Yeah. Not as fancy, but they've got a pretty good one here."

"So this Miss Chun was a *kisaeng* girl?"

"Yeah. You'd be getting a good deal. Man, she's a lot like Adja, too. I'm not saying I haven't had problems with her, but she really does keep me going."

"Well, Oyster, if you're happy," I said with a shrug, "what's so bad about that?"

"Yeah, that's what I say." He gave me that big sloppy grin. "Do you want me to call Adja and tell her to bring along Miss Chun?"

"Naw, I really appreciate it, but I want to take it easy."

All of this while the room hummed away. There were no blips in our Tolsan area, but a good number were being plotted over the rest of the board. It was all friendly, yet traffic of interest. You didn't put it all up, just stuff you had an interest in. The friendly traffic was plotted with white grease pencil. Red was hostile, and yellow was yet to be identified either way. Flight plans, pre-filed by both airlines and military, formed the basis of identification. Get off course far enough, and you might have fighters scrambled on you.

If you had radio contact with a bird, he could switch on his transponder for IFF, identification-friend-from-friend, that made his blip paint bigger than the raw radar return. You could dial up a code and tell him to set his "Parrot" to it. Then he'd paint a bigger yellow radar blip on the screen. It made ident easier, those parrots. Everybody flew squawking some code or another on the "SIF," Selective Identification Feature, the IFF.

I was watching a Korean surveillance sergeant following a track that was squawking mode 3, code 21. He gave a satisfied "Ha," and marked it on his scope with a black grease pencil.

"You're sure you don't want me to fix it with Miss Chun?"

"Naw, Oyster, I'm still not feeling too good from that bout I had with bad water bugs."

I really wanted to lead into the Academy thing before the day was over. "Did I hear Dubbs say you went to the Air Force Academy?" I said, fixing my eyes on the Korean sergeant as he followed the bird squawking 3-2-1 on the scope. Every time the sweep would pass over it, sweeping like a second hand, it would creep a little further across the scope face. He'd make a mark over the new blip position. That would soon give him the path of the airplane. You could then tell an adjacent site that the plane was heading a course of so many degrees at such and such a place on the GEOREF. I'd done it thousands of times. He and I were brothers of the radarscope, at least.

"Yeah, I went to the zoo. Dubbs always has to make sure people know that."

"Well, that's a cool thing to do, right? Pretty special school, I understand."

"Yeah, it's okay. I'm just not what you'd call a real strak zoomie."

I was still watching the scope. A radar picture was really a beautiful sort of an image. The first time I'd walked into a room like this I was struck by the yellow-greenish glow of the moving sweep. The sweep was a very bright line, moving like a second hand. The glow of a blip would fade as the sweep worked its way around the scope face. The sweep kept painting moving air traffic. Blip. Blip. Blip. It would paint big clouds and weather fronts, too. Tall smokestacks could show up as well as all sorts of other ground clutter. In large populated areas you could see the radio and television towers. But unlike the blips, they never moved, patiently awaiting the next sweep. Clutter was always there, in the same place.

The sweep looked a little like Tinker Bell's glowing pixie dust when she flew across the television screen Sunday nights on Disney's show. Radar: I had heard about it as a kid from the uncles who were in the war. Now I knew more about it. I could kill with it.

"What are you doing in controlling if you're an Academy grad?"

"I SIE'd out of pilot training. They slapped me into Tyndall faster than you could say 'bullshit' when I did that." Self Initiated Elimination seemed to me like his chosen lifestyle.

"How come you quit? Didn't you like flying or what?"

"Aw, I really don't like to talk about it too much, but, yeah, I never really . . . well, at least I found out flying wasn't for me. I got sick every time I went up. I shoulda never done any of this." He was shaking a little bit. The guy was always as nervous as a cat. I couldn't tell if it was my questions or just another bad day. He was doodling with a grease pencil, and I imagined he couldn't draw a straight line, even if he tried. "The only good thing was meeting Adja."

"Mmmm, I see," I said, still watching the grease pencil dots creep along the scope face below me as the blip continued a course of about 270 degrees. Due west. A good controller could pick out heading and approximate speed, after looking at just a few sweeps on a blip. This one was subsonic, about 250 knots.

Often, when I'd have to spend long shifts on crew, I'd just sit in front of a scope and follow tracks like that. I'd pick out a couple and put grease dots down over their steady, plodding paints. After about a half hour you'd have tracks all over the scope. They were ghosts of flights you really knew very little about. Just commercial stuff, taking people here and there. They didn't know you were watching them. The pilots knew they were on radar, but they probably couldn't care that somebody was just aimlessly following them on a modern yellow glowing crystal ball.

You could fool with the dial on the SIF and see who was squawking what. You'd look at 3-2-1, and 3-3-2, or any of the other combinations. But no matter what you had dialed in, code 3-6-6 would automatically come through. That was an emergency squawk, a Mayday distress signal. Harder to catch was a guy flying a triangle pattern, an emergency who had no transmitter or parrot. You'd be lucky to catch that. How many guys had fallen into the sea on the last leg of an equilateral triangle?

It was phosphorus that made the yellow air picture possible. That and an electron gun made for a cathode ray tube that let us eavesdrop on the sky's traffic. In everyday life a civilian air controller kept the blips apart. We ran them into one another on purpose. The other guy was a hostile target, a bogey, not a fellow airliner.

Sitting there with Oyster made me think about controlling, the way of it. I hadn't sat at a scope since I took leave and then followed my orders to Korea.

These Korean controllers and surveillance scope sitters would be fun to swap stories with, I thought. When Packer had told Dubbs that the day's fighters had crumped, I felt a familiar feeling in my stomach. You always felt queasy and apprehensive before a fighter mission. You'd have hundreds of those missions a year, but you always felt the same uneasy nervous sensation before each one.

You'd come in the morning to find out that you'd have, say, three F-106 fighter jets out of some base or another and you were going to pick them up on the scope and talk to them over your air-to-ground. You'd ident them with the IFF and then fly them in formation to an airspace training area you'd get from the FAA for just that purpose. Then you'd peel one of the three off and put some miles between him and the others. Say he was target for the other two, you'd turn them into each other, and guide pursuer to pursued, friendly to hostile, defender to attacker.

They'd paint on the scope, the sweep telling the truth of the course you'd set. The cursor was another bright line that appeared on the scope face with the flick of a switch. That was an electrical yardstick, with two dots on it. By putting one dot on the end of the cursor over the fighter and running the other one out to the target, you got a readout in a little window of how far they were from each other. The line and its dots were controlled and moved all over the scope face by a joy stick that made a machinegun-like noise when you'd push it and cause it to move the cursor. Turn the stick like a knob and the cursor would sweep like the sweep with the end dot as the axis.

The other tool you used was a handy-dandy, a piece of plastic that looked a little like a draftsman's triangle. On it you'd draw up attack vectors. And you'd let the blips follow the course you drew on it, telling the pilot headings and corrections so that the blip would follow the grease pencil line. The handy-dandy would use the cursor as a base. Angle off and range would be called out to the pilot, along with headings. And if everything was right, he'd see the target on his own radar and call "Judy," a code for airborne radar lock on. You'd hope he'd call "MA," mission accomplished, and ask for a breakaway steer. Then you'd set them up all over again.

Sometimes we'd be in big air defense missions where SAC bombers would attack large portions of the American continent. We'd run those late at night. The fighter scramble would be very real. And sometimes your pilot would whisper into your radio ear that you just ran him against a United or Pan Am flight, and neither of you gave a damn because his radar camera would only show that you'd made a good intercept. The colonel would be happy because he'd think you got the fake invader. As long as the commercial airliner didn't get a tail number, you were safe. As a matter of fact, they almost never knew you had done it because the attack was from the stern in the darkness. What the Hell?

I wondered if these Korean controllers had done things like that. They must have. At least they knew the queasy feeling, just before the silence on your channel was broken by the call of your fighters. The goal was to have a good mission. Your pilots called for the mandatory debriefing, and you were feeling great if they liked your headings, your stranger call-outs, your scope savvy. If things went wrong, you were a scope dope, a bad controller. These Korean brothers of the radar fraternity would surely know what I meant.

"Thisa is the new captain?"

A Korean officer had walked up to us while I had been pondering the radar screen. His blue shirt had two silver diamonds on each side of his collar, the rank of first lieutenant. His nametag was written in both Korean and English.

"Lieutenant Ko, this is Captain Whitman," said Packer.

The Korean thrust out his hand. "I very happy to meet you. We will talk when you come here."

I stood up. "I am so happy to meet you, Lieutenant Ko. I am very impressed with your operation here."

"You like this radar squadron?" he asked, a big smile on his face. "I think this one is not as nice as one in the states."

"No difference," I said, waving my arm around in a sweeping motion.

"Do you think Korea is as nice as your house?"

"I have only been in Korea a short time now, but I like it very much. We have many things the same."

"Many things the same," he laughed in a very nice way that said he took that as a compliment.

"Yes," I said, not really knowing what to say next. There now was a very awkward, sort of toothy-smile pause.

"When will you work here?" he said.

"He'll probably be up here all day tomorrow, Lieutenant Ko," said

Packer, now standing and beating his arms against himself in a warming effort.

"I will be here at that time. You will talk to me then," he said. "Now I must return to my squadron."

"Okay, Lieutenant Ko, I'll look forward to seeing you." And I shook his hand again.

He walked away and then turned and waved, "Tomorrow."

"Yes," I assured him.

Four-thirty came, which marked the end of the duty day. Packer took the wheel of our jeep, and down the steep winding road we went. Slowly. He shook behind the wheel, too, and I thought we'd both probably be a lot safer if I were driving.

A big open truck did come for the Korean shift change, but I noticed that many of them walked down in spite of that. In fact, the road was full of walking Korean enlisted men.

"One of them went over the hill just before I got here," said Packer, looking anxiously at the looming tailgater in the rearview mirror.

That big truck was behind us, very close, at about the midway point.

It was swaying back and forth. All of the Koreans were crowded in the back, pressing against the wooden high frame sides. I just prayed they didn't plow over us. No wonder many were walking. I'd be with them.

Packer was much more the courteous driver. As it was, the walkers had to form single file on either side to let us pass. They were neither negative nor positive as we went by. Rather, a neutral look came from them, breath making vapor clouds as they trudged.

Though Korea was known as a cold place in winter, the islands of the south were more mild. So far I had only seen clear days and nights, though Packer said it would snow on the island, too. That was becoming important to me as I thought about my inevitable navigations up and down this blasted hill come winter.

Finally we were down and made the turn through the gate. I got a better look at the sign. It was like a rainbow arch curved up above the road. The guard shack stood below the apex and supported the pole that gave it center strength. White Korean writing, below it an English translation.

"WELCOME TO THE 771st AIRCRAFT AND WARNING SQUADRON, ROKAF, TOLSAN-DO."

I was feeling a little better about the whole thing than I had the first time I'd passed under it, but I knew I'd ride under it, coming and going, a thousand times or more before the other side of the sign would bid me farewell forever.

5

Colonel Lee

I made a point to lay very low Monday night. Low profile was a thing I did to gain strength and put distance between me and my indiscretions. It was easy to do because Packer had headed downtown as soon as we parked at the Q. The Father had, indeed, stayed with his priest friends in the north of the island. Dutch's lady must have returned because I didn't see him at dinner. I ate alone at five. First one in the dining room, I missed Dubbs, too. Later, he and his Sue were at the movie, but I didn't even have to acknowledge them because I beat them in, scrunched down in my seat when they passed my row, and then zoomed out even before the lights went on.

Packer had said I'd pull duty the next day, so I just counted on that. I was up at five-thirty and had breakfast down by six-fifteen. No Dubbs yet, nor a Packer nor a Dutch. I walked over to the headquarters, but it was still locked. I went to Oyster's room, but the open door told me he hadn't slept in his bed, still neatly put together by the Kims. How the fuck did I get up the hill? It was 0630. Duty day started at 0730. I had an hour to walk it like the Koreans did. Fuck the jeep. I had no idea of where the keys were, or if anyone had thought about getting me up there.

So I joined the rest of the Korean Air Force, the Rocks, and walked the road. It was brisk, but it felt wonderful. The view grew with each step and I had a sense of my counterparts you didn't get from riding by them. I walked all but unnoticed, and that surprised me. I had two groups to listen to, one in front and one behind. They carried their tin lunch buckets and talked to each other enthusiastically. The sound of their language was delightful to hear there on that mountain road in their Korea on that early morning.

Their voices seemed higher. I could tell they were joking and jabbing at each other, young airmen full of life. Their language was melodious. The sound of its strange rhythm filled me. I was really in Korea doing the walk up the road. I wasn't just looking at it through a jeep window. I was walking a Korean road, on a Korean morning, with Koreans. I was an American military man in the field. How goddamn real could you get!

When I got to the top I walked out to the edge of the plateau the radars and ops building sat on. The Koreans had guard wire strung all around the perimeter, but there was one place where you could stand and look out over the island and on beyond to the sea. I could easily see the American compound, the Korean base, and the village near them. From then on outward it was farmland, small groups of houses, and the old Japanese fighter strip we used for a runway. Then the magnificent sea, so silvery in places, ran into the blue sky. There were puffy clouds here and there.

The only thing that ruined this placid scene was the big piece of pipe that was driven into the ground about fifty feet below my vantage point. That, along with a long slit trench, was the facility for the radar crews. There was a path down to it, access provided by the break in the wire. Koreans passed me as I stood looking at the view. They were coming to and from the facility. They urinated into the pipe and squatted over the trench. A bit of odor and weird, unavoidable voyeurism was the price you paid for the scenic view.

I turned on my brogans and went into the darkness and yellow glow of Benjamin ops, up the steps to the desk and radar set that made up the GI position. Benjamin 12 reporting for duty with time noted, my first log entry.

I sat there for at least an hour, just watching the Koreans. They all worked very busily at their scopes, reporting what little traffic there was, plotting tracks told them by the mainland and Japanese tie-ins.

Sergeants talking to young enlisted officer types coming into the room with papers to be looked at, and small groups of airmen gathered for a bull session between scope sittings. It all looked the same.

Yet these were yellowish men with black hair and exotic features. The uniform was different. There were strange smells and sounds in this ops room. It was like I was an invisible eavesdropper, watching these strange people talk with each other and carry out their tasks. It was a once-removed scene, something out of an adventure story.

"You walk up the mountain today?" said a voice next to me.

It was Lieutenant Ko.

"Yes, I walk. How are you today?" I said, turning in his direction. He was now seated at a long table across the aisle from me. We were only about five feet apart. He was at the ROKAF battle staff dais.

"How come you walk?" he said with a big smile. "We pass you in our jeep, but we have no room for you."

"Only way to know a mountain is to be on her. Just like woman," I said.

"Just like woman," he repeated, tickled with that. Then he said, "Do you never bring your jeep?"

"Yes, Lieutenant Ko, I will when I learn how to drive it."

"You cannot drive?" he said with surprise.

"I cannot drive the one with a stick and gears to shift."

"You never learn that?"

"Not you, too," I said.

"Not me?"

"No, no. It's just that my fellow officers cannot understand how it is that I cannot drive this one either. My father has had an automatic drive all of my life."

"Oh," he said with understanding. "So you need lesson before you can come up driving?"

"Yes," I said.

To communicate with the Koreans you had to speak slowly and use sort of an uncomplicated pattern of words. During my week in Osan I caught onto that and I knew I was going to be a good communicator. The Koreans I had met in the ops center there told me they didn't like GIs who talked fast. The idea was slow and simple, and imitate their way of putting words together in a sentence. It was like a side language, just a slight twist to the English language. It was fun to do.

Ko and I talked for hours, each of us turning away to scan the room and the large situation board in an almost unconscious pattern. You got into the habit of checking the area for tracks that might pose some threat. We trained that way in the continental U.S., where the hostile tracks were always simulated. In this place I was now sitting, it could turn real. In fact, Korea was always on an increased state of alert. No one ruled out the possibility that the North Koreans might come sweeping down across the 38th parallel again. Benjamin would not only be a target for sabotage and missiles, it might be the crucial suck-it-up-point where we'd control aircraft for a last ditch push back.

"My country is not safe like yours," Ko said with his ever-present smile.

"But maybe our two nations can keep it safe," I said. You got the feeling that just below the surface he was saying something else. He didn't so much talk with or to me. He kind of led me on, eyes searching for some soft spot he might hit. The more we talked, the more I suspected he had mixed feelings about America, about GIs.

The incredible thing was that Ko was not only a graduate of Seoul National University, but of its law school as well. He apologized for his English constantly, but I thought he was very articulate. At one point he actually got frustrated.

"If you could only hear me talk about the politics then."

"You do well enough," I said. "Besides," I added, "I feel like a stupid man because I do not know your language as you know mine. You pay my country great compliment because you learn English so well, I respect that."

He thought about that for a moment and said, "That is nice thing to say. You very much say a Korean thing. I think you know Korean thought."

That made him change the probing tactic just a little. We seemed more comfortable together after that. But I knew that a lot of Americans had made a string of impressions on Koreans stretching back to the fifties. That we could be "Ugly Americans" was well established even by our own literature and films. I could feel it just below the surface.

Packer walked up the aisle just then, with his parka hood over his emaciated head.

"I came to get you for lunch and then driver's school," he said, while he greeted Lieutenant Ko with a nod. "Ko, is this captain treating you okay?"

"Yes, he is very much like you, I think."

"Good. Us lieutenants hafta stick together." Yes, they were both first lieutenants. One a lawyer, one an Air Force Academy graduate. I liked them both, but I saw more future for the Korean.

The ride down was me on the brake pedal and in second gear. I didn't like that other pedal, that clutch. And I didn't like having to maneuver that damn stick. I had to do more of it once we leveled off, turned into the compound, rode under the arch, and then jerked to a stop in front of the Q.

"See, you almost have it," Oyster said, patting me on the shoulder.

"Can't you just put it in, say second, and leave it there? Couldn't you just do that for slow short trips?"

"No, man, you'd end up burning something up."

"I don't give a shit," I said, getting out.

"Zo you now learning dat jeep procedure, huh?" It was Dutch, stopping for us to join up with him. He was dressed in his work suit, hands resting on the backs of his hips. He looked the wise old engineer.

"He wants to leave it in second, Dutch. How do you like that?"

"He vants it to turn into a automatik, I tink."

"I'll do better after some chow. Let's forget the lessons for a while."

"Gut. Bud you call it chop here. Vee go get chop."

We headed for the dining hall and our chop.

On our way past the headquarters Quonset, we ran smack into a group coming out. I saw them exit as we joined up with Dutch. Inevitably, it became a collision course, they walking to the street and we toward the mess hall. There were five Koreans and one dumb shit American, Dubbs. I knew this was going to be Colonel Lee and his boys. It was.

"Gentlemen," I said with a snappy salute.

"Colonel Lee, gut day," chimed in Dutch.

That all stopped them in their tracks. Dubbs had no choice but to recognize us. He answered our salutes, but I was aiming mine at the Korean colonel. Taller than most Koreans, he was beaming at me. We hit it off right there in the middle of the compound road.

"Thisa new Captain Widman?" he said to Dubbs and me with the same glance.

"Yeah. Yes, Colonel Lee, this is Norm Whitman." He hated taking the time for this, I knew.

Lee walked over to me with his hand out. "You just now come to my squadron?"

"Sir, I've been here about five days. I got in on that last choggy."

"Yes my controllers said they meet you today."

"Sir, I spent the morning in your operations room as a matter of fact."

"And what do you think of my squadron?"

"I'm impressed, Colonel. They told me at Military Assistance Institute how skillful Korean control was and how good your squadron would be. It's everything they said it would be."

Lee turned to Dubbs at that and said, "I think he must be with your State Department. He knows how to say very happy words to a commander."

"Now all we have to do is learn him how to drive a jeep," Dubbs answered with a laugh.

Lee turned back at me. "You also now can meet my operations officer, Major Moon." The major stepped forward and gave me a big shake. "This is my communications Officer, Major Park."

"Sir, I'm glad to meet you," I said, taking his hand.

"And Mr. Chung is my administrative officer."

"Glad to meet you, captain," he said with a GI ring to his voice.

"Mr. Chung," I said, shaking his hand.

"And this is our doctor. Like me, he is a Lee."

I shook the doctor's hand with a smile and a nod. He didn't seem to speak as much English as the others.

"Well, we better get going," said Dubbs.

"Mr. Dutch, Lieutena Packer, how are you?" said the Colonel, not seeming to hear Dubbs.

"Ja, fine, sir. I give your civil engineer our cement mixer."

"Yes, I am very appreciate that. Do you think that cement will set now?"

"Ja, I tink zo. I vill check on him."

Lee patted the old Dutchman on the shoulder. "I think you are a good person for our compound."

"Sir, he likes to pour cement almost as much as he likes to pour OB," said Packer.

The Colonel laughed at that. "But we use water in the cement I hope?"

"Ja, vee don't vaste beer dat vay, you can be sure, Kolonel."

"So, then, I will see all again. Captain Widman, again I welcome you to my squadron."

He gave us all a raised hand gesture and turned with the group. The others all nodded and smiled. Meanwhile, Dubbs was reading a letter he had pulled out of his pocket. He had been reading it as soon as the introductions got past my jeep driving. They all turned the corner around the headquarters and headed for the Korean side.

"They have a meeting once a week. They'll take Dubbs over to their chow hall now for some tea and lunch, not that he did anything for them to reward," said Packer.

"He's a consistent ass," I said as we resumed our course for lunch.

The rest of my first duty day consisted of driving with Packer up and down the hill in the jeep. I shifted, putting in the clutch and putting out the clutch, and I jerked, jerked the damn thing twenty round trips or more. I learned the routine. By three o'clock I could do it pretty well. Oyster beamed at me and said, "Well, now you're a goddamn jeep driver." So I was, I guessed.

And when I made my final trip down the hill, I swung into our parking slot with a great deal of élan and confidence. I was surprised, however, to see a bunch of Land Rovers parked in front of the Q as well.

"God save us all," said Packer when he saw them. "Now you're going to meet the biggest bunch of scallywags you've ever seen in your life."

"Who?" I said, shutting down the jeep.

"The other Fathers on the island. They're Irish missionaries, the chaplain's buddies, the ones he goes to see."

When we opened the Q door, an outpouring of laughter, cigarette smoke, and booze fumes hit us. There was quite a party in progress. Packer and I walked up the hall to the Q bar.

Once there, we walked into a room filled with burly looking characters, dressed like lumberjacks or some kind of farmhands. One did have the traditional black suit and Roman collar on. Father Fisher was behind the bar, dressed in his fatigues.

"Ah, there you are, Andy and Norm. Andy, you know everybody. Norm, come here and meet the Fathers, the Columban Fathers of Tolsan," he said like he was a parent showing off a son to his business associates.

Andy was greeting the group with "Hi" and "How are you, Father?" I walked over to the chaplain.

"Now, Norm Whitman, Captain Whitman, here's Father Ryan O'Donnell."

"Hi, there," he said, raising up a glass.

"And Father Danny Callahan, and Father Regis Riley, and Father Pat Flaherty, and Father Tim Grady."

They were a hearty bunch and gave me big "Hi, Narms" all around. Their faces and hands were large, noses and cheeks reddish, and each one had a big-toothed smile.

"And over there resting by the fire is none other than the famous Father T. Patrick Sullivan himself, in person, otherwise known as T.P."

And there sat a very old priest, in the easy chair, with a straw hat on his head, cigar in one hand, and drink in the other. His nose and face were a spider's web of broken red veins. He feigned irritation at the introduction.

"I'll ask your forgiveness, Captain, for not gettin' up, but these beyes have me worn from the ride down here."

Putting his cigar in his mouth, Father Sullivan shook my hand with a surprisingly firm shake. "Father Paul tells me you're a good Catholic bey, and I'm glad of that."

"Well, I'm overwhelmed by the size of the clergy down here, I'll tell you that, Father," I said.

"Ah, Narm, get away from himself now before he starts tell'n you about his arthritis. He's always hope'n he'll find 'a good Catholic bey' to listen to his troubles. Come here and have a beer, what the hell," said the collared priest, Father Ryan O'Donnell.

"Yes, go over with the troublemakers," the old man said. "They're the new church that shoves the old people down by the fire."

With that the others let out groans and noises of glee. The old priest pulled down the brim of his hat. "Ah, the bunch 'a ya," he said.

I took the beer O'Donnell handed me and broke my alcohol fast. What the hell, indeed, it was handed to me by a man of the cloth. Now I had six priests to drink with, I said to myself. When I did write that letter to Angie, she'd think I'd been placed personally by our Lord in a literal sanctuary. And was I ever ready for a beer. Was I ever ready for a party. Was I ever. They could put it down just like I did. It didn't take me long to get right into the thing, enjoying the security of my new drinking companions of the one true church.

These Columban fathers were from Ireland, assigned to Tolsan-Do for life. Ryan O'Donnell, dressed in his black suit and Roman collar, was the local parish priest for the town right outside the gate. He was the pastor and only father at St. Angela's. His was a life of keeping an Asian flock of Catholics in a land that traditionally held with Buddhism and Shintoism.

The old man, Father Sullivan, was pretty much retired, but still performed priestly duties with young Father Grady up in Tolsan City. They all called the old priest "T.P." It wasn't long before he tilted his head and fell fast asleep in front of the fire. O'Donnell told me the old gentleman had been on the island since the 1920s and had been imprisoned by the Japanese in the thirties and then held through the end of World War Two. They all loved him very much. To the Koreans on the island he was a legend.

Father Flaherty had a parish in a town called Moklepo, halfway between us and Tolsan City. But the best story of all was that of Danny Callahan and Regis Riley. They were two of about five fathers who ran a huge pig farm owned by the church and operated to teach the Korean farmers how to raise pigs. The farm was located about ten miles to the south of us in an area known as Soopoo. They looked the part.

There was no doubt about their being Irish. They were so much the stereotype of the hard-drinking Irish that I thought I had been transported to some pub in Dublin on St. Patrick's Day. But it didn't take me long to see not only the priest in them, but also the fierce dedication they had to the job of bringing their beliefs to the Koreans. They were blowing off steam like people who paid hard dues on a grinding schedule.

And they were fast mates, as they put it. Like a group of fraternity brothers, they'd jab and jostle at each other, playing tricks behind the backs of the unwary. Their Yankee brother was both pal and provider. Fisher would bring them to the compound, a place where they could unwind and not worry about doing it in front of their flocks. Our place meant some good drinking and eating, a high pressure shower nozzle, an American movie, and a night's sleep away from the demands of either parish or pig farm.

We decided we'd eat in the NCO club because the party went through the mess hall's four-thirty to six dinner schedule. At six-fifteen, they woke up T.P. and we carried the revelry to Goldman's dining room for burgers and French fries. They were worried about getting the old man fed. If he hadn't been along, I don't think food would have mattered. He put down a big cheeseburger with great relish, along with a big glass of milk.

We all had burgers and beer. In a moment of inspiration, I picked up the tab for the whole thing.

"Ah now, look what Narm's gone and done, won't you," said Father Callahan. "You're invited, on this spot, to a grand dinner of fish and potatoes at the farm on the Friday after next."

"Here, here," they all chimed. "Mother Air Force's sent us a grand man for the cause of advancing the well-being of good Catholic men here on the island."

"Amen," said old T.P. "And I'll personally see to it that he's made to understand how much that means to us all."

"And that means he'll be getting you off in a corner to ask you if you'd mind get'n him a box of cigars, Narm."

"Aw, go on, Flaherty," the old man said, milk mustache and all. Somehow Goldman had gotten into the middle of all of this and with a great show of flair he and the bartender were putting shot glasses in front of us.

"From your local Jewish representative, gentlemen, a bit of Irish Whiskey that I had flown in at great personal expense. We're awfully sorry about that mix-up in Jerusalem. We hope this will make up for anything we might have done. Perhaps you'll think about taking the crosses down off the walls. Bad publicity, you know."

We were all seated around a large round table. There were three like that in the NCO dining room with three small square tables, too. But our party was the only one going. Soon Goldman and Mr. Kwak had a shot glass in front of each of us, filling them with a brownish liquid. Irish Whiskey.

Goldman was running his mouth a mile a minute, speaking to each priest as he poured. Everyone was very animated. I looked around at my dinner companions with a sense of wonder. Round flushed faces, in various stages of age, enjoying to the utmost the burgers, the ceremony of the shots, the entire affair. It was a remarkable group.

Father Regis Riley got up and put his arm around Goldman. "Gentlemen, if you please, a wee toast. Ahem . . . a wee toast," he yelled above the several side conversations and general uproar. The old man, T.P., banged a fork against a beer bottle.

"Much better, thank you," said Riley. "Now, I give you Sergeant Martin Goldman, a man from the Old Testament who traces his roots to Moses himself."

"Here, here," we all responded.

"He's given us a taste of another glorious heritage. Tip your glasses now, to the likes of Goldman and the South of Ireland."

Bottoms up. It was the first Irish Whiskey I'd ever tasted. It was good. Much like scotch, I thought, but milder and easier to put down.

"Hey, that's great," I said.

"Well, then, pour the man another," said Fisher.

"You took the words right out of their mouths," said Goldman. "I'll be surprised if I have to put this back on the shelf."

He didn't have to. One fifth of Irish Whiskey makes the rounds about four or five times and then it's finished. And the stuff really puts a nice edge on a beer base. It surely put a twinkle in our eyes and made those Irish faces glow like firelight.

The movie we saw that night was *Tammy, Tell Me True*, a re-release. I had seen the thing when I was a kid, but the missionaries loved it. And all of the prostitutes loved it. It was the kindest audience the movie had ever played for. Debbie Reynolds never enjoyed such critical acclaim. She was, hands down, number one box office actress of Tolsan.

On the way back down the street Ryan O'Donnell and Regis Riley were singing, "Does my lover feel, what I feel, when she is near? I'd sing like a violin, if she were only here." The harmony was good, tempered by the last of the Irish Whiskey that we had carried over in paper cups.

Once we hit the Q, the party started up again. Over and over the theme was sung. But without old T.P. Ryan's company. O'Donnell had tucked him in bed in one of the empty rooms. In fact, the care he gave to the act reminded me of putting one of the kids to bed, right down to carrying in the glass of water.

Dubbs made one appearance. He called Fisher out into the hall, and the two of them talked quietly for a few minutes. Father Pat Flaherty spotted that conversation and yelled out, "Major Dubbs, you must come and share at least a beer with us all, sir."

"No, no thanks, Padre," he said. "I gotta get up with the chickens tomorrow." He was three quarters of the way nice. It was because he was outnumbered, I thought. "You all enjoy yourselves," he said, and then he left the Q altogether, going out the door.

Nobody paid any particular attention to him leaving. The singing and the party just kept on going.

"Father," I said, pulling Fisher aside, "what was that all about?"

Fisher smiled at my concern. "Nothing really. He just wanted to make sure I collected two bucks a head for sleeping here. That's no problem. But the bad news is that the boys have lost their postal privileges. They can't send or get anything through our post office anymore. I'm sure Dubbs asked for a reading on it and the answer from Osan was to cut it out."

It turned out Dubbs had gone downtown after he delivered the news about the postal service. Good thing, too. That was the night we wrecked the club.

What happened was that we got good and drunk and pretty soon Goldman came waltzing into our midst. "Found one more bottle of Irish," he said, pulling off his parka. When you're drunk like that it's always great to see somebody pop in. Everyone yelled, "Hooray for Goldman."

And after we polished that off, in walks Packer, kicked out of his hooch for one reason or another. But he was met with cheers and pats on the back. God, he looked like death warmed over.

"Lieutenant, I gotta hear what happened. What was it this time?"

"Naw, nothing big. See, Sue and Adja are like sisters, and Sue came down to stay the night with her. I couldn't stay there with them. It wouldn't be right."

"So he's got a kitchen pass," I said.

"No, wait. I've got a feeling there's a detail or two more," said Goldman, waving for quiet. "How did Sue get down there, Packer?" Goldman had his cupped hand on his ear, the other ear motioning for speech from Packer.

"Well, Dubbs, of course. Somebody give me a beer or something. Geez, I'm thirsty." He was trying to change the subject.

"And Dubbs drove the two of you back here, right?" said Father Paul.

Packer didn't say a thing. He just started to pour that careful, jittery stream of beer into a glass. The silence was telltale and everyone began to laugh and say, "Oooooooohhhh."

"Aw, Packer," Fisher said, slamming his glass down on the bar. "Don't tell me Dubbs is staying with the two of them while you're up here."

"It's okay. There's not enough room for everyone."

"Do all three of them sleep together, then?" O'Donnell said, with his red eyebrows raised.

"No. No. I shoulda never got mixed up with all of you. Dubbs and Sue sleep in the big bed and Adja takes the little couch. Geez, do I hafta tell you all the details of everything?" He was pouting. He was all sweaty and hairs were sticking to his forehead. There he sat, drinking beer, annoyed at being caught the asshole, the dupe of Adja, Sue, and Dubbs.

That's when Goldman took his glass and threw it into the fireplace. "That actor Ronald Coleman, or somebody always did that at a time like this." It made a nice sound when it hit. There was even a fire in it. I liked the way it looked and sounded; so I got up, went around the bar, took down a wine glass, went over to the fireplace, and threw the glass into the flames. *Packer Gets Took*, scene one, take two," I said. With that, Packer got up and slammed his beer glass into it.

And that's how it started. Everybody was throwing, pitching, and lobbing in all sorts of glasses. It was most enjoyable, with people making statements after each throw.

"That's for the time my Uncle Sean wrecked our gate," said Danny Callahan. Clank.

"For the dirty who keeps stealing from the church," said Ryan O'Donnell. Crash.

"A girl named Maureen, and I'll say na more," said Tim Grady. Smash.

"To Saint Luke's soccer team," said Pat Flaherty. Clink.

And finally the end of the first round of oaths came with the crash of an empty beer bottle, flung by Regis Riley, who said, "To the stubbornness of God's pigs."

We broke every glass in the little Q club. Every glass. After a while we didn't even throw them into the fireplace. We threw them at the walls, the floor, the doors, other glasses, and each other. And we continued to drink. After the glasses were gone we drank beer, filling up the empty bottles with the whiskey if you wanted something harder.

There was all manner of conversations, odds and ends of things. I talked to Goldman about being a doctor, and to Father Ryan O'Donnell about teaching English at the local school.

Father Tim Grady had relatives in Pittsburgh; we were sure I knew them, but now I don't know why. And Packer asked me about thirty times or more if I thought he was a fool, to which I answered, every time, an absolute "Yes, fool."

It was one of those times when I couldn't remember the next morning when or how I'd gotten to bed. Morning brought me one of those exquisite hangovers my body was famous for. The guilt, the shakes, and the nausea all came with it.

One good thing that happened was that I learned a little more about the Kims. Up until that morning I'd only occasionally passed Mr. Kim in the hall as he carried the clean and dirty wash back and forth, or made his rounds of the rooms. He kept our beds made up with clean sheets every day, and he swept up. You could throw stuff all around your room and Mr. Kim would have it washed and hanging that evening.

In my restless sleep of the next early morning I could hear a scratching sound, like the tinkle of glass being swept. And that's what it was. When the Kims had come in and spotted the broken glass and God only knows what else, they immediately went about cleaning it up. When I staggered out into the club area, they already had the glass up, the floor vacuumed, and all of the wood polished. Parts of the rug were still wet from a good scrubbing. Some of the seat covers were off and drying outside.

Packer had gotten up to pull hill duty, but not before he'd performed a miracle, too. As club monitor for the little bar, he had given the Kims a couple of boxes of brand new glasses. They were all lined up where their deceased brothers had stood the day before. Dubbs would never know that we had torn the place apart. That was good.

The busy Kims gave me a big smile when I walked in. "Gooda morning, Captain, sore," Mr. Kim said with a very knowing smile. Mrs. Kim bowed and hid her mouth.

"You two are wonderful," I said, bringing my hands over my face, rubbing the hangover itch I always got over my entire face. "I think you keep us from big trouble."

"Big time party," Mrs. Kim said behind her hand.

"Yes, very big time we have last night. I wish you were there."

"Oh, no, sore, I get cut, I think," said Mr. Kim, shaking his head, but still giving me that big smile.

"Are the priests still sleeping?" I asked.

"No, sore, Shimboo Nim all get up very early and leave for their housa."

I just shook my head at that. I could no more get up early after a night like that than stand on my head. Just thinking about responsibility made me want to throw up. Lucky I didn't have the hill to do.

"Is Father Fisher up, too?"

"Yesa, he go to breakfast with Lieutena Packer. He and Shimboo O'Donnell go to town."

"Dubbs not back yet?"

"No, sore, Maja not back."

I didn't deserve this kind of luck. It was probably the priests that brought it. Safe. I'd get myself a couple of shots and maybe a beer after the Kims were done, to get well on, and get some more sleep. By lunch I'd be better.

"Sore, you know when old Mista Dutch come back?"

"Gosh," I said, wondering where the hell he was. "I haven't any idea."

"He say he go Tolsan City."

It was his *yobo*. She was probably flying back from Seoul.

"I think you probably see him maybe tomorrow."

I went back down the hall and just lay on my bed, looking up at the curve of the ceiling. Over on the dresser was a color picture of the kids, looking out at me with those dear little smiles. They looked like angels. A big black and white of Angie stood next to them. I had been here almost two weeks, I thought, and then I started to cry. I was a long way from them. I needed them. Hell, they could be dead for all I knew.

When I heard the Kims shuffle back down the hall toward the john and their workroom, that was my cue to get up. I was very dizzy. I had tears going down my cheeks. I wanted to vomit. Instead I slowly eased my way out of the room and up the short distance to the club area. Once there I made my shaky hands pour a shot of Jim Beam, and I got a small beer out of the cooler. One, two, I put them into my stomach, and it wasn't long before I felt a bit more relaxed.

This wasn't really drinking. It was get-well time. It was medicine. I could sometimes make myself over with just a little touch of booze in the morning. If I could get food down, and keep it down, I sometimes didn't even have the hangover. I was beginning to feel like it was going to be one of those days. The booze was staying down. I would be okay. Aspirin would come later.

6

English Lessons

And that was the beginning of a routine for me. In the next weeks that passed, I pulled my shift on the hill, talked with the Korean controllers, and drank a fair share with Doc and Father Fisher at night. Movies were every other day. They were most fun to watch when you were half snockered. The priests came down once a month. I made sure I ate at least two times a day, with several burgers at the NCO club being the best way to get food down.

It was hill duty, party, day off, hill, movie, party, day off. The days strung out like that. Letters from Angie and the kids came in droves when the choggy flew in. I tried to get one on each plane, but sometimes I'd miss. Though I thought about them, they seemed in another time.

I lived in a brown world with people who belonged to no one. Dubbs just talked when he had to, and he was happy as long as we pulled our shifts. Packer was downtown most of the time. Dutch's *yobo* did come back; he was in his hooch in the evenings with her. But Paul and Goldman I could depend on. They and the priests and the booze and the movies made up my circle of influence. As Goldman said, it was your mind or your liver. So, I made the best of it and counted the days.

I did discover one way to pass the time that was less destructive than drinking and more productive than the movies: giving English lessons. One brief snatch of conversation I remembered I'd had with Father O'Donnell was about giving lessons to people in his parish. He remembered it, too, the fox, and after a good meal in his rectory one evening, while the brandy was poured, he hit me with the idea again. We sealed it with a "Fine, Narm, fine." I'd give the lessons every Wednesday night in the back of the church.

He had an old blackboard set up back there, with a variety of stubs of colored chalk to write with. My first Wednesday was a big event. There were about thirty-five people there, ranging in age from small school children to some old mamasans and papasans. When O'Donnell brought me in, both of us walking down the aisle between the folding chairs, it was like a grand entrance. The people smiled and looked at each other with a "Here's our teacher" look.

O'Donnell introduced me to the group. These priests had been here so long that their Korean was said to be flawless. He'd actually go for months without speaking any English at all. But he looked like any other parish priest I'd ever seen, making an introduction to a church group. But the language was Korean, and the people certainly weren't Irish.

He'd say something, and they'd whisper "Ah, ah," and once in a while I'd hear my name come out with a strange sounding twist to it. It sounded like "Widitman." Then they'd say "Ah, ah," again.

These students were very nicely dressed. They'd probably put on their best clothes for the lessons. They'd paddle around town in outfits of every description, but lesson night had the oldsters in long, full Korean dresses or suit and tie. These suits, many of them, looked like the stuff I'd seen on the rack of the Salvation Army or Goodwill when Angie took me hunting for antiques. But this was a gesture of respect, very high fashion for where we were and who we were.

Everyone applauded. "Narm, I told them you were going to give them superior quality instruction and that you were a good Catholic man to be doing this for them. The class is all yours."

I put out my hand and took his in an exaggerated handshake. "Thank you . . . Father. Now I teach English," I said slowly, slowly.

I could see a lot of them, especially the ladies, moving their lips in imitation of my words. Some even said, "Than-ka you" very softly.

"Ah, you're just the teacher I thought you'd be. I'll come for you when it's time," said O'Donnell, and with a wave to everyone he walked back through the seats and out the door, his long cassock swishing with his steps.

The first night I did things like "I am Mister Whit-man," pointing to myself. Then I'd point to some of them and soon we were getting "I yam Mista Kim" and "I Mista Moon." The women didn't really like to recite, but they pushed their little children into it. They had "Thank you" down pat and even volunteered "Okay" and "Gee Eye," something I hadn't even said. They were all very bright it seemed to me. Their faces were alive and all toothy. The skin around the eyes looked tougher.

The smell in my classroom was the same smell I lived with in the operations room. They had *kimchi* breath. The national dish peppered the air with the smell of fermented cabbage and spices. It made the air close, I thought.

I wrote the letters of the alphabet on the blackboard, easy to do. I'd write the letter, say "Bee," and they'd repeat it together. The women would do that. It was an easy operation. "Gee," I said, watching the toothy replies, hot *kimchi* breath coming up from below, blowing over the cords, and over the buckteeth. In a way they looked like skulls repeating after me. Chamois skin, yellow chamois skin, stretched over toothy skulls that repeated letters to me. But they were not scary skulls and they smiled often, even giggled with delight at the strange sounds they were uttering.

Once I even said, "Okay, skulls, now you say 'Zee' and you'll be at the end of our lesson for tonight." The skulls all said "Zee" dutifully. You might have to work like hell for a teaching certificate in the states, but I was now a certified English instructor at the Saint Catherine's School for Talking Skulls.

I got that skull image teaching them that night and that would sometimes come back to me when I'd be with Koreans. Yet most times they seemed perfectly normal. Sometimes I'd swear they didn't look different at all. I mean you can spend so much time with them that you don't see any difference anymore. One of the sergeants had said once that the Korean women looked "whiter and whiter" as the months went on. Crude, but I understood what he meant.

The last thing I did that night was to say "Good night, Father" over and over again with them. I'd point to the direction of the rectory and say "Father." One old man said back, "Yes fath-er." The test came when O'Donnell arrived for me, and I cued them all. Out came the best "Gooda night ah Father Norm Widman."

O'Donnell laughed his Irish red laugh and said, "It's a good thing you're doing with these ones, Narm, even down to taking my job."

I missed very few Wednesday night lessons the entire time I was in Korea. It was a very private rewarding thing. They never caught the skull thing, and I'm glad of it.

I hadn't been giving English lessons at the school long before Lieutenant Ko asked me about it. We had been together on shift one morning, and I sensed from the start that something was on his mind.

"You teach some persons down in the town English lessons?" he said, probing. It was like he was trying to catch me off guard, put in such a way that I might have been caught red-handed doing something I hadn't wanted anyone to know.

"Yes, Ko, every Wednesday now I teach to people in Saint Catherine's Church."

No sooner had I gotten that out than he quickly came back with, "You can teach ROKAF officers, too?"

Suddenly I saw my life filling up with one English class after another, but how could I refuse.

"Yes, I would be honored to teach ROKAF officers. Do you want to organize a group?"

"Yes, you will teach us some Mondays in your BOQ," he said.

7

Pearl

When Goldman closed down the NCO Club every night, it was a matter of routine for him to drive the club employees to their homes in the town. They'd all climb in the back of the ambulance, and that gave Father Paul and me a perfect excuse to climb in front and take an excursion downtown. We never came right back. Though they had been just about everywhere down there, my coming to the site had given them the excuse to see it all again. Taking me around gave them renewed interest in all the spots.

They had introduced me to the icehouse early on. But now it was the round of teahouses. These were little one- and two-room affairs with tables grouped around a potbellied stove. They almost never closed, and there was always a group of Korean men sitting around sipping tea, no matter what the hour.

The tables were very fragile wooden ones, rather smallish for a restaurant in the States. The chairs—none of which matched—were also smallish. They were wooden, too, except that once in a while there'd be one of those chrome jobs with red vinyl, the kind you'd find in a cheap restaurant, diner, or dairy store back home. Both the tables and the chairs would creak and sway if you put any other than direct down pressure on them.

The floors and walls were cement, unpainted, and dampish. You felt like you were sitting in a basement. The floors always had wet patches because both the customers and the waitresses would dump out cold tea on them.

But the tea was always good, and Goldman said that this was the one time it was okay to drink local water because they kept it at a boil until you put in your order. There was a wide variety, but I liked the standard green tea the best. You could also order OB or Crown Beer, or a pot of hot rice wine they called *chung jung*. I was usually so looped by the time I got there that the tea was a welcome comfort, especially if the next day had me pulling duty on the hill.

We'd often meet the young ROKAF officers in those places. They were very much like 18th century English coffee houses in that conversation was the occupation, and each one catered to a certain steady crowd. When we'd show up, these young Koreans would invite us to form our chairs with them in a conversation circle. Often we'd sit there, enjoying the tea, and talk until two or three in the morning.

The conversation always had to do with our two countries. They had a lot of questions about America, mostly about how we lived. They never tired of hearing about us. After we went through all of that, we'd all re-fight the Korean War and speculate about the future of Korea. You had the feeling you were treading on thin ice when it got around to America's role in Korea. I think they had heard so many negative things about our being there from the GIs themselves that they wanted to test you to see how you felt about it.

I guess I gave rather disappointing answers. I held that we belonged there as long as we were welcome. I answered questions like, "You mad because we take you from your good house?" with "No, I must go remote somewhere. It might as well be someplace good like Korea."

After we had a couple of sessions like that, they became more relaxed and they'd tell you what was on their minds. I could get individuals, like Ko, to do that on the hill, but it was much better in a group situation. You'd get a wider viewpoint, and you could see them bounce ideas off each other. They liked to talk, and they enjoyed our attention. Goldman and Paul and I enjoyed their thoughts. We were a good audience.

These young men were very proud of Korea, but at the same time they were frustrated with their lot. For one thing, they were very well educated. They came from high- to moderate-income families. But their education had been dead-ended in that it was very difficult for them to find jobs in their country that fitted their studies. Many were engineers, for example, but there were not enough engineering positions to go around. Others, like Ko, had gone on for graduate degrees, like law, and were unable to find work. A commission was the best thing open to them; in a way they resented having to trade the prospect of being a philosopher, engineer, or lawyer for a uniform.

Korea was not a true democracy, either. It was ruled very forcefully by the regime of Park Chung Hee, a former general who had supreme power. These young men believed that the people should be given a choice for other leadership. But that was dangerous talk, especially for military officers, which they found oppressive. I gathered from their outspokenness that some of their professors had encouraged free speech and freewheeling ideas, but once outside the walls of academe they found a society not so tolerant of such talk.

But even though they'd let their hair down, the teahouse atmosphere was still tense. I discovered one night just how easy it was to put your foot in your mouth. In my mind I felt a bit ashamed of the image that America was like some powerful big brother that kept Korea free. I got the feeling they felt intimidated by that. So, I tried to give the impression that Korea was really strong enough to take care of herself.

It was the worst thing I could have said. It almost started an out-and-out melee. There were some older men sitting by us who never gave a sign they understood English, but when I let out with, "Korea does not need America to help her. Korea is a very powerful nation," I was surrounded by some very angry people.

These guys had been KATUSAs, which stands for Korean Augmentation to the United States Army. They spoke good English. And when I said that Korea didn't need America, they literally threw me out of the teahouse. It was weird. While they were very proud, they still wanted America in Korea. I was trying to save them face and damn near lost my ass. I had had it with teahouses for a while.

That's when Doc came up with the idea of going to the *kisaeng* house, the Korean version of the geisha. I objected on the grounds that I had made a promise with myself that I'd be straight while I was away from home. But Goldman reassured me by saying that all the girls did there was to help you have a good time. It was all very high classed, he said. You didn't have sex with those girls. Just like in Japan.

Now I'd heard of the Japanese geishas and I'd seen all those movies. But the Korean version was like seeing a Broadway show in Peoria. The *kisaeng* house was a rundown affair, a tattered copy of what went on in Tokyo. But it was a lot of laughs.

You went in from a porch where you took off your shoes. A mamasan and her giggling young ladies, all dressed in long full gowns, met you and took you to a little room with very fragile rice paper sliding walls. The floor was warm because heating pipes ran under it. You ordered beer and nuts and rice wine and they'd also bring in a table full of food. It was a good time. The little ladies would sit next to you and feed you with chopsticks. Harmless.

I could never tell just how many little *kisaeng* girls worked in the place. They came in and out of the party room many times an hour. There were perhaps five party rooms in the place. The same handful of girls was working all of the parties at once. The rice paper walls were thin enough so you could hear the same girls laughing it up with Korean guys.

They'd bring in the beer, sit with us a while, and then they'd split. Ten minutes later they'd come in with a table. On it would be more peanuts, dishes of eggs, and sauce. They'd break out chopsticks for us again, feed us a little, and then go off again. They were probably doing the same thing in all the other rooms.

Some of them spoke pretty good English. They were very childlike. They'd play little hand games with you or encourage us to chug our beers. That'd give them an excuse to go off to bring us more.

The room had a bare light bulb that hung down from the ceiling. All of the walls were rice paper. One night I wrote "Gamma Alpha Sigma" on the wall. Father Paul wrote something in Latin. Goldman took the pencil and wrote his initials, along with a Star of David. They served *chung jung* at the *kisaeng* house, too. We'd belt that down with the beer. It was nice to sit on that warm floor, shut off from the rest of the world by the rice paper walls. We didn't care if the girls stayed with us or not. It was just a chance to get away and enjoy a good meal. We learned a lot about each other down in those rooms.

The Father liked to talk with the girls, and Goldman enjoyed patting them on the ass. To me they were like little schoolgirls. I can't explain why, but they just didn't turn me on. But they were a lot of laughs. We picked up words and customs from them.

It was in that *kisaeng* house that I learned about the priest. On one of those late night expeditions he told Goldman and me all about himself. We'd get shut up in those little rice paper rooms, resting our butts on the heated floor, and it was like the world outside didn't exist anymore. You were just there, sipping beer and *chung jung*, talking to your friends. No matter if the little dollies kept popping in and out, the language barrier kept everything private.

"December seventh is the most important date of my life," the priest said, pouring us all another round of *chung jung* that was kept on a little burner in a tin teapot affair. You drank it warm.

"I was seventeen years old, a flight sergeant for the Seventh Pursuit Squadron at Wheeler Field, Hawaii, and I had the world by the tail. And then the Japs came along and messed up my world."

"You were there in Hawaii when they hit Pearl Harbor?" I said in wonder.

"Yes, but not Pearl. I was at Wheeler, in the center of Oahu, next to

Scofield Barracks. Pearl gets all the headlines. People remember Pearl. But Hickam and Wheeler got the shit kicked out of them just as badly, you know."

"Yeah, yeah, *Here to Eternity*, I know," said Goldman.

"Do you want to hear about it or not?"

"He's just being crabby. Go ahead, I really want to hear about it," I said.

"Yeah, Padre, we do," said a contrite Goldman, giving me one of his sidelong winks.

"I lied about my age and got into the Army Air Corps in 1940. If you had half a brain, then, you'd be sergeant in no time. I wound up in Hawaii with a great job at the Seventh Pursuit. Had my own room in the barracks there at Wheeler, and I was taking courses at the University of Hawaii off duty. It was swell."

"Then the attack, huh?"

"Yeah, and it was just as eerie as you've probably been told, or seen in the movies."

It really seemed incredible that he'd lived in that time. He was looking into his shot glass with that far off look he'd get once in a while, but I wanted him to keep going with the story.

"Where were you when the attack came?"

"I was coming out of church."

"God, you had it in your blood even then, huh? I thought you were going to tell us you got religion after the attack. Hell, you're probably the only guy who walked out of church into the Japanese attack."

"No, smarty, Sergeant Rimmel, Henry Rimmel was with me. He was the administrative NCO for the squadron."

"When did you guys know it was an attack?" I asked.

"We thought it was the Navy at first. The Navy guys used to like to mock strafe us, and overfly our base a lot. Our guys simulated attacks on their ships. It was a regular game. It was good practice for everyone, and fun to watch. They'd always come through a place in the mountains we called gunsight pass, and that's exactly where this bunch of planes came from."

Even Goldman was listening seriously now.

"But when they flew over the runway, smoke and fire came up after them. And then the whole area was just a mess of noise and smoke and confusion. I pointed to the rising sun on the planes. Henry and I just stood watching all of that without saying one damn word. Not a damn word."

The little dollies suddenly slid open the door and carried in a small table loaded with peanuts, fried eggs, and other assorted *kisaeng* hors d'oeuvres. They were suddenly so Asian. Their distant cousins had been in the planes flying over Wheeler, but they only brought us food and smiles.

The girls settled down next to us and started making sauce for the eggs, but I didn't want that to stop Paul's story.

"Go on. Go on. Noise, Smoke, and confusion."

"Then we hit the dirt and sort of crawl-ran to our squadron. There were a lot of wounded and dead lying everywhere. I think I vomited every ten paces. It was awful. But we were obsessed with getting to our squadron area."

The girls were saying things to us and giggling. They wanted us to eat.

Between bits of egg, Paul finished the story. When he and Rimmel got to their area, half of their building was blown away. "Guys were holding up machine guns and trying to shoot the planes down. All of our fighters were destroyed on the ground. You could just feel the intense heat from the fuel burning. And you could smell the flesh."

He wasn't really in the room with us. He was back there, in the middle of it. He'd let a girl put egg, dripping with mustard sauce, in his mouth; but the real him wasn't there at all.

"God, you guys, half of our boys were just killed in their beds. My room was blown half away. If I hadn't been to mass I'd have been blown away."

"Then what happened?"

"They just went away. They left us with the fires and the smells and our pants down around our legs and our busted planes and squadron, and they turned away and flew back to hell. We lined up all the bodies in rows all the rest of the day and tried to identify them. We spent the next two days tending to the dead. We lost half our boys."

"And then you went to fight in the Philippines, right?"

"Yes, I did. I got a chance to fight back."

"Norm, did you know he won the Silver Star two times in the Philippines?" said Goldman in a gentle way, letting me know that he'd heard it all before.

"Father, that's something to be very proud of. I mean, I'm truly impressed."

He was sobbing now, and the little *kisaeng* girls were cooing about that, one laying her hand ever so gently on his shoulder.

"They've been through this a couple of times, Captain. When he gets really snockered, he tells it. That's how I know he's zonked. We all go back to 1941."

It wasn't long until the priest was sleeping on the floor while Goldman and I talked. I was to make the trip back to Wheeler a few times more before the assignment was over. It took on a different look after that story.

8

Working Girls

Mondays and Wednesdays I taught English. Every other night I was out on the town drinking beer and rice wine. Or I was in one of the rectories, drinking beer, Irish Whiskey, and sacramental wine. Mornings were rugged, especially if I had to pull hill duty.

Sometimes we'd go to Packer's hooch, or even over to Dutch's, probably among the best homes in the town. By stateside standards they were dumps: concrete houses with tin roofs. But Packer and Dutch had the insides fixed up in a kind of plush Chicago whorehouse deco that would make any poor Korean envious. The floors had warming pipes made from soda and beer cans that were welded together, and the furniture was expensive. There was the standard big stereo outfit, hanging lamps, and a huge bar. The beds had lush canopies over them, and mirrors were everywhere. The decor was James Bond wet dream fantasy all the way.

They carried fresh water from the compound, and they both had small fridges. You could get a good drink at their places and the girls were pretty good at setting up a big Korean meal. When I'd be down with them, drinking their booze and eating, I'd look at them and their hooches and wonder what the people back home would think of all of this. It was another world.

The girls liked to decorate in red, and they'd put red light bulbs in some of the lamps. So, you were always sitting in a slightly out-of-reality environment where people looked a little better than they did in the daylight. Even Packer had better color in his hooch.

Dutch's girl was Miss Cho. She was a longtime hooker on the compound who spoke excellent English. She had a hard, world-wise, look about her. Yet, I always thought she was the pick of the litter. And she treated old Dutch like he was a king. They made a strange, reciprocating arrangement with each other. He laid out good bucks for her and kept a fine roof over her head. She laid down for him. He didn't have her come out to the compound every night for the bar and movie routine. She was very tired of that. Dutch liked to come home in the evenings, listen to music, have a few drinks, and enjoy the pleasures of the flesh.

Packer and Adja were different. She was a tall beauty, with long black hair that went down to her tail. You'd catch her looking you over when she thought you weren't looking at her. She did a lot of wild things when Andy wasn't there; and she'd get smashed right along with us, which would end up with her throwing a tantrum of some kind, telling us that Packer didn't give her enough money. She was always screwed up by the time the evening was over. But Packer adored her. The more she'd shit on him, the better he'd like it. Before I had gotten to the island, Goldman had put eight stitches in his cheek because she had slashed him with one of her high heels.

The sergeants had hooches like these, too. Usually the girl and the hooch came together. The new GI would take over the rent, kick in living money for the girl, and add pieces of furniture to the place. Some girls had been at this for fifteen years, living high. Forty dollars a month in Korea was a superb salary. These gals got twice that much, plus the rent. They were survivors in a sparse land.

Girls like Adja, Miss Cho, and Dubbs' Sue were the working girls of Tolsan's small military district. They even had what they called a Working Girls Association. That simply meant that no new trade would be tolerated. They paid the local police to stay away, and Goldman gave them a monthly VD examination. Goldman's signed certificate updated their cards in the police station. Everything was covered. Let a new girl try to horn in, and it would be the local police who would chase her away. In Korea everyone pays everyone for the right to a little piece of established territory, the action.

Up on the mainland all of this was bigger. Places like Seoul and Osan had thousands of prostitutes, living with GIs or working out of clubs that lined the streets near the bases and posts. Once again, payoff kept it all fairly safe for the GIs and legal for the girls. Sears catalogues kept the girls in the latest fashions; the exchanges carried tons of rubbers and enough hair spray to satisfy the city of Chicago; and there were enough nylons to supply the working girls for years. We were very small time on Tolsan.

Goldman had seen a couple of cases of syph since he'd been site medic; Adja did give Packer the clap once. But the VD rate on Tolsan-Do was nothing like it was in Osan or Seoul.

On the mainland, at a place like Osan for example, the morning VD line could have a hundred guys in it. Some were five-time losers, called aces. Everything was fine as long as you weren't an ace. The medics would then warn you that you were doing something wrong. They sent aces to special VD classes.

When you reported in, you got a lecture on VD. I was in a room full of officers who were in-processing in the hospital and this flight surgeon told us just how we could avoid VD. "Make sure you always use a rubber," he'd said, "and urinate after intercourse as soon as possible. If you're worried about the girl, then you may want to flush the penis with a mild antiseptic solution. You might be able to wash syphilis away before it begins digging in."

So, I was content to party it up at any of our local watering holes. I could watch Packer suffer through his love affair, or even pinch the *kisaeng* girls on the ass. But it was going to stay in my pants. Lucky I had the priest as a sidekick. He wasn't going to steer me wrong. Goldman liked to play the field. He was a butterfly. He had sampled a lot of the local girls. That was his little piece of the action. He did that when they were waiting for another GI to take the place of one that had departed, or sometimes when they came for their VD checks.

I'd think about that when we'd be down at Packer's place, drinking his booze and listening to his records. Goldman would be right there, the life of the party. Poor Packer. He didn't have the brains to see beyond the front door.

One of the things that you had to put up with when you were at Packer's place was an unexpected visit from Dubbs and Sue. Sue and Adja were "sisters." That meant they had done a lot of living together in the business of surviving in Korea. They had started out somewhere in Seoul and then wandered down to Osan where they had been hostesses—a fancy word for bar girls—in a place called the Five Spot.

This was Dubbs' second tour in Korea; he had been Sue's beau that first time, too, up in Osan. When he came back, he brought her with him to Tolsan. Adja came along. Their devotion to each other, these two prostitutes, was fast. Dubbs saw to it that Sue got to see Adja at least once a day, and so it was that Packer was more tolerated by Dubbs. Packer, likewise, vacated the place so Dubbs and Sue could spend the night with Adja anytime they wanted.

Depending on how drunk we were at the time, one of these drop-ins by Dubbs and company usually meant Doc, the Father, and I would set sail for other parts of the town. A couple of times we were so shot that it didn't matter. Dubbs would park his ass in the best chair, mooch booze, and just jump right into the conversation. I'll give him credit, he did try to be halfway civil. He was better if he'd been drinking.

It was on one of those nights that I really got my chance to see what old Dubbs was really like. Up until that infamous evening, I only knew him as the grudge-holding asshole that kept distance between us and had tried so hard to make me feel unwelcome on the site.

This particular Thursday—and I remember it was a Thursday because there wasn't any movie—Dubbs and Sue came in. We were drinking beer and listening to the stereo. When they came in he seemed too friendly; his weaving walk told me he had a good bellyful.

"Hey, buddy, how's it going?" he had said to me.

"Just great, Major," I said, letting my eyeballs roll, up into my head. "You're just in time to get this party off the ground."

"Well, I'm always for drinking up the junior officers' pay. Packer's always good for a free drink. Right, Andy?" Dubbs said, kicking the sole of Oyster's brogan a couple of times.

"Sure, sure, help yourself."

"But he ain't generous enough to help little Adja get started in the teahouse business," Dubbs said, pouring himself a stiff one at Oyster's little teakwood bar.

The music and drunken confusion stole away a lot of Dubbs' taunting, but I was taken with that jab. Old Packer was just giving his drink that simple-faced smile of his, but I could tell he was bothered enough by what Dubbs was saying.

Dutch was telling the priest some big story about Indonesia. Sergeants Mountain and Ellis, making up some kind of soup and snacks. Assorted girls were sitting either on chairs or the floor, talking or staring off into space. The music was blasting away. But I moved in on the conversation Dubbs was sending in the general area of Packer, Adja, and Sue.

"Tell him, Adja. Cut off his pussy if he don't help out," Dubbs was saying.

"Honey, you hava some money. Why you no help buy my tea housa?"

"Aw, shit, Adja, I can't be spending everything I've got. Save what I give you, and you'll have it in a year."

She was hanging around his neck, kissing him and looking at Dubbs and Sue. She was winking at them, and then she'd kiss Oyster on the cheek.

"You give me money to get started, honey? You help us get started?"

"Naw, come on, let's just have some fun and forget teahouse for just one night."

"No, No." She said, pushing him away and turning her back on him.

"Oyster, you should help her now," Sue said, turning to Dubbs.

"Look, Packer, we could get this started if you'd chip in now. Hell, man, we'll make money on this deal, and you'll be giving her a future. Compared to investing in the States, this is a piece of cake. It's only going to take a couple a thousand apiece. That's all, for a hell of a deal."

The three of them were looking at him hard. Though I was just on the chair across from them, it was like I wasn't there. I had the perfect vantage point.

"Naw, I'm standing firm on this one. I give her enough as it is."

Adja got up and crossed the room, walking toward the kitchen. "You a bad numba ten GI shit," she said to him.

"That's right. You are a chicken shit at that," said Dubbs.

Without even looking at Dubbs, Oyster got up and went after Adja. He was drunker than I thought. "Honey," he said, "let's just have a good time with friends tonight. Tomorrow we talk teahouse."

Dutch and Paul stopped their conversation and looked up at Adja and Oyster. "Not another spat, huh, kids?" said Paul. Dutch was laughing and shaking his head.

Goldman saw the two of them at the kitchen doorway and stopped his stirring. "Come on in and taste this, Oyster, sir. If you live, then I can serve it to the important guests."

"No, you get out of my housa," said Adja.

"Aw, Goddammit, Adja, knock it off," said Andy, grabbing her by the arm. "Just cut it out."

"You no hurt my sister," yelled Sue.

"Christ," I yelled, "let's take up a fucking collection so she can buy a teahouse, and we can all get on with the party."

Dubbs looked at me, but said to the room in general, "Adja wants everybody to get the hell out of here, now."

That made her go nuts. She started kicking at Packer and yelling, "You son-of-a-bitch gee-eye. You get out of my housa."

Paul was on his feet and breaking them apart, but not before she hit Oyster a good one with her hand. Dutch was in the middle of it too, saying, "Ja, now, Adja, don't be zo zilly." He took a couple of pointed shoe tips in the shins for that.

Then Dubbs was on his feet, shoving his shirt into his pants and acting like Mr. Law and Order. "Ladies and Gentlemen, I think that's about enough for tonight. In other words, everyone get the hell out of Adja's house, now."

The two sergeants had their girls on their arms by that time and were already heading for the door. Goldman was making soup, stirring, and tasting it like nothing was going on. Paul and Dutch did a double take, and I got up from the plush red chair I was sitting in.

"Attention, everyone, the party will now move to the street for other directions," I said.

"Yeah, that's about right," said Dubbs.

"But just as I had dinner about on the table," Goldman said, lisping the words and gathering his apron around him in mock nervousness. "This family. I just don't know," he said, giving it a sob with the apron pushed to his eyes.

"Sergeant Goldman," Dubbs said pointing, "you get your ass out now."

"We're all going aren't we, Oyster?" said Father Paul, grabbing Oyster by the arm.

"You're damn right, Padre," said Packer. "I've had it this time, and you guys be my witness. I mean it."

"Good for you, Andy," I said, walking past Dubbs and Sue, who both gave me dirty looks. "Let's all get the fuck outta here."

Adja was yelling, "Good, go out you numba ten gee-eye shits. Go out. Go out." And we did, ragtag mob of guys and Korean hookers filing out of a hooch in the late night, one crazy guy in an apron carrying a big pot of steaming soup.

9

Saints and Sinners

That night was the first time we'd ever seen Packer so determined to call it quits with Adja. He went out the door with us and stayed away from her. We couldn't believe it. He stayed away for days, and those days added up to weeks. He'd mumble something like "Korean bitch" when somebody would congratulate him on his resolve.

"Andy, I didn't think you had it in you," Paul said one night after we'd all seen *The Pink Panther*, plus a Bugs Bunny.

"Yeah, but I'm just better put'n it all out of my mind. This is okay, just work'n and having a few laughs. I'm getting over it good. I'm getting over it good."

We all felt good about it, walking along the compound road without a care in the world. At least I felt in that kind of a mood. "Let's go celebrate somewhere," I said.

"He's right, Padre," joined in Goldman. "We've got to toast the new Lieutenant Oyster."

"Chicken to take the ADOT jeep downtown," said Paul.

"Just get in, the three of you, and I'll be right back with the keys to the open road," I said. Dubbs was out in the AFAG jeep, it was Friday night, and I knew we'd be all clear. It was just a good night to go on the prowl. I brought back the keys and a six-pack of cold Bud. That would get us where we were going.

Even when I was in high school, Fridays were the greatest. So were Saturday nights. But Fridays meant cartoons the next morning and a big breakfast. And, Saturday night to look forward to. There was no school, and you were safe for what seemed like then a long time.

We drove down the road to Choipu with that same Friday night feeling. Beers in hand, freedom and adventure in the air, we were on our way to good times. We highballed down that hard-packed dirt road in the pitch black of night, headlights cutting through the darkness. There were no streetlights on these roads, no house or shop lights to light the way. You just drove through the tunnel of lights the jeep made. Overhead the stars were bright, and off in the distance the lights of the town marked the target.

"Ancestor toast time. Stop and drink a toast to the ancestors, I say," shouted Paul above the grind and humpty-bump of the jeep.

"To the ancient Korean ancestors," I said, bringing the jeep to a stop with a fast turn toward the wall that led into the town. I kept the headlights on, but turned off the engine. And there were the ancestors, hundreds of them crawling and running in and out of the spaces in the rock wall. Rats. More than I'd ever seen in my life. The walls were alive with them, as they weaved together in constant motion. Tails and legs. The ancestors. You could stop at any wall near town and see them make the walls live with their presence.

"To the Korean ancestors," we all toasted. If you thought about it too much you'd feel a gag coming on. "To the ancestors."

Off on the open road once more, knowing that the ancestors were still on both sides, Paul suggested we drop in on Ryan O'Donnell. That was a great idea. Irish Whiskey was just the ticket, I thought. But we didn't want to go empty handed, so we stopped off at the icehouse and took on a good supply of cold OB. When we pulled up in front of the St. Catherine's rectory, we spotted several Land Rovers parked there.

"Oh, Mother of God," said Paul, "are we all sure we're strong enough to do this?"

"As if he couldn't wait to get in there with the rest of 'em," snickered Goldman.

"I'm ready to drink the IRA right into the ground tonight," I said.

"The bigger the party, the better," said Packer.

And in we went.

"Aw, it's himself and the beyes," shouted Ryan. "Come in, come in, and tell us you've brought reinforcements."

"OB for me and thee," said Paul.

"A blessing on your house," said a red-nosed Danny Callahan.

And there was Riley, Flaherty, and Grady, too. I knew it was going to be a real Friday night at that.

"It's a post funeral party you've come to," said Ryan. "Only this marn'n I buried one of the triumphs of my work here, Goldman. It was a man who had been a Shinto all of his life, but took the dar Lard three years ago."

"A victory, a convert, huh?" said Goldman.

"Yes, yes, Doctor, for you see he brought a lot of souls with him. And now he's in consecrated ground, and the Lard's made His point."

And we all toasted to that.

"Now, just a touch of someth'n special, beyes," said Ryan, bringing out a holy water bucket filled with ice, chilling a bottle of champagne.

"Ah, ah," the crowd said, with Ryan speaking for us all, "We'll all have just a drop of this fine bubble water in honor of his dead self, out there in Saint Katie's cemetery."

Pat Flaherty followed him in with a tray of long-stemmed glasses. "Now each of yah take a glass in your hand, and Ryan'll fill them."

With that, Ryan came around the room, bucket in one hand, bottle in the other, pouring out the pink champagne.

Once we were filled, he put the bucket on the table with the dead soldier nestled in it. "Now, gentlemen, if you will, raise your glasses to the likes of Chee Yun Hol, may God bless his immortal Korean soul."

"To Chee Yun Hol." The glasses were raised high. "May God bless his immortal soul." And down the hatch went the pink champagne.

For just a moment we were all very silent. Hell, I felt the loss even if I didn't know old Chee from Adam. It was a very moving toast.

Then Ryan said, "Beyes, he did wonders for this parish. And he'll keep on doing wonders for it, God love 'im."

With our respects behind us, things went back to the normal chaos of a rectory party. We all sat in the living room, swapping stories. That was the best part about being with the priests. They loved to talk and tell stories. You'd hear all about county this and county that and the teams that played Gaelic football, hurling, and Rugby against each other. You heard about uncles who could drink barrels and about wondrous fights that made Irish history. And after a while you'd get the tears and hear about sweet old auntie, or, God help us, somebody's mother, still alive in an old thatch house somewhere on the Emerald Isle.

As the occasion wore on, Packer felt the effects of the beer and the champagne and the inevitable Irish Whiskey. He was telling the priests about his brother, Walt. He had them in stitches.

In the middle of the story, Father Ryan put up his hand to command silence.

"Listen, will ya. Listen, it's herself, outside."

Some didn't pay attention.

"Beyes, beyes. Pay attention. Listen there, outside. We've got a visitor."

He went over to the front window. "Sure it's herself. Look here will you now," he said pulling back the curtains.

We all followed and grouped behind him, craning for a look out the window. At first I couldn't tell what was out there, but I could hear what sounded like a drum and somebody singing.

"What the hell is it?" I said.

"It's the witch, the witch."

"The witch?" I said, looking around at the others.

Ryan was intent on what was going on outside. He was answering me but putting his concentration on looking through the glass. The light inside made him gather his hands to either side of his head so he could see clearly.

"She's the old Shinto witch woman, coming to get old Chee's soul from the cemetery. I won him over from all ah that, Narm, you see."

I looked at Callahan. "To be sure, Narm, she's a real one all right. She and old Ryan have been fighting it out for years."

Ryan pulled up the sash and yelled out in Korean. The cold air rushed in, along with the clear drumbeats and a high-pitched Korean voice that was chanting something over and over.

"Norm," said Paul, grabbing my arm, "let's go upstairs. We can have a grandstand view."

"Right," I said, following him out of the room and up the stairs.

Goldman was talking to himself in the middle of the room as we passed him. "Witches, priests, and drunks. God, what I wouldn't give for a peaceful night at the synagogue."

Upstairs we turned into Ryan's room. It was handsomely done in hardwoods, with big sturdy, old-fashioned dressers. The bed was a large oak four-poster. Everything was wood and solid.

Paul had the curtains drawn and the window up. We could really see her clearly now. And we could hear Ryan exchanging loud language with her, although I couldn't understand it. But it was easy to tell they were in a heated verbal duel.

I watched, with Paul busting his sides. Then I realized that I had to take a leak something fierce, so I took advantage of Ryan's bathroom right there off the bedroom.

"Norm," yelled Paul, "get back here and look. Ryan's throwing holy water at her and she's waving some kind of a painted stick at him. It's grand."

I was in midstream. Couldn't move. I had the image in my mind though.

As I waited for the bladder to empty, my eyes wandered to his medicine chest. I opened it with my other hand. Inside was all that you'd expect to find, bought at our BX, of course, including some of that good Johnson and Johnson's white first aid tape. I love that stuff. You can use it like electrical tape and for a million other things, including making yourself up like a monster.

When I was a kid I used the stuff to tie my ears forward, tape my nose up, and gather my eyelids together. The effect is terrific, especially the nose. Just attach one end of a strip of tape under the tip of the nose and then attach the other end to the forehead. It pulls the nose up. Looks like a pig's. Do likewise with the ears and the eyes and you look really weird. A variation on the eyes is to attach one end to the baggy part under the eye, pull down, and then attach the other end under the jaw. Pulls the eyes down.

After I washed my hands, I took Ryan's Johnson and Johnson roll and did my face up. Then I came out of the bathroom and said, "Father Paul." He was still having wonderful fun with the activity below, but when he turned and saw me it gave him a start.

"My God, that's creepy, Norm."

"Look at this," I said, taking Ryan's heavy black coat from a hook on the wall. I put it on and pulled the collar up. Buttoned to the top, that black coat really made me look good.

"Give her a shot of it," Paul said. "Maybe she'll see you. Go ahead."

When I got to the window I could see her clearly. She was giving Ryan hell, and I could look straight down and see his hand coming out of the opened window below. He'd fling holy water at her with his Aspergillum, dipping it in the bucket that had held the champagne. I wasn't sure if that was new holy water, or the melted ice that had been cooling down the bubbly.

Anyway, I made my entrance. I just stood there, a specter in the top window. I concentrated on her very hard, willing her attention.

"Does she see you?" Paul was saying behind me.

"Not yet, but any minute. Wait . . . now some old guy in the crowd does, and he's really doing a double take."

The sight of me slowly caught on among the group of onlookers out in the street behind her. In the midst of her screaming, she felt their attention going upward and her eyes scanned the front of the rectory, and then she looked up. Voom. She looked right at me. Her wand just stopped in mid-swing.

Now I had her undivided attention. She knew she was looking at something she'd never quite seen before. And then I slowly brought my finger forward and demonically pointed it at her. With one hand on my coat at the throat, gathering it in my fist like Bela Lugosi used to, I made a menacing gesture with a pointing finger. Then I said, "Yoooouuu."

She cut a quick choggy for town, looking back over her shoulder at me as she ran. She couldn't believe that angry horrible thing up there still pointing a finger at her.

"Norm, that did it."

I was still standing at the window. Then I turned slowly and pointed at Paul. "Priest, we will keep this secret to ourselves, or I'll seek you out."

"My lips are forever sealed, poltergeist. We'll let Ryan think his blessed ice water did the trick."

"He knew he was getting help from above," I said. "It just didn't come from the highest levels."

When we got back downstairs, Ryan was jubilant. "It was toe-to-toe, so to speak. But my Latin proved the best of the match."

"You were in great form," said Packer, with wine stains down the front of the shirt he was wearing.

"Narm, get a beer or something and we'll all toast Mr. Chee's soul again. Paul, get a drink. Beyes, get a drink. It's been a perfect day."

Nobody knew we had left the room.

10

For the Birds

One Monday morning Dubbs called me on the hill phone. "Hey, Whitman, I'm sending up the file on the lodge. That's going to be your deal. Read up. There's the first part of your crew coming in a week or so from Japan."

"Yes, sir, I'll beef myself up. But can you give me an idea about what's involved?"

"You'll run the hunting lodge and see to it the hunters are taken care of. The Japan crew'll take them out in the bird wagons and all that. Korean help'll do the shit work. Hell, just read the file. I don't have time to go through the whole damn thing on the phone." Click, he was off the line.

About an hour later Packer came up and handed me a brown accordion folder crammed with official looking papers.

"Here, Norm," he said. "Your headaches are about to start. I wouldn't have the lodge for anything, man."

"Great, Oyster," I said, "nothing like helping me off to a terrific start."

After he left for the bottom of the hill, I spent the next two hours reading the file. Dubbs had given me a surprisingly succinct rundown of the job. The tremendous pheasant hunting on the island did turn our little compound into a number one tourist attraction for the brass.

Those lodge buildings by the Q had dozens of rooms in them that would soon hold generals, admirals, and ranking civilians from all over the Asian Pacific Theatre. Big trucks with pheasants painted on them would transport the VIP hunters and their guides around the island in pursuit of the big tasty birds. For the most part the guides and house people would be local hires, regulars who showed up every season. The drivers, dog keepers, and extra support people would be furnished by rec services in Japan. Our dining hall, club, movie, BX, and the rest would provide everything else. They'd fly in on the choggies we controlled in from the hill. The fire department would be there in case the worst happened. All very neat and ordered. As I had guessed, I was stationed at a hunting lodge.

I had fun getting the place open. Dubbs put Packer by himself on the hill to carry the load alone. I had been freed up to get the lodge operation underway. It turned out that Goldman's chief bartender, Mr. Kwak, became boss of the Koreans who worked the hunting operation. He helped me immensely. One by one he had the lodge employees report in to me, and as they were in place the buildings were scrubbed down and put into order. House girls were soon busily washing sheets and making up beds, along with everything else it took to make the quarters ready.

Meanwhile, a C-130 flew in from Yokota loaded down with hunting dogs, shotguns, baggage, and four rec services types. The master sergeant in charge was named Clinton Davis, a burly man from somewhere in the Deep South. His accent was so thick you could cut it.

"Sur, you jest worry about overall housekeep'n, and I'll get them birds in the wagon. I take real good care of everyth'n for the OICees. Never mind about the hunt'n part," he told me the first time we sat down in my little office in Lodge Building One.

"That's just fine with me, Sarge. I never went hunting in my life, and I don't really think I'm going to start, either."

"Well I'll tell you one thing, sur, I'll see to it ya get plenty of bird on your plate."

"Sarge," I said, getting up from the chair.

"Sur," he said, still looking me over with a cautious eye.

"I'm going to stay out of your way. I know you've been running this thing for five years and that's the way it's going to be again this year. Right away I want you to know that. Like the new officer you have every year, I'm only here for that year. I want to get through this, go home, and forget about it. Is that about what you hoped I'd say?"

He gave me a big grin and put a big beefy hand out. "Captain, I've had some that didn't have your brains. They's things you can do to look good on this and I'll tell ya when. I 'preciate your attitude. Goldman said yu's alright."

And that set the tone for the hunting season. Old Clinton was a joy to work with from that first day on. He had the dogs in their kennels and the place humming. His three helpers jumped when he said jump. They had Sergeant Camp and Airman Biggs get the bird wagons in shape, and those wagons were soon running all over the site, helping with the grand opening. The place came alive.

I liked it that way. We had something to do, something to look forward to. Even Goldman was excited about the revenue he'd get from the hunters. There would be about twelve of them in roughly every other week, so Goldman told us that regular drinks and food prices would go down a lot because of the increased trade. The more the merrier.

But Dubbs didn't share my enthusiasm. "Shit, now we just have a lot of damn rank coming down here. We don't need that. Just remind them they have their own shithouses and steamer up in the lodge. Let 'em use the NCO club. Keep them the hell outta the Q, Whitman. Got that?"

"Yes, sir," I said. "I'll take care of everything."

"That's what I'm afraid of."

The bird wagons Clinton and his crew used were wondrous vehicles. One of the Air Force guys would drive, and there was a Korean guide assigned to each one. These guides were little Korean men who dressed in sporty hunting jackets, pants, boots, and hats. Mr. Cho, Mr. Jung, Mr. Hwang, and Mr. Dong all walked very proudly with a cased shotgun in one hand. They acted like they were the cocks of the walk. And Mr. Kwak, who managed them, took on a new air of importance as the season approached.

The wagons they rode in were trucks with big boxed-in rears, something like a big milk truck. But they weren't painted white. They were Air Force blue, with a big pheasant painted on each side of the box. On the front bumper each sported a number, one through four, and the words, "TOLSAN R and R." You opened up the rear doors, and there were two padded benches on either side, gun rack in the rear, and plenty of space to put dead birds in the big compartments under the padded benches.

There was a ceiling light in there, with a single bulb wrapped in a protective wire grille. In addition, there was a heater and a cooler for beer and water and soda under the rear gun rack. Four of them. Bird wagons.

They had four-wheel drive, and Clinton told me he could go just about anywhere on the island in them. Hunting party attack configuration depended on the composition of the parties. They'd either go out all together, or in pairs. Sometimes a single truck would go it alone. With two-way radios, they were in constant contact with each other, or the base station back in the headquarters Quonset.

They were a ball to ride around in: Big deal for the GI and the hunting guide, especially. If you were a Korean, employed by the U.S. Government, you were something pretty special. And to ride through a town in a big bird wagon, hunting clothes on and eyes looking forward, well, you were a big man on Tolsan. You had a good job. You were somebody.

I was popular at the lodge. Not because I was the OIC, but because Clinton Davis had put his brand of approval on me. I knew my place. I was an officer he could tolerate. He told me, as a matter of fact, that he was going to make me "look good." I was glad he and the rest of the crew knew what the hell they were doing. I was just satisfied to look on and ride around town in the bird wagons with them. They were fun to get drunk in.

Those things made any number of trips downtown each day, either picking up employees or taking them home. And, of course, there was always "stuff" to get. They needed, well, things, and that gave everyone an excuse to go along, which meant that we'd end up stopping at every little icehouse, teahouse, and hole-in-the-wall bar along the way. Good OB and good fun. It turned out I liked being the hunting lodge OIC a lot.

On one of those trips it was just me and Clinton up front. Goldman, Father Paul, a couple of guides, and the motor pool boys were in the back. We all left with a cold Bud in hand, though I had belted down two good shots of Jack Daniel's, to get the pump primed a little better.

"Sur, I have one other thing you and me has to discuss, sur. "

"What's that, Sarge?" I said, while a bump made my beer slop out over my chin and down my neck.

"It's about letters and messages, sur," he said, looking very serious, almost bashful.

"Letters and messages?"

"Yes, sur, you've been pass'n them on to me with notes and such and I 'preciate that. I know you're pass'n them as soon as they come in, sur."

"Damn right, Sarge. You're the honcho. I just read and initial as the big guys say. And I make very little editorial or otherwise comments, you noticed." I could hear the occupants of the padded benches breaking out in song, even over the noise of the road. "The only reason why I'm asking any questions on the memos is because I'd really like to learn something from you. I figure if I know, then I can help you if you need it." I finished the beer, crushing the can. "I hope that's okay," I added.

"Hell yeah, sur," he said, looking forward very intently. "Only thing is I don't know what questions you're ask'n about what."

"Well, you know, about why Japan's sending what they are and why the hunting manifests are made up the way they are. You know. "

"I don't until you tell me and then ask me, sur," he said, getting a little impatient.

I just rode along, watching him. I really didn't understand what he was trying to tell me. And then the light went on. Tell him. Ask him. Hell, he couldn't read, I thought. The guy couldn't read. This was a good guy who couldn't read. Now I had a chance to help him with something I knew how to do as well as he shot a gun.

"Sarge, you want me to read the messages and letters and questions to you?" I said looking at his reaction.

"Yes, sur," he said, like he'd been caught doing something despicable.

"Well, I'll be proud to. You just made me feel useful. Now I feel like I can do something to help out." I put the crushed can in my pocket because I knew he wanted those wagons to be spotless. "I'll tell you the truth, Sarge, I didn't feel like I was pulling any weight at all. If I could read the stuff that comes in to you, then I can learn the lodge business from A to Z and maybe even write what needs to be answered."

He didn't say anything for a while. Then he said, "You'll need a hat and coat like ours. So's you can greet the VIPs at the airplane with us, you be'n OIC and all." Then he added, "Would you wear the things?"

"Hell yeah," I said. The outfits were special parkas and even had a place for your name and rank. But the best part of all was that they had a big pheasant patch on one pocket, and on the back it said, "TOLSAN GUIDE — FOLLOW ME." I was in.

"Sur?"

"Yeah, Sarge?"

"Back home we call people like you gentlemen."

I just sat for a minute. Didn't know what my comeback to that should be. Then I said, "Aw, you're just trying to butter me up because I'm in so thick with Major Dubbs."

"Yes, sur," he laughed, "ya guessed it, sure 'nough."

Hunting with bird dogs was big in Virginia, and Clinton told me Packer was really handy with the dogs. "He's a good handler, sur," was the way he had put it.

"Well, Sarge, I'd really appreciate it if you'd let him help out with the dogs, because the lieutenant needs something like that right now," I said.

"Yeah, sur, I know about that cunt he's trying to get over. Don't worry, he's really a help. I'll use him all I kin."

And it was a very good thing. Packer probably had the best couple of months of his life helping out with the lodge. He'd get back from the hill and head straight for the kennels. Then he'd take out one dog at a time for exercise or a brushing. They were nervous things with strange brown eyes, but to old Oyster they were beautiful.

He especially liked the one called Dolly. If I was around, he'd yell at me to watch old Dolly do some damn trick or another.

"Hey, Norm," he'd yell, "watch her get this." And then he'd throw some kind of a rubber bird, and old Dolly would go get it, racing after the thing on her thin legs. "That's how she grabs the birds," he'd say, like a beaming father.

"Well, Oyster," I had said one night, "she's treating you a lot better than another dog I know." And after I did, I felt like a bastard. I regretted it as soon as I had said it. That kind of a line wasn't my style.

"Yeah," he said, "this is one bitch that's all for me." He was a good-natured guy. I shouldn't have taken a poke like that, but he just took it. So, I left him with, "Packer, you deserve the best," as I went into my office in the lodge. He just went back to the dog, crouching down to scratch her ears. I looked at him through the office window that evening, thinking how pathetic he looked. He and the dog were both thin, both so easily pushed around. Yet I thought the dog had a hell of a better chance making it than he did. I'll probably always remember him the way he was with Dolly that night, a thin figure in the Korean twilight.

11

The Brass Arrives

It was just about a week after that when I read the big announcement to Clinton. "Here it is, Sarge, the grand opening," I said, waving a newly arrived letter at him.

"Read it, sur. Is it General Pitts?" he said as excited as a little boy. Pitts was his commanding officer in Japan and an old friend. Clinton had told me that they'd been on the same bomber crew together during the Second World War. Pitts had put Clinton in the job and had been the one to set up the lodge idea in such grand fashion.

"You bet, Sarge," I said, with both of us sitting down in my little lodge office to better enjoy the big news.

"It says, and I quote, 'General Pitts plus party of five will arrive Tolsan via Osan choggy, 18 November. Please prepare for ten-day visit and coordinate flight times with flight operations. Note manifest and insure minimum protocol for distinguished guests.'"

"Who wrote it, sur?" he said, leaning forward to look down on the letter.

"It's signed 'Forest Belford, Lieutenant Colonel,'" I answered.

"That's the genrl's eckzek," he said. "He's a nice guy."

To which I replied, "Nice guy, for an executive officer, huh? There's more," I added, pointing to bold black handwriting under the colonel's signature. "This note says, 'Clint, get the birds and the other birds ready, I'm coming in for the whole nine yards.'"

"Hot damn," said Clinton, smacking his hands on his thighs. "The old man's ready for hunt'n and putang."

I looked over the manifest. The general was on the top of the list; then Belford; two other LCs, Coates and Yates; a British brigadier named Norman L. Rushworth; and a Mr. Price from the American embassy in Tokyo. I read the names to Clinton.

"Colonel Coates and Yates are fighter pilots, sur. Old drinking buddies, thick with the old man. The brigadier is with the Brit embassy, another old crony. I think he knew the old man even before the war, and he sure as hell was a lifesaver when we flew out of Alconbury."

"You knew the British guy?"

"Hell, yessur. He was with our bomber group as some kind of lee-a-soon. Just a Brit leff-ten't then. But he took good care of us all." He looked at the written names, but I knew they didn't register.

"And Mr. Price, he's with the embassy in Tokyo, but I'll tell you, he's a CIA agent. Nice guy. He and the old man are thick too. This is what we call the clan here, com'n in."

I was damn glad he knew how to take care of them.

Finally, 18 November came. Everything was all set up. I was looking forward to being there at the airstrip to meet the general and his party. But late on the 14th, Dubbs came by the lodge to tell me the news that I'd be on the hill, bringing in the choggy.

"But what about Packer? Isn't he on the hill so I can handle the lodge?" I said.

"I need him to run up to Osan on the turnaround. There's a controller meeting up there for a countrywide mission that's coming up. They want a rep from every site to get the brief and bring the battle orders back. He's it." He had a big toothpick in his big fat mouth.

"Sir, you'll get Dutch Elm's disease chewing on those," I said, trying to be a little civil.

"You'll get hunter's disease spending all your time up here. You pretty well have the place open now. Start pulling hill every other day again."

"Yes, sir," I said to the back of his parka. Who gave a shit anyway. We were up and running. Clinton needed me like a hole in the head. Hill was fine. And I could still do a lot for the lodge every other day, and nights, too. Yet I was just a little pissed that Dubbs had taken the fun out of meeting the first hunters. You can bet he'll be there for General Pitts, I thought.

That was one of those nights when Father Paul was at one of the rectories, Moklepo, I think. Goldman and company were mixing it up at the NCO club, and I just sort of decided I'd eat in the mess hall and lie in the Q and read. Made up my mind I'd just sip one or two beers and read from a volume of John O'Hara short stories I found at the little site library.

I did just that, but around nine o'clock I heard a rap at my door.

"Come on in," I said, lifting my head up off the pillow, leaving an O'Hara character on a train with a pretty girl.

"Norm?" It was Oyster. "Are you awake?"

"Yeah, Packer, what's up?"

"Oh, nothing," he said, coming in and putting himself down in my one chair, the metal one that went with the table desk we all had. "God," he said, looking around the room, "you don't have anything in here hardly at all."

"Yeah, Dubbs once told me I should fix it up, like home," I said, putting the book down on the floor next to my bed. "Home my ass, Oyster. There's no way this is ever going to be home."

"Yeah, I know." Then he looked down at his knees and smoothed his khaki fatigue legs down over them with his hands. "Adja sure made that old hooch look like something, though, you know."

"Oyster, you're not thinking about going back to her?"

"Naw, no, no. Really, I was just thinking, that's all. You know when you were talking about something looking like home."

"Yeah, I know," I nodded.

Just then the hound dog came through the door, pushing it open with her nose.

"Dolly? Where'd you come from," I said, sitting up on the bed.

"Oh, Clinton lets her stay with me at night. She likes sleeping in my room." And the dog nervously ran around my room sniffing everything and jumping up on him, on me, and then sniffing around again. He turned his attention to her.

"Packer." No reaction. "Packer. Are you going up to Osan on the choggy tomorrow?"

"Oh, yeah, Norm. Going to a controller meeting," he said, all the while scratching old Dolly's ears and head. The dog loved it, moving its ass and hind legs around, holding its head fixed in his hands. What a pair.

"What was it like at the Academy, Packer? Was it a good place to go to school?" I said, watching him make love to the hound with his fingers.

"The zoo? It's okay, I guess."

"No really, I always thought it'd be something to get there sometime and maybe teach or something. Is it cool?" I had never really been able to get him to talk about the Academy, and I wanted to see why in hell it didn't seem to have made much of an impression on him. Christ, he was such a mess. You just thought Academy grads would be more or something.

"I made it through that place by the skin of my teeth. I almost quit about five thousand times. My old man pushed me in there. Retired Air Force." He paused for a minute to let the dog go back out into the corridor to chase down the hall, probably back to his room. "Well, I did it. I stuck it out, but I'm not a lifer. I'm hanging it up as soon as I get the time in."

"Geez, they really motivated you, huh?"

"They teach you how to be a cadet. It's got nothing to do with this crummy BOQ and the crummy job we do on this fuck'n island."

"But what about tradition and all of that. Man, I thought Academy grads were ready to be generals when they graduated."

"Some guys probably are. The straight guys. But not me."

Then I didn't know what else to ask. He made it all sound so damn uninteresting, poor, pale, fatigue-clad skeleton.

"Norm, I'm going to get so much pussy in Chicol Village that my pecker's going to surrender like an Italian infantryman."

"You can probably milk four or five days out of it, right?"

"Yeah, and if the weather's bad I could luck out even better if they cancel the flights back here."

Chicol Village was the military sex playground. Before I got to Korea I heard about it: A man's paradise. With nearly fifty clubs to visit, all you had to do was go in, buy a drink, and decide which dollie you wanted.

In some of the places in the Ville the dollies wore numbers. A GI could pick out the number of his choice and she'd be his for the night. She'd take you to her little room somewhere in the village, and you banged away until you either passed out or fell asleep. Next morning you got up and went back to the base for duty. Just don't be late. But you probably fucked her again before you got dressed. And for all of that she got 350 won, or about five U.S. bucks. She could survive another day, feed her child. You got to fuck your brains out. It continued over and over again, without end, every night. GIs came in and went out, putting in and finishing up their thirteen-month tours. The Koreans and American powers-that-be looked the other way. Everybody made out, I guess.

"Norm, I know this cunt up at the Five Spot named Judy. I'm heading for her first thing. I had her the first time I hit the 'Ville. God, she bucks her ass so good you want to scream. I'm going to fuck her first, man." Packer was obviously looking forward to his trip to the mainland.

"Well, Oyster, I guess you deserve it. Everybody's here is so proud that you told Adja to shove it," I said, looking at my watch to see what time it was.

"Yeah, Norm, Christ, I shoulda played around more. This country's too full of cunt to get hooked up with just one. Man, I really let her take me. I just couldn't go for that teahouse idea. That's a lot for cunt, man."

"Well, Oyster, you get up there and have a ball. Fuck one for me."

The next afternoon I was on the hill, watching the radar for a blip headed from the direction of Osan and listening on frequency for a call from the Osan choggy. Every five minutes or so Dubbs would call me, always asking the same dumb question.

"Whitman, this is Major Dubbs. Anything yet?" he said for the eleventh time since I started making a grease pencil mark on the scope.

"No, sir. No inbounds yet. We'll call you as soon as we get contact." Contact simply meant positive radar and radio. The choggy would call in at about a hundred and fifty miles, giving everyone at least half an hour to get to the strip.

We'd get an estimated time on choggies early in the week. Then the comm with the mainland would go down, as usual, which left us in the dark. You could never get a confirmation of takeoff. All you had was the day and estimated wheels up time.

So they'd fidget down below, always thinking you had contact and you weren't telling them. My God, when the controller did give them the word it was a madhouse down there. The first announcement over the site loudspeakers that the choggy was one hundred and fifty miles out miles out would send the fire engines down to the strip. Meantime, everyone else held momentarily until the controller relayed the critical answers about cargo weight, mail, number and sex of passengers, any VIPs, and movie titles. That info determined the number of support vehicles and personnel needed at the strip.

Once all the calls were made, it was fun to go outside for just a moment to see the engines, trucks, and jeeps tearing for the strip. The speeding convoy made so much dust in dry season that the dirt road to the strip looked as if it were on fire. All along the route Korean mothers would pull their children in off the road to keep them from being run over. Men would curse the dust. And I would look down on it and say, "Jesus Christ, the Osan choggy drives men's minds to the limits."

Finally, the 18 November choggy called in: "Benjamin Control, Benjamin Control, this is Dragon zero-one, angels seven, heading one-seven-five degrees, squawking three-two-one, over." The calls always sounded like somebody was talking into a glass.

I responded with a "Roger, Dragon zero-one, this is Benjamin one two, stand by." Then a search on scope for a blip squawking his mode three, code two-one IFF. Soon it appeared. Easy, because there never was a hell of a lot flying in our area.

"Zero-one, squawk stand by," I said, meaning that we wanted him to turn off his IFF. If the blip on the scope you thought was him disappeared, then you had him. It did.

"Zero-one, return three-two-one. Positive radar contact at two-eight past the hour."

"Roger, contact, returning parrot three-two-one."

I put the origin of the cursor over him, and turned the line so it intersected Tolsan. At the same time I ran the cursor dot out until it rested over the airstrip. That gave me his bearing and range to the landing point. You read that out of a little window on the scope body.

"Zero-one, you're one-five-zero degrees Benjamin strip, now, one hundred fifty-five miles."

"Understand steer now one-five-zero for strip?"

"Zero-one, affirmative. I'm leaving frequency momentarily to make first call."

"Roger, Benjamin." And he knew I was alerting the compound below to send off the fire engines. We also hoped he'd never need them. Choggy pilots were the bad boys of the pilot roster in Korea, but took pride in their grass strip landings and super hangovers. Still, they hoped they'd never need the engines.

"Dubbs," he said, picking the phone up on half of a ring.

"Contact, sir, Osan choggy one hundred fifty out."

"Is the general on board?" he said. "Did you check about the general?"

God, he knew that came later. "Sir, I'm about to make my second transmission. I'll call you right back," I said.

"You should have that. This is special."

I just hung up.

"Roger, Benjamin, code-seven aboard, plus five other biggies." I got the pounds of baggage, and the number of mail sacks, including the message that our movies were *Mary Poppins*, *Shot in the Dark*, and *The Russians are Coming, The Russians are Coming*.

I dutifully reported it all and then I went out to watch the show. By the time I got outside, Dubbs was halfway there, trailing dust. I left Lieutenant Ko to flight follow zero-one onto the ground. It was procedure for us to give them the training experience of talking to U.S. aircraft. Besides, there was nothing we could do once they were on final. It was just the choggy and the old Japanese strip until the wheels were in the chocks. I had to be back with them from takeoff until I lost radio contact. Then they made their way back north for radio contact with Osan.

It was neat to see the bird come in and land. The hill was higher than the altitude the flight took over the island. So it was like some kind of expensive toy, with a fabulous airplane that flew over a toy island onto a toy strip. Toy trucks and jeeps would rush to it. Even *Mary Poppins* was on board.

They were on the ground just long enough to unload. That took about twenty minutes, just like the day I arrived. Only today, *Mary* and the general would get off, and Oyster Packer, Air Force Academy class of '64, would get on. I watched for a while and then went back in for the takeoff.

It wasn't long before I got the first transmission. "Benjamin, this is Dragon zero-one, requesting latest mainland forecast and permission to takeoff." The voice sounded familiar. I picked up the weather Ko had gotten for me. Somehow they could always talk to the mainland, even though our comm was down.

"Roger, Oyster," I said, "Osan high, thin, scattered. Visibility unlimited. Present altimeter two-niner-niner-one. Takeoff when you're ready."

"Benjamin one-two, how'd you know it was me?" Packer's squeaky voice said.

"Because you're one in a million, Benjamin one-four, one in a million."

They were letting him sit up front for the trip. One of the pilots was probably sitting in the unused navigator seat, just aft of the cockpit, right side. I knew Packer fit right in up in the cockpit, sitting with the rough-edged choggy boys. God bless him, he was having a big trip from the very start.

And off they went. Packer talked to me the whole time, making all of the transmissions from Dragon zero-one. At about a hundred eighty miles, I lost them on scope and said, "You're fading my crystal ball, zero-one. Do you still read Benjamin?"

I got back a faint, "Just barely, Benjamin. I'll say hello to Judy for you. Think of me . . ." And the radio faded.

Yes, you poor bastard, I thought, I'll think of you tonight, drunk and panting above some Korean moose, her bucking her ass and you pretending she's Adja. "Happy landing, Oyster zero-zero." I muttered under my breath.

12

Holy Matrimony

I went back down the hill at four, parked the jeep, and headed straight for the mailroom. Sure enough, there were about six letters in my box, all of them from Angie. They were her typical letters, stuffed full of little school papers and messages from the kids. And, of course, there was always seven pages or longer from her.

Those envelopes made me head straight for the Q. I needed the quiet of my room to read them. And as I walked across the street they started up inside me the feeling I always got when I saw that mail, a mixed feeling of both happiness and sadness. I both looked forward to and dreaded the weekly mail. They were so far away. Hell, they weren't even awake when I was.

I opened each letter and read it with relish. Angie had a way of gently folding the letters and little papers in such a way that made the envelopes seem even bigger and fatter. I always folded a letter right along invisible measured pressed lines, going back over the folds with my thumbnail and index finger. You could almost rip my folds apart, like the pretreated tear-outs you find in magazines. I called her folds "rolling folds," gently made so as not to break the letter's spirit.

With all of those letters opened and read, I had a huge pile of paper in front of me. It was incredible. And I loved every page. I couldn't bring myself to throw them away. I couldn't bear to have these little drawings and crayon-lettered messages go into a wastebasket, or even be burned. I couldn't let them out of my protection for fear they'd be by themselves in this strange place so far from their senders.

Angie's letters were so sweet. She and the kids were busy enjoying the wonderful times she made for them. She talked of little plays at school, dear little things that the kids were doing and saying, and of the sewing projects that kept her busy. I thought about the noise and smell of all of that and about the nights she and I shared together. She was a great mother and still a damn sexy lady. My cock and I both daydreamed about that, about her warmth and her passion for us both.

Angie was the best thing that ever happened to me. Ever. Thoughts of her and of our life together came rushing to me. The letters always brought that on, and I didn't fight the remembering and the fantasy. I just allowed myself to remember and relive the moments that made the letters so special. They represented so much. Sitting there in front of the pile, I thought of Angie.

I met her during the last few months of high school and from that time on there was never anyone else. It was just like we were made for each other, from the very start. She was a blind date and, somehow, I had a feeling that she was going to be the one, even before I saw her. When I did see her it was from the shoes up as she came down the stairs into the living room.

We got along well. Too well. That was the summer before I went away to Maynard. That summer was filled with the discovery of her. I had been way behind in dating and lovemaking, but Angie made up for all of that. She was so bright, alive, and very affectionate. We were always together. We explored each other with passion and innocence. Whole parts of me grew up. I felt like a man. It was the best summer of my life.

Then that great summer ended. I headed for Maynard College, bolstered by my 4.0 high school record that saw me graduate first in my class. I was sure to become the great healer I imagined. Angie would be a hundred miles from me at Sacred Heart, and that was to be unbearable.

I didn't waste any time in being a fuck-up at college. At Maynard I signed up for pre-med, drank, joined Gamma Alpha Sigma Fraternity, skipped classes, hung in there with marginal grades, and thought about how much I missed Angie.

That first college year we saw each other every chance we got. Times like Christmas and spring break were the best. We had yet another great summer between our freshman and sophomore years. Then back to school, and more of the same separations and frustrations.

Before that time Angie and I had done just about everything, except "it." As the second summer of our college years came to a close, we sat on her back porch and decided it was time. But how? We needed a good place. Back seats, blankets in the woods, or the car parked in the garage all seemed too cheap. Not fitting. We were special, and the first time was going to be special. Then I hit on the perfect plan. We would tell our folks we had been invited to

Bob and Jane's place on Lake Eire. They were a young couple we knew who were married and going to school. They were very religious Catholics, and Angie's parents thought the world of them. Theirs would be a place where they would let us go without a second thought. So we did invite ourselves, and the weekend was all set. We told the folks we would spend Friday, Saturday, and Sunday with Bob and Jane. We told Bob and Jane we'd be there Saturday afternoon.

Now the second part of the plan involved a masquerade. After a lot of thinking, I figured out a way for us to be welcomed into a nice hotel without any suspicion. How could two young people like Angie and me do that? As newlyweds, of course. So, after driving an hour and a half toward Lake Erie, we stopped off on a back farm road near Maynard. We decorated my dad's car with crêpe paper and streamers, wrote all over it "Just Married," and tied shoes and tin cans to the bumper. For the sake of realism, I tattered some of the props so it would look as if we had driven with them for some good hard miles. The job looked great. We laughed with glee. The five-and-ten-cent-store rings completed the package. Angie said she even felt like the real thing. We were.

Back out on the road people would speed up, pass us, beep their horns, and give us knowing smiles. We loved it. We were in the right frame of mind. It was our wedding day, dammit. The whole world was wishing us well. How much better this was than trying to sneak into a motel, or get turned away from some flophouse. Even if you got in, the worry of getting caught would ruin the whole thing. This was fresh and out in the open. I discovered very early in my life that the world responded positively to accepted norms and symbols. You could open any social door with the right key. And the key could be forged.

We drove right into the driveway of the best motel near Maynard. It was called the Wagon Wheel. I wasn't even parked in front of the office before both the man and the woman who owned the place came bounding out of their little office to greet us with big happy smiles. "Well, how wonderful," said the gray-haired lady. And we both just smiled back, Angie looking down, the way a young bride will.

We got the best room in the place. It was all country style, with bright reds and whites. It smelled fresh and clean. The guy took us in and got down on his hands and knees to catch a cricket he heard chirping under the desk. "Finally got ya!" he said. I thought I had once read that a cricket on the hearth was good luck. After again wishing us well and telling us just to ask for anything we didn't see, he and the little cricket left. We were in.

I picked the Wagon Wheel because it was nice and my favorite restaurant, the Fireside Inn, was also across the highway. I could get a big martini there, and they had the best bleu cheese dressing in the world. They never carded me and I love bleu cheese dressing when it's pared with a good gin buzz. We had a great meal there and got caught up in the tremendous feeling of being alone with each other. It was just the two of us, all to ourselves.

That night, the faux wedding night, was a little awkward, but a time of closeness and new smells of each other. Angie had a negligee her godparents had bought for her trousseau that made her look simply beautiful. The combination of her long black hair, brown eyes, and silky nakedness was overpowering. We made love well into the early morning.

So I wasn't really surprised when she called me from school that October to say she'd missed two periods. The doctor's test showed up positive. After a little research, I found you could get married in Detroit, if you were eighteen. Detroit was only a day's drive away. I told Angie I'd see her at her dorm on October the 7th, not to worry. I told her to pack a bag; I was going to take her to Detroit.

I was rooming out of the Gamma Alph house that semester with two guys I thought the world of. John Temple and Ray McGill had rescued me from my pre-med misery. It was Ray who convinced me to switch to history when I flunked organic chemistry. When I got Angie's call, he helped me with my Michigan elopement plan. He was more than willing to let me use his Fiat, but the damn thing had a stick shift! My old nemesis, the same stick shift curse that would follow me to Korea. I had never learned how to use a stick shift. I knew I had to learn how pretty fast if I was going to pull off the trip to Detroit.

We took the car out on the roads for an hour, and I got checked out just enough for me to drive on flat terrain pretty well. I had a hell of a time with hills, however; that was something that would come back to screw me in the future. But the drive to Pittsburgh to do the right thing was mostly flat and straight down US Route 19. I left with a full tank of gas and a small suitcase filled with what I'd need for a weekend on the road.

The Fiat worked well throughout the ninety-mile drive to Pittsburgh. But when I got there, I was faced with its famous hills. Angie's school, Sacred Heart, sat atop the mother of them all, known as "the bluff." I tried seven times to get that Fiat up the bluff, each time backing down and putting it on the curb. Every time I'd make a run I'd hit a red light or have to stop for a car, and then I couldn't get it back into first gear. Cars would blow their horns and there would be passing and name-calling. I had come all that way and then stopped by a hill.

Up there—on the bluff—Angie was waiting for me and there I was, stymied. But not for long. I got out of the little car and I headed down the street for a cabstand I had spotted. There was a Yellow Cab parked there.

The cab driver was a black guy. He was eating out of a paper bag. It was probably his dinner break. He was really preoccupied as I came up on the driver's side. Even though the cab windows were rolled up, I could hear disc jockey Sir Walter Raleigh's distinguished accent over WAMO.

I knocked on the window—rap, rap, rap—and he turned around in surprise. He gave it one of those hey-what-the-hell kind of looks.

I said, "I need to talk to you," but he shook his head in a big N-O and pointed to his brown bag with a sandwich in his hand. I came back with, "Hey, man, just let me talk to you a second." I knew he really couldn't hear what I was saying, but he was by now annoyed enough to roll down the window.

"Hey, man, what's a matter which you?" he said, giving me a penetrating look. "I'm eat'n man; get another cab."

"Look," I said, "I'm sorry I'm bothering you, but I really need your help. I don't really need your cab, but I'll pay you to drive my car."

"What the hell you talk'n about?"

He looked like a pretty good guy, so I stood my ground and explained the whole thing to him. I pointed to the Fiat and told him that it was urgent for me to get up the hill so I could pick up my girl and elope. As I told him more and more, he lost interest in his sandwich and WAMO and began to grin. "So, if you could just drive the car up there, we could pick her up and I'd bring you back down to your cab," I finished, pointing back up the hill.

He liked it. He just sat there for a good long moment, laughing and repeating parts of my story.

"Okay, man," he said, "let's elope." The sandwich went back into wax paper and into the brown bag. He was out of the cab and locked it up. And then the two of us walked over to the Fiat and the edge of the hill.

We started up like a song, both of us sticking our elbows out of the windows, the Fiat radio now playing WAMO, enjoying the idea of the thing.

About halfway up, though, another cab was coming down. My new driver put out his arm, beeped the horn, and flashed the lights on and off. As soon as he recognized his fellow cabbie he stopped and backed up.

"Hey, man," he said, laughing. "This cat and I is eloping with a college girl." The story was passed from the Fiat to the Yellow Cab, it made a U-turn and followed us up the hill.

Now, everything I had ever read or heard about eloping would suggest that it was a kind of discreet operation, with the girl easing out of the house, or in this case, the dormitory. But when we all came pulling up in front of Our Lady of Mercy's Residence Hall, there was Angie and half of her sorority standing on the steps. It looked like a group photograph. Her suitcases were right there out in the open. When Angie saw it was me, she was all excited and smiles. Somebody said, "You're going in a cab?"

I said hello to everybody. They were all in a festive mood. A nun came by and made her way up the stairs, past the lively little group. She smiled and said, "Angie, are you going home for the weekend?" Everyone answered, "Sure, Sister." The two cabbies grabbed and jammed the suitcases into the Fiat and we were on our way. My cabbie wouldn't take my money.

According to my plan, we would have just enough time between then and Sunday to have the blood tests, get married, and make it back in plenty of time for me to make my eight o'clock on Monday. I had already paid a month's rent on an apartment in Freeport and still had sixty bucks left in my bank account. We had it made.

It was an all-night ride to Motown, but it was great. The turnpike was fun to drive. We stopped at every Howard Johnson's on the way. We'd drive and then stop for coffee and then drive some more. The ride was all straight and flat.

The Detroit operation was a breeze. In one day we got our blood tests and everything we needed. It was like a payoff operation. Once the ball got rolling, each step along the way sent you on to the next. For example, the blood lab sent us to a dingy doctor's office because we needed a medical certificate. The doctor was an old white-haired guy who took each of us into his office separately and asked us if we had VD. We said no. He filled out the papers we needed.

Angie had always been a good Catholic girl; she wanted us to be married in the church. It was okay by me, but all of my life getting connected up with the Catholic church had meant problems. In Detroit things weren't any different. We got all the tests and paperwork done on Friday, including the marriage license. There was a judge who was marrying people right there in the courthouse, but Angie reminded me of my promise. So we left the courthouse and stayed overnight.

Bright and early on Saturday we found the nearest Catholic church. The priest, Father Bob, was really nice; he said he'd help us. So we got a crash marriage instruction course and he started to make the arrangements for a real church wedding. Just one hitch. We had to have our parish priests vouch for us. Hell, we eloped to avoid our home parishes, parents, and all of that. But no Diocese of Detroit church wedding without Pittsburgh nod.

We made it back to the courthouse just in time. At four o-clock in the afternoon a bushy-eyed judge passed good civil words over us, with two Michigan state cops acting as the witnesses. Angie raised her left hand instead of her right. That made us giggle through most of the ceremony, which was more like a swearing in than a wedding. But we got the job done.

All the way back to Freeport we laughed and had a wonderful time talking about how easy it was and how nice it felt to be married. I kept thinking: what was ahead? Yet another overwhelming feeling. Church wedding or no church wedding, I felt like the whole thing was blessed.

It was. My falling grades took an upturn. I couldn't wait to get home to my bride after classes. We had a first floor, one-bedroom apartment in a rickety old frame house on Jefferson Street, but to us it was a palace.

The first night we spent there was incredible. Angie loved the place. We discovered that the old mattress was stuffed with newspapers, she had to turn our first breakfast potato pancakes with a saucer, and the stove was one of those early cast iron jobs. But the place cleaned up under her direction, and we even got the landlady to get us a new mattress. Every day brought a new domestic challenge, but we worked them out like an old married couple.

1960 was a time when an elopement and a pregnancy were both tough for the traditional family to understand. That was the tough part. I phoned my mother to tell her the news; my dad and grandfather got drunk. We went to see Angie's folks. Her dad and little brother were watching the World Series on television when we came in and made the announcement. It was the first time I actually held her dad's complete attention. Anything else would have paled next to the series. He cried. It made me feel terrible. On the way back to our apartment in Freeport, we still felt good about ourselves.

We learned a lot that first year together. I had a professor who'd eloped as an undergraduate, at the same school, years before. He was my history advisor. When I told him the news, he gave me a big pat on the arm. "No kidding?" he said. And he said it with a reflective, sad look on his face. It kind of scared me.

We were disowned. That was to be expected. I had heard that time healed all wounds; and most of all, especially with the baby coming, I steeled myself against the old folks' rejection. I knew I had to do my duty by Angie.

Right off the bat I learned that sixty bucks in the bank isn't much, even if you did pay the rent for two months in advance. We got wiped out financially one Saturday after we had only been married two weeks. John, my old roommate, came by and told me I'd have to pay my share of rent for the last month, plus the big phone bill I'd run up planning out the elopement. The grand total came to exactly the thirty-three bucks we had left. Exactly. John couldn't carry us. After he left, we looked at each other and said, "We're broke!"

Then the miracle happened. The next day another fraternity brother came by. He was a married senior who was also married. Because he was going to graduate at semesters, he asked me if I'd like to take over the campus sandwich man business. I'd forgotten about the sandwich man. He was a married student who came around the dorms every night yelling "sandwiches" up the stairwells. He carried a big wooden box full of great homemade sandwiches.

He wanted twenty-five dollars for the business and even said he'd wait to get paid. I didn't know what to say, but Angie jumped on it. So, Fred, the sandwich man, my fraternity brother, came by with a truck that night and put an old, beat-up refrigerator on our sun porch and leaned the well-worn sandwich box next to it. I was now the sandwich man.

It was a miracle because the next day a guy driving a Sealtest milk truck came by and asked us, "How many pints do youse need?" He was talking about milk. I didn't know what to say, so he suggested that he should bring us forty pints of white and forty pints of chocolate a day.

You pay at the end of the month. He also said the deep freezer would be there soon. What deep freezer? The one for the Sealtest ice cream bars, along with the dry ice. The bread man came, and the meat man, and the man with the mayonnaise and mustard.

After the last deliveryman left, we had all the sandwich makings. I ate until I felt like a dairy store. Angie gave me that bright laugh of hers and said: "See, I told you this was a good idea. Now, let's make the sandwiches."

And we did, around a hundred of them. And I walked two miles up Main Street to the college and yelled "sandwiches" up the stairwells. My fellow students came down and bought the sandwiches, the milk, and the ice cream. We weren't broke anymore. Every night we made the sandwiches; up the hill I went. Angie even added cookies. We lived on cheese, ice cream, milk, cookies, and sandwiches. It was all delicious.

The nightly routine was making the sandwiches. Ours were good. Sales went up. Angie even started roasting big turkeys for fresh turkey sandwiches. She baked cookies for fraternity and school events. We added lemonade. We went big time and hired a guy with a car to drive to campus and sell. We got two boxes, new ones, and had two agents. I didn't sell anymore. I just made sandwiches. We were even putting money away. Our new-found culinary skills got us through the school year.

Then the summer came and the students left, but Angie came through again. She heard at the little store around the corner that Grand Lake Amusement Park would hire college students. So from being the winter sandwich king of Maynard College, I became the summer operator of the Flying Coaster, the biggest, newest ride at Grand Lake.

The Flying Coaster was a big wavy track with cars that rolled over the track and up into the air. Each car was connected to a spoke that joined the others at the center of what was a big wheel. It had a big engine driving it, all brand new with fresh paint. School kids would come up to it and say, "God, six tickets!" Most all of the other rides were only three. It was something special.

I'd start it up early in the morning and we'd go until ten at night. It was a long day. You got an hour for lunch. There was this guy, named Sleepy, who came around and relieved you for a break. I liked him a lot because he'd come by and relieve me almost every hour and tell me to take my time.

As time went on, I got to know the other ride operators. They all had nicknames, derived from the rides they operated. There was Scooter, who ran the scooters; Moonie, who had the Trip-to-the-Moon ride; House, who took tickets at the haunted house; and my favorite, Horses, who kept the Merry-Go-Round spinning all day long. At night we'd all go to the main office with our collected tickets in long sacks that looked like the kind sailors carried. The boys who worked in the park hotel would nudge each other and say, "There's Horses," or whatever, as we went by. I was Coaster.

We'd carry those bags high on our shoulders with the tie strings knotted several times. That was profit. The fastest way to lose your job in the park was to get caught with tickets in your pocket. You were out if that happened. An Australian guy was our boss. He was redheaded and the down-under nickname for that is Blue. Blue would remind us every day to "Keep 'em sacked, mates, or you are O-U-T, out!" He also had a motto: "Get the last nickel."

I was the youngest ride operator, the college kid, and was soon adopted by Horses and the gang. Our lunch hours were rarely the same, but when things would slow up at night we'd all congregate near the Merry-Go-Round ticket booth and shoot the bull. You could see your ride from there and after Blue had made his rounds it was safe to gather for a session. It was a pretty time of night, too. Colored lights were strung along Ride Street. Off in the distance the activity down on the midway made a nice sound. The evening air was always a little chilled, and there were few riders after seven.

It was at one of those bull sessions that I got my carnival-man education. It had to do with the relief guy, Sleepy. Everyone was standing around with their hands in their pockets. On Ride Street, when the air was chill, you did that, and it was done in a special way. The hands were thrust deeply into the pockets and the arms were not allowed to bend. This made the shoulders climb higher and narrowed them inward. You also put your head forward and looked downward. We all stood like that, facing each other, and talking. Movement was with the feet in a shuffle.

At one point, old Horses said to me, "Coaster, do you milk 'at ride?" I looked at him and tried to shrug my shoulders, but that was impossible, of course. "I mean, do ya check the seat bins for tips?" he said.

"Horses, I'm not sure I know what you mean." They all looked at each other and gave it one of those I-thought-so looks.

"Boy, your pay's only half the money out here. The other money's in the ride, and you got one 'ah the best," he said. Scooter joined in with, "You betcha." And then they gave me a lesson that increased my earning power right on the spot.

Because of what Horses called "centriffica" force, the coins and loose objects in the riders' pockets tended to part company with their owners and fall out onto the seats. As this wonderful force continued, it also caused these objects to creep down the seam formed by the seat cushion and seat back and then fall through the crack between the leather and the metal wall. If you put your hand between the seat and metal wall and pushed it down to the bottom of the metal box, there would be the money. It was a vault!

It became clear to me that, though I wasn't doing this, Sleeper was. "That's why he's so damn good about com'n down to relieve you," laughed Horses. "Yeah," said Scooter, "he don't give no damn about you. He's take'n ya."

In the weeks that followed I became very good at milking the Flying Coaster. But I didn't see as much of Sleeper. I'd shut down the ride every half hour or so, to "check out things," and I'd find money on the left inside corner of the big steel box that held the seats. Also, if you ever notice a carnival ride operator going to great lengths to help you out of the seat, it's because your money didn't take the full trip down into the innards of the seat casing. He's distracting you with helpfulness so he can quickly push the coins down until it's time to milk. A nice, crew-cut college guy, I could do the help 'em off bit quite well.

Every night I'd come home and Angie and I would put the nickels, dimes, and quarters in neat piles and know that we were going to make it through the summer just fine until it was time to make sandwiches again.

Now the nickels and quarters and dimes were fine. It wasn't really like you were stealing. Most of the time you didn't have any idea whose change it was, except for the few times you helped it down. It was okay. It was all very impersonal. It was like a donation. They probably didn't even know it was gone. I could see my own dad saying, "Geez, I thought I had some quarters. Oh, well, take this dollar and get some more tickets." No harm at all.

But something the ride operators never talked about was wallets. I knew that all the other guys must have gotten wallets, but they never said a word. I wanted to bring it up a thousand times, but somehow it seemed a forbidden subject. Did they take them, or turn them in? I told myself I had to develop a wallet philosophy, a wallet stance before it happened. But it happened before I got a chance to think it through.

I had never had even one wallet, and then—bang—I unloaded and there were four of them on the seats. It was dark when it happened, a warm night when dads would ride. I didn't know they were there until I took a walk around. Some of them could have been there for half an hour. And I found them late. There were no riders waiting. The whole ride street was quiet. Horses and the rest were forming out near the Merry-Go-Round. I grabbed the wallets and put them in my lunch bag where I was saving a cookie and a plum.

When I did it, I felt a shock wave hit me. I had wallets! I turned back to see if anyone was looking. Horses and the others were all standing with their hands in their pockets not looking my way. God, I thought, I have four wallets here. I must act casual and get these home. I'm committing a crime! But, I told myself, I have a wife and little baby to support. Go through with it.

When I closed up that night and walked down to turn in tickets at the office with the others, I felt sure they knew. I thought they were all waiting for me to hand them in at the last minute. In fact, everyone I saw looked at me like they knew. The old lady who took the ticket bags looked at me a little harder. I was sure she'd press a button if I didn't turn them over. I almost did, but then—like a common thief—I pressed the sandwich bag to my chest and turned away from the window. Horses dropped me off in front of the house. I made it. Unless they were watching me.

I didn't go right in. There was an old garage out in back of the house and I went there instead, where I could look over my take. As I went through each one I pulled out real bills. By the time I had gone through the last one, I had fifty-three bucks! I really hit the jackpot, I said to myself.

I put the money in my pocket. Then I had the problem of what to do with the wallets. No problem. There was a big sewer on the corner. I walked down to it and tossed them in. Nobody saw me. Then I headed for the house. Rich!

On the short trip to the house I tried to tell myself I was a cool guy, a real operator; but when I got there I started to feel like a crook. I came in and Angie was standing there with that wonderful, glad-you're-home look she always had for me. She said, "Look, I've got a surprise for you." And, on the table was a big chocolate cake, with "Daddy" on it. She was holding little Mikie in her arms.

God, I felt like I wasn't worthy. Here they were, cake and all, and I had just committed a crime. I felt like the guy in the movie who's got the cops on his tail and he comes home to his wonderful family knowing that it'll soon all be gone. And that made me panic. God, I had to get those wallets. I had to get them, put the money back in, and turn them back. I just looked at Angie. I could have cried. I said, "Wait, honey, I'll be right back," and I took off back out the door.

I went back to the garage where I kept some tools. In quick order I hammered a nail into the end of an old broom handle to make myself a wallet spear. I took a crowbar, too, so I could pry off the sewer lid. I had experience with that from my old days in Pittsburgh when we kids would lose our baseballs down a sewer. Then you were a real hero if you were the guy who went down into it to get the ball.

I got the lid up, and I didn't even have to go down. It turned out that the sewer was filled with dry dirt and the wallets were only about three feet from the top of the sidewalk. I didn't even need the spear. I got them all.

Angie was concerned when I came back in. She said, "Honey, what's wrong." I confessed. She said I was a good man. I felt more worthy.

Now I was faced with the problem of how much money went back in each one. So, I read through the cards in them and looked at the pictures. After a while I had an idea about what each person was like. One guy was a lawyer, one a student at the University of Pittsburgh, and another was a member of the meatpacker's union. I couldn't figure out what J. S. Filbert did, but he had five really great-looking kids. I finally gave the first three ten bucks, and put twenty-three in Filbert's. I thought he had the greatest need. After that, Angie laughed and hugged me and I held her and little Mikie in my arms. We ate the cake. It tasted good.

The next day I gave the lady at the bag pickup window the wallets at noon. She didn't even show any emotion one way or the other. She just took them. She didn't say something like I was the most honest young man she knew or anything like that. She just nodded and took them. I said, "You'll see to it that they are returned." She nodded again, like it happened every hour on the hour.

That night at the last bull session I confessed what I had done to Horses. He listened with a half smile on his face. He was such a good old guy I knew he'd have something to say. He did. He said, "God, kid, I'll never make a carnie man outta ya." He told me I was lucky to have a wallet ride. "And it didn't help 'em suckers any to give them to old Mary, you know, because she'll just pocket the money herself." I still felt good about doing the right thing. I didn't want little Mikie to have a crook for a father. I wasn't going to be a carnival man anyway.

Once in a while I'd relieve another ride operator when we were short or real busy. I enjoyed that. It gave me a chance to work different gadgets. As a matter of fact, I went around on several of my lunch hours and rode everyone's rides. They thought I was crazy. But I had to do it. When you're little you promise yourself that you'll buy fifty candy bars when you grow up and eat them all. You say, "Promise me, self, that you'll do it." Well, I did. I rode everything. Once I had forgotten my lunch and Angie got a ride out to the park to give it to me. I was on my ride when she got there. She couldn't believe it. I waved.

You got double fun when you relieved House at the Fun House. He had a lady in the ticket booth with him so that he could make a walk-through every half hour or so. It was done just to make sure everything was working and also to chase the creeps out. Weird guys would go in there and hide. They'd stay for hours if there wasn't a "flusher" to push them along to the exit. Sometimes they were guys who'd grope the girls coming through. That was easy to do because it was dark, there was a lot of noise and confusion, and the girls weren't expecting it. They could grab a handful of ass or tit, and then be gone.

We carried a flashlight to flush. You checked under the stairs and in the corners. You told people to move on if they lingered too long in front of the mirrors or a scary display. I got so I could go through that funhouse with my eyes closed. I had the "events" down in a set order. There was first the mooing cow that made a loud moo and leaned forward like it was going to get you. Then you went up the crazy stairs. The screaming devil came at you after you got to the top. Then there were the air blasts, especially attractive to leg freaks.

Through the crooked hall and into the slanted room, I could walk through all of this without losing my balance or missing a step.

One night I had just gone past the slanted room, and I came up on these two huge guys who were kicking in the laughing clown. The clown was full-sized, with a big plastic grin, and he'd light up and laugh at you as you carefully made your way down the hall. He was fixed well back into a cutout box and had a heavy screen in front of him. One of these jokers was holding onto the frame above the screen and swinging his heels full force into the laughing clown. By the time I got there the screen was almost kicked in and already hitting against the clown.

No sweat. I put the light on them and said, "All right you bastards, stop it!" I sounded good. For just a split second I startled them. Just for a second. And then they turned in my direction and went for me. I was the authority, right? Not for long. They were coming at me and I ran like hell in the other direction. I had to go back against the crowd in reverse order. I said, "Oh, God, let me get outside." I knew I had the advantage, but I had to do it backwards. Let's see, through the slanted room to the . . . hall . . . and then was it moving floor or crazy stairs? Air blasts, screaming devil, crazy stairs, mooing cow, and outside. I got it right. I was almost ready to pass out, but I got to do something fantastic. I got to yell, "Hey, Rube!"

It worked. Everyone hearing my call came at once, including the two midway cops. When the two came out, and they did it like there was no danger, the cops grabbed them. The old man who ran the hit-the-stake-and-ring-the-bell had his mallet at the ready while the cops questioned the two big guys. They were drunk and mean. But there were about twenty of us carnies gathered around them. I felt scared, yet good about having them under control. Somewhere I had dropped my flashlight.

I liked running the Coaster. All during the school year there was either a paper to write or a test to get up for. Standing out in the summer sun in a country amusement park was a good escape from all of that. Though I had pressing responsibilities, I was doing okay. Money was coming in. It would be another school year until I graduated. All I had to do was run the Coaster. Another year, my senior year, would come soon enough.

Grand Lake got what you would call a high-classed crowd. The country people in the area were very wholesome, and the city people had the money to stay at the park hotels or spend vacation in a cottage by the lake. In spite of those two mean drunks there was rarely any trouble. In fact, it was a rather easygoing environment, as long as we all got that last nickel.

During the day I ran the ride and watched the people walk up and down Ride Street. Off in the distance I could hear the race of the big Roller Coaster and the screams it produced as it went crashing downward. Then there would be a pause as it slowly worked its way up another incline; this was accompanied by a straining, clicking sound. Though the riders were quiet, you could hear their expectation. Then, screaming, back down another stretch they'd go. Horse's Merry-Go-Round was a beautiful thing and played snappy calliope music all day. Added to all these sounds were snaps of shots from the midway, the motors and wheels of the other rides, and talk and laughter everywhere.

At night the streets were lighted with colored lights. The park owners had patterned the night lighting after Disneyland. Large colored balls were placed in the trees here and there. The summer nights, the noises, and the people walking in the glow all made the place into another world. I was only passing through, just a visitor. I savored it all.

I had one rider who showed up again and again, all summer long. He was a sad looking little child. He had been burned or something, or maybe he had a birth defect of some kind. He was about eleven or twelve. He had no hair and only stumps for ears. His eyes bulged. There were no eyebrows. His lips were malformed. Just a slit for a mouth. It was like he was leaning to one side, with one shoulder higher than the other. He always wore the same black shoes, old-fashioned with laces that went up to the ankle.

He loved to ride the Coaster. He would wait in line with his head down, not looking at anybody. The kids in line would stare at him, sometimes even make faces. But he didn't seem to see it. He wore thick glasses. If you caught a look into his eyes straight on, they looked huge, wide, and kind of wondrous. I'd take his ticket, and he'd get on. And then he would be a different little boy. I'd turn the handle slowly, and it would hiss because the controls were operated by compressed air. I could see the rubber tubes running from the control handle stiffen as they bulged with pressure. And around the cars would go, up and over the coaster track and into the air. Because I rode it myself, I knew that feeling you got in your stomach as it went over the track and up. You were lighter than air for an instant, and your gut fluttered in the wake of it.

My little crooked rider would be in a car all by himself. He'd be in a world all his own. He would squirm and laugh and scream a soundless cry of delight from a lipless circle of a mouth. And I loved him for his joy. I was glad to see him when he'd appear. He made my day.

He would only ride one time when he came. Just one time. He'd show up about once a week. I had the feeling he lived nearby and that the money for the ride was hard to come by. It was his big event of the week. Once he left the car he would be twisted again, very silent and shy.

Once I didn't see him for a week. Then the next week I just happened to look over by the side of the Merry-Go-Round and there he was, standing back on the grass and watching the riders on the Coaster. His big eyes were fixed on the cars as they went over the top of the incline. They seemed to smile. But he didn't come over to get in line. Then he was gone. The next day same thing, and then he was gone for three days.

When he appeared again, I waited about fifteen minutes to see if he was going to ride. He didn't. So I waved my hand in his direction. It took me some waving, but he caught my hand out the corner of his eye. I got the big eyes straight on. I motioned for him to come over. He just stood there. I felt like I was being sized up by a cautious deer.

Very slowly he started moving. He kept on coming. Then he was right in front of me. My God he was a sight. I just looked at him and said, "Ride?" He shook his head a slow no. Then I said, "No ticket for you today. You're my guest." He understood that. Not because he nodded or answered or anything, but I knew he understood. When I unloaded, he went right out and got into a car. When I walked past him to snap the safety bolt on the seat rail, I said, "You can just stay on as long as you like. Don't get off until you want to."

He rode for about half an hour. It was a good thing old Blue didn't come by because I'd have to explain why this kid stayed on between the rides. Man, he had a ball. He squirmed and held on with his hands working up and down on the rail. And that little O on his face sent out happiness from every part of him. It was his day. And old Coaster zinged around like the slick machine she was.

I have no idea when he finally got off. I just saw that he wasn't there anymore.

About four days later, around eleven o'clock on a Saturday, I felt a tug at my sleeve. It was him. He looked right at me and handed me a huge paper bag, the kind you get groceries in. Then, he was gone across the street and out of sight. When I got the chance to look inside it was filled with this great lunch. There were two chicken sandwiches on thick homemade bread. I knew sandwiches. These were from freshly killed chickens. And there was a big apple, some homemade fudge, and this big chunk of peach pie. It was still warm. And there was a note, written on the same kind of brown paper. It said,

"Sir, thank you for being so nice to David. He don't have many people that will. Enjoy this food."

The only other thing that happened of any consequence was the undertaker's convention. They set up big tents near the park, on the large grassy areas near the lake. The tents were the open-air type, right out of King Arthur. All around them there were parked hearses, along with huge metal vaults. They would hire summer workers for five dollars a half hour to lie in the caskets inside the big tents. Undertakers would come along and view the caskets. Once in a while they'd comment on the lining or something about the way the box showed off the corpse. They called us corpses. I did it lunch hours for the week the convention was there. Kind of a strange experience. They liked me because I slept.

When the summer was over and I went back to school, sandwiches and other jobs like selling Christmas trees paid our bills.

Through all of that Angie and I grew closer as we faced the realities of making it on our own. Sandwiches, carnivals, odd jobs, and putting all of the pennies together bonded us. It was more fun than work. We just kept moving toward the goal: graduation.

Senior year I got a job on the local radio station, writing copy and doing the late night news. That made me feel like I was somebody. Angie could hear me read the copy at home over the blue clock radio we kept in our turn-of-the-century kitchen. I picked up two bucks an hour for that.

The little rundown apartment in Freeport was the best place in the world to be. Angie made it such a home. And our door was always open to the brothers of Gamma Alpha Sigma. There was always something going on. Angie liked the fraternity crowd to come in, especially since it was the Gamma treasury that had financed all of our household goods.

When we got back from our elopement to Detroit, my fraternity had us up for dinner the Monday after our weekend marriage. After dinner, Temple stood up and told everyone how happy they were that I was finally under control. He looked at Angie and wondered aloud how I had rated such a wife. I remember he added something like, "Knowing Norm, he hasn't thought beyond the honeymoon. He doesn't know that they'll need pots, pans, dishes, brooms, sheets, and all of that to keep them going." He was right.

He gestured to the hallway beyond the dining room, and there was a full table of all of that being carried in. They had spent a couple of hundred bucks getting us set up. Angie cried. She never forgot that, so we always had an extra sandwich or ice cream bar for the brothers of Gamma Sig.

After graduation, I thought maybe I'd stay on and try the radio thing a little longer. WPEL, the voice of Freeport, it was. I worked full-time. No more sandwiches. It was like we held onto the first world we made together for just a little while longer, but the money was not good. I wanted us to have more.

I looked around, took interviews, and imagined I'd take corporate America by storm. I got two offers: the telephone company and a drug company. History majors just weren't in demand. I couldn't stand the thought of either prospect. Finally, Angie whispered to me one night that maybe I should try being an officer in the Navy for a while. So I went to the recruiting station in Pittsburgh. On the way up to the Navy office on the third floor a guy in the old familiar blue suit stopped me. We talked. I came home to announce that I'd be in Air Force Officer Training School at Lackland Air Force Base, Texas, in September.

Never to be the great doctor, I was now sitting on a bunk in Korea, a long way from Angie, the kids, and the early days in Freeport. I sat and thought about all of that, letting the memories rush over me, hands cupped together between my knees. Suddenly, a cold, wet nose pushed itself into my palms. It was Dolly. Her buddy was gone for Osan, so she was looking to someone for comfort. I patted her head and knew that I was a long way from those wonderful memories.

13

Let There Be Light

The screen door banged and somebody walked down the hall toward my room.

"Captain?" It was Sergeant Clinton Davis.

"Hi, Sarge," I said, getting up. "Were you looking for Dolly here?"

"Both of ya, sur. The gener'l's here. I wanna introduce ya."

"Oh, okay. Yeah, that's great. How did the arrival go?"

"Just fine, sur. Major Dubbs tried to act like he was the big welcomer and all, but I've known the gener'l too long to let him get snowed by an asshole like that."

I combed my hair and took my parka out of the lighted closet.

Clinton, Dolly, and I walked into a very cozy NCO club. It was dark outside, and the late fall chill was considerable. Coming into the club, the fireplace and the warm glow of the place gave me a good feeling. Fresh beer was in the air, mixed in with the smells of the grill. Whammo, I was in the party mood.

Instead of the usual crowd of airmen and their moose sitting on the chairs and couches by the fireplace, the general's party had quite taken over the fireplace area. Goldman was sitting with the group, along with Dubbs and Dutch. The dog got to them before Clinton and me.

"Dolly's ready to go, boys. Lookie here, she's ready to go," said the guy sitting in the overstuffed chair. He was grabbing her by the head and giving her a mock tussle. The dog was loving it.

"Gener'l, sur, I want you to meet Captain Whitman here. He's the OIC this season, sur." I was the OIC, officer in charge of nonsense as far as I was concerned.

General Bobby Pitts was the good old boy type. Jolly looking, he came right out of the chair, with the dog jumping up on him. He was bald on top, crew-cut sides, red cheeked, and ruggedly overweight. He didn't really look like a three-star in his hunting outfit, but he did look like a pretty good guy.

"Whitman, glad to meet ya," he said, giving me a hard grip.

"Sir, my pleasure, I can tell you that your visit has been the big event around here for weeks."

"Well, we 'preciate everything. Sergeant Clint here tells us you did us a lot of good work."

"For sure, sur," said Clinton, beaming at what was surely his patron and hero.

The others all got up on their feet. That surprised me, too. I was just a damn captain at a two-bit radar site. The general and his guys had manners, large manners.

"Look here," Pitts said. "I want you to shake hands with the rest of the group."

"Forrest Belford, Norm," said a tall, lanky guy with prematurely white hair.

"Sir," I said, shaking his hand, "your letters all got here."

"Yeah, Whitman, but what about the dancing girls?" he said, laughing.

"Never mind, Bel, we'll get in enough trouble ourselves," the general said. "And this is Colonel Coates. And Colonel Yates."

We exchanged handshakes and hellos.

"And Brigadier Rushworth here. And meet Mr. Price."

They were all very cordial. I was impressed.

"How 'bout a round, everybody?" the general said, as we all settled down into a chair.

"Mister Kwak," yelled Goldman, "we all need a reload."

"Sergeant Goldman here has been keeping us all entertained, Norm," Pitts said. "He says you're the other half of his comedy team."

"Sir, I'm his straight man, and when Father Fisher's around he has two."

"Who's Father Fisher?" the Brigadier asked.

"He's our site chaplain, sir," Dubbs said, trying to reassert his importance in the group. "He does a lot of work with these missionary priests they got on the island and that's where he is now, working at one of the churches up island."

"Well, we'll be able to go to mass Sunday then, ah, Captain Whitman?"

"Yes, sir, he'll be back, probably Saturday night." That was Belford who had asked. Now Paul would have more attendance at mass.

Kwak came, and we ordered up. General Pitts made it clear he was buying. Most everyone ordered a hard drink. Not bashful, I took a double scotch on the rocks.

It was a grand experience talking with our visitors. It had now been two months since I'd seen anyone else but the people on the island. These guys were good company.

Clinton was obviously a favorite with them. He gave them a rundown on where they'd go on the hunt, who would go with whom. He sent Kwak over to the lodge for two of the guides, Mr. Cho and Mr. Jung. They came over proud as could be and got to sit with us. Their English wasn't bad, and eventually they were answering questions about how the bird population looked this season.

I breathed a sigh of relief when I saw Sue standing by the bar giving Dubbs the high sign. The group was pleasant enough with him, but I could tell they had the word he was a clod. Clinton did good work, I thought.

"General Pitts, I'm gonna have to excuse myself," Dubbs said, standing.

"Oh, yes, major," the general said, "I'll see more of you, I'm sure. Thanks now for meeting us."

Dubbs nodded to the rest and went off and out the door with Sue, who gave the group an over-the-shoulder glance as they went out the club door.

"Well, at least he's got good taste," Pitts said, laughing his cheeky smile.

We had more rounds, and then a plate full of burgers was passed around, a product of Goldman's genius. He put salt, pepper, and Heinz Ketchup from my hometown on the little coffee table by the fireplace. Later on, the cooks brought in three or four plates of French fries. It was all delicious.

"You don't ever go anywhere with the Yanks without a hamburger and chips," the Brigadier said, laughing.

"The Brigadier used to have his cook make 'em for us in London, Sergeant Goldman," Pitts said, holding up his burger.

"But not so delicious as these, Sergeant," Rushworth added, putting up his hand. "These we know are made from real beef. Those War Two burgers were likely to have mysterious ingredients."

Pitts wanted to pay for the food, too, but Goldman shook his head. "No, sir, this is on the club. I just want some of those pheasant when you start bagging them."

"Goldman, I'll tell you what. You keep your oven hot 'cause I'm gonna bring you back enough birds for the whole membership."

"You're on, sir. And I'm glad Captain Whitman's here because I want him to see how a truly generous officer conducts himself, sir."

I toasted them all with my drink.

Belford said, "I propose that we all make an inspection of the local sights."

"We'll take the bird wagons, sur," Clinton said.

Yeah, these were my kind of people.

We took ample cases of beer, climbed into the wagons, and hit the road for Moklepo, a little town twenty miles from the site. They had a high-class *kisaeng* house there and some really plush tourist hotels. The General and his boys wanted to get laid.

I rode in the second wagon with Goldman, Lieutenant Colonels Coates and Yates, Cho and Jung. Clinton and the general had all of the others in the back of number one. "This is a good way for the old man to blow off steam," Yates said to Goldman.

"Don't worry, sir. Whatever happens goes no further."

"Bud, Sergeant Clint was right about these guys," Colonel Coates said, taking a long drag on his cigar.

We bounced over the Moklepo road, talking about Korea. Both pilots had flown in the Korean War, and they were telling me how good the Korean pilots were up at the Republic of Korea Air Force base at Suwon. "Since the war these guys have really gotten their act together," Coates said. "I'd fly any war with a Korean F-5 driver."

"I wish we could get more training sorties with them," I said. "Our ROKAF lieutenants need the work."

"You ought to talk to old Virgil Canada," Coates said. "He can get you the missions."

Colonel Virgil Canada was the head of ADOT, the air defense operations team up north at Osan Air Force Base. The big Boss. Dubbs reported to him. I had only seen him through an office window during my orientation week at ADOT headquarters.

"Do you know him, Colonel?" I asked.

"Virgil? Hell, yes. He's part of the old pack. He and the General are very good friends. Matter of fact he almost came on this trip."

"Put in a good word for us, will you?" I said.

"I'll do that, Norm, for sure. We'll see him on the way back through Osan."

"Canada's a little straighter than we are, Whitman," Colonel Yates said, "but he's sure one fine individual. Hell of a record in World War Two."

Coates told us Canada had flown P-51s. "Came from a real poor background," he said. "There's a great story about how he heard his mother was dying just about the time he was getting shipped overseas. He flew a Mustang to South Dakota, where the family farm was, had his old man drive his mom to the nearest paved highway, and he set it down right there."

It reminded me of a Norman Rockwell painting.

"Yeah, and this old boy sheriff had both ends blocked off so Virg could get away with it. His kid brother climbed in the cockpit and kept the engine revving while Canada said goodbye to his mother."

Great story. You could see it. "Did his mother die?" I asked.

"Yes, matter of fact, she passed away about two months after Virg got to Europe. He was damn thankful he did it," Coates said, finishing off a Bud and reaching into the ice compartment for another. "You need to meet him, Whitman. He's a square shooter. He got the word on your Major Dubbs."

"Well, if you could lie a little and tell him the captain's good, it would probably help us all," Goldman said.

"Hell, Sarge," Coates said, "the captain's got you to protect his ass."

"Yes, sir, but who protects my vital interests?" Goldman said, shrugging his shoulders.

"Fair enough," Coates said with a wave of his cigar, "we'll tell Virgil that you two are just f-a-n-t-a-s-t-i-c."

Just then we stopped. The doors opened and the noises and lights of a side street in Moklepo came rushing in. The others were already standing outside in a group.

"Clint says this is the best place in town, Bill," the general yelled to Colonel Coates. "Get your asses over here and let's go run 'em."

"Yes, sir. Yes, sir," we all said in staggered response. And with the wagons locked up, we all filed up a set of broad wooden steps leading to a large multi A-frame building. The roof was painted red. The wall panel windows were glowing from within. You could hear traditional Korean music and a lot of voices. My kind of place.

Once on the large porch, there were two mamasans and a papasan to greet us. We were almost halfway up a Korean island nearly ninety miles out at sea. These folks didn't see many Americans. Their customers were either wealthy Koreans or sometimes a few Japanese tourists. The locals tolerated the Japanese. But Americans were generally number one.

Because we were so far away from the commercial sex and fun of the Seoul and Osan red light districts, we were a special group of round eyes. You could tell the mamasans were delighted to see us. They were all smiles.

They didn't know word one of English, so Cho and Jung went right to work, speaking to them a mile a minute. They'd talk, and the mamasans would listen, nod, and cover their mouths with their hands. They were being told that this was a high man's party, an American general and his boys.

The papasan was obviously impressed. He very ceremoniously shook each of our hands and bowed. "They say you come in. They will give us very special *kisaeng* women and food. You take off shoes," said Mr. Cho, basking in the glory of being Korean guide to these important visitors.

All the while I could see pretty little faces peeking at us from within. The *kisaeng* girls would peek, giggle, and then scurry away. There was a lot of excitement spreading around on the inside because of our arrival. My big black military brogans took for damn ever to get off.

A pretty little *kisaeng* girl saw me doing an awkward balancing act out there on the porch and floated past everyone at the entrance to come to my aid. She giggled and snuggled under my left armpit, holding me up. One of her arms went around my waist and I reciprocated. She smelled and felt wonderful. I got both brogans off. There was a lot of laughter and giggling over my awkward dance.

Then we went inside, my little friend still clutching me around the waist. I felt like Gulliver being led by the little people. Good thing I had those ample fatigue pants on because my helper had given me an erection.

Our group was escorted into a beautifully done room. All rice paper walls, with black varnished wooden framing. The floor was spotless linoleum, heated from underneath. Our hosts seated us around a beautiful black low table that had inlaid mother-of-pearl dragons, flowers, vines, and clouds.

Little sweetie pie sat right down next to me. Other girls came in, bowed, and sat down with the rest of our group. General Pitts went wild when a tall *kisaeng* scooted next to him, her hand over her mouth, with eyes cast down.

"Well, look at you," he said, putting his arm around her. "Boys, she's an angel. Just look at you." He was all red in the face, his stubble crew cut bulging around the sides of his neck and head. His bald spot glowed. I was reminded of that right jolly old elf part in the *Night Before Christmas*. He was just beaming over the sight of her.

Rushworth, the British Brigadier, got a tiny *kisaeng* with great almond eyes. She'd look at him, then turn away, and laugh with her hand over her mouth. You could tell that she had probably never been this close to a round eye in her life. "Hello Miss Smith," he said in his strong English accent, not cracking a smile. She looked down at the table and said, "Heloo," and laughed with glee. "Yes, h-e-l-l-o, Miss Smith," he said back, trying to get her to look up at him. But she turned away, too shy to look at this strange man with the booming voice.

The girl sitting with Price, the CIA guy, was gently pulling the hair on his arm and cooing out embarrassed "Oooows" of wonder. That prompted all of the other girls to look at the hair on our forearms. Korean men don't have hair on their arms. My little partner began rubbing my arm in wonder. "Hair," I said. That made them all laugh.

Goldman was looking his girl over while she tried to avoid eye contact with him. She'd look at the others, move away from his stare, and then bury her face in her hands. "This one's Jewish. I know she's Jewish. You can tell by the nose. My mother, my rabbi, they'll be so happy I found a nice Jewish girl in the USO."

Meanwhile, Colonel Belford and the two Korean guides were trying to order us some drinks and food. "Everybody, listen," Belford said. "This lady here wants to know what we'd like." A smiling mamasan was standing above him with the Korean *kisaeng* version of a waitress order pad. "Listen up!" Belford said again, and put his fingers in his mouth for a good old-fashioned, two-finger, American-GI, New-York-taxicab-stopping whistle. It was loud and shrill. It made everyone stop midsentence, and the girls broke out in delighted laughter once more.

"Okay, Forrest," Pitts said, "well done. Let's get some order in here."

"Gentlemen," Brigadier Rushworth said, "our leader has called for order."

"Yes, sir!" we all said together, squadron meeting style.

"What do we want to make merry with?" asked Belford.

"*Maekchu* and *chung jung*," I yelled out. "Beer and rice wine, Korean style."

The old woman nodded. "*Neh, maekchu* and *chung jung*," she said, with approval.

"Good, Norm," General Pitts said, "and have Cho and Jung tell them to bring us whatever food they want us to try. Tell them it's on me, and give us plenty of local Tolsan-Do fare. Like seafood. We'll try what they think is their best. It's all on me."

"Yessa, I tell hor, Genaraul," Cho answered, with professional seriousness.

The mamasan and our guides talked back and forth, shaking their heads in mutual agreement as they appeared to be checking off a list of dishes. Then mamasan clapped her hands together, and the girls got up on their feet quickly.

"They go now to bring us what we order," said Mr. Cho.

"You tell this one to come back poly-poly," Pitts said, grabbing on to the traditional full silk dress his girl was wearing.

"*Neh, neh,*" she said, chirping the Korean word for yes. She knew she was a big hit with the high man of the group.

Just before my dinner companion got up, she put her hand right on my crotch, and then said something to the girls. They all laughed.

"What'd she say, Cho?" asked Goldman.

"Oh, she said Captain Whitman has a big one, sore."

That announcement made, everyone turned to me and gave out here-heres and hoo-rahs all around.

"Hey, come back here Miss and measure mine," General Pitts yelled.

"Young officers can always be depended upon to make us old men feel our age," the Brigadier said with a dramatic sigh and tone of resignation.

"Hold onto it, Captain," Price said, "because you've got to wait until the party's over."

"It's all a bluff, sir," Goldman said. "He's still a green bean, Korean cherry. I know because I'm his personal physician."

"Don't worry, he'll fix that tonight," said Clinton, giving me a big salute.

Finally I said, "I don't know what she's talking about." That just got me some catcalls.

It wasn't long before the ladies returned with another table loaded down with a fantastic array of food that could have been on the cover of an Asian gourmet magazine. There were egg dishes, fish dishes, meat dishes, and sauces. The colors were just beautiful.

Two guys took away our bare table and the girls put the table laden with our feast in its place. The transition was flawless. Nothing was spilled. And on the heels of the food came the OB Beer and the hot pots of *chung jung*, along with sparkling clean glasses. Before you could say bon appétit, we each had a glass of foamy beer in our hands and a little Korean dollie fondling our crotches. It was a hell of a way to begin a party.

After ample portions of beer and rice wine, we all agreed that there wasn't a loser in our band of brothers. The more Pitts drank and groped Miss Lee, as her name turned out to be, the more entertaining he became. Any time the booze or food got low, he'd call for more of everything. He loved to party.

We learned all of the girls' names. The big difference about a high-classed *kisaeng* house and the clubs up on the mainland was the names the girls went by. Up at the Five Spot or the Arirang in Chicol Village, the girls had adopted American first names. You met Judys, Sues, and Carols. Here it was Miss Lee, or Miss Kim, or Miss Park. These girls wore very traditional dresses called *chimas*, but the moose up in the GI clubs wore tight skirts and sexy blouses. I had once seen a guy and his *yobo* going through a Sears catalogue, picking out her clothes.

Miss Lee liked her general. She didn't understand a word he said, but she laughed at every joke he told us. She fed him whole fried eggs and crab with chopsticks and kept his glass full. But he waived off a *chung jung* refill saying, "I'm not going to let myself drink too much Missey Lee because I got to be able to get it up for you later on." She giggled at that like she knew exactly what he was saying.

Goldman had a real beauty. She was Miss Ihm. "Do we speak to the rabbi about our relationship?" Goldman asked, pretending to be very serious.

She looked him square in the eyes and replied, "No, I do not think I was born in land of Christ."

That got our attention. "She speaks English," said Price. "She really led you down the path, Sarge."

But that didn't faze Goldman one bit. He came right back with, "You mean you're not Jewish? I've already made so many plans. I was gonna call my mother. My God, what did I almost do?" He was not one to get out of character.

But just as quick as he was, she said, "You neva going to find anybody as good as me anyway."

So Miss Ihm became the translator. And that was a good piece of luck, because it wouldn't be good form to ask Cho or Jung to act as our romantic go-betweens. They did have dollies sitting with them, but you could tell that they were relating to them differently. It wasn't the same version of give and take the round eyes were playing with their girls.

"I hava been telling my sisters everything you gee-eye say," Miss Ihm announced with pride.

"Then Missey Lee knows I'm going to get into her pants before the sun comes up tomorrow," Pitts retorted with a big wink, then hugging his very receptive *kisaeng*.

"*Neh*, all gee-eye are same-same," laughed our translator.

So we spent the next few hours playing little grabbie-feelie games with the girls. They dutifully stroked our crotches when we took time out from the games to chug down our drinks. The only time they brought their hands up from under the table was to feed us generous chopstick delivered bites of the special Tolsan-Do banquet food.

Miss Ihm taught us a game that involved learning the Korean word for various parts of the face. It started out with the girls touching our noses and saying, "*ko, ko, ko, ko, ko!*" Then their fingers went to our lips and they'd say, "*eep, eep, eep, eep, eep!*" Once they taught us the words, we were supposed to do our own pointing when one of them would yell out a word. The pace was fast. Most of us couldn't remember squat, so you'd end up pointing to your ear on *eep*, instead of your lips, and everyone would laugh.

There we were--generals, pilots, college graduates, roughneck sergeants, and even a cloak-and-dagger CIA guy--playing games like children in kindergarten. I saw this same loving touch the hookers had in the clubs up on the mainland. The American GIs and the Korean girls. There was this crazy, warm relationship. God help us, I thought, if our wives, mothers, teachers, sweethearts, aunts, and nuns were to see us. They wouldn't believe it. They wouldn't understand. And why the hell should they.

I was stinking drunk. We all were. The beer and rice wine kept coming. My bladder was about to burst.

"I gotta bleed the goose," I finally said. "I gotta go," I said, nudging my companion. But Miss Ho didn't understand. "Miss Ihm," I yelled across the table, "tell Miss Ho I've got to take a . . . that I've got to go to the bathroom."

"He's got to take a leak," General Pitts said to her. "Get the boy to the WC, Miss Ihm."

She looked blank for a minute and then the light of understanding came into her eyes. "Oh, he need *binjo*," she said. "You need *binjo*!"

Miss Ho nodded and mumbled, "*Binjo, neh, neh, binjo.*" Then she got up and dragged me by the arm.

"I go *binjo*," I said, waving goodbye to the crowd.

"You make sure you hold it all by yourself, Whitman," Colonel Belford yelled. "No fair gett'n ahead of us."

The door slid open and we were in the hall. I was still being led by hand. After we navigated the halls and landed at the door, the next problem was to find my brogans. There were shoes and boots everywhere.

Miss Ho and I looked all over the porch. I went down on all fours to get a closer view. Meanwhile, a small group of Korean men and girls was taking all of this in, which led me to stand up and give them a big bow. My audience responded as you would a circus clown, laughing with approval. But I did notice that a few well-dressed guys were regarding my shenanigans with a scowl. I guessed they didn't want us round eyes at their party house.

"Tough shit," I said, getting back to the job of finding my brogans. Somebody behind me said, "shit," but at that moment I spied my brogans. It was time to get to the *binjo*. It was time to bleed the goose.

Miss Ho and I went down the stairs and around a path to the back of the main house. I was reminded that on Tolsan-Do the narrow path between the street and one's doorstep was called an *olle*. This *olle* would lead me to relief. There was a full moon. It was so bright I could see everything. It was quiet out there in the crisp night air. All of that sobered me up just enough to see that I was out there with a very attractive woman leading me down the *olle*. We were walking almost single file, her arm leading me from behind her back. I stopped, came up behind her, put my arms around her waist, and buried my face in her long black hair. It felt wonderful.

"*Binjo, binjo,*" she said, breaking away, and pulling me on.

"Yes, *binjo*, " I said.

There was nothing exotic about the *binjo*. It was just a large outhouse. It could have been behind a farm back in rural America. It had two sets of doors. My grandfather would have called it a four holer. It had four oval holes evenly spaced over the do-your-business boards you sat on. But all I had to do was urinate. And thank God, too, because it smelled like hell in there, even with the nose-numbing buzz I had on.

Up to the first hole on the right I strode, unbuttoned my GI fatigue fly, and brought out the goose. When I looked down into the hole to take aim, there was a face looking up at me.

"Jesus Christ!" I said, stepping back. "Christ!" I said, looking back out the door at Miss Ho. "There's somebody down there!"

"*Twaejigogi,*" she said, laughing. "Oink, oink, oink," she said, forming a snout with her hands.

I stepped back into the *binjo* and looked down again. Sure enough, it was a goddamn pig, looking up at me. They let pigs come into the bottom of the outhouses, I thought. Hell, yes, they let the pigs eat the shit in the outhouses. God, no wonder why they tell you in the country arrival briefing that you shouldn't eat the pork.

"I don't have anything for you, you ugly son-of-a-bitch," I said to the pig. "Get the fuck outta my way. Get out, oink." But the pig stood his ground, making snorting sounds.

"Okay, you shit eater, here's a drink on me," I said, letting go with a strong stream that hit his snout dead center. The force of the stream made a sound that reminded me of the time I took aim at a Halloween jack-o'lantern on our fraternity house lawn. But that still didn't make him move an inch. He just kept looking up, letting me piss all over his face. "You dumb ass, lap it up, good to the very last drop," I said. I guessed it wasn't his first golden shower.

"God, Miss Ho," I said, as I buttoned my fly, "just when you think you have the shit end of the stick you find out you coulda been a pig in a fucking Korean outhouse."

She just smiled and took my hand.

"So long, pig," I yelled over my shoulder.

Back in the *kisaeng* house, Goldman took in my big grin with, "I know, don't tell me, Captain, you pissed all over the poor swine in the crapper."

"What swine?" I said.

Just as I settled back down at the table, the general announced that the party was over. "Ladies and gentlemen, Mr. Cho has very professionally taken care of the necessary arrangements. We'll all retire to the hotel across the street. It's time to sow our wild oats."

As he spoke, he was patting Miss Lee on the ass, and she was motioning the rest of the girls to stand up. Angie was a long, long way from all of this, and I was just drunk enough to go with the flow. Fuck it, I said to myself, if Miss Ho crosses the street with me, I'll lay her.

But nothing's simple in Korea. You learn that very quickly. You just don't grab Miss Ho by the arm, go to the hotel, rent a room, and plank her. Not so fast, GI. Those four steps require a lot of translation and negotiation. In this case, our two Korean guides were the negotiators. The first step involved *kisaeng* house hallway conversations between our guides and the management. Meanwhile, all of the girls had disappeared.

General Pitts and Colonel Belford got into the mix--giving instructions to Cho and Jung, who then relayed the words to the mamasans and papasans in Korean. It all had to do with *How much? How long?* and *Where?*

Goldman was standing next to me. "Sir this could spell the end of your cherry if they ever get this worked out."

"You have the best one, Goldman," I said, avoiding any further discussion of my cherry. "She speaks English."

"Sir, cunt's cunt."

"Yeah, well, it'd be nice to talk and get to know her."

"Wait, Packer's back. You're sounding like Packer. What'd you do, agree to play his part while he's on the mainland?" He said, with exaggerated frustration. "You don't talk to them. You fuck them. It's lust, sir, not love."

"Okay, everyone, it's checkie-in, checkie-in time at the Royal Palms," Colonel Yates announced.

On our way across the street, I took Goldman by the arm and motioned back in the direction of the path that led to the *kisaeng* house *binjo*.

"Goldman."

"Sir?"

"You know, you could fuck the outhouse pig and not say a word to it either."

He put his arm around my shoulder. "Sir, that's why I like you so much. You're so intellectual. So profound, Sir Profound. But my religion prevents me from getting that close to pork."

"Cunt's cunt, Goldman."

That exchange took us to the hotel lobby, where I witnessed the tail end of checkie-in, checkie-in. There was a huddle, it broke up, people scattered, quarterback Belford pointed to me, and I was whisked away by a little Korean guy who led me through a maze of rice paper hallways. We stopped at a sliding door, soft white light coming from within. He slid the door open, and I walked in. But when my stocking feet hit the smooth, heated floor, I skidded, lost my balance, and fell backwards. I landed on my ass, half in the room and half in the hall. That set me on a laughing jag, with the little guy trying to shoosh me. It sounded like, "*da-da, na-na, da-da, na-na-na.*"

Strong for his size, he managed to get me back into the room, put his finger to his lips, stepped into the hall, and slid the door shut behind him. I sat there alone, feet and legs spread out at sixty degrees or more, and looked around. Above me, one bare light bulb hung down on a long cord. It looked like something you might have found in Thomas Edison's old New Jersey laboratory. Not frosted, I could see the glowing filament ovals inside. Very appropriate for skid row.

The floor I had skidded on was shiny linoleum, like Packer's hooch, heated from underneath by pipes that were often made from lengths of beer or soda cans that were welded together. Over in one corner there was a round jar with a lid. You peed in that. In the center of the room was a sleeping mat, neatly rolled up, sitting atop a folded quilt. That was the bed. Next to it was this beanbag thing, harder than hell. That was the pillow. Yes, friends, make yourselves at home in one of our luxury rooms, complete with all of the conveniences you'll need for a restful and relaxing stay.

I took off my parka. Its extra weight reminded me that I had shoved a bottle of beer into each pocket. It was hard to believe I hadn't broken them when I went down on my tail. A quick check of the breast pocket, and there was the opener I always carried because I never learned how to open a beer with a quarter.

I opened the first beer and started to drink the suds when all of a sudden the door slid open and in came little Miss Ho, bowing and hurriedly closing the door behind her. Well, I thought, here it is. This is the moment of truth. I'm going to break my Korean cherry.

She didn't make eye contact with me. Instead, she started unrolling the rolled up mattress. Once done, she spread out the quilt on top of it. I just sat there, chugging on my bottle of Crown, the second most popular brand of Korean beer. I was glad that I had something to do and that she had something to do, because I didn't have any idea of how to get things moving in the direction of sex. But when her domestic task was finished, she turned toward me and got into the traditional sitting position--kneeling with her pretty ass resting on the back of her heels. I was still in my legs out position, as if I was about to begin the seated toe touch exercise.

I finally decided that a more romantic atmosphere might get things going. For that I needed to turn off the light. When I finally struggled to my feet, I went to the light. It was just this little unfrosted bulb, screwed into a plain, black bakelite socket. No switch to be found, I quickly unscrewed it, ignoring the heat on my fingertips. "Ouch!" I said to Miss Ho. "Very, very hot."

Mission accomplished. Darkened room, with just the right amount of romantic light coming in from all sides of the rice paper walls. Perfect. But Miss Ho unfolded like a fan and shot up on her feet. She was on me in a panic, poking me on the arm and pointing up at the disabled bulb.

"Miss Ho," I said softly, "calm down. The day's done. It's time for us to retire."

She did freeze for a quick moment.

So I put my hands on her shoulders. "Sit down like a good little Miss Ho, please, and take that lovely *kisaeng* dress off so we can join together in an ancient tradition common to both of our cultures."

But she didn't sit down. Fully animated again, she started gibbering away in Korean, pointing up at the light bulb, which was way out of her reach. Christ, I thought, she's hard to deal with, a fucking nagger. Maybe she was some kind of a light freak, standing there with her hand mimicking the twisting of the bulb in clockwise motion. She wanted that light on!

"No. No. No light. N-O light, Miss Ho. We go bed now," I said, twisting the goddamn thing all the way out of the socket. But that only fueled Miss Ho's passion for the light, miming as if she was inserting it in the socket and twisting it back in place. Marcel Marceau couldn't have done it better. In appreciation of her skills as a mime, I formed a socket with my closed right fist, screwed the bulb in, and raised it in the air. "Statue of Liberty!" I said to her. "Give me your tired *kisaeng*, your panties and your bra. Give me the business, Miss Ho."

I guess we were both getting kind of loud because I thought I could hear rustling noises in the other rooms. Up to that point, I hadn't thought about other hotel guests. But then I held my lady-liberty stance and listened silently. Yet Miss Ho didn't shut up, and that brought on low, guttural mutterings from the hallway.

"Aw, go back to sleep," I yelled. "This is just a little lovers' quarrel over a damn light. Miss Ho here wants to do it with the lights on." That only brought more hallway shuffling and whining, probably telling us to cool it.

Then behind me there was a soft rapping at the door.

"*Yoboseyo*," I said, "who's there?"

"Captain Whitman? It's Goldman," the voice said and the panel slid open. He was standing in the hall in his bare feet, no shirt, dressed in his GI fatigue pants only. Behind him were half a dozen onlookers, including the papasan who had checkie-checkied us in. The guy looked pretty agitated.

"Look, Norm," Goldman said, squinting to get a better view of Miss Ho and me, "You've got this whole part of the hotel awake and pissed off. It's three in the morning, and this guy's seriously thinking about throwing you out on your ear."

"Well, Christ, Goldman," I said, holding up the light bulb. "I unscrewed this damn thing so we could . . . you know . . . and then she went nuts on me. I was trying to get her into bed, that's all. She's all riled up about the goddamn light."

Meanwhile, Miss Ho just stood there like a figure in a wax museum diorama. Now she was quiet, downright impassive.

Looking past me, the hotel manager spoke some very direct words at her, none of which I could understand, of course. That brought her to life, and the two of them exchanged sharp-pitched sentences for several minutes. Every once in a while, she'd gesture toward me, raising the pitch of her voice as she did. Then they both looked at me and scowled. Goldman watched it all like you would a tennis match.

Then Mr. Cho showed up on the scene with the little guy who had taken us to the room. He was probably sent to get Cho.

"I can't believe this," Goldman said, rolling his eyes. "You've got the whole place up, sir."

By this time, Mr. Cho, the two hotel guys, and Miss Ho had a conference going. They were talking and making points in the air, punctuated with dirty looks in my direction. Voices from all around the hall were joining in.

"Sir I think it's the light thing," Goldman said, turning to Mr. Cho. "They're upset about the light, right, Cho?"

Cho broke off his conversation with the manager. "Yessa, they say captain make too much noise and he make girl upset by the light."

Goldman nodded with a knowing brow. What a showman. "Captain, the lights stay on all night in these places. The Koreans don't sleep in the dark. They sleep in the light. You started all of this when you doused the light."

"Shit, Goldman, that's crazy," I said, looking at the little bulb in my hand.

"No, Captain, it's not crazy. It's crazy to sleep in the dark, sir. That's crazy. See?"

All without looking up, I responded to that by reaching up and behind me to find the socket, found it, felt for the opening, took some volts through the thumb, and then successfully screwed the source of all this misery back in place. Presto. Let there be light.

And there was. You would have thought that I had just lighted up the national Christmas tree. I heard a soft, unified "Ah" come from the crowd in the hall.

"Good man, sir, "Goldman said with a snappy salute. "You just did wonders for Korean-American diplomacy."

"Christ, I'd hate to see them in a power outage," I said.

Then, one more short conference, with Cho acting as spokesperson. "Manager man say you please keep light on, sore. And please be very quiet. Many people now wish to sleep."

"Mister Cho, please tell this number-one manager I very sorry. I did not know Miss Ho here would go nuts when I turn out light. I make noise only to get her to calm down."

"God of Abraham," Goldman said, looking down and shaking his head. "Why do you send them to me? Why must I get these cases?"

The two hotel guys gave me halfhearted bows and went back down the hall, gently motioning their other guests to return to their rooms.

"Godda night, sore," said Mr. Cho, preparing to exit as well.

"Good night, Mr. Cho. Thanks for helping."

"Yessa, sore," he replied, giving Miss Ho a raised eyebrow and frown that very clearly said, cool it and get things under control. Then he was gone.

"Do I have to undress you two now and tuck you in?" offered Goldman, with his hands on his hips.

"We're fine, Martin, fine," I said, smiling confidently.

"You'll leave the light on, please sir? You'll whisper, sir?"

"You won't hear another peep out of us, I promise," raising my right hand up to heaven, avoiding any hint that I was reaching for the light.

He started to go down the hall, but then stuck his head back in. "Sir, one question before I depart?"

"What?"

"Would the pig have been any easier, sir?"

"Good night, Goldman." And he was gone.

I turned my attention back to Miss Ho who stood about two feet from me, looking innocent and humble. "God, Miss Ho," carefully whispered, "you're hard to handle. You bet your ass I take it very easy with you."

She whispered something back, her face showing no expression. But she did slowly slip out of her full dress, folded it neatly, and put it in the corner. Underneath, a silky full-length slip. Laying back down on the pallet, she motioned to me to do the same.

"I'm getting down there with you, Miss Ho," I said, "carefully. I'm getting down there with you, not even thinking about the light. Easy, Miss Ho. No sudden moves. No surprises."

I made it. I was sitting next to her. She turned on her side and gave me a great big smile. She looked great in the full light.

Pulling the quilt up over her, she got out of the slip. Packer had told me that paradoxically these girls were very modest about nakedness.

"Not too dark in there for you is it?" I whispered.

From under the quilt she giggled two or three muffled sentences. It sounded cute, that little voice under the quilt. Ah, Miss Ho, the unpredictable Miss Ho. At last she was relaxed and at peace. I crawled over the floor to the corner of the room to grab the beer I had carefully stowed near the door. After a good slug or two, I got down to my underwear and joined her under the quilt.

She pulled the top of the cover down to our necks, and the realization that I was lying next to a warm, naked broad came on me with a rush. I turned and pressed my legs against hers, she snuggled against my chest, and I pressed my lips onto her forehead. I had been away from Angie for so long that this was almost like something I'd never done before. I was holding a very beautiful woman in my arms, moving my face from her forehead to the soft skin of her neck. On the way down was a path of long black hair that smelled like a garden. It was woman.

I wanted to see her body, so I pulled the cover top and reared myself up for a good look. But she pulled it back up. "God, Ho, " I said, "I just want to see all of you, just for a second."

But she shook her head back and forth and said some sharp words.

"Okay, okay, okay, Miss Ho," I said, letting go of the edge of the quilt. It was the modesty thing. "Take it easy. I no look. I no look. No noise," I said, smoothing down her hair. Man, her mood could turn on a dime, I reminded myself to be very careful with her. Handle with kid gloves.

Yet she let me touch all I wanted. My hands described breasts, leg, ass, back, and tummy to my brain. But I was cautious about touching her cunt. Somehow, that seemed to me to be right up there with light bulbs and peeping under the covers. My plan was to have little hand accidents at her thighs and carefully work my way over. The more I explored, the more the fires of passion rose. Even though the sermons of sin replayed in the back of my mind, I knew I had to screw her.

Over at the *kisaeng* house I hadn't really noticed how beautiful she was. I breathed hard and tried to focus my eyes for a close-up of her face, but my head was spinning. She got softer and more desirable by the minute. Caught up in my building lust, I wanted to kiss her on the lips. There was a faint hint of *kimchi* on her breath, but that made her even more exotic. My breath surely smelled of beer. Maybe that's why she would turn her head each time I tried to kiss her. When she turned back to face me, she'd put her hand over her mouth. At the party table, the girls would hide a laugh with the same gesture. She did willingly let me kiss her neck and ears, and seemed to enjoy it.

Right on course, I worked my briefs down to my ankles. Though I was still pretty well blitzed, my hard-on was immense. As the underwear passed my toes, she had spread her gorgeous legs apart, and I moved myself fully above her. We were in the classic Missionary position, with my cock poised directly over the target. She was gently caressing the back of my head and neck. I eased about a third of myself into her and tried for another kiss.

But just before our lips touched, just before I made the final push into her very warm and slippery pussy--she said something with a mix of English and Korean. It sounded like, "Meapa."

I stopped the action and breathed out, "What you say, beautiful Ho, you?"

"Me *appo*."

Appo? Appo? I ran it through my beer soaked mind. Did she say A-P-P-O? Wasn't Appo the Korean word for . . . sick? I knew that because medic Goldman often said so-and-so was appo when he talked about the patients he had treated that day or even somebody so ill that he had to put him on bed rest. "You appo, Miss Ho? Appo?" I asked, frozen in place above her, one-third in, rapidly losing pressure in my overly inflated organ.

"*Na-mani-appayo.*"

My God, Goldman also used appo to describe a girl who had . . . the clap . . . or syphilis. He'd say Miss so-and-so was appo and she had given some GI the clap or syphilis!

"Me appo, " she said again, staring up at me as I was reviewing the situation. And then it hit me, Jesus, she was trying to tell me that she had a venereal disease. She was trying to save me, warn me, protect me. And I was already one-third in. Christ, I was about to screw a syphilitic whore.

In that instant, the in-processing VD briefing all GIs got at the doorway of our Korean assignment came rushing back to me. The briefing doctor had said, "Guys one big thing to remember above all--use a rubber, never screw without a rubber." Hell, I didn't have any rubbers. I didn't carry rubbers around. Now there I was, rubberless, sticking it into a syphilitic.

Zonk. I pulled it out fast. I got off her. I got up off that mat. Once up, I stood, no pants on, thinking about the rest of the VD briefing, in panic.

One big thing, use a rubber, he had warned. Well, I broke that rule. But if you screwed up, broke the big rule, then you were supposed to pee right away, so you could flush out your urinary tract. It was an emergency tactic, a straw to grasp at. So I raced over to that beautiful jar, took off the lid, and peed hard. Thank God for all the beer I had chugged. It was a good flush. Full bladder. Good, hard flush. I counted one-thousand-one, one-thousand-two as I peed, and felt so grateful that I ended up pissing for over a minute.

While I peed, I remembered something else the doctor had said. "Guys, if you didn't use a rubber, then it's also a good idea to wash your penis as thoroughly as you can. Do that right after you pee. I can't guarantee that it will prevent a case of syphilis, but it does help to wash the head of the penis with soap and water. That's where the spirochetes enter and they move very aggressively. Therefore, we think it only makes good sense to immediately wash the penis anytime you engage in sex with a Korean national, *ESPECIALLY IF YOU FORGOT TO USE A PROPHYLACTIC.*"

But wash with what? No sink. No water. God, there wasn't anything to wash myself off with. I panicked. I thought I could actually feel those creepy bugs boring into my penis.

Then I remembered the other full, unopened bottle of beer. That beautiful full bottle of Crown. Not only was it a watery brew, but the alcohol in it could certainly kill germs on contact, just like Listerine mouth wash. Alcohol. The greatest antiseptic known to man. Crown beer had lots of alcohol.

The opener was right by the bottle. I snapped off the top and went back to the honey pot. Out of the corner of my eye I could see Miss Ho sitting up on the pallet, tightly holding the quilt over her breasts. Syphilitic Miss Ho, wide-eyed and watching me in wonder. I didn't know if I hated her or not, but at least she had warned me.

I centered myself over the jar and skillfully poured every drop of Crown over the head of my penis. It went glug, glug, glug over me as it cascaded down into the jar, creating a sudsy amber mix of beer and pee. Some of the beer missed the jar and puddled on the shiny floor. Hell with it, this was an emergency. Glug, glug, glug. Good strong alcohol killing whatever Ho had shared with me.

I wasn't especially keeping track of Miss Ho. The next time I looked around she was fully dressed and putting her white socks on. She was muttering to herself, but I could have given a shit less about what she was telling herself. I would have given anything to have the opportunity to go back in time and kick her ass out of the room when she started raising hell about the light.

I had promised myself that I'd keep my Korean cherry; but no, I had to be like everyone else and fool around with the dollies. I thanked God that Angie wouldn't know about this night gone so wrong, even as a much agitated Miss Ho flew past me and out the door, both hands grasping the front of her full skirt in the interest of full speed ahead. Good riddance, I said to myself.

I walked back to the pallet, empty bottle in my hand. I sat down, dried myself off on the bottom of the quilt, fished for my underpants, and pulled them on. Suddenly I was tired, no, I was exhausted. The last stages of too much beer were coming on as well. I just sank down on the mat, tossed the beanbag pillow away, and fell into a deep sleep. I prayed that all of this was just a bad dream and that I'd wake up next to Angie, long before I signed up for the Air Force and went to Korea.

Sadly, when I woke up, I was still in Korea, and standing over me were Goldman and most of the others. I gave them a sluggish smile.

"My God, look at 'im. Isn't he a beauty though," said Belford. They all had beers in their hands.

"Sir, here's your breakfast," said Goldman, handing me a cold, fresh Crown. "This works wonders on him, gentlemen. He'll be up in no time."

"Are you going to drink that, Whitman, or pour it all over your cock?" somebody said, and that brought on uncontrollable laughter around the room, punctuated with remarks like, "Oh my God, I'd have given anything to have seen her face," and "I'd have given anything to have seen the whole thing, period." And then from Goldman, "I told him to stick with farm animals the next time."

My reaction to all of that banter was to wonder how in the hell they got the key details about my misadventure with Miss Ho. I felt like a child sitting there on the floor. I never could stand it when I'd be in bed and someone who was up and dressed, come in the room, and look down on me. That happens when you're young, like when the doctor comes in, or when your dad chews you out before you get up for school. I felt like a dork.

"Look, you guys, thanks for breakfast and warm greetings," I said sheepishly. "I'll get my duds on and be right with you. Go on ahead."

"Not before you tell us what the hell you did to make a perfectly beautiful Korean moose say that you're the nuttiest guy she's ever met," said the CIA member of our group."

"Well, if you must know, she's a very sick girl. VD. And she's nuts, too. Goldman you witnessed the trouble she caused over the light. I had to tell her to leave," I said, reaching for my fatigues.

Goldman followed my explanation with, "Sir, once she . . . ahem . . . voluntarily left this room, your Miss Ho came busting in on me and Miss Ihm early this morning. Ho fucked up the rest of my time with Ihm because she had to tell her buddy about the madman she'd been locked up with. I got the blow-by-blow English translation, which will help you better understand your take on things."

Putting on my pants, I said, "Oh, I know what happened and I know what she told me."

"She has a sore throat, sir. A bad sore throat. She was trying to tell you not to smooch her because she didn't want to give you a sore throat, sir. That's what she meant. Sore throat," he said, pointing a finger into his open mouth.

Then someone said, "I can't take it. Isn't it beautiful." And everyone cracked up.

"She had no idea, Captain, of what in the hell you were doing. She was aghast at what evil, weird, perverted ritual you were performing over the room slop jar. She told us that she got the hell out--in terror, I might add--at the thought of what you might next do to prepare her private parts for whatever mating rite you practiced in your part of America."

Everyone had joined in on the flood by this time.

"Well, all I heard was appo, Goldman."

Then the general said, "Everyone, get up on your feet. You, too, Whitman, for I will now offer a toast."

We all got up on our feet.

"Gentleman," he said, with raised beer in hand, "I give you the Appo Kid."

"Hear, hear," everyone responded. "The Appo Kid."

I made a deep bow, embarrassed as hell.

14

The Banquet

Those kinds of things can go either way sometimes. I've seen guys get their asses booted right out of the Air Force for fucking up on an overseas tour, but this was Tolsan-Do, and General Pitts was a long way from his big maple staff table in Tokyo. Instead of sending a twix to the Pentagon recommending I be shot as the biggest drunken clod in uniform, he put his arm around me and said, "Come on, old Appo Kid, we're goin' to buy you breakfast." I received numerous pats on the back on the way out of the room and down the hall.

We had heaps of eggs, real toast, juice, fruit, and fish, and then we headed back to the site in the wagons. It was bumpy, but the beer we stocked up on kept our stomachs on even keel. For the most part I just sat and thought, not saying much. The two light colonels talked to each other about how they'd start the hunt the next morning, and then they got into a deep discussion of how the fighter squadrons were being distributed throughout the Pacific. They were worried about Vietnam. They were worried about "the sphere of Russian influence." It all seemed a long way from where we were.

When we got back, General Pitts told me he never had a better time. "Appo, you come along with us 'n hunt anytime this week you want," he said.

"Well, sir, I'm not a hunter," I said, with a sheepish grin.

"Yeah, and I learned last night you're not much of a fucker either, but next time I go to a *kisaeng* house you're com'n along. That's an order, Captain," he said, winking to the rest.

"Thank you, sir. I'll make sure I bring an extra beer."

General Pitts and his crew spent a great week of hunting. The old bird wagons rolled out of the compound every morning at 0530, with Clinton Davis and his merry men keeping everything under control. I had hot coffee and rolls sent over to the lodge for them in the wee hours of the morning.

Lunch was packed in paper sacks, and they'd be back by dinner with twenty pheasants or so in the bird boxes under the long seats in the wagons. The hunting was superb.

Dubbs saw to it that I pulled hill duty the whole time, so I didn't get a chance to ride along. In fact, it was beyond Dubbs' dignity to pull common hill duty, of course. But I did have a good time sitting around with the hunting party at night. And those were fairly quiet evenings, because they couldn't hack any more wild nights and still get up to drive out at the ungodly hour of 0530, often referred to as "Zero Dark Thirty."

Father Paul got back from visiting up island, but he didn't come back alone. On the way through Soopoo he stopped to pick up Father Danny Callahan and Father Regis Riley at the pig farm, and they all told Father Ryan O'Donnell to meet them at the BOQ bar. When I got down from the hill, one hell of a party was already underway. By that time, however, Pitts and company were all tucked away in bed, ready for their final hunt on Saturday morning.

I was tired, too. Even though it was great to see Paul again, I just had one beer with them and went back to my room and crapped out. I was into one of my semi-good, semi-quiet periods when I'd just sip a few beers, eat well, and sack in early. My exploits of the Friday before had made me want to lay low for a while. Though I had gotten over the hangover, I didn't shake everything off. Most everyone in the Air Force picked up a personal call sign. Mine was to be the *Appo Kid*. General Pitts and one Sergeant Martin Goldman had seen to that.

So, against the protests of my ordained friends, this good Catholic boy was long in bed by the time Paul and Danny began to chase each other with the fire extinguishers. I don't know how long they had been doing it, but my clock said 0416 when they woke me up running down the Q hall and out the door. They were hooting and hollering, punctuated by the sound of the CO_2 blasting out of the extinguishers. It was a hell of a racket. Callahan and Riley were right behind them, trying to chase after the action. And whichever of those two got to the door last went right through the outer screen door. I wondered if Dubbs was in his room or in his downtown hooch.

I fell back to sleep before they got back, but just before I drifted back off again, I thought it sounded like they were running around the hunting lodge grounds. But I was too tired to care. I was also very thankful not to be involved. The General and his boys liked me, and I didn't want to mess that up. Paul would have to fend for himself.

Next day, Thursday, was uneventful. I got up, ate breakfast, and spent the better part of it writing all the letters I knew I owed Angie, the kids, and even my mom and dad. Sunday would be a rest day for the general's party, and the choggy would be in on Monday. All that mail asking why I hadn't written would come in on it, and I was determined to put tons of letters on board. Packer would come back on it; Pitts and his crew would leave on it.

Once I went by Paul's room and he was still asleep. Ryan's Land Rover was gone, so he must have gone back to Choipu. Fathers Regis and Danny were sacked out in two of the empty spares. I walked around lightly so I wouldn't wake them. To protect their lily white asses, I brought inside the one empty fire extinguisher I found out on the Q lawn. Dubbs had obviously checked out for the weekend.

I wrote eight separate letters, and I back-dated them criminally. I wrote Angie things like, "The choggy didn't come last time, and I just pray there will be one tomorrow." Then I'd write another one, a follow-on, that sounded like it didn't come again. It was a system that kind of worked, just kind of worked. But, knowing Angie, she used it to keep from thinking the worst. I must admit it did beat the hell out of regular letter writing.

I wrote the kids some letters too; I even sent them some funny pictures, making the artwork follow their style. And I wrote Mom and Dad, reassuring them that I was fine. My pop just couldn't understand how a guy who had gone to college for four years could end up in Korea. Before I had left, his last words over the phone were, "I only had to get to fifth grade to make me eligible to crawl around in the mud in France in 1917."

But I got them all written, and I was one proud guy to drop them through the mail slot in the HQ building. It was a great relief. I finally felt like I was worth something.

On my way back to the Q, the hunters came rolling in. Wagon number one stopped just long enough for Clinton to stick his head out and yell to me, "The Genr'l wants to see the captain ASAP." Boy. ASAP. As soon as fucking possible. That didn't sound good.

"Okay, Sarge," I yelled after it, hotfooting it for the lodge.

Though I wasn't surprised when Pitts said, "Who in the hell was that bunch that woke us up this morning? They sounded like some kind of foreigners."

"Sir, I'm sorry if they bothered you." I didn't want Paul to get into trouble. Dubbs had already told me Paul had been kicked down to Tolsan for bad behavior. I was afraid something like this, pissing off a three-star, would do him in for good.

"Well, I'll tell you, I'd like to rip their assholes right out of their frapp'n bodies for gett'n me up like that. I never did get back to sleep. Got up once to grab their asses, but they were gone. Who were they?"

"Sir, believe it or not, they were just a couple of priests having a little night. You see . . ."

"Catholic priests?" he said, cutting me off.

"Yes, sir, remember we told you Father Paul has these wonderful fellow priests here on Tolsan who do all this great work for the Koreans?"

He smiled. "By God, they sure can let off steam, can't they?"

"Yes, sir, but they're really the greatest."

"That's what I heard. The Irish brogues. Irish brogues. I'll be damned."

I could see that he had a pretty good temper, but the idea of who it was that had spoiled his night's sleep pretty well defused his three-star revenge. "Let it go, Appo. Don't say anything to them," he said, absentmindedly running a comb through his hair. "Don't even tell them I said a word."

With an obedient and relieved "Yes, sir," I got out of the lodge living room and headed for the NCO Club. Everything was okay. God takes care of His own.

The club was deserted, except for Goldman and the crew. Mr. Kwak was washing glasses. The big jukebox was playing Tijuana Brass. Goldman was sitting at the bar, reading a paperback.

"Mr. Kwak, two beers for the captain. Have a drink and a prophylaxis, sir."

"Okay, Goldman, enough," I said, sitting down opposite him, leaving one stool between us for room.

We just sat there for about an hour, making small talk. I especially liked sitting in the club when it was uncrowded, watching the fire and listening to the jukebox. And Goldman was good company. He was very happy about the fact that I'd made a hit with General Pitts.

"You may need him, Norm. It doesn't hurt at all to have a general who knows you if you get your ass in a crack."

When the dinner hour rolled around, I told Goldman I was going over to the mess hall for the meal. He was going to go over the club books with Kwak, so I walked over by myself. Even from the club stairs, something looked different about the mess hall windows. The light coming out of them seemed pale. As I walked closer, it looked like there were candles on the tables. Candles? On a Thursday night?

I opened the door, and the place was full of people. It was the General,

Belford, Coates, and Yates, the Brigadier, and Price. They were all dressed with at least a sport coat. And just as big as life, all smiles and sweetness were Fathers Fisher, O'Donnell, Callahan, and Riley, decked out in their best black with Roman collars. They looked at me, beaming.

The tables had been pulled together for one big banquet setup. Fresh linen was everywhere. There were candles every three feet. Wine bottles were as numerous, along with extras of all kinds. The place actually looked beautiful.

"Norman," Father Paul said, "General Pitts is treating us all to a sumptuous pheasant banquet, and you're a special invitee."

Callahan put his hand on the back of an empty chair between himself and Colonel Belford. "This one's reserved for the Appo Kid," he said with a grin.

I thought to myself, you bunch of con men. You're just lucky old Mr. and Mrs. Pitts had their baby baptized a Catholic. Some WASP lieutenant general would have been serving you all up on a platter about now.

The conversation was lofty. Between sips of good wine and forkfuls of the best wild game I'd ever tasted, Pitts and the priests talked about the missionary work on the island and the need for that throughout the Far East. Pitts was really a Mick. In fact, he got it out that he'd been in a seminary for a year and a half himself before the Second World War. He was thrilled with the four priests he had brought to dinner, especially the three Irishmen.

Regis Riley explained to him that their farm was really a starter program that provided young pigs to farmers and trained them to raise the little porkers for profit. The Koreans spent a couple of weeks with the priests, learned the how and why of raising pigs, and then went back to their own land with a half dozen or so piglets. In addition, they got their feed for free, supplied by the church farm. If things went well, the Korean got more pigs and corn. The hope was that pretty soon he'd be successful and become independent. It was the dream of these good fathers that the trainees would soon be breeding and selling healthy fat pigs for good money.

"But you see, General, sar," Riley said with a swig of white wine, "we fight against many odds here. The black market, as an example, offers aur beyes a ready fist of cash for the wee pigs and the carn as soon as they arrive back in their villages. It's all uphill, sar. All uphill."

I had heard them talk about their work many times before. I was always impressed with their patience and their strength. To a man, each would spend his entire life on the island, except for a year's leave every seven years. At least that gave them a chance to go back home, see Ireland and the people they loved so much. But it would be back to Tolsan-Do and ultimately to a foreign grave there that their strong faith and dedication would take them. They were utterly unafraid of that, completely accepting of it. In Korea the grave was often referred to as *The Happy Mountain*.

"At leest we become a paart of their community, sar," Callahan said. "We larn the language and speek it very well, and they know we're hare with them and not just pass'n through. Aur people tell us when things are not right, the few, that is, who do fallow the right path."

As they talked I watched their faces and studied them, these dedicated priests with their large farmer's hands. They had only the comfort of each other and their work to keep them going in a country so far from Ireland and the life of a typical pastor. They had this wonderful blind faith, this absolute dedication to who they were and what they were doing. Jesus was flatassed real. Period. They were doing His work.

"Well the charch contributes, af caurse, but we also produce our own park for profit. You must also har about our wool aperation, too."

"You have sheep, too?" I asked, surprised.

"Narm, you'll come to stay some weekend. The faarm's more than ya think it 'tis. Yes, sheep and even a convent of sisters who make the finest Irish linen and wool sweaters you've aver seen."

"Could we maybe come down before we take off Monday?" Pitts asked enthusiastically. "I'd love to bring some of that back to Japan."

"Heavans yas, sar," Riley said. "After the mass at Father Ryan's, you all could come down for Sunday dinner and see the hale place. Narm and the beyes can bring you. It's a grand idea."

"Is there a special mass tomorrow, Father?" said Pitts.

"Sir, tomorrow is the Feast of Saint Catherine's, the big day for our own Saint Catherine's Parish in Choipu, just outside the gates here. We're all going to celebrate high mass with Father Ryan, and I'm asking everyone from the compound who wants to join us to come on down."

"Well, the boys and I'll be there for sure," he said, looking down the table.

"Wal, that's fine," Ryan O'Donnell said, obviously pleased. "My peaple will feel so speacial when they see all of you at mass. They feel very close to the saint herself, and this will make Saint Katie's feast day all the mar impartant."

Then Father Ryan paused very thoughtfully, and leaned close to the inside of the table, making the signs of one who is about to reveal intimate thoughts. "As a matter of fact, the paarish has never been so close in its faith as just now. And it's all due to an incident that Narman and Father Paul saw themselves."

Everyone else leaned in toward the center, too, not wanting to break the intimacy of it all. We knew we were in for a good story. The Irishman's own dramatic sense and the candlelight added to the moment.

Father Ryan continued, in a very soft voice made almost melodious by the pheasant and wine. "One of my flock was buried by myself in aur cemetery, and the local heathen witch woman—ah, they have such things hare, General, sar—challenged that with a ritual right outside the paarish house the very night of the funeral."

For a second, Father Paul and I exchanged glances. Everyone else was spellbound.

"From the lower window of the paarish house I threw haly water at her and said prayers in Latin, all the wile the villagers looked on. It was a great test for the charch, it was. She brought the devil himself to the very dar of Saint Catherine's."

What an atmosphere Ryan was building. Nobody talked or moved. The only thing anybody did was to discretely take a sip from their wine or water glasses, bringing the glass only just high enough to drink from, head low, eyes trained on Father Ryan's face.

"It was back and farth, back and farth, and then all of a sudden she let out a shriek that'd chill you to the maarow. Something had caught her eye from above. When she finally could tear herself away from the sight of it, she fled down the street toward the town." He took a sip of wine himself, and wiped his mouth.

"Now I didn't know at the time what had caused it, but I knew she had been driven away by something vary haly. And the beyes were at a loss, too, because we were all downstairs looking out on herself."

Father Paul and I exchanged another look, but this time I nodded my head ever so slightly. He looked down into his water glass and smiled ever so slightly.

Ryan continued with his story. "The day after, the mystery cleared up a bit, for some of the good Catholics that were watching from the street told me that a strange, wonderful lady had appeared at the window above mine, the one just below the peak of the paarish house roof. She was dressed all in black and had a terrible look about herself they said. Well, it was enough to chase away the witch. For sure'a what she saw was no lady of this earth and none of the lower regions, either."

"That's incredible," said Price. "Surely you don't think it was . . . well, a ghost or a spirit of some kind?"

"Well, my flock thinks it was Saint Catherine herself, coming to protect the soul of aur departed Mister Chee. And I don't think the Haly Spirit wants me to rebut their revelation, for it was them that saw and not myself. And I do believe there was something there, Mister Price."

Then he really leaned in on the group, making us most aware of the total blackness of night coming in the mess hall windows, broken only by the candles. We were a pale yellow island surrounded by the stillness of the Korean night, joined together in the brotherhood of the Irish priest's tale.

"But I meself have me own theory about what went on that night and hare it is: When I questioned my peaple, and there were a fair number who had witnessed the sight, I had them very carefully describe to me every feature of the woman. Each stary was the same, and a sure pattern emerged."

This was the open-your-mouth-for-better-concentration part, and Father Ryan was playing the suspense to the hilt. Tears were even beginning to well in his eyes. Pitts was on the edge of his seat.

"Gentlemen, as I sit here before God the Almighty I know by all that's true that the spirit in the window could have been none other than me own dear departed Grandmother O'Donnell, come to help me rid the paarish of the evil eye." And he slammed his open palms on the table before him, tears filling his eyes, his nose changing color and almost swelling from the emotion.

I looked at Father Paul. He took his wine glass, ever so discreetly toasted in my own direction, and broke the silence by saying, "Gentlemen, can there be any doubt but that God does indeed work in strange ways?"

"Here, here," everyone said. O'Donnell excused himself, pressing a table napkin to his eyes, and went into the men's john around the corner.

"This was a touching moment," General Pitts said to the group. "I think the whole dinner has reminded us lay people just how vastly important the religious side of man is. I, for one, will carry this night in my heart for a long time."

"Here, here," the CIA guy said, followed by encouraging words from the others.

Wow, I thought to myself, Ryan's grandmother really must have been ugly. But, better yet, I'll bet his "flock" knows better than to fuck around with old Saint Angela. I was betting on a full house in church the next day.

We all gradually got up from the table and started making motions to go back for some time in the Qs before the movie. Father O'Donnell returned from the john, and Pitts shook Ryan's hand and told him how much he enjoyed the story. We looked for all the world like we were people who had been to an AA meeting or something, saying goodbye until the next one.

"We'll all meet in the movie," Father Paul said. With that, the two groups left and headed for either the lodge or the Q.

"Oh, the General's a fine man," Riley was saying. "We'll show him around tomorrow, eh, Danny?"

"Lord's grace yes," Callahan said, pulling Riley over to his side. "I'm hope'n he might have some spare parts for the tractor, Ryan, do you suppose?"

I just walked along very contentedly, and then said, "It doesn't hurt to know a general at all, and that's what Goldman says, too, gentlemen."

"It's the truth," Ryan said, "It's the Lard's own truth."

When we got back, the priests packed up their black overnight bags because they'd all go back to Ryan's rectory after the movie, including Father Paul. The rest of us would follow the next day for mass there, and then the trip to Soopoo in the bird wagons. Everybody would be Catholic tomorrow, I thought.

The movie was going to be *Mary Poppins*, and I was looking forward to it. I thought I'd take a steamer, as Dubbs called it, before I went, and I had about forty-five minutes to do it. A quick check of his end of the Q revealed he and Sue were gone. You could count on that every weekend. He and his Suzie baby would be down in their hooch sucking on each other. So, I'd use his shithouse and have it all to myself.

Soon I was sitting in the sauna letting the heat pound on my body. It was a wooden room with wooden benches running along the walls in step-like fashion. The higher you sat, the hotter it was. To keep the steam going, you poured water on these rocks that were constantly being heated by a gas cooker. When the stream of water hit them, it was like a volcanic eruption. You'd pour and, gaboom, gaboom, these billows of steam would rise up from the rocks and fill the whole wooden room with scalding cloudy steam that would take your breath away. After it settled down, though, you felt pretty good.

When I'd pour the cold water over the rocks, I'd imagine that I was in hell or the underworld of Mythology. I'd get into the billowing steam cloud and imagine I was Vulcan or somebody like that. The pouring part was the best thing about the whole operation. After a while, though, you've got to quit pouring because you'd cool the bricks down. You've got to give them a chance to heat up and boil off all the water that collects at the base of the pile.

I sat there, taking in the steam, staring at the hot rocks and then the thought suddenly struck me: what would happen if you took a piss on those rocks? A weird thing to think about, but, nonetheless, the temptation to find out really started working on me. And, besides, I told myself, the simple answer was that nothing would really happen. So, why not do it?

I waited for the rocks to heat up, boil off every drop of water, and get hot and dry. When they were perfect and ready to make steam, they looked like desert rock baking in Death Valley.

At that point Vulcan stood up and let go on them. Instantly it was pow, kazboom. This big, hot cloud of awful smelling, greenish steam damn near knocked Vulcan further down into the lower regions. God, it smelled awful and for just a moment I thought I was going to be asphyxiated by it. Then I panicked. Christ, I was going to die from my own urine cloud in a sauna In Korea.

I got out of there fast. When I opened the door, the steam came out with me. Worse yet, the smell came, too. It filled old Dubbs' shithouse, every corner of it. And it was rolling up the hall toward his room. The vengeance of the urine cloud, I thought. Killing everything in its path, it would seep under Dubbs' door and wait for him. Yet, I sure hoped it would be gone before he did get back. Wouldn't it be terrible if he found out, I thought.

But then I listened to the Q. Not a sound. Paul and company had no doubt gone to the BX so the Irish priests could stock up on the hard-to-get items we'd let them buy on the sly. Not a soul around. I probably had gotten away with another stupid move.

Mary Poppins ended up depressing the hell out of me. I kept thinking about the kids and how much fun I'd had when Angie and I took them to see it only a few months before. The "Feed the Birds" part had been one of their favorites, and we had sung that while they threw bread out for the birds that came to our back yard. It did me in.

After the movie Pitts asked everyone to come up to the lodge for a final brandy, but I begged off. I was glad we were going to the mass, and I just wanted to sleep on that. My eight letters were in the mailbag. I knew I just wanted to go back, sack out, and think about home. Funny thing, I used to look for opportunities to sneak off and have a few with the boys when I was home. Now I was sneaking off from having a few with the boys to think about being home. Crazy.

15

Night Visitor

I went right to sleep, like a log. But my deep sleep yielded to the conscious awareness that something was going on in my room. I came out of it like a guy taking a fast elevator from the first floor to the thirty-third in twenty seconds. I didn't move a muscle or open my eyes, though I was wide-awake. Somebody was in the room. I wasn't hallucinating this one. Somebody was there.

Well, I thought, this was going to be it. We knew that infiltrators were coming into South Korea. Here I was, lying in my bed, an American officer, and some North Korean agent was probably going to stab me as I lay there. I was going to die in bed, the victim of North and South Korea's violent situation. And I could literally feel the agent poised over me.

With every ounce of courage I had, I forced myself to open my eyes to at least make him look me eye-to-eye as he put the blade in my chest. I opened my eyes quickly. My God, there actually was a person standing over me. I felt my chest pound, and I almost lost control of my bowels. I gasped.

It was Adja. It was Adja, standing over me, looking into my eyes. Packer's heartthrob, standing over me. I just went all limp and realized that I had broken out in a cold sweat.

"Adja," I said, running my hands over my damp forehead, "what are you doing? You scared me to death."

"I come see you," she said softly, giving me a flash of that big row of chiclet teeth, letting her long black hair fall onto my face.

"Why you come see me? You no hear from Packer?"

"No not Andy, I come give you *testo-testo*, thena you want me to be your *yobo*. Andy leave me. I want you anyhow. I come show you short time. You *testo-testo* my pussy." Then she sat down on the edge of the bed and began unzipping her skimpy red dress. That made me go from the cold sweat to that warm stirring in my breeches some wise poet had described a long time ago in a poem whose author or title I couldn't remember. Just for an instant I almost grabbed her. But only for an instant.

"No, Adja, you wait. Packer is my friend. He will not like me anymore if I *testo* you. He will say I am number ten." Telling her that, I sat up, my hand out in the standard school crossing guard stop position, made to stop cars at an intersection and now to stop Adja from taking her dress off.

But she didn't heed the command to stop. She was down to bare chest and panties in a flash. She did not share Miss Ho's modesty. I saw everything and noted that her nipples were almost black. She was put together. No wonder why poor old Andy Packer lusted after her so.

"You sucka my tits," she said, pressing her boobs together in her hands and shoving them into my face. "Then I sucka your dick."

That almost made me blow my wad. I'm a pushover for legs, too. She still had her red high heels on. Her legs were crossed.

Think of the "Feed the Birds" scene in Mary Poppins, I told myself. Imagine Mikie and Shelly singing, "Feed the Birds," as they throw bread crumbs to pigeons in a park. No, think of them almost getting run over by a bus or a truck. Think about a burglar stealing their Christmas presents. Think about being on a Candid Camera gag right now.

I rolled to the other side of the bed and dressed as quickly as a fireman responding to an alarm. Under my fatigue pants, I was still stiff as a board.

"You son bitch," she said with narrowed eyes, "whatta you, some queer person? You numba ten."

"Look, Adja, you sneaked on base like slicky boy. If we go checkie the log at the gate, I know I find you not signed it. You need Andy to sign you in. If I tell base police, you can get arrested. They can take you to jail downtown."

She put her dress back on, poly-poly quick. "I tell Major Dub on you," she said.

"I don't care what you tell Major Dub, Adja. You can tell him I don't let butterfly Adja in my room. You go find teahouse money from some other GI sucker."

"You tell police?" she asked, knowing there were no more aces to play with me.

"No, I now take you back downtown in jeep. I take you back to your hooch."

She had to go with me, or risk the chance that I'd raise hell about her getting on base. She probably slipped the ROKAF gate guard a few won or told a story of some kind to get on. Now she'd need me to get out.

"Get in," I said, opening the passenger door. The air outside was cold. My watch said 0230. When I glanced back at the lodge, I saw only dark windows; the pig farm Land Rover was gone. This would go undetected. I wasn't a Jodie, a buddy fucker. Packer would never know his precious Adja tried to make an end run on him.

I cleared the gate and headed downtown. We passed the stonewalls, always alive with their tribe of rat inhabitants, and in about ten minutes I pulled up in front of the hooch old Packer rented for his *yobo*. As soon as I cut the engine, she started to cry. It was pretty loud, but I didn't give a damn.

Then, bing, on went the lights inside. That was her cue to pull out all the stoppers. She turned on the tears for all she was worth. You'd think I had beaten her or . . . aw, shit.

When a woman's voice yelled from inside the hooch, Adja answered with more sobs and bursts of words. She didn't get out of the jeep. Then I heard the worst. It was Dubbs' voice talking with the woman inside. What a fucking mess. In GI slang it was CATFU, completely and totally fucked up!

He came out. All I could do was sit in the jeep and watch it happen.

"Adja?"

"He is bad GI," she said, looking in my direction. "He numba ten."

"Who is that? Whitman?" he asked, pushing his fat face in her side.

"Yes, sir, she came to my room, woke me up, and I just wanted to get her back downtown," I said, with both my hands on the steering wheel.

"What you got this jeep off base so late for?" I didn't respond to his question, except to make a point of looking at the other Air Force jeep parked in the alley next to the hooch.

"She was in the compound without being signed in, past midnight curfew for nationals. For Packer's sake I wanted to save her ass from trouble. I could have turned her in." I was starting to get pissed off. I didn't belong to this crazy red light world. This was for jerks like him and Packer.

"All I see is one goddamn scared, innocent, and highly vulnerable Korean national female sitt'n in a U.S. military vehicle for no apparent official U.S. or Korean government business, Captain," he said, with a real mean look on his bloated red puss.

This bastard is giving me the business, I thought. He's standing here giving me a hard time, and we could end up slugging it out. This whole mess could end up getting us both in big trouble.

So I put the heel of my hand on the horn, pushed hard, and left it there. Jeep horns are loud, especially in a quiet Korean town like Choipu at three in the morning. It blared out with a nice steady pitch, so loud you could feel it vibrate on your body.

I just kept leaning on it. He was dumbfounded.

"The horn's stuck," I yelled. "I better get this out of here before the town cops come to see what's going on." Surely Dubbs knew he couldn't afford a big stink downtown.

He was saying something, but the horn was drowning him out.

"Get her out of the jeep, sir," I motioned. "I'll get this back before we have the whole town down here." I didn't let up on the horn.

When he yanked her out, I was afraid that he'd come around to my side. So I cranked her up, pushed in the clutch, put it in first, and let it peel out like the rubber-laying-son-of-a-bitch you saw in those old moonshine runner movies. I kept my hand on the horn. When I turned the corner, I let go . . . but it didn't quit. I really had gotten it stuck. I had to bang on the damn thing almost all the way back to base.

In spite of the commotion, I never saw a cop, a car, or a living soul. My only fear was that he'd be pissed enough to follow me back. So when I got into my room, I shut the door, locked it, and propped the desk chair up against the knob. I nodded off and the next sound I heard was my alarm going off. The chair was still in place. It was morning. Dubbs would still be sleeping off his booze and wouldn't show his face until way late in the day. For me, it was time to get ready for the Feast of Saint Catherine's.

That day turned out to be one of the best I'd had on the island. Had I thought to take my camera, this day's activities could have been the slide show you'd want the folks back home to see. Too bad I forgot to bring the camera.

The church service was impressive. The place was packed with people. Saint Catherine's looked like any Catholic church I'd ever been in, so it felt like I was back home attending mass. The only difference was that there were no rows of pews, just a beautifully polished wood floor on which the Korean congregation sat and kneeled on soft, embroidered rectangular pads.

Way in the back, however, there were two rows of regular wooden pews. That's where we all sat, even Goldman and Brigadier Rushworth. General Pitts was wrapped up in the mass, kneeling up straight when it was appropriate. I was the kind of kneeler who rested his butt on the seat and let the knees gently hit the kneeler.

The sermon was in Korean, but Father Ryan took just a minute or so to tell us in English how happy he was that we could all be there that Sunday.

"I'm especially praud to have his generalship with us this marn'in, and I've mentioned that to the congregation, sar."

Pitts smiled broadly and nodded. I wondered to myself when they'd hit him up for the tractor parts.

After the mass, we went to the rectory for coffee and these great Korean rice cakes. A bunch of the Korean congregation was there, and there was another little reception in the room where I taught English. Ryan went from one place to another, shaking hands and talking with his flock. It made me feel very good about life.

A lot of the people who came to my English lessons were there. I exchanged "Hello, how are yous" with them, along with some of the other phrases we were doing. Some of the little children would peek around their parents' legs and say, "hello, hello," laugh, and then disappear. Everybody was dressed in Sunday best. Saint Catherine was very proud, I'm sure.

About an hour later we all headed for the farm in Soopoo, in a convoy of two Land Rovers and the two bird wagons. The coolers were empty. Yet, the conversation never stopped all the way down. The only thing I missed was a window to look out of.

Like most towns on the island, Soopoo was on the seacoast. There was a dock and a cluster of fishing boats at anchor in the little harbor. Saint Bridget's was the parish there, and the pastor was a priest I'd never met, Father Michael Francis Henry. His fellow Tolsan priests called him the old grouch. He was in charge of the wool operation and the convent of nuns. All of the parish buildings stood behind very sturdy iron gates.

Father Henry was pleasant enough, yet he was somewhat unlike his other countrymen. My mother would have explained it this way: he was hard to warm up to. But he did show us around, and we met three of the twenty or so nuns who turned out the sweaters and the Irish linen. Sister Mary Elinore, Sister Katherine, and Sister Ann Margaret more than made up for Father Henry's standoffishness. They showed us the woolen factory with great glee and kept the party well occupied for upwards of an hour. Pitts and his boys ended up dropping about three hundred dollars total on cloth and sweaters. I told myself I'd be back, so no need to buy today.

I liked the nuns. I guess I didn't feel sorry for the priests at all. They had made a sacrifice, of course, but it was still a neat, adventuresome thing they had chosen to do. But these dear little Irish ladies were so far from home. They, too, would spend a lifetime among the Koreans of Tolsan-Do. Somehow it made me sad.

While we took the tour and the group made their purchases, I saw Father Henry giving stern glances in our direction. I also detected some sharp words between him and Callahan. I didn't think I was going to like this guy Henry, and I was glad when we all left for the farm. It sat on the high ground above the actual town, about two miles inland. From it you could see the town, the harbor, and the steeples of Saint Bridget's.

I was glad Henry didn't come with us.

"The nuns cook for him, Narm," Callahan said, "which means he doesn't have to watch us corrupt ourselves, eh, Regis," Callahan added, looking toward his fellow pig farmer.

The tour of the pig farm was impressive. Clinton Davis said he felt like he was back on his father's place down in deep Mississippi. Pitts added, "Hell, Clint, I never intended being anything but a farmer, and I wouldn't have left my dad's place if it hadn't been for the war. Where do you think I'll head when they finally give me the boot?"

As it turned out, Coates had been raised on a Texas ranch and Yates in the wheat fields of Kansas. So Pitts' group was really a band of farm boys who had gone to fly. Belford was not a country boy; he was the son of a Chicago lawyer. He had gone to the University of Chicago and studied English. They needed his skill with prose. He was the executive officer. But he did wear pilot wings.

The pigs were, well, pigs. There were lots of them, all running around in large fenced-in fields. They also had these long buildings they went into. The ground they ran around on wasn't a mud pit as I had anticipated, but it was pretty well chopped up from their hoofs. They were hairy, kind of dirty, and their noses were moist. They were just okay.

The little pigs were better. They were squirmy, but very cute. Certainly a lot more likeable than the bigger ones. They didn't have all of that wiry hair on them.

There was a full Korean contingent on hand to run the place. They seemed a very happy bunch. And I think they really liked the pigs. The guys who showed us the little ones treated them like they were pets. They laughed at their antics like someone would for a cute dog or something. And the guys in training—the ones who would take their pigs home—seemed just as enthusiastic.

"This would be a nightmare my grandfather would have," said Goldman. "All of these pigs attacking him, pigs everywhere. All of these chops and bacon strips. It's an Orthodox nightmare."

"Well, Sergeant, we'll have bread and vegetables for you to eat this afternoon," Callahan said.

The dinner was a real feast. We all sat around a huge oak table they had made right there on the farm. It was designed to accommodate all of the Fathers on the island and must have been fifteen feet long. It sat in the middle of an equally impressive dining room in the large, two-story farmhouse. As a matter of fact, the entire place smacked of heavy furniture and lots of rugged living space. By contrast, the lace curtains on the windows added a soft touch. The entire effect was most pleasing.

If there was large farm work staff, the house help was ample, too. The kitchen was full of cooks and servers, and we met two housekeepers who kept the place as clean as could be. Everyone kept an eye on our needs. Ask and you got it, from water to more bread.

Yes, there was roast pork, tons of it, piled high on four different platters. But there were also pork chops, and for Goldman a choice of fresh fish or steak. He took both.

The delicious meat choices were supplemented with potatoes, carrots, beets, beans, and salads. You could even have orange sections and apple slices, mixed in with nuts and mayonnaise sauce. Applesauce, of course, and these large pitchers of milk. There was homemade bread, served along with coffee, tea, and wine. You ate it all with real sterling silver from fine china plates. What a banquet! Fit for a saint, a general, or a kid from Pittsburgh, Pennsylvania, who hadn't been to a restaurant until he was out of high school. If they could only see me, those people back on the block, I thought. I'm sitting in a rectory on a pig farm in Korea with a general, a British brigadier, three priests from Ireland, a CIA man, a couple of sergeants, and three fighter pilots. Crazy.

Right then I wished I was a painter. Somebody like Norman Rockwell could have really made something out of that farm table scene. All of the big hands, passing plates and bowls filled with colorful food, some of the fingers shiny with grease and butter. The faces, most of them big-boned, smiling and chewing, and then the Irish faces with red hair, and crooked teeth flashing. Pitts' crew-cut stubble. Goldman's strong Jewish features. Korean faces looking for bowls to take and refill. A celebration of smells and foods and differences and likenesses and eating. What a painting it would have made.

After the feast, we adjourned into the living room for a smoke and talk of what the priests would do with the farm in the years to come. The air was blue from pipes and these fat cigars Callahan brought out. The brandy we all sipped cut a relieving hole in the dinner we had packed away and also served to fuel up our vocal cords and helped us to say profound things. The Victorian table lights, with their heavy-glassed shades, added to the warm light of a huge crackling fire that burned below a large portrait of the Holy Father in Rome. Everything else was heavy oak, lace curtains, and the feel of good overstuffed couches and chairs. Almost all of the furnishings came from Ireland.

Finally, Pitts winked at me and said, "Let me see what I can do about those tractor parts, and I'll let the Appo Kid here know what I find out. I don't see any problem. I can't think of a better project." And then he looked at his watch and Belford nodded. We all just slowly got up and shook hands.

Riding back in the bird wagon, Colonel Coates said, "Boy, this sure was some day." He said it all.

Next morning I said goodbye to them at breakfast, and General Pitts took me aside before I left for the hill. "Whitman," he said, "I really appreciate your hospitality. I know you helped Clint a lot with the lodge, and he 'preciates that. It's not easy com'n over here every season and not knowing what kind of officers there'll be on board. It's a new site every time. Thanks."

"Well, I had a ball, sir. You let me know if there's anything you need," I said, popping him a salute.

"We'll be back a couple of times. And I'll be getting ahold of you on those parts for the Fathers," he said smiling. "Aren't they the most charming bunch of hooligans you ever saw?"

Then I was up on the hill. The choggy came in at 1300 (one poor soul aboard, thirty-four hundred pounds of cargo, movies, and four mail sacks) and departed with the general's party at 1415. Just before we lost radio contact with them, the pilot said, "Benjamin Control, the code-seven aboard says relay to Appo Kid much thanks for everything."

I really had a case of the letdowns when I brought the jeep down the hill and swung in the parking space in front of the Q. It had been fun and exciting to have the Pitts party with us. Now we were going to be back into the same old rut, not to mention the fact that I was going to have to see old Dubbs. And there wouldn't be any friendly three stars around, either. The Feast of Saint Catherine was definitely over.

Dubbs must have been counting the minutes before my return, because I had no sooner gotten out of the jeep than I saw him come out of the headquarters Quonset. He was walking with his shoulders squared and his chin forward. What a horse's ass. I gave him a snappy salute when he got into range.

"Afternoon, sir," I said, with a properly subordinate smile.

"You don't ever tear up the town like you did the other night, Mister, you hear?"

I hated it when he shoved his fat face in mine. The bastard was totally wrong, but I had to live with him. For better or worse, there was really nothing I could do about him. Yet.

"Sir, I'd rather not tell Packer how I . . . I screwed up." If Dubbs lets it die here, I thought, then I'll let him save face.

"He won't hear it from me. He don't fuck Adja no more anyway."

"Then you can bet I'll be damn careful in town from now on, sir."

"You bet your tail you will," he said, brushing by me. Then he turned and said out of the corner of his mouth, "General Pitts thinks you did a good job. Well, you snowed somebody, anyway, Whitman." And he was gone into his end of the Q.

I walked over to the mailroom and my spirits picked up a bit, for there were those wonderful letters and packages from so far away. When I went to my end of the Q to read them, there was old Packer, throwing a brand new dog toy for Dolly. He had probably bought it somewhere up on the mainland. It was one of those rubber hot dogs with a squeaker in it. The old hunting mutt was loving it.

"The return of Oyster, ladies and gentlemen," I said. "Though he went to the bright lights of Osan, he still thought enough of his comrades to return and die with them on Tolsan."

He looked up, grinning as usual. "Hey, Norm, it's great to see you."

"Did you have a good time on your TDY?" I said.

"Yeah, yeah, man. I fell in love twenty-two times, and never once thought about this place." He actually did look better. He wasn't as pale.

"Listen, I want to hear all about it. I can get over my frustrations listening to your adventures. Let me read this mail, and then we'll go over and have a Goldmanburger and a beer, okay?"

"Yeah, I'll take old Dolly for a walk, and I'll be back."

The two big boxes Angie had sent me and all of the letters were my Christmas, I just knew it. She was worried about getting it to me in time, but I had pushed Christmas way back into my head. I had mentioned it to them in my letters, but I hadn't really done anything about it. Yet here was my Christmas, early.

Lovingly and carefully I set everything on the table that doubled as a desk. I was glad I had an excuse not to open any of it. I'd wait until Christmas

Eve at least. These things had come from a place where I was so loved, so accepted by these dear souls that trusted me so much. It was difficult for me to think of them and then think of the way I was. Angie wouldn't believe that I had almost laid Miss Ho. The kids wouldn't even understand why their Daddy was falling down drunk in a Korean hotel. At least I had driven Adja's ass back downtown. And that reminded me of Packer, which prompted me to go find him and put off thinking about all of this until 24 December.

Oyster and Father Paul were out front talking to Dutch.

"*Yobo sayo*," I called to them.

"*Yobo sayo*, yourself," Paul said. "We understand half the cargo on the choggy was for you."

"Yeah," I said, "ashes for my stocking."

16

Happy Holidays

With the first hunt over, we were left alone to have our Christmas. Paul, Oyster, Dutch, and I sat together at a table in the club that 23 December, sharing thoughts on the Yuletide season. Goldman joined us, too. We sat at the table, sipping beer, talking about Christmases remembered, and we also absentmindedly watched the other GIs at their tables talking with each other, the girls with that waiting-for-the-movie look on their faces.

I had heard that Korea was one of the coldest spots on earth, but our southern island had a much milder climate. It was nippy all right, but up on the mainland there was already a bunch of snow for the 25th. That late fall weather had helped me to push Christmas into the back of my mind, that and the week of the first hunters.

"Did you know dat I vas prisoner of var?" Dutch asked.

"Japanese?" somebody said.

"Ja, I was kaptured in the Marianas and spend two Kristmasees in bad camp. I joined da Dutch Army right out of Indonesia. A first lieutenant I vas," he said, lighting up that wonderful carved pipe of his.

"Did you ever talk to old Father T.P. about being a Jap prisoner?" Paul asked, very intent on the subject.

"What's the story?" asked Goldman.

"Well," said Paul, "T.P. has been here since the 1920s. When the Japs finally turned this island into a fighter base, they put him in a cell up near Tolsan City. They sort of tolerated him for ten years or so, but he spent the whole Second World War and then some in that same cell. That's why he's so crippled up. The dampness."

"Ja, dey treated him like shit. Ve haf often talked about dem. Dey can be terrible kaptors."

"You know," Paul said very seriously, "he told me that the biggest thing he worked on all the while was getting himself to the point where he could honestly tell God that he loved them." He paused. "And he did it. He did it. To this day he loves them."

"Do you love the Japanese, Dutch?" I asked.

"Ha. I'm no holy man. But I guess I just grow olter. I'm in this part of the world zo much I guess I just used to how cruel it can be, even sometimes not on purpose. It's hard place, ja."

"I know it's against everything I am, but I can't get seven December out of my skull that easy," said Paul. "I went through the Pacific campaign for the whole war, and I still don't regret one bullet I fired."

"An eye for an eye, eh," put in Goldman.

"Vell, you know you haf company here in dis Korea, Fatter. Dey hate the Japanese vis passion. Too many times dey occupied dem and tried to take kulture. Dey still hate Japs."

"You know what Colonel Lee told me?" Paul said, draining his beer glass. "He said the worst thing you can call a Korean is a *wanzingi*. You know why?"

"Da monkey," Dutch said, laughing and puffing.

"Right," Paul said, pointing at him. "Monkey, right, Dutch."

"What do you mean?" I asked.

"When the Japs had Korea occupied during the war, they would sometimes go into a town or village where the people weren't doing quite what they wanted. They'd line the people up and get this trained monkey out there in front of the lineup. They'd pretend to ask the monkey to point out who the bad Koreans were, and then this monkey would just go up and down the line pointing, just randomly, of course." Paul was really bitter about this. He was shaking ever so slightly. "They trained the little bastard to point at those poor, innocent people."

"Then what?"

"Those the *wanzingi* pointed to were shot right then and there, that's what, Norm. Shot, because a monkey pointed at them."

There was an awkward silence for a moment, I guess because you'd expect this kind of anger to be more a part of 1947 than 1966.

Finally Goldman broke the silence, looked around like he didn't want anybody to hear the hot information he was going to pass along, and said in a low voice: "And if you guys think that was something, let me tell you about what this guy Hitler did when his SS clowns lined my relatives up in front of a slit trench."

"Ha, ha," laughed Dutch.

"Well, if you want to get in a fight here in Korea, just talk about how great the Japs are. Or, call somebody a *wanzingi*," Paul said, refilling his glass.

"You know," I said, "as we sit here, this Vietnam thing is really getting hotter and hotter."

"I'm glad to be right here in Korea," Paul said. "I've had my fill of jungle fighting."

"You know," Goldman said with a remarkably serious tone, "I'm thinking about becoming a search and rescue helicopter paramedic and getting into that one, no shit, I am."

"You're already serving your overseas remote, Sergeant," I said. "There's no need to ever get involved in Vietnam."

"No, I'm serious, Captain Whitman. I'm more than halfway thinking about it."

I thought it was odd the way he addressed me so formally.

"Well, look, you guys," I put in, "and, Father, I'm stealing your job, I know, but Vietnam and the Second World War and pointing monkeys are all pretty far away right now. I'd just like to toast the upcoming Christmas season and with it good old peace on earth and good will and all of that horseshit."

"Ja, ja, gut," puffed old Dutch, raising his glass up like mine. "But I yust add dat ven you look beyond da season and all dat has been, you look at real problem. Russia."

"Good," said Goldman, holding up his beer, "let's toast to Christmas now and the future occupation of Moscow. God bless us everyone."

Together we clinked our glasses and said, "God bless us everyone." The timing was beautiful.

And then Christmas actually came. When I opened my boxes, I found a little artificial tree in one, complete with a string of tiny lights and ornaments. The kids had made little decorations for it, too. I opened that box on four or five good belts of Scotch and that had me uninhibited enough to not be able to hold back the tears. I set the little tree up on my desk, put on the ornaments, turned on the lights, and sat looking at it, crying like a mental case.

The homemade ornaments were of two kinds: paper and dough. The paper ones had messages on them like "Merry Christmas, Daddy." The dough ornaments were cut into figures: snowmen, gingerbread men, bells, and little Christmas drums. They were all beautiful.

When I got to the presents, there were slippers, socks, and a smoking jacket robe Angie had made herself. There were little treats as well: candy, cookies, and my favorite kind of pretzels. Some of it was pretty well beaten up, but every crumb tasted like heaven. I could almost smell Angie on the food.

I must have sat in the dark with that tree all Christmas night. My present from the site was that nobody bothered me. Paul had said mass in the morning and then took off for the big celebration and dinner up at Corpus Christi in Tolsan City. Again, I was invited, but passed. Goldman was getting stoned in the NCO club, and Oyster was down at Dutch's hooch for dinner. I was invited to it all, but I wanted to sit in front of my little tree, drink a fifth of Scotch, eat the goodies, and just revel in the sheer misery of being away from the best Christmases I'd ever known.

Around five in the morning I had relived all of my seven Christmases with Angie for about the hundredth time. I was full of booze and cookies and pretzels, and I had my new socks and slippers on, along with the robe. The little tree was still lighting the room, and I crawled over onto the bed. It wasn't long before I went into a deliberate deep sleep that took me away for endless hours of escape. It got me out of Korea for a little while. I wasn't home, but I wasn't awake, either.

The entire week between Christmas and New Years was a blur. Oyster and I pulled hill duty on alternating days. I stayed pretty well lit on booze. The movies were something I could look forward to each night. We had gotten a slew of them, sort of a gift from rec services up on the mainland. They had TV up there, and they had USO shows. We didn't even have good communication lines, but they did send us movies.

I was careful about one thing, though. I stayed out of Dubbs' way. I timed my trips everywhere in terms of where he wouldn't be. And I only used the jeep for the shift on the hill.

I had the duty on New Year's Eve day. Of course it wasn't the big New Year's Eve in Korean culture, but they sort of acknowledged it. At least they tried to make us feel good by wishing us a Merry Christmas or Happy New Year. Lieutenant Ko and some of the others brought me some tea at my little dais position about an hour after I'd been on duty.

"Now thisa ginseng will maka you a good new year," Ko said, giving me that big chiclet smile.

"Oh, I thank you so much. I especially need this since I am having a big head this week." I stood up and bowed to them. The tea they handed me was hot on my cupped hands.

"I think your head will also be suffering this night."

"Yes, Ko, tonight I will probably tip a few." After I said that and took a slug of that good tea, I got an inspiration. "You are invited to my BOQ for a New Year's Eve party."

They loved it. A Korean loves a party and he also loves to be invited to a GI party. I couldn't have said anything better.

"Yesa, we come, and we bring our brother officers."

"Look, bring anybody you want. It's going to be my treat."

I lost my case of the blues. I was going to throw a blast. After some mental planning, I picked up the phone and called down to the Q. Paul answered, and I told him the plan. He loved it.

"Okay, I'll go over to the BX and buy up a bunch of food for snacks. There's nuts and assorted goodies over there from the last choggy. I'm splitting with you fifty-fifty, man." He was excited.

"Get Packer in on this, Paul."

"Okay, okay, and maybe Ryan'll want to come up, huh?"

"Great. Great," I said with tremendous anticipation.

And then he was off the phone and on the errands that needed completing for the party. It was going to be a blast.

I made a few more calls, too. I called Goldman and ordered forty cheeseburgers and a couple of big platters of French fries for about ten o'clock.

"Oh, I understand, sir," he said, "an officers-only party at the BOQ."

"Come on, Goldman, you're welcome as hell and you know it."

"No, sir, we enlisted swine will survive somehow. Besides, we're doing a pig out back, and just for the hell of it I'll send over a platter or two of that with the burgers."

I paused a minute. "Goldman?"

"Yes, sir."

"I'll be over to help carry that stuff, and I want you to follow me so we can all toast you for just one drink, okay?"

"Sounds good, sir. In spite of everything I've been taught, I somehow see human qualities in you."

"Okay, we'll see you later," I said and put the phone in its metal holder.

All I had to do was wait until party time. We would have everything needed for a good blast, including roast pig. Goldman was a genius.

When I arrived at the Q, Paul and Oyster had the place fixed up in style. Goldman had given them some extra silver tinsel chain he had for the NCO Club and that was neatly strung back and forth under the curved Q ceiling.

Mr. and Mrs. Kim had vacuumed and polished. The glassware was sparkling.

"Lookit this," Oyster said, opening up the frig door for me. "I put four cases of beer in here and I got four more waiting in the wings. I restocked the bar completely." We bought the booze for our little Q bar from the NCO club. We paid cash for it, out of a kitty, and then sold it to ourselves to keep the fund alive, a common practice on radar squadrons.

Paul suggested we dress up in our class A blues, the uniform with coat and tie combination. He was sure the Koreans would do the same. When party time arrived, the old Q was full of Koreans and Yanks, all in uniform combination one, coat and tie. Father Ryan O'Donnell made it, too, with Roman collar and black suit, his combo one.

It was a success from the very first beer. Lieutenant Ko introduced us to the other Korean officers we hadn't spent much time with. We had a nice crowd: Nine Korean officers, three American, and one Irish Catholic priest. Not a teetotaler in the house.

Seems like you always end up playing drinking games. Drink chug-a-lug is always first, and then a popular Air Force drinking game called dead bug, where you hit the floor on the command "dead bug." Makes little sense, but when you're loaded, it's the greatest. Most of the Koreans had done all of this before and they hit the deck with yelps and great relish. I always kept a few raw eggs in the frig for my egg-in-the-beer thing. After I demonstrated, we dispatched Oyster to the dining hall for more eggs. Everyone wanted to prove to me that it was easily duplicated. On his return, they did, indeed, prove it. Gulp, gulp.

Next we did the Korean drinking thing, which involves a guy pouring a mouthful of hot *chung jung* rice wine into his glass, but handing it to you. The glass pass is done with the right hand, while the left hand supports the right arm joint. You then bow, take the glass, and belt it down, whereupon you fill it and hand it back to him. Soon, everybody was passing a glass to someone. The object of the game was to pass and receive from everyone in the group. It was symbolic of mutual respect, and it also got you blitzed quicker than if you sipped on your own. It was very good for Korean-American relations.

Around nine-thirty we were all blood brothers, sworn to defend each other's homeland at the drop of a 38th parallel. Even Father O'Donnell was giving his blessing to a push northward by President Park Chung Hee's forces. In reality, the only one of us in the room who had seen combat was Paul, but he was more interested in encouraging the Koreans to overtake the Japanese economy. His personal gripe was still against Japan.

While we put together our Korean expansion plans, I spotted some figures coming through the doorway. It was Colonel Lee, and with him were Majors Moon and Park. I shouted, "Officers, Attention. The Commander!"

Everything came to a halt. Paul gave me a wink that said, "Beautiful move, son."

"Be at ease," said Colonel Lee as he moved into the room and right up to me. "My officers and I wish you a most Happy New Year."

Ko didn't tell me he had invited the old man. Well, why the hell not? This was the whole reason for our being there and it was about time we all got together like this. I'd been on site almost four months, and this was our first Korean-American blast. Yeah, I thought, about time.

Oyster came up with three full glasses of beer. Lee and his two chief staffers took them with ceremony.

"Sir," I said, "may I propose a toast to the Republic of South Korea?"

"To the Republic of South Korea," we all said, and then filled them up again.

I knew most of these guys from the English lessons I gave. The radar intercept controllers I knew best. But this party was a lot different from standing up in front of them and slowly pronouncing English phrases. We were together, on New Year's Eve, rubbing shoulders and tying one on.

Colonel Lee was very gracious. He gave the party real class. "I think you are a very good officer to my staff," he said to me, nursing his second drink. Then he added, "Where Maja Dubbs now?"

"Sir, I think he is downtown tonight." I felt like adding a thank God, but I left it at that.

"So, you cannot celebrate with your commander?" he said.

"You are our commander, sir," I said, and handed him my freshly filled glass. He took it, drank it down, and the room applauded. I got his in return and belted it down. And then we shook hands, and everyone else started passing around glasses all over again.

So we welcomed in 1967 in grand style. The club called, and I brought back the burgers, the roast pig, and a celebrating Staff Sergeant named Martin A. "Doc" Goldman, who poured everyone a shot of brandy from a new bottle he brought with him. It wasn't long before everything was gone, including the bottle.

At midnight we toasted to a great new year for America, for Korea, for our families.

17

Bridges

The party was a stroke of genius, more than I knew at the time, because that new year delivered a series of events that would bring Colonel Lee and me closer than I could have ever guessed. The English lessons and the bull sessions on the hill had broken the ice, but our big New Year's blast established a tone that was to last.

Relations were getting better and better, and yet some real frustrations were built into this Korean-American radar assignment. For example, we could all communicate with each other pretty well. There wasn't any problem with small talk, or even finding translators for longer conversations. But controlling fighter pilots in English was a different ballgame.

The problem was that the Korean controllers had to run missions using English as the language. Likewise, the Korean pilots had to understand and speak back in English. So, whenever we were controlling the F-5 fighters out of Suwon, an all-Korean unit, English was the language of the mission. They controlled and flew in a second language. Thus, the Monday night English lessons were important. I imagined how hard it was for them to have to do such a complicated thing, two guys who shared a common culture and language, speaking to each other in a foreign tongue. The pilots and controllers were well-educated, high-born Koreans. But they had to fly, control, and speak in English. That was so the allies could work together, though I often wondered to myself why we never made the attempt to learn their language.

I'm sure if I was told to talk to another American in what little German I know, I could go along with the game as long as it wasn't for very high stakes. But if that guy and I were controlling a target intercept together, I think we'd revert back to English the first time we faced a head-on. My Korean counterparts proved to be no different.

We'd often have practice Air Defense exercises that were held Korea-wide. All of the sites would play together and tie in with the chief control center in Osan. Usually, you'd know a week or so in advance if there was to be an exercise. They were built to simulate the way the real thing would start, complete with a script, or intelligence brief, that would describe the day-to-day breakdown in international relations. Finally, things would go to hell, and we'd simulate either a world war, or an attack by the North Koreans on their southern cousins.

Colonel Lee and I composed the senior battle staff, along with Major Moon and a few other senior Koreans. He'd be hooked into the headsets that allowed him to talk to his commander in Osan, and I'd be connected with the American commander there. Though we all talked in English, each talked to his own. Lee and I, like our counterparts in Osan, would confer with each other as the air battle progressed. Though we talked to different elements at headquarters, we really did share a good deal. I'd pass on info from my people, and vice versa.

It was during one of those exercises that he asked me if I had read the operating instructions for the Air Defense Operations Team. I said I had. It was simple enough: we were to advise the ROKAF radar squadron commander and his staff on air defense matters, or on anything else they might need.

"The part of your order I wish to talk about is the part that tells about what you do when Korea goes to war," he said, as he turned his attention away from the big board to me.

"Well," I said, "it lays out options for us to follow."

"No," he said very softly, "more than options. If war, it say you will become the commander of this Korean radar site."

I just looked at him. I knew what it said.

"You will never do that when that time come, even if you think so," he said with stern resolve.

I looked into Lee's hard eyes for what seemed minutes. He was very serious about this. This was his country, his command. Up in Osan I had been given a copy of an operations plan to read. It said whoever was on duty was to take command from his Korean counterpart in time of war, and now here I was sitting alongside a man who'd seen more war then I'd ever read about or watched John Wayne wage. He was old enough to be my father. I felt like a kid.

"Colonel Lee," I said, "you're a colonel, and I'm a captain. We're allies. I salute you and call you sir. Military tradition pretty well defines our relationship. I said it all on New Year's Eve: You're the commander, come hell, high water, or war."

His face relaxed, and he knocked the desk with his knuckles and sucked in a good breath of air. His only reply to my answer was, "This island famous for three things: Rock. Women. Storm. All over Korea they say, 'Tolsan is rock, women, and storm.' But I will show you even more than these things. No gee-eye must hold his nose here because the farmers put fish on their fields, not night soil. And they are very good at farming. If they just hava high skies and fat horses, they are very happy. And they say to each other, 'I wish you hava high skies and fat horses in this year.' I will show you rock, women, and storm. I will show you more. You will hava high skies and fat horses in this year."

It wasn't long after our conversation that a call came on a Saturday afternoon over the radio communications system saying someone on the U.S. team should immediately go to the hill and dial onto the command line. Naturally, Dubbs was nowhere to be found. So, I jumped into the jeep and cut a choggy for Benjamin radar control center. When I got there, everyone was in place. The room was a hub of activity. Lee was in position, already talking on headsets. It seemed like they had been in place for some time.

He waved to me as I sat down and patted me on the shoulder. "Big mission," he said. And then he continued talking on his headset—in Korean. As a matter of fact, when I put my headset on and listened in to the positions all around the room, I found that everyone was talking in Korean.

A Korean sergeant tapped me on the shoulder and said, "Sore, you hava call on your line."

I punched the Osan switch and heard the voice of Colonel Virgil E. Canada on the other end. "Whitman?"

"Yes, sir."

"They talk'n Korean down there on Tools'n."

"Yes, sir."

"Okay, boy, stay on the line. We'll get back to ya."

I rogered that. I knew he had turned his attention to the general sitting next to him in the big Osan situation room.

Lee was tense and chattering excitedly on the phone. But the big Plexiglas air picture track plotting board at the front end of the center was translator enough. I could see the plotters behind the glass plotting the progress of four parallel tracks with their white grease pens. Tracks were given numbers, so the plotters had to be expert at writing backwards. These tracks were headed out toward the sea from the Suwon area. That meant there were friendly fighters headed out of Suwon, flying out over the South China Sea. They seemed to be in orbit, maybe engaged with a target. They were just south enough that they were within our range, our area of control. When I switched on air-to-ground, I could hear the unmistakable chatter of airborne traffic speaking in Korean. Lieutenant Ko, at radar scope one, was talking to them.

My Osan switch lighted up, rang, and I answered, "Benjamin Control, Captain Whitman, sir."

"Whitman, that's four ROKAF F-5s working their way down toward you. They have contact?" said Colonel Canada.

"Sir, I think the ROKAF controllers here are talking with that flight."

He paused at that. "Can ya make out what they're up to?"

"No, sir," I said, "but doesn't it seem like they're orbiting some seaward point?"

"Yes," said Canada, "that's our picture too."

There was some muttering on the line. Canada was talking to the man on his right. "Whitman?"

"Yes, sir."

"Ask Lee what they're look'n at."

"Colonel, pardon me. Can you tell us what your fighters are doing there?"

"In time. Please now to be quiet," he said, putting his hand on mine.

"Yes, sir."

"Sir," I said over the Osan switch, "I'm sorry, but I can't really get an answer at this time, sir."

"Okay," said Canada, "same here," and punched off.

With that, everyone in the room stood up and began to cheer. Koreans are better about showing emotions than Americans. They were hugging each other and jumping for joy.

Colonel Lee turned to me and pointed to the board with his finger. "I very sorry I not tell you so soon, but we very busy only now with mission. At splash point was North Korean gunboat who want to take a South Korean fisherman's boat to the North. Our Air Force found this thing out, and my general sent Korean man in fighter to stop this. No time to speak English. No time to clear. I can tell you that Captain Kang has shot the boat from the water, and he is Major Kang now."

"Congratulations, sir," I said. "I'm proud to have been here to see it."

"You are invited to my Officers' Club to celebrate for Korea. We make Lieutenant Ko a captain."

Ring, went Osan switch. "Whitman, do you know the story?" said Canada.

"Yes, sir, I understand there's a promotion party at Red Squadron, Suwon, tonight."

"Yup," he said, "and can you imagine he did that with a 20-millimeter cannon? We're going to give General Dai here official holy hell for breaking every goddamn rule we've got set up. Then I'm going to go over to the club and toast to people who still got spine. See ya, Norm."

Geez, I thought. He called me Norm! "Yes, sir," I said, and hung up Osan switch and my headset.

The room was quiet now, with most of the crew now piling into the waiting trucks outside. They'd break down now to the usual Saturday skeleton crew. There were smiles everywhere ear to ear. I thought they did just swell. And I liked the sound of Colonel Canada, though we'd never met.

Then Lee came from nowhere and said, "I ride back down with you in your jeep. We did a good team job today. You did just right thing for advice to me. I think you are a very good American counterpart."

When we got to the bottom of the hill, we had a hell of a party. We drank many a beer-and-shot to the glory of Major Kang and Captain Ko.

My rapport with Colonel Lee, his majors, Captain Ko, and all the rest kept climbing. They did a great deal to expand my horizon. Instead of spending my time with only my American site mates, I found myself going to little ceremonies on the ROKAF compound and sitting in on the ROKAF controller meetings. They spoke Korean, of course, but being the kind of people they were, they always found a way to make me feel included. Someone who spoke English would always sit with me and translate. Sometimes, the speaker might even stop and clarify something in English.

At the controller meetings, for example, I could follow the chalk diagrams of standard target interceptor tactics being drawn on the board. They'd be running through fighter attack profiles (stern, frontal, beam), or debriefing a mission Benjamin had controlled. My interpreter would keep me filled in. The briefer sometimes would say to me, "Captain Widman, do you think thisa speed ratio would work with our F-5 on MIG-21?" I'd put my two cents in, with a delayed voice translating for me. Damned if I didn't feel useful.

Lee's two majors, Moon and Park, were an interesting pair. You saw them with him all the time. Everywhere he was, so were they. They were his shadows. I'd never seen such loyalty. Didn't matter if it was ten at night, Lee would have Park and Moon with him as he went about his compound. The memory of the Korean War, the presence of the unpredictable North Koreans just above the parallel—all of it put a certain sense of realism in the air.

Lee was emerging in my mind as a very tough and conscientious commander. I made it a point to be on the Korean side at least once a day. Dubbs, the guy who should have been doing more of that, just sat in his office in the GI Headquarters Quonset, doing only God knows what. He could close the door on himself, and the frosted glass he had Dutch's people put on the door window held the secrets of his workday. I'll give him one thing, though. He was in there at 0730 every morning, but I had a suspicion that was just in case he'd get a call from Colonel Canada up in Osan. Dubbs' big motto was "Show up and be around." I thought: Do as I say, not as I do.

I was reminded of that motto once every week or so. "Hey, Whitman," Dubbs had said to me one Thursday afternoon, "why the hell don't you put more time in over there." He was pointing to my desk, sitting out on the floor of the Quonset, along with Packer's and Mountain's. I was walking through the place when he caught me taking a shortcut to the Korean side. Only Mountain was in place, typing a letter to his wife.

"Sir, I was going over to the weekly controllers' meeting. Since I watch most of the intercepts, I like to be there for the debriefs." The backbone of success in the target intercept game was PBED--Plan, Brief the Plan, Execute, and Debrief.

Dubbs smiled a sarcastic smile and shook his head side to side. "They don't need you over there. But we need you over here. The slopes can take care of their own business without us nebb'n in. When you get involved with them, they just need our stuff. They're con artists, parasites. You'll have Lee over here trying to get our stuff."

"Well, I promised I'd go to this one. It'd look funny if I didn't show up," I said.

"Whitman, who writes your effectiveness report? Colonel Lee do that?" he said, walking out of his doorway so he could put his face into mine. Now he was going to threaten me with my ER.

"No sir, but isn't it based on how well I work with him and his people?"

"Hey, no. It's based on you right there at that desk, put'n out for me. And I can tell you that you're never at that desk."

"Well, all I can say is that I thought I had an idea about what I was supposed to be doing over here." No horn to drown him out this time, I thought.

"Why not ask me about that? I tell you what your job's all about. And it ain't spending time in slopeland. Packer's here when he's not on the hill. Today's your day here. Mountain's never away from his desk. In a nutshell, Captain, take off your hat and acquaint yourself with your job." He turned and walked back into his office, shutting the door behind him. I just stood there. Dubbs was always referencing "here" or "there."

"Write a letter, sir," Mountain said, giving me a smile.

"No, I need a specific job for today, Shirt," I said, walking over to Dubbs' door. I knocked.

"Yeah. "

I opened the door and looked in from the doorway. "Sir, do you have anything specific for me today?"

He looked up from reading *Stars and Stripes*. "Yeah, you and Mountain can inventory all the classified. Do that."

"Yes, sir," I said, and shut the door. Inventory the classified. Inventory the classified. A standard busywork job. We really had some pressing things to do here at our little desks, didn't we, I thought. But the boss has the real responsibility: read all of the back issues of *Stars and Stripes* before the choggy brings in the next batch of old news and sports.

So Mountain had to interrupt his letter home, and we spent the day going through the classified. It was mostly procedures and lists of frequencies. There were also exercise packages, those scenarios we'd follow that told the stories of make-believe wars that would be fought between the allies and their enemies. There were little odds and ends, too. Just a little drawer of material, all items found and accounted for.

Just as we finished, Dubbs came out and said, "Now you've seen it all, sign for it. You can be the classified custodian now."

Oh great, I thought, that's just what I need.

Next day, I had the hill. As soon as I showed up, Ko asked me why I hadn't been to the controller's meeting. "I sorry, Ko, but I had an unexpected mission in GI compound. Was it a good meeting?"

"Yes, but my commander was sad that you not there. He wanted you to meet visitor from our headquarters in Seoul." I could tell from Ko's face I had lost face by not showing up. Goddamn, Dubbs was always fucking up my life in some way.

About an hour later, Lee himself came through the darkroom. That made everybody sit up real tall. A Korean commander is an all-powerful god to his troops. Discipline in the Korean armed forces is tough, superb, and has teeth. Ko had translated a little sign for me that hung just above the big plotting board. It said, "The more you sweat in peace, the less you bleed in war." Lee and his people practiced that.

But they did some bleeding, too. The first time I saw a Korean sergeant knock one of his troops down to the floor, I was aghast. Fuck up in the ROKAF, and you got the first shirt's fist in the chiclets. Officers weren't exempt. Park and Moon had both been known to lay a roundhouse on an errant lieutenant. It was their way. I accepted it.

When Colonel Lee spotted me, he headed up the steps. I stood up as he approached. "Captain Widman, you not to our meeting yesterday? You sick?" He was very polite.

"No, sir, I had mission in compound. I am very sorry I missed the meeting. I did not know you would be there."

He smiled at me. "No, no, no, I just want you to know that my controller like very much you there with them for those meetings. You first gee-eye to meet with us in long time."

"Well, sir, I learn a lot from them. The debriefs in your squadron are just like ones at my last base. I think it makes for good control."

What I really wanted to find out was who the visitor had been. I was afraid he'd told somebody I would attend the meeting and then lost face because I wasn't there.

"You can have some tea with me now?" he suddenly asked, gently hitting my arm with his blue hat.

"Yes, sir. I can leave the dais if the commander invites me."

He laughed the laugh he did when I referred to him as my commander. He liked it, of course, because there was really no such line of authority. And he liked it because his officers who understood English had heard that on a number of occasions. Even a shitassed American captain was a big deal to them. My saying that gave him something to feel a little pride about. Well, what the hell, he *was* the commander as far as I was concerned. Dubbs couldn't make a patch on his ass.

I followed Lee out of the darkroom and down the corridor to the administrative offices of Benjamin Control. There were a lot of places around there I'd never been in before. It looked like any admin section, with uniformed workers walking paper in and out of the offices. Though it smelled a little different, the floors were as polished as ours. The mood of the place was like any military operation I'd ever been in. The differences were merely cultural; "slopeland," as Dubbs called it, didn't bother me one little fucking bit.

We ended up in a nice little room that had a carpet on the floor, regular chairs, and a beautiful coffee table in the middle of a group of chairs. In the corner there was a wooden cabinet that held cups and saucers, a couch was set up against one wall, and a little potbellied stove was burning away under the weight of a half dozen little chugging teapots. It was warm and smelled spicy good.

Lee's walk down the hall made workers press against the walls. When he walked into this little tearoom, the officers relaxing and drinking tea shot to ramrod attention. I said, "Hi" to everyone, but his sharp Korean words to them had the place evacuated in about three seconds.

"You sit down please," he said, gesturing to one of the chairs around the table. He sat down with me, and that instant we were joined by Major Park. I knew either he or Moon couldn't be far away if Lee was in the building.

"Hello, Major Park," I said.

"Uh, Captain Widman, I am glad to see you. I still have big head from New Year party," he laughed.

"Now, what kind of tea you like?" Lee said, taking his pipe out of his blouse pocket.

"Today I would like to try your favorite," I said.

He laughed. "My favorite not here in thisa place, but anyway we try this one I will show you." Then he said some quick sentences to Park, which were answered by a grunting sound of approval and his move to the boiling pots. He worked over there for a few minutes, and it wasn't long before I had a little cup and saucer in my hand, filled with fragrant hot liquid.

"Ah, ah," I said after taking my first sip. "This one is the best, sir."

Park smiled and said, "I think for a communications officer I am good *kisaeng* tea maker."

"No wonder our communication at Benjamin is so good," I said. "Our comm officer can do anything." He liked that.

We just sat there for a silent moment. Lee had something on his mind. "Yesterday my classmate from ROKAF academy comes here. Too bad you miss him. He is also a good friend to Colonel Canada. I tell him about you." Lee sipped his tea. "We agree that you are a very good man for my site." I just nodded, and he sipped his tea like he was getting the next bit of information out of it. "He will tell Colonel Canada, I think." That was good to hear!

"Sir, I am grateful that you like my performance." Then I thought for a minute and added, "I really am glad I have this assignment. I am proud to be a part of this important mission. Your squadron is a very professional place for me to work and learn."

They both nodded at that. And they smiled. It was taken the same way it had been given. They knew I meant it. Koreans have very good shit detectors.

We sipped our tea. I enjoyed sitting there with the two of them.

"Colonel Lee, you went to the ROKAF academy?"

"Yes, even before Korean War One was cadet. Hava you been to my academy?"

"No, and I wish I can go see it sometime." He was a real soldier, I thought, in a country where it counted.

"You were in the war?" I asked, probing for more about his background.

"The war came even while I am cadet. Then my whole world turned on its end. Do you want to hear?" His eyebrows went up with his question

"Please, sir. I'd very much like to hear your story." You bet your ass I wanted to hear.

Lee had been the son of a professor at Seoul National University. His full name was Lee IL Dong. Lee was his family name, the second was his generation name, and the last his personal name. To Americans, the Koreans only used the family name. The system seemed to confuse the GIs, who had trouble with last names coming first.

Colonel Lee was born in Seoul and spent his youth there. He adored his parents. He described his father as very wise, a teacher of philosophy who had attended French schools. His mother was a beautiful woman who played the cello.

Lee admired the military life and wanted to be an aviator. As a young boy he had taken a trip to France with his father and had seen quite a bit of Europe. He loved the strangeness of the Western civilization he saw, and he also marveled at the rise of aviation everywhere. He vowed he'd be a pilot and fly to all of the capitals of the world.

He worked hard on that dream, going through all the steps of Korean education, including an appointment to the Korean Air Force Academy. That was in the fall of 1949. The important thing about those times was that Korea had finally been freed from occupation by Japan. The four thousand years of Korean culture were again flourishing, and there was great hope everywhere.

"But my country was divided in two. South was given hope for new future, but North now in hands of communist fanatics. Your people still cannot understand what fanatics they are in North."

Park sucked in a loud breath of air and mumbled approval. He had already gotten us a second cup of tea.

"When the push across border came, it was sudden. South Korea very surprised. Seoul was run over by many forces. Everywhere there was sound of war, and we not ready. I tell that to you with embarrass."

"But it is well known that Korea caught its second breath very bravely," I said, trying to gloss over his hurt about that first big punch his people took.

"Because your President Truman send help. We were not so good then. I ashamed of how we were. You musta never forget that your country save us. You kan be very proud and I will tell you that your people died everywhere on Korean ground." He was moved by his own words, and there were tears in his eyes.

"What happened to you, sir? When the attack came."

"We were cadets and joined with Army. There no time to say blue uniform or green. We were put into artillery unit, and we retreat and retreat away from Seoul for days. All Korea on fire. Our hearts were sad." The pipe had been in his hand, so far unlighted, but now he held a match above the bowl, puffed, and got it going. He smiled and held it out, showing it to me. "I get this from American artillery officer during that time. He teaches me to pass time with it." Then more smoke. It joined with the heavy spicy smell of the room.

"Finally we go back to Seoul, but we all wonder what we will find. Someday I will take you to Seoul, my city, and show you. There is big bridge there that crosses the Han River, and it is there that I first came back to my city after the Americans finally drive the North back. My age then is nineteen years, and I stand looking across the Han. I am first praying thanks that bridge is still there. Only is American vehicles crossing it. Much smoke on other side. Things still on fire everywhere. Many building all broken." He reengages his pipe, reflects. I felt privileged to hear this.

"I am even afraid to cross bridge, for I maybe might not want to see my house. How can it escape all of thisa destruction I say to myself. But I walk, and I find all of the street of my city I know so well. Pretty soon I am very close to my house. There is smoke and brick everywhere. As I come downa my street, I cannot see the end because of smoke. When I reach end, my house is just like it always was. Can you imagine how I feel?"

Park was looking at us both as Lee told the story. He'd watch Lee tell it, and then check me for a reaction. I think I must have looked very intense. I could almost see what he was telling me; it was all so vivid.

"And then I go to door and push open, and there are my mother and my father sitting there, having tea like we are. World begin to come back on its axis once more again. But I swear that it will never tip again, not while I can fix."

I was very moved. Real. I might be stationed at a hunting lodge, but these guys were in the business of keeping their country free.

"Colonel," I said, giving him a handshake. "I am honored you would share such a moving story with me. I was just a young boy when all of these things happened. But even then I heard how brave Korea was. You and your countrymen will not let that happen again."

He nodded and shook my hand firmly. "But we stilla need America to help us keep Korea, and we are proud to say that. Sometimes I worry that America do not understand how important that is."

"Colonel, those who count will always care," I said. I was open to this. Receptive. Maybe I had an advantage because I had been one of the few who had been sent to a thing called the MAI, Military Assistance Institute, before I shipped out for Korea.

There's really no rhyme or reason to the selection process that goes on in the mysterious Air Force Assignments Section. We joked that our assignments were determined by dartboard. Attached to every hundred or so officer remote duty assignments would come orders to report to the MAI for a month prior to your PCS, the Permanent Change of Station. The dart hit my name, and I went to D.C. to learn about Korea.

The MAI was unique, located in a group of nondescript high-rise buildings on the Virginia side of the capital, across the Key Bridge. If you drove by there, you'd think you were looking at an apartment complex where some of Washington's thousands of government workers lived. It was so typical of the Washington area, that the buildings were almost invisible.

The MAI itself was located on the basement level of one of those nondescript buildings. You got off the elevator at B and there was a guard sitting at a reception desk who needed to see you wearing a badge before he'd let you go any further. My badge said: Captain Whitman, USAF, Korea. All of the badges were the same shape, size, and had a standard coding. The only difference was rank, name, service and country of assignment. If you had the badge, you went on into the school.

What you walked through was a vault door that sealed the school off when it wasn't in session. I liked the vault and the super-secret procedures because it reminded me of a popular prime time network TV program, *The Man From U.N.C.L.E.* So, the best part of the day for me was walking through the checkpoint and into the school through the vault way. But then it meant a day of school and that made everything go downhill from there until four o'clock.

Most all of the major assignment countries were represented at the school. The badges said Korea, Congo, Philippines, Turkey, Thailand, and Vietnam. For each country there was a group of students and a specific classroom. Above the door you'd see the country name. Inside, the desks and chairs and blackboards were all alike, only the maps and the decorations were different.

The pattern reminded me a little of grade school. At Holy Rosary in Pittsburgh, each grade had its own room, and you had that room and that nun for the whole time. Likewise MAI. We stayed in the Korean room most of the day, with retired Army Colonel Hubert A. Hoddington as in command as any nun I'd ever had in school. In fact, the similarity in classroom styles was remarkable. It only needed a crucifix.

Hoddington had seen a lot of Korean duty. He had been there even before the Korean War, fought in it, and ended up being a military governor after the hostilities. He knew every inch of the place, but his view of the country and its people was very much filtered through the lens of a pure one-hundred-percent infantryman who measured history through the eye of West Point tradition. "I'm infantry, my father was infantry, and his father was infantry before him. West Point, every one of us, of course." And that's how he introduced himself to us. That's how he introduced Korea to us. I called him Sister Mary Infantry.

I could have learned a lot more from old Hoddington, except for the fact that there were just too many diversions pulling at me. The MAI was the first lengthy stay I'd ever had away from Angie. The pattern I set for myself there put me in great training for my excursions with Paul, Doc, and the hunters. In short, I was on the town every night until three or so, walking around the MAI in the daytime like a zombie.

By some wonderful, or terrible, stroke of coincidence—depending on how you looked at it—my roommate upstairs at the MAI, in the hotel part, turned out to be Captain Ed Peterson, U.S. Army, and a brother in the bonds of Gamma Alpha Sigma. He was an ROTC graduate from the University of Kansas and shared my enthusiasm for the adventure and good times to be had in the bars of Georgetown. What a pair we were.

Ed was Korea-bound, too. We were alike in so many ways. He loved his wife, Marge, very much, and he was equally crazy about his little twin sons, Jeff and Jimmy. But they were back at her parents' home in Manhattan, Kansas, and, like me, he thought we might as well enjoy batching it in D.C. Bedford was close enough to D.C., however, to enable me to spend one weekend home with Angie and the kids. It also helped that I would have three weeks with them before my port call. So, D.C. was an interlude to be enjoyed with my good fraternity brother.

Enjoy we did. As soon as school was over, we'd be out the vault and headed for a quick change. It was a Yellow Cab and barhopping. The hell with homework. Fuck it. We were going to pay thirteen months for our country, thirteen months away from home. It was time to enjoy life while we could.

So, with that kind of a nightlife it was hard to concentrate on old Hoddington. I never did pass the map test, and I barely got through the "match the U.S. military unit with the Korean city" test. I guessed and pulled it off. Hell, I'd see it all firsthand, anyway.

But some of the things old Hoddington told us made an impression on me. I liked to hear about the people. He had a good repertoire of stories. Some were good, some were bad, but always colorful.

Hoddington liked Korea. He liked Koreans, too. But you got the feeling he liked them the way one of Rudyard Kipling's regimental colonels liked the Indians. White man's burden, and all of that, you know, pip-pip. He admitted their strengths, their determination in battle, but he also regarded them as barbarians not blessed with Western values.

"Fellas, they can be amoral thieves. Thieves," he said one day, strutting as he often did, back and forth in front of the class. "I well remember one night—I'm in my little house in Seoul, asleep—when I'm awakened by sounds in the next room. An intruder. Thief. I grabbed my Browning, always on my nightstand in Korea, fellas, and I walked into the living room. I sleep in the raw. I'm naked as the day I'm born. Door's open. Noise outside in the courtyard. Korean going up the wall, a silver platter that was my grandmother's in his hand. Moon's out. Everything clear between me and him. Bam, at the top of the wall he catches one forty-five caliber slug between the shoulder blades." Like all of his stories, Hoddington told this one in a sort of crisp, telegraph-message style, delivered with much pomp over his deeply tuned vocal cords.

"Never made it over. He fell backwards into the court. I retrieved the silver platter. The Koreans took him away. Never saw another thief, fellas. They understand force, you see." He liked to pause and walk a few dramatic paces after a pronouncement like that.

"Not now. Not now, though. That was nineteen fifty-four. I was a United Nations type. No questions, fellas. Now, there's a Status of Forces

Agreement. Be careful. You can be tried in a Korean court. Be careful, unless you're wearing a MAAG badge of some kind. Air Force Assistance Group. Army Assistance Group. Purse strings. Money. Immunity. No curfew. No questions. But be careful even then . . . because we've got liberal sob sisters in this town that'll let you bite the bullet. They'll sell your asses right out from under you if you're not C-A-R-E-F-U-L."

I leaned over toward Ed and said, "I'll bet he had a hard-on when he shot the guy."

Ed whispered back, "Yeah, *both* guns went off at the same time."

Hoddington had a color 35 mm slide of every American installation in Korea. We spent days looking at them. The MAI sent him all over Korea once every two years so he could update his info on the country and keep his slides current. It was hard to stay awake during those sessions. Dark rooms made my late night outings catch up with me. More than once I slept through a whole battalion.

But his best show was a real eye-opener. When he gave his lecture on prostitution in Korea, he really had a good bunch of slides. "Now these are pictures of the kinds of Korean moose you'll find everywhere." We watched slides of girls, girls, girls. They were slides taken at every unit, at all times of the day and night. Sometimes they'd be walking or standing alone. Others would be of groups of girls, or girls with their GI dates. All of us were awake for those pictures.

"Whadda ya want, fellas. Ava Gardner? Jane Russell? Teenager? Big girl? Small girl? Tits? Legs? Smoke a cigarette with her cunt? Whadda ya want? Make one up. She'll do it. She'll be it."

In addition to girls, girls, girls, we saw his collection of moose. Some looked like they were posing for the photographer, like someone they had been walking with had just said, "Stand right there. I'll take one of you with . . ." Of everything we saw, this series of slides was his pride and joy. He obviously worked very hard on this presentation. It was in order by geography.

His grand finale was this great vertical shot of a longhaired beauty, one high-heeled foot up on a chair, smoothing out her stockings over a luscious long leg. Looking into the camera, her lips showed just enough tongue so that you got the idea of what she'd be good at.

He put it up on the screen for thirty seconds and then he cautioned, "But sometimes chancy. Risk involved. Goes to the police and swears out a warrant. Reasons? Sodomy. Promises of marriage. Rule that says 'live together and you're married, soldier.' Disease on the ones you pick up for a one-nighter.

Next day you'll feel like you're pissing on an electric fence in South Dakota. Black market a danger, too." Then looking over his glasses, he gave the stern warning: "There's drugs now, gentlemen, and she might be on something." Long pause for the final point. "It's up to you. Individual decision. But for God's sake protect your troops. The hooker might be the enemy. I'll end with a direct quote out of the communist manifesto of 1919: 'Corrupt the young, get them interested in sex. Make them superficial; destroy their ruggedness.' Lights up."

Hoddington always managed to work moose into whatever lecture he was giving. As he reenacted his trips to the Asia, he'd throw in a description of what the moose were like in whatever part of the world he was talking about. We learned that in Hong Kong there were high-priced English hookers who would shop with you all day and knew just where to go for the best prices. If you had your wife's sizes, she'd pick out things especially for the little lady. Just tell her hair color, likes and dislikes, and she'd make your bride happy. "Fact is, you can read the sizes over the phone when you order such a companion, and she'll be your wife's size. That way she can model the dresses for you," Hoddington told us.

To that Ed whispered, "That means old Hoddington probably traveled around with a fat-assed Englishwoman built like a fireplug."

"No," I said. "He's definitely the-bring-the-sizes-on-a-three-by-five-card-type."

Those hookers, by the way, Hoddington told us, always gave you a little present for your wife: Something from one girl to the other. My only thought was how in the hell do you explain that?

We'd sit in a bar at night and talk about Hoddington's lectures. I suggested he could have a very successful TV series called "Hubert A. Hoddington's Moose of the World." It could be run in a format like those zoo programs, with one guy to sort of play off of old Hoddington's bullshit. "Gosh, Colonel H.," he could say, "what whorehouses do you have in store for us tonight?"

Old Hoddington could come back with, "Phil, this week it's chicken in the basket at a centuries old brothel in Singapore where it's rumored that the crew of the HMS Bounty once spent a week before pushing back out to sea." The possibilities for the show were as many as there are different types of moose throughout the world. Ed and I even got the idea that a condom company could sponsor it. As sidekick announcer Phil comes out of a whorehouse somewhere in the world, old Hoddington could say, "Good thing Phil had the protection of Ramseys, because that place is known to be infected with syphilis. Not one whore in there is free of syphilis, but Phil's safe, thanks to Ramseys."

Often we'd get to leave the little classroom and go into the big school auditorium for a lecture from some expert. We'd hear the experiences of ambassadors and ranking military people who had things to say about being stationed in a foreign country as an advisor. Sometimes they'd have good things to tell us. One such lecturer was a fellow by the name of Bernard Fall, the author of a book called *The Street Without Joy*. It was all about how Vietnam fell under the influence of communism.

After you heard him talk, you understood why we were having such a hard time there. It only took a few communists to go into a village and make believers out of the people in it, especially after several local families were disemboweled and hanged in their own village square. Fall said he saw the same thing starting up in South America. It ran a chill down my spine. In spite of Hoddington and the MAI, it was after my talk with Lee that my MAI diploma seemed legitimate.

18

Scarlet Butterfly

I was indeed an advisor, and just as they had promised back in Washington, the Koreans were intense on talking about their country, its needs, and its problems. It really happened as they said it would. They needed an ear, even a shitassed captain's. They were rolling high for stakes. It was serious business.

So, I made myself stay involved. I kept the friendships burning. I knew Dubbs hated the Monday night English lessons. Dutch said he'd heard him referring to me as a "slope lover." It was only January, with nine months to go. It seemed like a long time to go, but I could at least be grateful that Dubbs himself would rotate to a new assignment in June. Whoever replaced him was bound to be better: I could do the last four months standing on my head, anyway. Above all, I was going to do the job.

You learned Korean food traveling around with Lee and his officers. You saw more than bars and *kisaeng* girls, though I must admit Majors Park and Moon loved those things as much as their GI counterparts. But when you were with Lee, you saw the sights featured in the travel books. You saw traditional Korean plays and real Korean homes. He was a great host.

At least once a week there would be something going on in some nearby town. As the senior military commander on the island, Lee was a favorite invitee to things like school plays, memorial dedications, new construction unveilings, and civic events. He liked to bring me along. I called myself his trained American.

These occasions were always great fun. Events with kids in them were the best. I loved to watch them sing and dance around in their little outfits. Oftentimes, the children in the ceremonies had their faces painted in a way that dated back thousands of years. "Ours is a culture four thousand years old.

Yours is a two-hundred-year experiment that's going well. You must work at making it last long time," Lee said to me at one of those occasions.

Once Park and Moon took Packer and me fishing with them. Oyster loved to fish. He had often said that his hometown, Oyster, Virginia, looked just like the fishing village of Choipu. "We have the same old boats tied up everywhere, except we also have dredging boats that harvest clams and oysters from the beds. The shuck'n houses are right by where I live. I used to work in one." Oyster told us about the beautiful inland waterway that stretched for miles with all sorts of flounder and drumfish. He told me about the huge rays that roamed those waters and all of the oysters, clams, soft-shelled crabs, and blowfish his mother would cook up just right. "In high school we'd have these big parties and roast clams and oysters. You never had anything like it. The open water's something else. Kill ya if you're not an old hand. Geez, we did it in little rowboats with low horsepower Johnson Seahorses. I feel right at home here. I've known a fish town like this since I could crawl."

"Then we take you with us to catch fish," Park said, and that's how we ended up on a small rock island about three miles off Tolsan's coast. We were taken there by a friend of theirs in a big wooden scow with eyes painted on the front.

"One thing we wouldn't do is paint a boat blue. That's bad luck. But these eyes'd be okay," Oyster told us on the way out. Park and Lee nodded, but were intent on the water and the island we were headed for. "Yeah, this is just like home," Oyster said to me, scratching Dolly's head, whom he had insisted on taking along.

The fishing was good. We used rec service rods. Sliced up squid was the bait. Old Park and Moon started hauling in fish as soon as they threw out their lines. Mostly, we caught a beautiful fish that looked like trout. About a foot long, they hit hard and steady. "See, they have swim path right out there," Moon said, pointing out to the water in front of our rocky shore. We had brought out fresh water and beer in a cooler and I had put some snacks in, too. Park and Moon kept a stack of firewood out there, so we built a fire toward late afternoon. It was near the end of March, but it wasn't a bad day. There was hardly any wind.

I was putting the fish on a stringer, when Park grabbed two and started filleting them with his knife. After he was done, he had four beautiful fish steaks, not a bone to be seen.

"Major Park," Oyster said, "you're about the best damn fish cleaner I've ever seen. As good as any of these old boys we have back on the Chesapeake."

"Now you eat," Park said to me, handing me a healthy sliver of the raw fish.

I knew they ate it that way, but I also heard you could get all kinds of parasites from eating raw fish. So I hesitated.

"Look," he said, and popped a sliver in his mouth.

"You will like," Moon said, urging me on.

Anything for good Korean-American relations. I took it and ate it. And then I pumped down some beer, just in case there were bugs in it. But I liked it. It was tender and very tasty. "Good," I said. "Yes, gentlemen, this is the way to eat fish."

Then Oyster followed suit saying, "Yeah, I've eaten it this way since I was a kid. It isn't bad."

It wasn't long before we were putting it on crackers I had brought, cutting up fish as fast as we could catch them. We worked on the big bottles of OB I had brought along, too. It was just a damn nice day, a damn nice time. Even old Dolly enjoyed running around the rocks, chasing these weird little crabs that ran like hell when she'd come up on them.

"My buddies and I back home always have days like this," Oyster said. I knew he was loving it.

I think about that time a lot. It was just the four of us, away for a few hours to fish and enjoy.

I can still see Oyster throwing out his line, seagulls flying over him as he gave the water one of his big smiles. Dolly was cautiously putting her nose in the water, deciding whether or not she should go in after whatever he had thrown. Park and Moon were yanking in fish and laughing with each other, probably at Packer's wonderfully awkward casts. I got hooked on eating raw fish fresh from the cold waters of the East China Sea, dressed by a Korean major who used his razor sharp knife as well as any European chef. It was a special day. One of those Saturdays that ranks high on my list of all-time memories.

Two days after that, on Monday night, I was teaching English to the Korean lieutenants. We were reading British poetry, the Romantics. I had pulled hill that day and had sacked in really early the night before. I hadn't seen anybody since Paul said mass Sunday morning. Oyster had gone somewhere, but I hadn't paid attention.

I was talking about how Lord Byron was really a weird character, when Goldman and Paul came into the Q and motioned to me. They looked white. Something was wrong. God, I thought. Something's happened to Angie or the kids.

"I think I must do something with my people now," I said to the group.

Paul nodded yes to my dismissal. We had been at it for two hours anyway.

"Come back to my room, Norm," Paul said. His hands were shaking.

"Look, Father," I said stopping, "is something wrong with my family?"

The Korean lieutenants were not leaving very quickly. I could tell that Paul didn't want to share what he needed so desperately to tell us.

"No. No. Get that out of your mind. It's something else, and I want to tell you in private."

So he and I and Goldman walked down the hall to Paul's room. Goldman was deeply somber.

He closed the door. It was oddly still in there. Paul looked at me for a minute and then at Goldman. "Oyster's dead."

I waited a long moment, looking into their faces. "Dead! What the hell do you mean? How do you know?"

"He went downtown to see Adja. He was drunk." Paul stopped and his lips quivered.

I felt like crying. "Well, how, though?" I asked.

Holding back his own tears, Goldman said, "She castrated him after he passed out. He bled to death." Then he grabbed my arm because I was going down on the floor to just crash through and never stop trying to sink myself in some dark pit. "The whole thing was about his butterfly time in Osan. She found out about all the girls he'd been with."

"Jesus Christ," I said. "She's a fucking whore. She's probably screwed six hundred guys." I was caught up in this blackness. I could see Paul's face, and Goldman's, but I also saw Korean faces. They were strangely mixed in with the large jars they kept things in. It was like the faces and the jars were rising up. Everything, even the jars, had wide-open eyes. It was like all of that was making a humming noise.

"Where is he?" I asked, breathing in short shallow breaths that had a sulfur taste about them.

"Still at the hooch, but they've got the place closed off. We can't find Dubbs, and the Police Chief wants the senior guy. It's not me," said Paul.

"Where's Adja?" Suddenly that was my focus. "Where is she?"

"They found her sitting with him. She had his head in her lap. She's totally out of her mind," said Goldman.

I knew I was starting to go off the deep end when the thought that we should kill her passed through my mind. I must have said something like that out loud, because Paul shook me by the shoulders.

"Listen," he said. "You're needed, pal. You've got the clout with Lee to at least get that poor boy absolution. I haven't been able to get in there. Get Lee, Norm."

I ran back out into the hall, but the Koreans were already gone. I turned and raced outside. "Captain Ko," I yelled.

"Sore?"

"Ko, come back here, please." They came back double-time.

"Ko, do you know where Colonel Lee might be now? It is very important I meet with him now."

"Oh, yesa, sore, I can get him."

It wasn't long before I heard the sound of Lee coming up the street. Somehow, I could hear his hat, or the brass he wore.

"Colonel," I said, saluting. "You must help my American Compound. A bad thing has happened to us." I quickly told him the story, the parts he needed to know.

He looked very sad. "We musta go in my jeep."

It wasn't long before we were out on the town road, Paul and Goldman behind us in the ambulance.

He sucked in a breath and said, "I very sorry this happen."

I was wiping tears away with my flight cap.

"You musta let yourself know it all now and not try to push it back. Sadness is something that man musta take all in as it come, or you will have it in little pieces for long time. Put it all in your heart now."

It seemed like forever before we came up on Packer's hooch. In some respects, it was like any other incident in any town or city you could name. There was a crowd outside, with the neighbors standing in doorways staring at the action out on the street. When things happened on my block back in Pittsburgh, the people gathered and stared just like this. Trouble. It wore the same face everywhere.

But there were no sleek police cars and wagons, just two police jeeps. The big rotating lights weren't painting the walls here with broad red strokes. This was a country town in the East China Sea.

Because it was a small Korean town, I knew the police probably didn't know at first just what to do with what they had found. Hell, I didn't know myself. I just wanted to wake up. I wanted this to be one of my drunken dreams. I would have suffered a million of them to make this one of them.

Lee put his hand on my sleeve. "You stay here only at first. I musta see the chief of this police," he said, pointing to a tall man with a hat covered with gold braid. He wore stars, like a general, but the uniform wasn't military. It was the standard black Korean policeman's uniform with white piping around the pockets.

"Norm?" It was Paul leaning in the jeep. He and Goldman got in the back seat. "Just get us in there, Norm."

"I will. God, I will, Father." We all looked in the direction of the hooch.

"Doc and I were at Mr. Kwak's house. His kid heard about it on the street." Paul had a black leather case clamped firmly in his hand. "We came right over, with Kwak to translate, but the cops wouldn't let us in. Even the ambulance didn't faze 'em."

"Then how do you know he's . . . he's dead?"

Goldman leaned forward and spoke softly. "They sent the local medic out to talk with me. It must have happened late yesterday, sir."

Lee stuck his head in the driver's side. "Captain Widman, you come now."

"Can we join him, sir?" Paul asked, leaning forward.

"Just wait for some short time, Chaplain. Captain Widman will take you soon."

Lee was very firm, but his voice had understanding in it. I'd heard that kind of tone in the large men who were the fathers and uncles in my old neighborhood. It was big-handed and blue shirt. It had been to wars and could make things go right around strike time or when somebody was in need.

I got out of the jeep, and Lee took me over by the side of a building opposite the hooch.

"Now you musta understand that this chief and his mayor have never had thisa kind trouble in this village. Lieutena Packer is American, and Korean has done a terrible thing to him. They do not know what will happen. They sorry. But they also very afraid about not doing right thing."

As Lee and I walked toward the hooch, I hesitated. "Sir, I must find Major Dubbs or else I must make a phone call to my command post in Osan."

"You do not hava time." He motioned me to continue walking, and it wasn't long before I stood looking into the face of the Police Chief. "This one is Chief Lim," Lee said, nodding to him.

I put out my hand. The Chief took it, and we shook firmly, both bowing slightly. Then I gathered my senses, stepped back, and saluted him. That did the trick. His face softened and he started to rattle sentences off to me.

Lee translated. "He says his investigation is almost complete. He has taken pictures and his doctor has been very careful to gather facts. His best men now make final investigation, and the Korean head attorney is on the way from Tolsan City to see him. After that time, when things are complete, you can move Lieutena Packer."

"Sir, please ask him if I and my medic and chaplain can go in now."

There were more words exchanged. "Yes, he will take us in himself."

Now I was going to have to face what was inside the hooch. Like the town officials, I also prayed that I'd do the right thing for the sake of everyone--for the Americans, for the Koreans, and especially for Packer.

The Chief and Lee led the way, with the three of us Americans trailing behind. Along the short route across the street, the Chief stopped to talk with a few of his uniformed officers. With his men were two guys dressed in fairly nice business suits. I guessed they were the Tolsan equivalent of detectives. A little more chatter, and then we crossed the street.

The whole hooch was lighted up. Through the windows you could see Korean profiles busily walking about on the inside. As we got to the front door, I noticed poor Dolly tied up outside by a rope. She looked forlorn and confused. Her ears were back, and she cowered in the corner. "Dolly, Dolly, good girl," I said, bending down to pet her. She was frantically glad to hear her name and smell someone with the compound scent on him. The sight of her, tied there, was chilling.

We were in. The first thing that hit me was that it didn't smell like Oyster's hooch. It smelled like a hospital. It had that antiseptic smell about it that made you think of white porcelain and stainless steel containers. Korean guys were everywhere. They had set up little office areas and moved familiar tables around to accommodate equipment, notepads, and black boxes with red felt insides. There were several pair of rubber gloves thrown on the coffee table I had put my feet on at a dozen parties.

Korean guys were sitting on the chairs and couches, grouped together in conversation, going over notes and clipboards. They paid no attention to us. I wanted to throw them all out on their ears, every one of them. They were moving, disturbing Oyster's home. They didn't have any place here. Christ, somebody was always moving in on Oyster's turf. I was overcome by the intrusion on my poor friend's life.

Then I heard a strange moaning coming from the kitchen. It sounded like Adja, still in the hooch. Another moan told me I was right.

Doc and the priest were standing next to me, not saying anything. They were as dumbfounded as I. "Father, we'll go in soon, okay?"

"Just say when," he said, still clutching his leather case with a look of determination.

"Goldman, you're going to have to do something in there, right?"

He was crying, God bless him. Big tears were welled up in his eyes, and he looked lost. He looked like Dolly out there, I thought.

"I won't let you down," he said. He looked down at the floor. "I'm just not going to be able to talk for a while, okay?"

I hugged him. I just put my arm around his small, skinny, parka-clad frame and hugged him. It was like he was all horn rimmed glasses and staff sergeant's stripes and bones. He was a good troop. He was sad sack. No, a deflated Groucho Marx.

"Chief says, do you want to see the girl?" Lee asked, drawing me out of my thoughts. That's when I had a little talk with myself. I instructed me to see everything, to know as much as I could, and to start taking notes. I was a damn poor excuse for an American officer, but I knew I had to try to do as much as I could to act like a good one.

"Yes, I see her. Can I have paper and pencil to keep record?"

He started for the Chief.

"And, sir. "

"Yes, Captain Widman?"

"My government would appreciate copies of everything he writes and maybe all pictures."

They chattered back and forth. Then the Chief looked at me and nodded.

The clipboard came. I wrote: *3 Apr 67, 2210 hrs, Captain Whitman, Captain Fisher, and SSgt Goldman in Mywong Street Residence with Col Lee, ROKAF CCR, local police officials. Girl, Adja still at scene. Told that incident is a Korean civil matter under status of forces agreement, promised copies of all investigation documents and photographs, and agreeing to abide with Korean authority in exchange for Lt. Packer. SSgt Goldman estimates time of death sometime on Sunday, 2 Apr 67. Planning to call Osan after I have seen Packer. NLW.*

After completing my notes, the chief motioned us toward the kitchen. Adja was sitting in a chair at the chrome kitchen table Packer had bought for the place. It had red vinyl seats and backs. The tabletop chrome was cheap mother-of-pearl. There were millions of kitchen sets just like it.

Her hair was a mess, and her face was sunken. She had this white silk blouse on, and it had blood on it. Her hands were resting on the tabletop. Her nails were painted red, and she had red on her arms and elbows, too. She looked like a child who had been finger-painting and had gotten it all over her blouse, hands, arms, and elbows. Adja always did have long red nails.

Three Koreans were in the kitchen with her, two in uniform and one in a suit. She looked as if they had put her through it. She looked terrible.

She was staring at the tabletop.

For some reason Paul said, "Adja, look who's here," but her eyes never left the table.

The man in the suit said, "Not to talk to her at this time."

Before I walked out, I took one more look at Adja, the source of Oyster's passion. It would be the last time I'd see her. Father Paul looked at her and made the sign of the cross, his blessing.

It was all red in Oyster's bedroom, his red swag lights still hanging from the ceiling. I'll always remember his hooch for those red lights. When we partied, it gave the place a total red glow—like an Amsterdam whorehouse.

Goldman introduced me to Doctor Yi, head of the Choipu Clinic, and whispered, "He's a pretty good physician, sir."

The antiseptic smell was strong. Sight somehow took on sound. Everything made a hum. And there was Oyster, lying on his side under the covers on the bed, fast asleep. He made the same humming noise. There was his head. Same sweaty black hair. His ears stuck out. He was serenely asleep. It wasn't terrible at all. It was just old Oyster, lying in his bed, making this humming noise in my ears. I went over to the bed and stood right over him, and Paul came up next to me. Lee joined us, and the three of us looked down at him. I looked into his face for signs or clues. But he was only peaceful, completely peaceful, and pale. I saw no pain, no evil, no malice, no suffering of any kind. Just Oyster, lying in redness. Crusted red, jellied red, on finger-painted sheets.

I put my hand on his forehead. Cold. Then I gave him a pat on the cheek. "Hey, man," I said. "We're sending you home." And then I was through.

Lee followed me back to the edge of the bedroom. We watched Paul kneel down by the bed and begin the last rites of the Catholic church. He kissed a long piece of cloth and then put it around his neck. Lee and I went out in the living room. I felt like ice.

A new voice broke into my chill. "I am Mr. Chong from the governor's office in Tolsan City." Lee and I shook hands with him; they seemed to know each other. My duty now was confirm for Mr. Chong that the man in the next room was First Lieutenant Andrew Oscar Packer, United States Air Force.

I needed to call Osan. Lee and Chong said they'd stick with me; order was starting to take a part in things. It was very dark outside. The walls and the rats passed by quickly as we rode back to the squadron. We were there in no time.

As usual, my comm lines to Osan were out, but Lee somehow got us through. I sat at my desk, listening to Korean voices making connections. I hadn't thought once about Dubbs.

On the line I could hear, "Canada. Canada." We were trying to get Colonel Canada. He seemed to me the person I should contact, the place to start. Then, like magic, he was on: "This is Colonel Canada, go ahead, Tolsan."

"Sir, this is Captain Whitman."

"Yeah, Whitman, I'm getting rumblings about an incident. What's going on?"

"Sir, Lieutenant Packer's dead. It happened in the local village."

I know he heard it, but he didn't reply; he was talking to someone there. "Okay, lad," he finally said to me, "don't tell me the details over these lines. But answer some questions either yes or no. Ready?"

"Yes, sir. And, sir, Colonel Lee and the Governor's attorney are here with me."

"Good, okay, but the questions. I've got you on a conference line. Are you ready?"

"Yes, sir," I said, looking over at Oyster's desk.

"Have you seen the body?"

"Yes, sir."

"How long ago do you think it happened?"

"Sir, the coroner here thinks it was yesterday, Sunday, sometime early morning."

"Have the Koreans moved him?"

"No, they said . . ."

"Just yes or no, Whitman, you're doing fine. Any of our people with him now?"

"Yes."

"Girl do it?"

"Yes."

"She still in town?"

"Yes."

"See her?"

"Yes.

"Major Dubbs there now?"

"No, sir, I'm sorry."

"Where is he?"

"On a pass up island, sir."

"You're the senior guy, right?"

"Yes, sir."

"Okay, now hold it a minute. This is Mr. Sims I'm putting on. He's our senior OSI agent, Whitman."

"Captain Whitman?"

"Sir?"

"Does your gut tell you there was a fairly good investigation?"

"I think so, sir. But I'm not anything like an expert."

"Pictures? Stuff like that?"

"Yes. They said they'd share."

"My problem is I want to see things as they are, but frankly that body must be moved before too long, Whitman."

"Sir, they had every window open, heat off in there. I think it was for that."

"Right, but you'll need more soon."

"Our medic's with him now, sir, looking. He is a great medic."

"You say Mr. Chong's there?"

"Yes, sir."

"Put him on."

I handed the phone to Chong who nodded and spoke to the OSI guy like they had known each other for years. Chong told him he'd cooperate. He answered some rather explicit questions for Sims.

"I think it all happen in that bedroom," Chong said, "and we have photos from every possible angle. I cannot commit my people, but it's all there. I cannot think of anything I wonder about. Very clear."

More talk, and then the phone back to me.

"Whitman? Sims."

"Yes, sir."

"I know Chong. He's all right. You go ahead and tell your medic to move the body if it's okay with Chong. He's got big clout. You have our permission to work with him. He'll steer you okay. Here's Colonel Canada."

"Captain Whitman?"

"Sir."

"We'll send a C-130 as soon as landing's possible. Expect us early and be down there to meet us. Leave the body where you put it tonight."

"Yes, sir."

"You took your time about letting us know."

"Sir, I wanted to get down there first. I thought you'd want answers rather than just . . . just hearsay."

"Okay, I'll talk to you."

"Yes, sir."

"And Whitman, I want Dubbs there."

"Yes, sir," I said, but the line was already disconnected. Lee, Chong and I headed back downtown. Everything was pretty much the same when we got back to the hooch, except Doc had put Dolly in the front seat of the ambulance. I could see her in there, pacing back and forth from one window to the other.

"Goldman, we can move him. Osan says you do that the best way you can."

"That's very good, sir," he said, with more control in his voice by this time.

"Where's Paul?"

"In with Oyster."

We were talking with each other in the living room. I knew Adja was still there, but I just didn't care about that. I said hello to the ROKAF doctor, Captain Yuk, who had gotten there while we were up on the hill. The local doctor was still there, too.

"I am going to take the girl now, Captain Widman. Here is my phone number in Tolsan City. Mr. Sims often visits me, so he also know how to get to me."

"Okay, Mr. Chong," I said, anxious to get Oyster out of there. "I am sorry we must meet this way. Colonel Lee says you are a very good person."

We shook hands. "We will see each other again," he said.

"Sir, the other docs are going to help me. Why don't you tell the priest."

"Father Paul," I said, coming back into the quiet room.

Oyster was still lying there. Paul was sitting in a chair next to him, a black prayer book in his hands.

"Let's say goodbye to him, Father, because Goldman's going to get him out of this place."

Paul stood up, leaned over, and kissed Oyster on the forehead. He said something in Latin.

I looked at Oyster and gave him a salute. "Let's go. They'll do this their way, Father."

Oyster was taken to the icehouse and kept there until the C-130 cargo airplane arrived. Paul, Lee and I left in Lee's jeep.

My head hit the pillow around two-thirty in the morning, but I didn't really believe I was going to sleep. Instead, I just lay there with all of what had happened clinging to me. Before I sacked out, I wrote about seven pages of log entries. Maybe it would help tomorrow, I thought.

For some reason, it occurred to me to check Dubbs' room. But he still wasn't there. I left a big note on the door, outlining the key facts and saying for him to wake me up if he came in. I didn't care that he wasn't there. He was allowed to take a pass. We all were. What the fuck did it matter anyway.

Then this old image hit me. I was in this big long room with all these other kids. They were all getting over something. Seemed like the rows of beds went on and on forever.

On one side there was Luther who had swallowed lye. He was the first black friend I ever had. On the other side was this bigger kid who couldn't walk. He always wore these green shorts with halter straps, knee socks, and a white shirt. We called him Pinocchio. Luther couldn't talk much, but Pinocchio would tell us things and hush me when I'd cry for home. I would always say, "Pinocchio, are you awake?" and he'd answer me and make me feel better. Then I could go back to sleep.

Except one morning when I woke up, the nurse was making his bed with new sheets and a different cover. When I asked for him, she put her finger to her lips and said, "shush." I never saw him again. There was no red, no blood, no nothing. He was just gone. Pinocchio just vanished. But Packer stuck around, making a humming noise.

"Whitman. Whitman. Wake up." It was Dubbs. It was morning. It was eight in the morning. "What did Colonel Canada say?"

Christ, he was practically shaking me out of my ribcage. I thought he was going to get in bed with me. "When did you talk to Canada?"

I sat up and ran my hands over my face. I felt that shitty feeling you get when you haven't gotten enough sleep. "Last night, late . . . nearly midnight."

"I want you to tell me what you said to Canada." He was worried about his own ass. The fuck was worried about his own ass.

"I told him everything that happened the best I could. Read that log over there," I said, pointing to the clipboard on my desk, with its seven yellow pages of lined paper on which were written my notes.

He jumped up and grabbed them, sat down in my chair and read. That gave me a chance to get out of bed and put my pants on. I can't stand people standing over me when I'm in bed.

"He knew I was on a pass. I phoned it in before I left. That's the procedure." He had the clipboard on his lap. Oyster's tale was all there, but he was only concerned about his tail.

"Look, sir, Colonel Canada understood that, I 'm sure. We were manned, covered. We took care of everything." I couldn't believe I was being calm. It was like the morning had erased everything. I knew it had happened, yet the morning seemed to make it a lie. Surely, Oyster was asleep two rooms down. This was just another silly encounter with Dubbs. Oyster had nothing to do with it.

"Okay, let's get the hell down to the flight line," he said. "I can't get through to Osan, but I've got the fire engines and most everybody down there. They could be here any minute."

He was horsing me. Bullying me. I had had enough. "Look," I said, giving him my eyes full-face, "Andy Packer is dead. I feel horrible about it, and I would expect you to feel the same. I spent all last night taking care of this shitty mess. Don't push me, Dubbs."

My ace was Canada. He didn't know what Canada was going to do or say. I had talked with Canada. He didn't want to push me too far, just in case I could fuck him with Canada.

"I'm sorry. Of course, I'm sorry. I just want us to handle things okay." He had on brand new fatigues, and his shoes were spit-polished. Instead of his usual baseball cap, he had a regular blue flight cap on. For all the world you'd think he was a halfway decent officer, the dumb bastard. He was afraid for his ass because he hadn't been around when the balloon went up.

I put on a set of fatigues, clean and neat thanks to the Kims. My brogans looked like hell, and I didn't have any idea about the whereabouts of my hat.

When we got to the flight line, everybody was there. Goldman had brought the ambulance. Nobody was saying much. The vehicles were parked in a line as usual. Normally, everybody got out and shot the breeze, leaning up against the fenders and bumpers. But this morning was quiet. They all just sat in the jeeps and truck cabs, not saying anything. All eyes were forward, watching the grass flight strip.

Dubbs and I did the same. Usually I'd be uncomfortable about the silence, but on that dark morning I didn't care one bit about whether or not we ever exchanged another word again. My thoughts were running over the scenes of the night before, and I was thinking about Oyster, at peace in the back of the icehouse where I had first met him. It was Adja then, Adja in between, and Adja now. His whole life had been about her.

Then I concentrated on the landing strip. It started on the beach, at sea's edge, and ran thirty-six hundred feet. It had been built by the Japanese before I was even born. To those of us who had come here so many times, waiting for

C-47 choggies and C-130s, the place held secrets: like the little mounds near the strip, the concrete domes with long horizontal slits, covered with earth and vegetation. These had held and camouflaged the zeros that had flown hundreds of attacks on targets in the East China Sea.

Like us, Japanese ground crews had waited here, too, for landings and the return of comrades. We who had been the enemy now waited on this grass strip for mail, movies, and cargo. On that morning in April 1967, we waited for Oyster's C-130, nicknamed the Hercules, the one that would take him home.

The gloom and the silence on that gray morning was broken by a loud humming noise. A big fat airplane shot in front of my eyes. There it was, the C-130. The others had already gotten out of their vehicles. I hadn't even noticed her. Neither had Dubbs. Or maybe it was that he wanted to delay it until the last minute. Finally, he pulled out and turned on his red light to lead the big cargo ship to the parking ramp.

The C-130 grinded around and followed us obediently. Turning at the end of its landing, engines blasting, it followed us back down the strip for engine shutdown, to pick up Oyster. This C-130 was painted for war; it may have even been in Vietnam the week before.

When I finally got out of the jeep, I came up next to the ambulance where Goldman was quietly taking in the parking operation. "You all right?" I asked.

"Yeah, I'm okay. But Dubbs grilled the padre and me for over an hour this morning, trying to find out everything he could."

I dug my brogan heel in the dirt, making a trough.

"He sure was interested in everything you did."

"He's worried I said something to Colonel Canada about him. He was raw paranoid this morning. I wish it was him down in that icehouse . . ." I scared myself when I said that.

The engines of the big bird were turned off. And no sooner had they stopped than the rear main loading ramp started coming down. It moved slowly and deliberately, finally resting on the Tolsan strip. It made a wide ramp and exposed the huge shell on the inside of the plane. People started coming off, and it startled me to see there was even an ambulance, a more traditional looking one, parked there inside the shell. It was blue, Air Force, with smaller crosses on it. It looked like the kind you saw in big cities. There were white-coated medics standing by it.

A tall full colonel walked briskly down the ramp, putting his wheel hat over short cropped white hair as he tramped down the incline toward the ground. A couple of other guys were hot in trail. He had silver lightning and clouds embroidered on his hat brim, the stuff we called farts and darts, and silver eagles on the shoulders of his blue coat. That was Canada for sure.

Dubbs shot past me and walked up to meet him. They exchanged salutes, but no handshake. Quick as a flash they both turned toward me, with Dubbs pointing his finger. I was the next stop.

I just stood there, letting them come up on me. It was Canada all right. Under all of the lightning and clouds on his hat brim, his eyes were drilling me.

"Sir," I saluted.

He returned it. Snappy. "This is Mr. Sims. We all talked last night."

Sims came up beside him along with two light colonels.

"You, me, and Major Dubbs need to talk. Sims and Doctor Clark here want to get downtown immediately." There was no farting around with this guy. He had it all worked out. He knew how it was going to be.

"Goldman," I shouted. He was there in two shakes.

"Sir, this is our site medic, Sergeant Goldman. He'll take these gentlemen downtown."

Dubbs just stood there, letting me either hang or whatever. He was acting like he was supervising it all. But he sure as hell didn't want to say a word.

Goldman saluted Canada and the doctor.

"Sergeant, I want to pull our ambulance out of the plane. We'll take it and follow you, okay?"

"Get going, all of you," Canada barked.

So the doctor, Goldman, and Sims walked to the plane, leaving us with Canada and the other LC.

"This is Colonel Judd. He's the JAG." The JAG was the Judge Advocate General, the high sounding name the Air Force gave its lawyers.

"Sir, we can go back to the compound and talk," Dubbs said, finally managing an input.

"No. I want to stay here. I promised General Paul we'd get in here and get out. Sims will stay with Colonel Judd and work the legal problems on the island."

"We have plenty of rooms, sir," Dubbs said to the lawyer.

Judd replied, "I expect we'll really be spending most of our time up in Tolsan City with Mr. Chong's people just as soon as we take a fast look downtown."

Dubbs had struck out twice with his suggestions. Not big deals, but, nonetheless, strikeouts.

"How about this little weather building over here?" Canada asked, pointing to the small square building the Koreans used for both flight line ops and weather observation. It had a weird dome on it that looked like an observatory. Instead of a telescope, it housed meteorological equipment.

"That's fine, sir," said Dubbs. He put his hand out like a host, and we all walked toward it. As we did, I saw Lee's jeep coming down the road. It and we got to the building at the same time.

"Sir," I said to Canada, "Colonel Lee is here. He was such a big help last night."

"Good," he said, breaking me off. "I know him."

Canada went off to meet Lee, and the rest of us hung back, letting the two of them exchange greetings and words. They looked very cordial and comfortable with each other.

"Captain Whitman," Judd said, taking me by the arm, "come over here a minute." We left Dubbs standing by himself.

"Did you hear anything about charges, or did the Koreans say anything to you about what they were going to do about the girl? Or anything about the lieutenant's conduct downtown?" I could read years of experience all over him.

"The only thing I remember was the Police Chief told me through Colonel Lee that the girl would be charged in Tolsan City and that she was involved with what had happened. That's almost a direct quote, but that's all they said."

He studied me. I was trying to break his stare by looking around, but every time I'd look back at him, he'd still be looking at me.

"What happened, Captain?" He was so direct he almost took my breath away. I jumped at the chance to get it out.

"Frankly, sir, Lieutenant Packer's been involved with her ever since I got here. She was an obsession with him, but about two months ago he broke with her. I thought it was clean. And I thought it was good that he got away from her. Matter of fact he went TDY to Osan in December. Well, he visited a lot of clubs and a lot of ladies up there. I knew he still wanted Adja, but he was staying away."

"And this weekend he went looking for her?"

"Yeah, and we had no idea he had either. It's insane, sir, but it was because he had . . . cheated . . . done the butterfly thing in Osan. She must have taken him to bed . . . he was very drunk . . . and she got her revenge. It's absolute madness."

He softened somewhat. "Whitman, this can be a madhouse. Crazy things go on sometimes. This is not the first time it's happened."

"He was a good guy, Colonel. Last night I saw what happened, and now today I'm just numb from it. I want to hit something or kick something in . . . I even wanted to give her . . ." Shit, I was going to cry. I was standing there in the daylight talking to a JAG, and I just couldn't hold it back.

"Thanks, Whitman," he said, walking me about ten steps down the runway, away from the crowd. "The suspicion always is that maybe there's more. Sometimes our guys get involved in black market, or drugs, or some kind of a deal. Do you think it was just as simple as revenge for butterfly?"

I thought about the teahouse deal for a minute. Oyster had made the break because of it, so there was no money, no deal. I decided to let it stay right where it was.

"Yes, sir, I think it's just that simple."

"You hesitated a minute. Something else?"

"No, I'm sure, sir. But I give you my word that if I ever find out there was anything else, really something, I'll report it to you immediately."

He smiled. "Fair enough, captain. Let's see what Colonel Canada's up to."

We walked back to the others. Dubbs had joined Lee and Canada.

"Colonel Judd, I want you to meet the ROKAF commander here, Colonel Lee."

"Sir, a pleasure," the JAG said, and they shook hands.

"Captain Widman," Colonel Lee said, turning to me. "I tell Colonel Canada you did very good job with Korean authorities last night, even though everything was so fast and sad." God, he was a real gent. He didn't have to do that, but it sure took some of the glare out of the situation. It put me more at ease.

"Sir, you were the one who made things go well," I said.

Dubbs dug his heels in the ground.

Canada's face went very serious. "Colonel Lee, I thank you, too. You know I 'm always available in Osan if there's anything you need."

Lee nodded. "Now you must talk in my operations building. I only come to give my sorrow." He gave that nod of his to us and got back into his jeep.

I knew he and Canada had talked, and his exit was right on cue. I blessed him in my heart for saying what he did, but at the same time I felt no better than Dubbs. Both of us were suffering from the same fear: our asses in the crosshairs. Lee had done something to help me look good, and I clung to it. I, too, had forgotten Oyster for a moment in favor of my butt.

We assembled in the operations building and sat around a wobbly wooden table ROKAF used to file flight plans and make calculations on weather. Canada took off his hat. He was still all business.

"Okay, now, we're going to get the young man's remains out of here and stateside as soon as possible. Sims and Judd will handle things with the Koreans. You guys are completely out of that, you understand?"

"Yes, sir," we both said.

"This is an absolute disgrace, this whole damn thing. Anytime the Air Force sends a young person overseas and a meaningless death like this occurs, we're all to blame and we all share in the shame. Frankly, I don't know what or how we'll tell his parents."

"Sir," I asked, "do his folks know yet?"

"They know their son's dead. That's all." He swallowed. "He was one of mine, and it's up to me to see how far that's got to go. Do you two understand that?"

"Yes, sir."

"Ask yourselves, what did or didn't you do as comrades—as officers senior to that boy—to prevent what happened. I want you to live with that. You were all remote together. He didn't make it through the tour. You can't ignore the fact that you had a share in what happened. You can provide leadership, and things still happen. I know that. But I still want you two to take yourselves to task. I don't approve of a lot of the crap that goes on over here, and something like this makes me all the more sure my concern is well-founded."

He was tall and he sat very straight. The hair was short and white. In his blues you got to see his whole career laid out over his left pocket. He had scores of Air Medals, a couple of Distinguished Flying Crosses, and even a Purple Heart. The top ribbon was a Silver Star, one notch below the Medal of Honor in importance. Command pilot wings sat on top of the row of ribbons. He was a World War Two fighter ace. He was everything the Air Force wanted you to be. He was John Wayne, Gary Cooper, Jimmy Stewart.

"Major Dubbs," he said, looking old Harold right in the eyeballs, "you were cleared for a pass. You had the site covered. It went the way it went. If I could have had it the way I wanted it to go, you would have been there. We field a guy to be in charge with the idea of having him there when things like this happen. Sometimes circumstances work against us. What could have been . . . what it was . . . that's over and done with right here. Closed."

I thought I heard Dubbs breath ever so slightly, a breath that said, thank you. Then the eyes turned on me.

"Captain Whitman, you responded to the situation. Things seem to have been done right. I think the thing I'm most impressed with is the fact you got Colonel Lee working for us." He leaned forward for the next part. "You know he was running things for you, don't you?"

"Yes, sir, I do."

Colonel Judd looked at each of us as Canada talked, occasionally squinting when Canada would make a point.

"As your commander, I'm taking full responsibility for what has happened here and for whatever will be the outcome." He turned to me again. "Captain Whitman, you'll be my representative as summary court officer. Colonel Judd here'll tell you what that entails."

"Yes, sir," I said, looking at Judd who nodded his head.

But Canada had more for me. "You just made captain a month before you came to Korea, right?"

"Yes, sir."

"Grow into your responsibilities. I think you learned something these past twenty-four hours, don't you?"

"Yes, sir, I did," I said.

Then he got up, and we all stood at attention. This had been an ass chew. You stood very straight and tall after one of those. Canada hadn't said a lot in terms of time, but he'd said a lot. I felt like I just had a bucket of ice water poured over me.

Our timing was perfect in terms of getting back on the strip just as the Osan ambulance pulled up to the Hercules. Goldman was following in our ambulance, and I saw Paul sitting in the passenger seat. He must have been with Oyster in the icehouse that morning before the pickup. That made me choke up.

We all gathered in front of the lead vehicle. Canada and Judd spoke with the Osan doc, giving me a chance to fall back and talk with Goldman and Paul. "In there?" I asked, pointing my eyes at the other ambulance.

"Yes, Norm" Paul said. "They were very good about it. I like the doctor who came."

I looked at Goldman.

"He's been treated with dignity, sir. It was as good as something like that can be," he said, moving me over to the ambulance.

I looked in through the side window. You could tell the coffin was lightweight metal. The Air Force could fly a whole cargo plane full of them. Vietnam was making that a routine operation. But Oyster was in this one. He'd fall in formation with those other coffins. He'd look like all the rest. You wouldn't be able to pick his out. Once home, though, the questions would be asked. Better he had taken a bullet in Nam, I thought, this poor soul who rested in the lightweight coffin, his balls tied up in a plastic sack beside him.

They drove the ambulance on board, and Canada thanked Goldman and Paul with handshakes and a pat on the arm. He nodded to Dubbs and me, the ramp went back up, and takeoff was almost too quick. As the bird circled and flew off out to sea, I caught myself waving. Goldman and I and Paul just looked at each other. There wasn't anything to say.

19

Secrets

Back at the compound, Colonel Judd explained to me that, as the summary court officer, it was my responsibility to go through all of Oyster's things and ship them to his home. The room would be sealed, and only I would have access. The Osan medic team had been to the room for Oyster's Class A blues, shirt, tie, shoes, and hat. But now the room and its contents would be closed for me. It was all laid out in Air Force Regulation 143-6, which Judd handed me, a brand new unused copy.

"The real critical thing about this is to sanitize the personal effects, to take anything out that might cause embarrassment on the other end. Do you understand?"

"Like what?" I asked Judd.

"Items. Things written down, magazines, anything you wouldn't want his mother or father to receive. You want him to be remembered well. Don't let anything get home that would reveal a private moment he wouldn't want his mother to know about. Read everything, look at everything, and destroy what your judgment tells you to. You were his friend. Protect his memory and his privacy. Read the reg. It's all there."

I understood.

"And nobody gets in there but you."

Soon after that, Judd and Sims borrowed a jeep and took off for parts unannounced. The only thing I could think of was to start working on the belongings. Oyster had been taken off the island, but somehow it seemed like I could reach him again if I went to his room. When I went in, I found poor old Dolly lying on the floor. For her, I'd make an exception to the rules of the summary court. She could stay. She could keep secrets.

When I went in there, it occurred to me I couldn't remember spending much time in Oyster's room. I had talked to him from the hall or even stood in the doorway, but I had never really sat down in his room and talked. Paul and I did that a lot, but Oyster and I hadn't. He had been in my room a couple of times, but only briefly. I really didn't know him at all.

Since Oyster was the BOQ manager, probably the worst additional duty to pick up, you could see that the Kims did little extras for him. For one thing, he had the nicest furniture in the Q. He had a lot of extra furniture and pictures. It was a nice room. I wished he had spent the previous Sunday in it. If only he had, then maybe I could be visiting him instead of his belongings.

Compared to my room, this one was a showplace. I still hadn't done anything to mine, except to put a picture of Angie and the two kids on my desk and tape up a couple of pictures the kids had drawn. I lived in austerity, self-imposed. The Kims scrubbed that austerity and kept my clothes clean and put away. Even Paul had fixed his room up with a stuffed chair and some warm rugs. Angie wouldn't have liked mine, especially if she had seen Oyster's or Paul's.

I closed the door. Dolly just lay there, head down, looking up the way a dog will with wrinkled brow. Sad eyes. She had inherently sad eyes. All hunting dogs did, I guessed.

It hit me then that I was feeling like an intruder. I was thinking about my room and a hundred other silly things to keep myself from getting to the point of my being there. I was supposed to go through his stuff and "sanitize it," as Judd had put it. So there I was, standing in the middle of Oyster's room, the sanitation man, not having the nerve to begin. Dolly raised her head.

There was only one way to get through it. I walked out and back down the hall to the Q bar. I grabbed a glass and a half-full bottle of Jim Beam. I needed more than old Dolly to get me through this job. Beam was just the thing. I'd just have a sip or two, enough to get the creepy edge off.

When I got back in the room, a healthy shot down the chute, I took the first step: I opened up Oyster's closet. Same as mine, it had that perpetually burning light inside it to ward off mildew. There were several items of clothing inside. Besides his fatigues and other uniform items, he even had two suits. Where in God's name would he wear a suit in Tolsan, I thought. Two yet.

Even though they had gotten Oyster's blues, there was yet another set hanging in the closet. He had a bunch of clothes. Funny thing was, I never thought of him as a snappy dresser or anything like that. For a guy stationed on an island a long way from the bright lights, he sure was prepared for any occasion. I looked through it all. All clean, it could be shipped just as it was.

But what the hell would his folks do with these things? He'd never wear them again.

The dresser yielded everything you'd expect: underwear, socks, shirts. I thought to myself, did Canada know how foolish I'd feel going through these things? Was this my punishment? Because I didn't give moral lectures to Oyster, did Colonel Righteousness send me to go through Oyster's underwear drawer?

That called for another belt of Beam. Actually, two shots seemed in order. God, it was quiet in that room. It had the quiet about it that you felt when you were a little kid and your mother had left you in the house while she went to the store or something. The house was especially big on those days. Quiet. You couldn't wait until your mother came back, and you were just a little afraid she was being killed at that very moment, never to put life back into the house again. It suddenly hit me that I had gone through all of the forbidden drawers and closets on those days. I had examined all of my mom and dad's treasures and secrets. Now it was an official duty.

In the third dresser drawer down I found something to keep from his mother: rubbers, three boxes of reservoir-tipped, sensi-creme lubricated Sheik rubbers. I pulled over the empty wastebasket and deposited them. Plop. Plop. Plop. They had been buried under sweatshirts and athletic T-shirts. One of the shirts had a tiger head on it with the number ten and lightning bolts. Under the emblem, it said "Tiger Ten." That had been his squadron at the Air Force Academy. We'd ship that.

There were assorted Korean trinkets in the drawers. Little dolls and pieces of jewelry, even nice pieces of crafted black coral, a specialty on the island, all mixed in with his shirts and pants. At first sight, I pegged them as presents he was gathering. There was really a lot of nice things, not to mention a couple of those Irish woolen sweaters and yards of the raw linen. All keepers.

As I continued my work, there was a knock at the door. Probably Paul, I thought. "Yo," I said, feeling my Beam just a bit.

"How are you coming in there? I told Dutch to make up some shipping boxes. How soon?" It was Dubbs.

"It's going to take a couple of days," I yelled. "It's coming okay." I could feel him still standing out there.

"What's the big deal. You just throw his sh . . . stuff in the boxes."

As he was talking, I looked at the door and the turn lock under the knob. At that point, he could have walked in. Dolly got up on her feet and walked over to the voice coming through the door. I slowly walked over, too, and put my right thumb and forefinger on the lock latch. Click. I turned it. The door was locked.

"What are you doing? Are you locking the door?" He heard the click. He must have been right up on the door. "What the hell did you lock the door for? I want to come in there, Captain." He was a mixture of surprise, panic, insult, exclusion, anger, and rejection.

"I'm supposed to seal this off. I'm sealing this off now," I said through the door. "Colonel Judd said that I was supposed to do this alone."

"That's just reg stuff. He says that because he's a lawyer. He knows you won't really follow that."

I silently poured and put down another Beam. "No, I'm doing it by the book. I'm going to do what he told me." I made faces at the door. I did a little jig. I stuck out my tongue.

"Okay, the book says the commander goes anywhere on his site. I'm the commander. Open up. Now." He had his best tough voice coming through the door at me.

"The commander on this one is Colonel Canada. I'm his representative. I'm the summary court officer appointed by him. You're interfering with that legally delegated responsibility, Major Dubbs," I said, my Beam providing the eloquence. Then I added, "This is Major Dubbs outside, isn't it? I'm talking to Major Harold Dubbs, right?"

Blam. He kicked the bottom of the door. "You bet your smart college ass you are, Mister. You're talking your way right into a big hole, too."

"Get Canada on the phone, or get ahold of Judd. If they say it's okay, sir, then I'll be most happy to allow you entry." I did another silent jig, and then forever broke it with him. "Otherwise, go fuck yourself, Dubbs."

I could feel restrained madness out there. The knob turned. He was twisting the knob so hard I thought he'd twist it right off. What you saw on my end was his frustration transmitting itself through the brass knob. I thought to myself that he was probably very good at getting ketchup and pickle lids off. But it didn't matter. It was that good old bolt that kept us apart.

The tension suddenly left the knob. It relaxed. Blam. Another kick at the bottom of the door, and he was gone. I heard him walk heavily back up the hall.

The window. He could walk around, stand on the hill in back of the Q and look through the window. I went quickly to it and pulled the cloth curtains Oyster had on them. They were good curtains, floor length, and very heavy material. I pulled them back just a little to check the lock. It was secure. There was a screen and glass. Both were locked. With the curtains pulled, I was safe from Dubbs. I was dug in. Safe from the big bad wolf.

I waited for a long time, standing and listening very hard. Everything was quiet. Asshole was gone. But where? I was beginning to feel just a little paranoid. Another belt of Beam fixed that.

Back to work. I went through the dresser carefully, drawer by drawer. The bottom one was a total throw out. It was filled with *Playboys* and a lot of other magazines that made Hefner's centerfolds look tame by contrast. And there were other pictures. Dog-eared photos of women taking sex in a lot of different ways. There were a couple of close-ups of vaginas and a weird one that had this gal taking on a mule. I'd heard of that, but had never seen it. But the worst of the lot was the stack that was tied up with a piece of blue string. There was Adja, posing in the raw, much in the same way as the ladies in the magazines and other photos. Polaroids. She had stripped down from the waist for me that night in my room. There were her tits, just as I had seen them. She was smiling brightly in all of the shots, looking toward the camera enthusiastically.

I was really surprised to find a couple of Adja and Sue together in the altogether. And low and behold, there was one of Dubbs, in his skivvies, holding a nude Sue and Adja, one on each knee. But the worst of the best was a shot of Adja performing fellatio on the person taking the picture. It made me feel sick.

I tore the pictures into a thousand little pieces, all except the one of Dubbs and the two girls. That one I put into my fatigue pocket.

I decided I'd put all of the throwaway stuff in bags and have Dutch's people burn them in the incinerator where we burned old classified. I had filled the wastebasket to the top and started a pile next to it. The last drawer had put me over the top.

Surprisingly, there was another rap at the door, but softer this time. "Friend or foe?" I shouted.

"Friends, friend," Paul's voice said.

"Goldman with you?" I asked, shutting the bottom drawer with my brogan.

"Yes, sir, I'm here."

"I can't let you guys in because I've locked Dubbs out," I said through the wood.

"He's in a rage. We figured you'd done something, but he isn't giving out details," Paul said.

"Well, I know I'm supposed to do this by myself and that's the way it's going to be."

"Anything we can do, Norm?"

"Yeah, bring me a cheeseburger and a box of those big pretzels from the BX."

"Okay. Be back in a little bit."

I had to take a leak in the worst way, but I didn't want to leave the room until it was really late. Because luck was with me, I spotted the little sink Oyster had in his room, the only one like it outside of Dubbs' room. That would do just fine. That reminded me that Dolly would have to be let out pretty soon, too. "Hold out a little while, girl, and I'll give you to Doc and Paul," I said. Her tail went back and forth slowly.

Two belts of Beam later, I was back at work. I went to Oyster's desk. He had a real one, not the table affair most of the other rooms had. I opened the top drawer: pens, ruler, paper clips, candy bar, and letters.

I went to the letters first. All to Packer. Some of them had an Oyster, Virginia, return address: Mr. and Mrs. Fred C. Packer, 121 Cliffmont. That was printed on one of those little labels you could order out of a magazine. It had a little American flag on it with blue and red borders. It had to be his folks. Some were APOs from Vietnam and Thailand. I figured these had to be from old Academy chums. I put the letters in piles, by return address, latest date on the bottom.

The first pile was from a radar site near Da Nang known as Monkey Mountain. The correspondent was First Lieutenant Chuck Bailey, a weapons controller like Packer and me. He was in Oyster's class at the Academy.

The thing that struck me about Bailey's letters was the fact that he was really doing the job. I knew Vietnam was getting hot, but Tolsan's routine, away from everything, made it seem so far off and somehow unconnected. Bringing in the choggies, drinking with Paul and Doc, hating Dubbs—that was my life. Benjamin Control, compared to Bailey's Motel Control, was Sleepy Hollow. The real action was in Southeast Asia.

Bailey was a pro. He loved to talk about what he was doing, and his view of how the air picture was set up in Vietnam was extremely concise. His first letter to Packer was written in November 1966. It read like a reply to numerous questions from Packer. It made more sense to me than anything I'd read about the war.

12 Nov 66
Monkey Mountain, RVN

Oyster,

I'm just off shift and if you can drag yourself out of that Korean Pu Tang long enough, I'll fill you in on this place here. It's nothing more than a board game, complete with rules and moving pieces. You could call it "Bugs Bunny and the Pirates," or something like that. The problem is that the rules are so fucking complicated. The way the board's set up is easy enough to understand, even for a little pawn like myself here.

Okay. You know I'm at Monkey. We're the primary control for all the air ops in the northern part of South Vietnam and the stuff that goes into North Vietnam. Action, roomie, action. We get our orders from 7th Air Force, down in Saigon. Once they make up the frag orders, we do all of the actual controlling for everything going in for a strike on the North, even stuff coming in from Laos or the Gulf of Tonkin.

There's also a control point at Dong Ha called Water Boy. They're on the east coast of Vietnam, south of us. They handle stuff going North, too, and they're also the guys who join thirsty birds up with tankers out over Tonkin. Mostly Navy guys going back to the carriers. Navy's got a control ship out there, too. It's called the Piraz.

To round things off, we've got these EC-121s flying around here called College Eye birds. They have radar onboard. They can control northern sorties and the Navy birds going to and from the carriers. But their radar stinks on land. Too much ground clutter shows up.

So, I sit at Motel for hours, running strikes on the North. I also keep our guys away from the Chinese border and I look for MIGs that might be sneaking up on them. Bad part is that I listen to them get their asses shot down by SAMs.

Now the other side's got hundreds of Soviet made radars, Oyster. Their MIGs are under positive control from takeoff to landing. No holes. And they have SAM sites and antiaircraft everywhere. Overlap up the ying yang.

Then there's the rules. They even call them the Rules of Engagement, Roomie. Simply put, our Rules of Engagement keep us from attacking certain places—like within ten miles of Hanoi because that's "a densely populated" area. So, the gooks put the SAM sites there. They can hit anything out to about thirty miles. And, Roomie, most of the sites and supply stuff we want to kill is within that kill area. We can't knock out the SAMs and we take heavy fire getting to the targets we're allowed to get to. Take Haiphong. We can't touch the dikes they have there. If we did we might flood the entire Hanoi delta. We'd kill civilians and ruin their whole rice crop. So where do you build the SAM sites? Right. On the dikes!

We can fire on the SAMs outside of the ten mile zone but within thirty miles of Hanoi only if they are firing at us. People again. They build them near dense areas there, too. And Haiphong town has the same ten mile rule, in addition to the dike thing.

So we have all that shit thrown at us, plus MIG 17s and 21s. But we keep on running in, getting what SAMs we can, and managing to do a pretty damn good job. The idea is just to hold the North in check. Victory, Oyster? Bullshit. Gotta go. Ball in your court.

Cheers.

"Beetle"

Bailey was articulate and all business in his letters to Oyster. They all contained detailed descriptions of missions against the North and the politics of targets. Christ, I thought, by all rights these letters should be classified TOP SECRET. Very little small talk, except for the last one, written in February.

15 Feb 1967
Monkey Mountain, RVN

Oyster,

I'm proud as hell to start out by saying that on 2 Jan we ran a little operation called "Bolo" against the MIG fleet up North. We got them with their pants down because they thought we were sending in a routine Thud mission against SAMs. Instead we launched twenty some flights of F-4s. We got seven MIGs. The Christmas stand-down is always a big maintenance time for them, so we had lots of MIGs up in the air to shoot at, all fixed up for us. Let us loose and we could do more than check them, believe me.

Now a word to you, from your old roommate. Nobody's a failure at age twenty-three. Not even us two flight-school wash outs. You've been on that rock too long. You need substantive action. Why not try for a consecutive tour here?

You can do more than flight-follow C-47s, pal. It's a great ego and career boost. Your problem is that you always look at the glass and say it's half-empty when it's really half-full. Off your duff, cadet, and peak that attitude. No more down in the dumps.

Cheers

"Beetle"

P.S.—Talked to Pete Boggs. He said you two are writing. Good show. He's the best Thud jock in SEA.

That was the Monkey Mountain pile. I learned more about Vietnam with each of Bailey's letters, but not much about either him or Oyster. It was like a Vietnam controller's notebook. His responses to Oyster's private life told me that old Packer had poured his heart out to his buddy at Motel Control. I guess Packer's problems seemed as remote as Vietnam had been to me. Next to Bolo, Tolsan was trivia. But Bailey was right, Oyster never saw the full part of the glass.

The letter written by Captain Pete Boggs was loaded with news about the war, but it had an added dimension. The adventure was there, but something else, too. Boggs had been an upperclassman, class of sixty-three. He would have been a junior and senior when Packer was a freshman and sophomore. It was evident that he had taken Oyster under his wing at the Academy. As I read those letters, I had the feeling I was reading the words of the person Packer most looked up to.

Packer had two Academy yearbooks on the shelf over his desk. Called Polaris, he had the sixty-three, -four, and -five class editions. I went to those after I read Bailey's letters, and sure enough I found Bailey and Packer, head and shoulder shots, among the class of sixty-four. I found Boggs in the sixty-three edition. Now I had faces to look at, plus the editor's small comment about each under the mug shot. They were in formal parade uniforms with belts and sashes.

Under the picture of a brighter looking Oyster, eyes staring to the right of the lens it said:

ANDREW OLIVER PACKER
Tiger Ten

Nickname: Oyster

Packer claims he's from a place called Oyster, Virginia, but nobody in the Wing has ever seen it. One thing we're sure of though is that his "Dear John" letters were real enough! They came in by the score from all over. But Oyster forgot it all, casting his homemade flies into Colorado's trout streams ("Our ocean's bigger, by gosh"). Headed for flight school, he made his mark on the fencing team.

Bailey's picture looked as bright, crew cut, and hopeful as Oyster's, with a line in his write-up that said "He's counting on shooting down a MIG before the end of the decade." Well, at least Operation Bolo gave him a chance to do it by radar, I thought. At least he kept on charging. Poor Packer ran right into a brick wall.

Boggs looked like a fighter pilot. He stared straight into the camera, jaw set and smiling tightly. This was the picture of a warrior.

The bio said he was a football player and Tenth Cadet Squadron Commander. Guys like Packer and Bailey probably thought he was bigger than life. His last letter to Oyster was impressive, though his English left something to be desired.

2 Jan 67

Oyster,

Thank you a lot for your letter and let me tell you buddie whatever you heard about driving a Thud through Hanoi was true. A lot of guys here say the flak is the heaviest in the entire history of air warfare. They got 37s and 57s going at you as well as SAM sites all over the place. I'm flying out of Korat, out of the 388th, and if you remember the Second Group AOC who was Col Bill Green then you'll know we have the best GD squadron commander in the world. Dick Poulton and your old friend (ha, ha) Major Robin Taylor are here too.

Dick says fuck you and Taylor would if he knew I was sending you a letter. You asked about Harry Plant and I'm sorry to tell you that he was shot down in the Hanoi area two weeks ago on a target run. Standard tactic is to come up on target and start the dive at 12,000 ft and then pull out somewhere at like 4,500 ft. You pickle then and that's when you are at a stable point between roll-in and pull-out and that's how Harry got hit. Taylor was lead on that one and said there was a chute. Hope to God he at least is captured for Betty's sake.

I'm now getting revenge flying Wild Weasel flights against the SAMs. Four of us go in, two with air-to-ground and two with bombs. We go ahead of the regular strike force and try to draw out the SAM site and put it out of commission before our guys get there. It is like a cat and mouse game and we have to get there just right. We do a lot of good when we knock one out as those SOBs are scary as hell with the only way to outrun one is to turn into it with a hard diving turn and then make a quick four-G rolling pull-up and keep your speed up while you are doing it or else.

In a word I'm doing what I trained for and doing it in a good outfit. And here I have talked myself onto another sheet of rag and did not even tell you that I gave old Annie a big ring before I shipped out for this place. In a couple of missions and a couple of months I will be sending you a wedding invite. So I am not working on the railroad or laying any ties (or Thais) as your completely worn out joke suggested.

Do plan on seeing us tie (ha, ha) the knot in a couple of months and I meantime hope you get out of the dumps. Your worried about that old honor board, your worried about washing out of UPT. You worry about things past too much. And Oyster I just cannot see you making any kind of life with a Korean girl just even only because I think you must solve your own problems first. Come on. Up. Up. Let Annie and me hug you and we will hit the town and talk things out. Wait that long. This is your old squadron commander talking, doolie. Things will get better.

Thumbs up,
Pete

I went back to his picture. Boggs was from Montana. I imagined him now, four years after graduation. His Air Force had turned out just the way he had wanted it. He had probably been a big man at the Academy, but his concern for poor Oyster was more impressive to me than the record he must have had there or the airplane he flew. I wished Oyster had waited for that hug. You got the feeling it might have done the trick.

The last little stack was from his mother, the letters from Cliffmont Street in Oyster, Virginia. They just oozed a mother's love. The funny thing was that they all pretty much sounded the same. The news was about things that were happening on what she called "the shore." Northampton High

School had done fairly well in football, the local crops were okay, and the migrant worker camps were getting worse in terms of violence and trouble. Dr. Brown had to stitch the hand of a lady by the name of Mrs. Crandell. She had cut it on a bread knife. Packer's dad had traded in the Ford for a new Chevy station wagon. It was a cold winter. His dad never wrote, but passed messages to Oyster in the form of "and your father says he still can't get that old Johnson to run as well as you can." I got the idea he was some kind of state inspector who worked with the fishing industry, but it never came through in so many words. The code was hard to break because the background, the foundation under all of these letters was well known by the writers and the reader and put together over a lifetime.

They didn't say things like, "As your father, the sixty-year-old fishing inspector, who was born in Virginia and only has one arm, said to me . . . your fifty-three-year-old mother who has dark hair worn up in a bun . . ." They just talked of small things, touchstones. You read between the lines, and you found out which high school and what church, but you didn't get the answers to a thousand other questions, the questions that might tell you why Packer washed himself out of flight school, met an honor board, and went back downtown to embrace death in a Korean whore's hooch.

I yelled out, "Who the fuck were you, Oyster?" That made old Dolly jump up and walk over to me. I looked down at her, held out a Mrs. Fred C. Packer letter, and said, "Well, these don't tell me who he was. They don't tell me a fuck'n thing." Dolly just put her ears back and wagged her tail. No answers from Dolly either. So I peed in the sink and threw the letters from Vietnam and Thailand in the trash. I'd leave his mom's in so they'd know he had read them and cared enough to save them. There were nine in all. No real answers in the lot.

Once again there was a rap at the door. "Hot food for the summary court," said Goldman through the fortress gates. "I don't think I can get it under. You're going to have to open it."

"Okay, wise ass," I said, turning the bolt and swinging open the door.

"You look like hell, sir," said Goldman, handing me a neat tray with everything I wanted and then some. It smelled great. Paul was standing there with him, looking past me and into the room.

"Norm, you'll be able to put a lid on all of this if you get it done, you know."

"Yeah, Father Paul, I know. I'm moving right along," I said, putting the tray behind me on the table. "You know, I thought there were going to be answers in this room."

Paul just winked and shook his head.

"Take the dog, will ya? She needs to go outside."

"Sure."

"Come on, Dolly. Come on," I said, but I had to push her out with my foot. "She'll probably pee for an hour."

"Norm?"

"Yes, Father."

"Dubbs is getting tanked over at the NCO Club. Your locked door probably isn't a bad idea." Paul said that with a worried look.

"I've got food, booze, regulations to follow, and a sink to piss in," I said with a salute. "I'm locked in for the duration."

"Good," he said, and then added, "but why don't you pack up all of those unanswered questions as quickly as you can and come out and join the living? You're breaking up the old gang, and there's nobody to remind the Koreans that somebody gives a shit. Okay?"

"Don't worry. I'll soon be done." And I shut the door.

The cheeseburger was delicious. Goldman had put fries on the plate, along with a generous supply of ketchup. I got my box of pretzels, too. They were good and salty. I sat down on the floor, put my back up against the wall, and slowly sucked on salty pretzel sections. I washed them down with another splash of Beam. Everything was quiet, except for my crunching.

I thought: if I were to go out right then, how much of my life would you be able to learn if you went through my stuff? And how much, I asked, did Father Paul or Goldman really know about me? Should you write something down? Leave a bio sketch in a drawer? That thought, plus a little help from the Beam, made me roll a cheap, black and white two-reeler of my life for myself, made up of what I thought were the significant events.

I decided that the first thing I could remember was an image. It was a small me standing in front of a wooden fence looking at a round, circular mosaic mass. I put my finger out and touch its center, and it scatters, swirls, by itself. Little bugs I guess, huddled together in that tight circle, made to scatter by my touch. Little round bugs with fast little legs. My first memory.

Then I'm sick. Polio. I'm in and out of hospitals and finally end up in the place where I meet Pinocchio and Luther, the place where the beds of kids stretched out so far beyond mine on either side. Pinocchio tells me what's happening down past him; Luther gives me the word from his side. The nurses tell and retell the story I say to Luther, "Are you black?" And he says, "I don't think so." Cute, they say, and they tell it to my mom and dad on visiting day.

From that place I have the memory of the artist, the wonderful guy who comes to see us and draws these great pictures on big sheets of paper he has on this big easel. He does it with chalk—different colors—and he draws what the kids yell out: "Draw a cow." "Draw a baseball player." "Draw a truck." "Draw a little boy riding a horse." He can draw anything. If he picks up on your idea, you're a hero and you get the picture.

Other images from there. Nurses change the small babies, and I see the difference between boys and girls. Once a nurse changes the diaper of a red-headed kid. The crap is the same color as the hair. For a long time I think that's a truth too, like the differences. And from Pinocchio I learn about death. From Luther and the artist I learn that colors are neat.

My two-reeler went on. I'm home. One of my legs is skinnier than the other, and I'm very weak. My mother works with me. My father has that worried look all the time. "I never thought I'd have a kid that had problems like this," he says to the men who sit with him in the kitchen and drink beer. They all work at the J & L steel mill and wear work clothes. Their hands are big and always dirty. They dare anyone to "mess with me or mine."

Everyone lives in the same kind of house. Some of the houses are row houses. Ours is a duplex. Mr. and Mrs. Schmidt live next door. She looks at my skinny leg and says, "Oh, my God." In both of our houses there are Infants of Prague and pictures of Mary and Jesus showing their hearts. The entire block is praying for my leg.

And then I remember that it's time for me to start school. My dad says, "How in the hell can a kid like that keep up?" The doctor tells Mom that I shouldn't walk.

So she pulls me in a wagon. Every day she pulls me to school and back in a wagon. I can get around okay when I'm there. "He's going to be an educated man," she screams at Dad. "Somebody like him can make it if he's educated."

All of the kids laugh at me because she pulls me in that wagon. I sit and look forward, but I know who they are. I'm six, and she pulls me. I'm seven, and she pulls me. I'm eight, and I can make it—both ways—by myself. The leg is filling out. I'm strong enough, and it works well enough that I can just about run away from the guys who laugh at me and run me home from school. I'm running, and it's "A miracle, Mrs. Whitman," says the doctor. I have to run.

But I'm taking names: Louie Hubchek, Bobby Lamanski, Freddie

Schmidt, Tommie Haluka, and Sam Husinski. Someday, I tell myself, I'm going to clean up on them all.

Meanwhile, my dad makes me watch the fights on TV and eat raw onion sandwiches. He was a boxer, and he shows me punches. The fights bore me, the onions are horrible, and his fighting pointers don't look anything like the brand of street fighting I'm seeing in the neighborhood. But I bide my time, turn out to be straight, and the leg keeps on filling out.

I go to Saint Philip's grade school. The schoolyard is rough. But inside I'm good. I can write, talk, and draw. I can especially talk. I get that from listening to the radio. I listen to the announcers, and I practice talking like them. *Jack Benny, Fibber Magee and Mollie, the Green Hornet, Hit Parade, Al Jolson, the Lone Ranger, Jack Armstrong*, and—best of all—*Edgar Bergen and Charlie McCarthy*. They teach me to talk. Their announcers give me the correct pronunciation. It's different from the street I live on. My dad says, "I never thought I'd have some kind of an egghead for a kid," to the men he sits in the kitchen and drinks beer with.

I decide to become a priest. One day, Sister Mary Placede says, "Now boys and girls, Jesus was the perfect man. He died at age thirty-five, the perfect age, and he was exactly six feet tall, the perfect height." I think about that a second and say, "How could he be exactly six feet, sister?"

"He was exactly that," she says.

"But from where?" I ask. "I mean skin compresses. You're taller in the morning than you are at night. And hair can be pressed down, too."

Memory. Image. She's standing in front of me. "Don't argue with me, Norman. Jesus Christ was six feet tall."

"He couldn't have been 'exactly' six feet, sister. And even if he were, that's not the big point anyway."

She takes the ruler and raps me on the knuckles. "Jesus Christ was six feet tall." Rap. "Jesus Christ was six feet tall." Rap. "Say it with me, Norman." Rap. "Jesus Christ was six feet tall." Bloody knuckles. I abandon the idea of holy orders.

But they were good days. Good images. I see the faces of Mom, Dad, aunts, uncles, and friends that flicker on the home movie in my mind. Days of playing in the summer. Days when kids come for you to play, pressing their noses against the screen door. It leaves a tic-tac-toe mark on the nose. By noon everybody has that mark, and, hopefully, a friend or two to play with from the effort.

And images of getting good and dirty. There is a great ball field near the house. The dirt there is refined, like silk. It covers you. A couple of times a summer some kid who is covered, coated with that fine grained silky dirt, would get hurt or mad or beat up and then he'd cry like hell. The tears run down the bare chest in rivers, turning him into a zebra. It dries. He would be a zebra all day, with African warrior designs on his cheeks: Zebra Boy.

And always during the grade school days I see my father worried about me. He'd been so strong all of his life he was unable to cope with "a sickly kid." Somehow he feels responsible. He takes my pulse all the time. He tells me not to get overheated, not to get wet. Fast heartbeat means trouble, he thinks. Getting wet can bring back polio. Stay dry and calm.

Mom keeps working with me. "He's coming along fine," says the doctor at the clinic. But dad takes my pulse, asks about my habits, and frets over my appetite. "You won't shit. You won't eat. You won't sleep," he says to me. And he tells the guys in the kitchen who drink beer with him that he'll "never have any more kids."

This party all the relatives gave came up on the memory flick. The party was so big that it was held in two houses. I see myself at Aunt Helen's with the older cousins. Some are in high school but others are in the union and working with dad at the mill. He got them in.

Cousin Andy—they call him Crazy Andy—is making up games to play. I insist on playing. They say no. I insist. So they put the funnel in the top of my pants, put my head back, place a quarter on my forehead, and say, "Try to get the quarter in the funnel." In slow motion I see myself bring the head forward, the quarter actually falls into the funnel, but it gurgles. I put two and two together. They have also poured water in the funnel while I'm bending backwards. It's a trick. My pants are soaked.

Out of the corner of my eye I see my dad passing a doorway. He sees it all as he passes. I see the look on his face. He also puts two and two together, and I see the anger on his face as he realizes that I'm wet. "Don't you fuckers know he can get polio again if he gets wet?" he yells at the cousins. They cringe. He's the tough guy of the family. They literally fear for their front teeth, their whole ribs.

"I ought to clean up on youse right now," he says with a big fist poised in front of Crazy Andy's face. But instead, he says he's got to get me home to dry clothes. So he pushes me out the door, to the house up the street, so we can get Mom.

All the way up the street I'm bouncing off the end of his foot. He's kicking my ass up the street. He loves me. He's worried. "Jesus Christ," he says from behind, "I tell you not to get wet and you get wet." Me and Dad, working our way up the street.

This car stops. The window rolls down and the driver says, "Hey, you, we don't treat kids like that in this neighborhood." Dad stops in disbelief. I know what's running through his mind. He treats me great. He loves me so much that he's out of his mind with worry about me getting wet. This is a life saving act here. He's getting me to dry clothes, to home, and kicking my ass because I've endangered my own life.

"Oh, yeah," he says, and he goes over to the car, gets the door open, and creams the guy over and over again before he can even think about what's happening. The engine is still running. The car is on the street. The door slams shut. I see the poor guy, blood on his face, just sitting in his car with this dumbfounded look. One eye is slammed shut.

"That's how we treat guys who push in where they ain't supposed to in my neighborhood," he yells at the guy, all beat up and sitting in his idling car. "This kid means everything to us," he adds.

My flick continues. Reel two. I go to the public high school. You can't tell the difference between my legs. I lift weights. I have good friends. I'm all As. National Honor Society. President of the homeroom. But I belong to one of the toughest gangs in that part of the city. Switchblade. Some of the Rules of Engagement: chains, no knives. Fists only. Anything goes. Whoever sees cops coming first sounds the alarm. Everybody scatters. Nobody rats on nobody. Pick an option and rumble.

One by one, I find the guys who laughed at me and ran me home from grade school. I bloody the noses and close the eyes of Louie Hubchek, Bobby Lamanski, Freddie Schmidt, Tommie Haluka, and Sam Husinski. I also win first prize in the citywide science fair ("The Use of Radioisotopes in Medicine").

The school—Inverse Mather High School—is known all over Pittsburgh. Just say Inverse Mather and the wimps from Mt. Lebanon give you plenty of room on the streetcar. Mechanical drawing is usually only offered in the fall because somebody is stabbed with the dividers and they close it down—again—until next fall. Our football team is awful, but we always win the big rumble behind the stands. Neighborhoods hold their breath when we play the local team and come pouring in, wearing our maroon-and-white Inverse Mather jackets or black ones, the kind Brando wears in *Wild One*.

I learn a lot from the guys I run with. Carver Washington and I talk a lot in wood shop. He's a "colored kid." He likes the way I almost strangled Tommie Haluka to death. He likes the reason: Revenge.

He tells me he doesn't have the same chance in school I do. I say it isn't so. "Watch the way she looks at me," he tells me in music class. He tells me secrets. Like about ash. Ash is the fine powder of dry skin a colored guy can scrape on his arm. White guys can't make ash.

Carver is smart. One day Miss Hadden says to him, "Thank God you're not like the rest of them." He tells her, "Hell, my mother is the rest of them. What the fuck do you mean—the rest of them?" Things get worse for Carver. One day in music the principal and two cops come to the door and say, "Could we please see Carver Washington?" He puts his hand on my arm and says, "See you later, man. Do something for both of us." And I never see him again. He goes to Thorn Hill. Armed robbery. He shot another black man.

Most of the kids in the school are poor. Carver is poor. He and a bunch of others stand at the bottom of the big stone stairways and stop kids on their way to the lunchroom. You get by them if you have "a dime, man." The wimps always pay up, or they don't get to the lunch ticket machines. Some guys steal hubcaps. Guys like my friend Bob Kelly roll drunks. Carver went too far.

I see us in class. Always a mess. Lots of horseplay and moving around. The teachers yell for order but they know better. I do the homework and give it to my buddies. Not all of it. They don't want every assignment. Just enough to pass.

There's Big Rod and Phil. These two guys have no fathers. They both wear blue shirts and black pants to school. The shirts say SUNOCO on the right side, with "Rod" or "Phil" sewn over their left pockets. They work the night shift, pumping gas, waiting until they can leave school. They help support their families. Rod is over seven feet tall. A giant. A freak. He wears glasses that look like the bottoms of Coke bottles. He stutters. But nobody comments on any of it.

On the day we have a substitute, it's always the same. Rod and Phil come in and go to their usual chairs in the back of the room. They have worked all night. They climb in the chairs and sleep, sometimes leaning up against the back wall on two chair legs. We all know to be quiet. The back row is theirs. The regular teachers know that, too. You don't bother them.

"Just a minute," the sub says. "What are you two doing?" Standing above Rod he pokes at the giant's arm. We all suggest that the sub should leave things alone. But, no, he pushes it.

Rod opens his eyes. They fill the big thick lenses with wide open amazement. The pupils seem as big as your fist. "What the fuck are you do . . . do'n?" he says, as much to the room in general as to the sub. He expects us to keep the order of things. "What the f-fuck did you let h-him wake me for?"

"This is a classroom, not a bedroom," says the sub.

By that time Phil wakes up and says, "Take it easy, man."

"Don't you talk like that to me, mister," says the sub.

"Look," says Phil. "We sleep here, and you teach up there. Nobody bothers anybody. Go back and teach."

Rod's limbs are filling with life by this time. He's slow and stiff at first in these situations. It takes time for him to be able to comprehend and become mobile. He's like a robot that needs time to start functioning. But finally he does, and he pushes the chair forward onto all four legs, and that lets him stand up. He towers over the sub.

"Shut the . . . the fuck up or I-I'll kill you," he says. "Leave us sleep or I-I'll kill you." And like always, order is once more restored.

On another occasion a teacher threatened to call his mother. Rod loves his mother. The call is never made. When Mr. Hathaway says he would flunk Rod, Rod promised instant death as well. He always passes. Just before he quit school we see a movie and in it this sheriff had broken the hand of a gunslinger. Rod changes his threat from death to "I-I'll break y-your f-fucking hands if you d-do."

My best buddy is Chuck Bateman. On the flick I see us getting drunk together, swiping beer and a mason jar's worth of whiskey from our dads' bottles. We are always drunk on weekends. Sometimes we nip at school. He works at Mr. Yates' hardware store. Yates has this old truck with a wooden railing built around the rear bed.

Chuck is his stock boy and makes deliveries. I wait on a corner for him and then we drive around together. It's like having our own truck. Sometimes he delivers sand. It doesn't take long for us to figure out that, if we get some money together and have me call fake orders in for sand, we can have the truck for our own use. The sand is incredibly cheap. In all sorts of voices, I phone orders in to old Yates all day, giving my address as far away as I can stretch it.

We even help Chuck bag up the sand. Old Yates is a hunchback. He never comes out to check. He never questions the orders. We put in gas and somebody turns the mileage back.

Now comes reel three. Maybe this will be the last one. The Beam is taking its toll. I go from Yate's truck to my favorite movies. We go to a lot of movies in those days. Cowboys. War. Musicals. They're all great, but the musicals bother me a little.

A lot of them star Van Johnson and Judy Garland. There's a plot all right, but in the middle of the action they often look at each other and start singing. It doesn't matter where, either. They could be on a boat, walking down the street, sitting in the park, or in the middle of a big store.

The other people, strangers, don't seem to think anything of it. As a matter of fact, they smile and even clap along—just drop everything—and clap along to the tune of the song. Never any problem with it, no matter where old Van breaks into song.

Not real. That couldn't happen in real life. I decided I'd test it.

Once Judy and Van looked into each other's eyes and broke into song in a drug store. The "Ding, ding, ding, went the trolley" thing had happened on an old streetcar. In both cases, the people in the drugstore and on the streetcar had joined in. The conductor really loved it; the soda jerk even pulled levers in time with the music. Nobody got worried when Van jumped up on the tables, or even the counter.

I choose Ralph's Drugs for my field test location. Ralph's is a dump, but it has the soda counter and a couple of booths and tables. It will do.

On the promise of a case of beer or two, plus some excitement, I talk Chuck and a few others into helping me. All they have to do is filter into the store, sit at two of the tables, and clap in time to the tune when my musical begins. I'll play the part of Van. There is no female lead.

The image of that Wednesday afternoon rolls across the screen. At one table there's Al, Art, Dave, and Ross. I come in with Chuck and a kid named Mike Hubcheck. Everyone is in place. Cue talent. Action.

"You know," I say, "this has been a great day for me. Everything went right." I say it loud. Ralph looks up from his place back behind the prescription counter for just a second. Some old ladies are looking around. One old bat is getting fixed up by Ralph. The other druggist is wiping up by the soda counter.

"In fact, I've never felt SO GOOD," I say to my table. It's loud. Then I start singing. "Zippity-do-dah. Zippity-A. My, oh, my, what a wonderful day. Plenty of sunshine going my way. Zippity-do-dah, zippity-A." I'm loud and it sounds pretty good. Ralph is transfixed, looking at me. The old ladies are raising their purses up to their breasts, clutching them there. That's a normal reflex reaction in the neighborhood.

The other druggist has turned around and watches in disbelief as I get up and walk around. I come up to an old girl, smile at her, and give it: "Mister bluebird's on my shoulder." Then I point to where he'd be perched. "It's the truth. It's actual. Everything is satisfactual." She's scared to death.

My buddies are clapping now and moving back and forth from the waist. But the rest of the store is reacting as if there's a robbery in progress. Some of the old girls edge their way out the door. Ralph still doesn't know what to do.

As my performance continues, I'm up on a chair, ready to mount the table that's empty. "Zippity-do-dah. Zippity-A," I sing as I hit the table edge the wrong way and slip off. That's it. Ralph is around the counter and the other guy follows his lead. I hear someone say, "Oh, My, God," another normal reflex reaction. As I go out the door, I laugh and shout, "Wonderful feel'n. Wonderful day." The others are already one block ahead of me. The musical comedy theory of life only works in the movies.

Things like that made me famous as a kid in the neighborhood. It got me elected class president. My grades were good enough for a scholarship. My dad's reaction is one of "I'll be damned" and "He's going to be one of them educated muckity-mucks." Both legs look exactly alike.

Reel Four: I meet Angie my senior year in high school. I see her for the first time on a blind date arranged by a kid in our school who somehow got going steady with a broad from a ritzy section of Pittsburgh. I infiltrate too. Angie and I hit it off right away. She comes down the stairs to the living room, so I see her feet, legs, waist, and breasts first. Then the pretty face. All great.

I was dating a girl who wore a blazer and went to Mt. Lebanon High School. Her father, the steel executive, is impressed with my scholarship to Maynard, a rich boy's school. For some reason, my third reel goes into that funny fast-speed mode. Like flicks of Woodrow Wilson, World War One charges over the trenches, and Charlie Chaplin shorts, I see myself go off to school, elope, make love and sandwiches, run rides, have two kids, work at the radio station, join the Air Force, and get off the Tolsan choggy. Finally little flaws dance across the screen, the picture fades and clouds, but just before the reel ends and slaps the leader against the projector I think I see a glimpse of Packer tipping an old straw hat at me.

Blank screen. Images gone. Beam making my head spin. Still in Oyster's room. I had reviewed the events of my life, what I would have left him to know, but I still knew nothing more about Packer. I only knew his wardrobe, his magazines, the words of his friends, the news from his home, and the looks of his room from a couple of angles. Oh yeah, I had seen the nude pictures of his mistress now in jail for his murder. The thought flashes through my mind that the one with Dubbs and the two girls needs to be published.

The clothes told me he had expected to dress for occasions. The pictures told me he searched for titillation. That he lived out sexual fantasies with Adja and even took pictures. The letters to his friends told me he was depressed and had been before an Academy honor board. The ones from his folks were touching. It was nice to know he had loving folks who followed his old team and remembered how good he was with an old outboard.

But I had a hard time coming to any conclusions. In the morning I'd pack up everything that wasn't on the trash pile and send it to Virginia. There wasn't anything more to do, except maybe have a few more Beams.

"Whitman. Open up." Dubbs was back. My watch said three in the morning. "Open up." He sounded on-his-ass drunk.

I stood up, reeling a little myself, and went right over to the door. A click and a pull, and there he was in front of me, standing there wild-eyed and white-knuckled.

"Are you through going through his stuff?" he slurred.

"It's done," I said.

He looked past me, at the desk and then on to the pile of trash. "I wanna look through that."

"You will like hell," I said, putting my hand up.

"You don't put your hand up at me, you little rich college boy, or I'll knock you on your ass."

That was it. I grabbed him by the shirt and pushed him out into the hall, with my clutch doing the moving. I held him up. I lifted him, and I pushed his chest with it. I had a real fistful of military fatigues. I wasn't playing around. We moved so fast he only stood up because I was holding him up. His shoes hit the floor like little puppet shoes. He was riding on my fist all the way down the Q hall.

As I traveled him over the linoleum floor, down the hall, I shouted at him. "I'm not rich at all, you dumb bastard, and no bully like you is ever going to kick my ass, anywhere, anytime. And you're not going to look at Packer's stuff because that's a finished job, and there's nothing left that has anything to do with you at all. I've absolutely taken all the shit I'm ever again going to take from you."

By that time we were in the Q living room. His door was right around the corner. I kept him off balance. "Now, if you're thinking about giving me a hard time, you just remember you tried to interfere with me doing a job I was appointed to do by the motherfucker in charge. And if that's not enough, let me tell you that I'm one of the great asskickers. I'll break your fucking hands if you don't get in your room right now and sleep it off."

I had the shit scared out of him. Then I softened and said, "You're done, Dubbs. Whatever it is, it's over."

He didn't say a word. He didn't look at me. He just turned and went for his room. He opened the door, paused, and said, "I'm going to be reassigned to Osan to finish up my tour." Then he walked in and closed the door behind him. We were almost even.

20

In Charge

I racked out in my own room. I had locked Oyster's room before I hit the sack, but somehow I didn't think it was now as critical. As soon as my head went down on the pillow, I was asleep; it was around four a.m., but my head was strangely clear and I felt very much at peace with myself.

When I woke up, it was eight in the morning, and even though I had gotten only four hours of sleep, I still felt clear and easy. I even went over for breakfast and found Father Paul there working on an omelet.

"I thought I heard some noise last night, Norm." Paul was concentrating on his food so he didn't have to look at me.

I could tell he had a sly look on his face. "Just getting those questions packed away, that's all. Took your advice and got the whole job done."

When old Dutch came in, I said, "Good," because I needed to get some items packed and others destroyed.

"Ja, sure, Norm. I send my boys to see you anytime you vant. Vee haf krates ready now."

The three of us spent the rest of breakfast talking about old Oyster, recalling funny, nice things about him: how he loved that old hound dog, the fun he had fishing, and all of the wonderfully eccentric things he had done to make us laugh.

By noon the boxes were filled. Dutch's people had done a beautiful job on them. He had called them crates, but they were really handcrafted redwood boxes, roughly four foot square, with hinged lids. Dutch's people had a stencil-making machine in the shop. After I had given the word to nail them down, this little Korean man sprayed the stencils with black paint. When he peeled them off, they said:

To Mr. and Mrs. Fred C. Packer
121 Cliffmont
Oyster, VA 23310

Dutch's guys put the trash in burlap sacks. In went the magazines, the torn-up pictures, and the letters I decided to pitch. I followed the sacks as they were carried up to the incinerator. It was already fired up and blazing. In they went. The burlap bags kept it all compacted together. It burned as a mass. They'd open a little metal door every once in a while and poke at the pile. On the inside of the pile you could still see centerfold girls yet untouched by the flames, but they'd ignite when the pokes tore away their protective shell of hot leafy carbon. Pretty soon it was all charred, burned beyond recognition.

Later that night I ran into Dutch going into the movie and he said, "Vee also made up krates for Major Dubbs, ja. He takes a move?" I just smiled and gave it the palms-up, raised-shoulders look.

The flick that night really left an impression on me. We watched *Zhivago* live through his times. He saw one world die and another come out of the ashes. Russia was a fucked up place when he was born, but the Reds didn't do much to bring things around. There was something about Russia itself, something in the people that scared the hell out of me.

One scene in the movie hit home. It involves this young shiny officer who gets up on a barrel and tries to stop a bunch of deserting troops, to persuade them to do their duty. He looks like a young aristocratic Russian. He's impressive, and they almost—just for a minute—obey him. But the barrel he's standing on caves in and he crashes through into the cold water within it. His whole image is destroyed. He takes this pratfall and that breaks the spell.

The troops laugh, and then somebody takes direct aim and shoots through the barrel a couple of times and he's dead, coloring the water with his blood. I thought to myself, you better be careful about the barrels you stand on. All of the enlisted guys were in the movie that night. I wanted to sink down in my seat just a tad.

The next day I pulled hill, and it looked like I'd be pulling it every day for a long time. I got a call from Osan that the choggy would be there the following morning and that I should be there to meet it. The sergeant in Osan didn't know why, but just be there. He also was told to ask if I had Lieutenant Packer's things ready to ship and I said that was "affirmative."

I hadn't been off the phone for a minute when it rang again. It was Colonel Judd, the JAG, calling from the site. "Whitman, I just wanted you to know that Mr. Sims and I are back on Tolsan, and we're ready to go out on that choggy tomorrow. Mr. Kim's got us fixed up with rooms in the Q tonight."

"Okay, sir," I said. "What's going to happen with Adja? Can you tell me, sir, or is that out of line right now?"

"Well, she'll go through the Korean system. She's been charged, but she turned up pregnant and that's going to complicate things."

"Who'd she say?"

"What would you think?"

"Packer," I said, feeling a little twinge of anger.

"Yes. Gee-eye get her pregnant, and she very upset because he no marry her."

"So she's off the hook?"

"Don't know, but this ain't going to be even a page five story, and that's really a Godsend. Nobody needs publicity right now."

"She'd have to be pretty far along for it to be Oyster's, sir. You know that, huh?"

"Whitman, listen a minute. Colonel Canada's going to be on that choggy tomorrow. He wants to see you and Colonel Lee. How about setting that up?"

"Yes, sir," I said, reading his signal that we weren't going to talk about Adja anymore.

"And, Norm?" he said with a softer voice.

"Yes, sir."

"Father Paul says you two can take Sims and me down to get some linen in Soopoo. Feel up to it?"

"Yes," I said, realizing how wonderful the idea sounded to get away and drive down the ocean road. "You bet I want to, sir."

"Okay. I've got to spend some time with Major Dubbs right now. We'll see you after your shift sometime."

I rolled down off the hill at four, gathered up Father Paul, Judd, and Sims, and we took off down the ocean road in the brightness of a Tolsan April afternoon. We didn't stop at the farm because of time. As it was, Father Henry hinted that things were shutting down for the night, but when he brought Sister Mary Elinore into the rectory parlor, just beamed at seeing us. "Af carse you can shop," she said. "I'll just open the near dar, and you can pick out all the linen you'd want."

They did. And I even bought a beautiful woolen sweater for Angie. But no invitation for dinner came from Michael Francis Henry, and I wasn't surprised. I heard him ask Paul if there "wasn't a bit of a death" at the site, and Paul answered that it was "a total death." He gave no more details.

We drove down into Soopoo after that and walked around by the docks. The Korean fishermen had thousands of these little fish laid out all over the dock area and roads. It smelled to high heavens. But some old guy who spoke pretty good English explained to us the fish was going to be fertilizer. Tolsan, he said, was one of the few places in the Asian Theatre where the farmers didn't use night soil, or human waste, to fertilize the fields. "They feed it all to the pigs," I said after he left.

We also watched a boat bring in its catch and unload it on the dock. The fishermen sorted all of these strange big ocean fish out into boxes, but I noticed that they were throwing away some big lobster-looking things. They looked for all the world like lobster, but they didn't have the big juicy claws that usually went with Maine lobsters.

Those guys didn't speak any English, and I couldn't find our friend who told us about the fertilizer, so I made gestures that tried to ask, "You don't eat?" They got it after a couple of tries and laughed and shook their heads no. With a pitching gesture, they pointed to the ocean. They were telling me they threw them back. "Can I have one?" I motioned. Yes, the nodding head said, and one of the guys even put it in a can filled with salt water. I gave him fifty won, about five bucks. He bowed and probably told the others I was crazy.

Paul said there was a very good restaurant near the docks that the farm Fathers had taken him to once. So we all went there and that turned out to be the idea of the century. The place was just great. It looked like any other teahouse-restaurant in Korea, but we got royal treatment and food that was out of this world. Sims and Judd were impressed.

"You see, you guys," Sims told us, "we can't eat much of the local food in the Osan area. But the docs say Tolsan is pretty much okay."

"It's because of that fertilizer system for one thing," said the lawyer. "I guess the pork is really the only thing you've always got to watch."

I thought about my friend up under the outhouse.

We had this great soup that night. It had spaghetti-like noodles and things that looked like wontons. It had a clear broth, with all sorts of vegetables mixed in. The main dish was something they call *pullkoki*, strips of beef you cook at the table on this brass grate filled with red-hot coals. It was delicious.

"Norm," Judd suddenly said in the middle of dinner, "I've been talking with Colonel Canada the past couple of days pretty regularly." He sucked in a mouthful of noodles. "And he talked a little bit with General Pitts the other day, too. I'd just make sure you're down on the flight line good and early tomorrow and looking your best." He chewed some more and then looked me in the eyes. "Just a friendly tip in exchange for the trip here and the hospitality, okay?"

Christ, I thought, I forgot to tell, Lee about the meeting.

But it didn't matter because he was already there by the time I got to the flight line the next day. He gave me his big smile and walked over to meet me as I parked the jeep. "So Colonel Canada again comes to my site?"

"Yes, sir," I said, showing my relief at seeing him. "He wants to talk to me and asks if you can also talk with him."

And just then the old goon made an initial pass over the strip. I hadn't been as early as Judd had suggested, but I was spit-shined and wearing my blues. Paul had promised to bring Judd and Sims down after an early morning shopping trip he was going to take them on with Goldman at the helm of the ambulance. I saw them, standing by the ambulance, further down the line, bags laid out and ready for the trip back.

Not surprisingly, Dubbs was decked out in his blues, too, waiting by the AFAG jeep. Packer's boxes were on one of the trucks, along with some others. It seemed like a lot of suitcases were with them as well.

"What's going on, sir?" It was Sergeant Mountain. "What's up? Major Dubbs says he's going to Osan."

"Well, Shirt, believe me, I have no idea. Colonel Canada's on board. I promise I'll tell you as much as I can as soon as I can. Okay?"

"Yes, sir, but this place is really getting to be too much."

"I know, Mountain. I'll let you know when I can."

He saluted and walked off to the trucks. We hadn't really said much to the guys about anything. I felt bad about it. Though I'm sure Goldman kept them posted.

Pretty soon I was back in the flight line ops building. This time it was Canada, Colonel Lee, and me. Nobody else.

Canada had given all of his attention to Lee right from the start. Even at this little meeting it was like I wasn't there. "Colonel Lee," he said, "we've made the decision to reassign Major Dubbs to Osan. In the meantime, Captain Whitman here will be your chief counterpart. He'll carry out both the ADOT and the AFAG function." He still didn't even look my way.

"That makes me very happy," Lee said. "Captain Widman is a very good man for my controllers."

"Well, sir," Canada continued, "I just wanted to make sure that was okay with you. And I wanted to say that if there's ever any reason whatsoever, you call me directly if things don't work out."

Shit. He really was pompous about that, like I was some kind of a bad character or something. I felt like telling him to shove it.

"No. I will never have to do that," Lee said.

Lee was worth staying for. I'd work my ass off for him.

"Okay," said Canada as he got up from the table. He shook hands with Lee, and I followed them out the door. We were all the way to the airplane when he finally stopped and looked at me. "I'll be sending you some new staff to fill up the holes pretty soon. When they get settled in, come up on the next choggy to see me and get the ADOT orientation brief from my ops officer."

"Yes, sir," I said.

"But make sure you let us know when you're coming and make sure you get on my calendar for an hour or so."

"Yes, sir, I will."

When I turned, I saw Dubbs, one bag in his hand, getting ready to walk up the ramp aircraft stairs and board his last choggy. He looked a little grim.

I reached into the inside breast pocket of my blues and brought out a sealed white envelope, folded in half. Photo size.

"Here," I said. "I'd like to wish you luck."

He stared for a minute, then took it. I shook his hand. And that was it. We were even.

Funny how things come to an end. You think there's going to be fanfare, bands, speeches. But it's always kind of unspecial. It just ends.

And beginnings are strange, too. The choggy took off; the trucks, fire engines, jeeps, and ambulance all headed up the road for the site; and I suddenly realized that I was the guy in charge of it all. Mountain's words to me had half sunk in. But with the airplane's departure, it hit me like a ton of bricks. My God, I thought, I was the site chief.

Nobody had come up to me after the plane took off, not even Doc or Paul. They were giving me a little room.

On the way back in the ADOT jeep, I damn near panicked. What the hell to do? Then I thought, what would I want me to do if I were one of the guys I was now in charge of? I'd want to know what I wanted people to do. I'd want direction. Okay. I decided to hold a meeting.

Mountain wasn't a dummy. When I came pulling up, he was waiting for me. It was only eleven-thirty.

"Sergeant Mountain."

"Yes, sir?"

"Movies come in on the choggy?"

"Yes, sir."

"What's the movie tonight?"

"I think it's *The Great Race*, sir," he said.

"Well, look, Mountain," I said, moving closer to him. "Do you think you could ask everyone to be there for sure for the movie and then to show up about a half hour early?"

"Yes, sir," he said with just a bit of a smile.

Well, I thought, I could maybe talk to everyone then and the movie might make the effort worth it. If they don't like what I say, then they'll still have a movie to watch.

After receiving Mountain's salute, I picked up five letters from Angie, put them in my room, and walked over to the Korean HQ. I wanted to see if Lee was in.

He was, and I half think he was expecting that I'd be over. "You come in my office, and I get tea," he said.

"This is my first call to your office as the GI site chief, sir," I said. "I only come to tell you that I am happy to have nothing between us any longer."

"We have already make our agreement when we talk before. That is still a good one for me," he said and put out his hand.

"Then for us, I hope high skies and fat horses together," I said. We both broke out in laughter. The tea came.

That night at seven o'clock I walked into a full theater. When I entered, Mountain called the room to attention. I didn't expect that.

"Take your seats, please," I said, coming up the aisle. "We'll do that once a year," I added.

I came around the front row and wished myself good luck. Goldman and Paul were front-row center.

"I was going to say something about how some men have radar sites thrust upon them, but decided it was too corny." Thank God they smiled at that. "This has been a hell of a week for everyone. Let me just say that Lieutenant Packer's death was sad as hell. I know you all liked him very much. God knows I did."

They were a good bunch, I thought. They were making it easy on me.

"Sergeant Goldman here . . . and Father Fisher . . . well, they did us proud when the heat was on. I'd just like to thank them. And I'd like to thank you for your patience with the way things have been unsettled lately. That's really what I want to talk about, and I'll make it quick so we can see the movie." I tried to look at each face as I spoke. "I realized too late that we might have had a meeting sooner so you could have known everything that was going on. But, in spite of that, this site never skipped a beat while we were working out our problems. I mean, it was just like today. You all had the plane unloaded, while the food was cooking, and the vehicles were being maintained, and people like Sergeant Ellis never misplaced a fork." I got a little murmur, a little laugh of approval on that one.

"So, I guess I'm saying that I just want all of that to continue. You all know what you're doing, and God knows you've been doing it damn well. For the past ten months or so, Major Dubbs has been here in case you needed a hand with something. I think he did a good job with that. He's been reassigned to Osan, so I'll try to fill in here for a while." I paused for a moment. "I'll support you, and I'm going to really need your support. Let's just keep doing what we do."

They applauded. I never felt so good in my life. Boy did they have a ringer for a commander now.

Yet things did go pretty well. I made up my mind that I'd keep a low and easy profile, putting my faith in what I thought was a pretty good bunch of people. That wasn't what you'd call military genius, but it worked. My people rose to the occasion.

Gradually, I did make a few changes. I gave Paul some responsibilities and encouraged Mountain to be more of a First Sergeant. We had regular coffee meetings with the sergeants in charge of the sections, and I generally let it be known that I'd like to help improve things where we might need it. One of the things I heard all the time was that the NCO club needed more income. The men bought things there, played the slot machines, and kept the till going, but it depended on the support of the tiny membership to keep going. Very little came in from the outside.

I gave that some thought and asked Goldman to come over to the Q and look at what I had in an old lard can.

"A rotten crayfish, sir?" he asked. "You called me away from my post to see a rotten crayfish? It smells. Why not collect bugs, or something less messy."

"Okay, okay, listen," I said, putting the can down on the grass. "Look at the size of that tail, Goldman."

"Sir. Sir. That's even too weird, too perverse for even you. I've never heard of such a thing."

"Come on, Goldman. I mean it. I'm trying to be serious here. That's the same thing that we buy frozen. Rock lobster. Right?"

He kicked over the big can and pushed it away from the crayfish. "Yeah. Yeah. It is." He was interested. "But what's next?"

"I think we could get these real cheap in, say, Soopoo, from the fishermen. Koreans don't eat these things, but I'll bet we can. I'll bet they're just like those rock lobster tails."

"And?"

"Let's get over to Soopoo, get a couple, and see what they taste like. For starters, we could sell 'em in the NCO club. If it works out, I think I might have another idea." What I had in mind was having the club offer a cheap lobster dinner the hunters could buy when they were here. The club's cheeseburgers and fries just didn't pull in any great food business. Most all of the hunters went after the dining hall food.

Goldman sent Mr. Kwak out for a couple of the big crayfish, and the tails turned out to be pretty good. As a matter of fact, they were delicious. The lobster dinner was soon the attraction in the NCO club dining room. For a while, everyone ate lobster like crazy, and the till started to grow. Problem was, it still came from our own guys. But we were ready for the hunters. I didn't know it then, but those old Korean crayfish were going to work out even better than I had imagined.

The reality of my new position was that I had been working my ass off. That was helping me forget Oyster's death, but I was also getting tired of pulling hill every day, all day, and then coming back at night to the headquarters to either catch up on paperwork Mountain had for me or to review the requests Colonel Lee and his people were making for specific assistance. I hadn't had a real drink for weeks.

To my rescue, one Wednesday afternoon, the choggy came zooming in, and there were two first lieutenants on board: Dick Fife, a tall guy from Norman, Oklahoma, and Carl Betts, a black from Los Angeles. They had both been about halfway through their tours at Osan and had volunteered to finish up at Tolsan-Do. I was glad to see them. I'd have regular shifts on the hill again.

They "sir'd" me to death the first hour they were on site, so I finally said, "Why not just call me Norm. I'm just the guy who makes out the work schedules and signs the paperwork." I was really kind of hoping Canada would send down a major. Being in charge was a pain.

We had three empty rooms in the Q besides Oyster's. I decided to lock that one up as long as I was on the island. But I did tell Mr. Kim to split his good furniture among my two new charges. They didn't have to know.

It seemed a shame to waste the desk and the dressers. I moved into Dubbs' old room. It had a living room and a bedroom. What the hell, the spoils of command.

Dick and Carl turned out to be good controllers. They knew the procedures in the Korean control environment, and they had already worked with lots of Korean controllers up in Osan. They were young guys, but very capable. Both around twenty-two. I think they looked on Paul and me as old men. Paul maybe, but I was still only twenty-six. Dear God, I thought, please make them send a major.

My new responsibilities were interfering with the good times I had with Paul, the other priests, and Goldman. Paul seemed to be a little moody about that. One night I came back to my room after cleaning up some work and found him staggering up the hall. "Well, Captain Whitman," he said through a snoutful. "I hardly recognized you. It's been so long since you've had time for the common folk."

Despite such annoyances, things were humming along. With three of us pulling hill duty, I started to find more time to do everything I had to do, and, best of all, Colonel Lee and I were getting together a couple of hours every day. He really did have a bunch of long-range needs, not to mention some regular day-to-day things that Dubbs hadn't paid much attention to.

21

"I & I"

I waited two weeks and then booked myself on the choggy for Osan. The place would never know I was gone. The hill was covered, Lee was happy because I was going to hand-carry some of his requests, and the site NCOs never needed me in the first place. As long as there were *yobos*, movies, beer, and lobster tails, I could leave without fear of an insurrection.

That was in the early part of June, and as we bounced down the strip for takeoff, I felt a surge of excitement at the thought of getting the hell away for a while. The old goon climbed away from Tolsan-Do and turned herself toward the mainland. The view of the countryside and the immense stretch of sea was breathtaking. There wasn't a cloud in the sky. Everything was bright blue.

We flew over the ninety miles of ocean that separated Tolsan-Do from Mother Korea and then followed the peninsula northward. The land below was mountainous, the Roof of Korea they called it, but everywhere you could see the Asian cultivation patterns and groups of thatch houses. Once in a while, we passed over larger, more sophisticated towns. They were made up of more familiar structures, mostly made from cement. There was a squareness about the shapes you saw in those towns. The predominant color was brown.

There weren't many trees below. The trees of Korea had been burned down and blown to the four winds by the ravages of the war. Park Chung Hee had millions of young seedlings planted everywhere, but they were still too young to give any color to the brown mountains and hills. Only the farmers contributed the bright greens your eyes loved to find in the middle of all the brown.

Finally, I felt the Osan runway hit the tires. We chugged around and parked in front of the Seventh Aerial Port Squadron, one of the main gateways to the Korean mainland. It had been my launching point to Tolsan-Do six months ago.

I grabbed my B-4 bag and walked down the stairs, thinking I'd lay low for the rest of the afternoon, kind of get myself ready for the ten o'clock appointment I'd made with Canada the next day. But there he was, standing at the bottom of the stairs looking up at me. My God, he'd come down to meet me at the plane. As Ryan O'Donnell would say, it was "himself" in the flesh.

"Hi, country boy," he said, returning my salute.

When he said it, I felt like doing that old classic turnaround to see who he was really talking to. But it was me all right. He even gave me a solid handshake when I got to him.

"Throw your bag in my car here, and we'll start off by getting you into the VOQ." Maybe he was just treating me this way because he wanted to soften the blow of my own reassignment to who knows. Maybe even Leavenworth, I thought.

But I wasn't being reassigned, or replaced for that matter. Canada, as usual, got right to the point as we drove to the VOQ. His attitude toward me remained incredibly personal and warm. "You might guess that I get my best intel about my site chiefs through the Koreans. Lee sends nothing but good signals since the switch, and frankly, before that you were turning around a very bad situation down there. Beyond that, I haven't heard any kicks from my enlisted spies, either. I'm leaving you in the job, Whitman." He was looking straight ahead, smoothly taking the big blue staff car over the paved streets of Osan Air Base. The windows were rolled up and the air-conditioning on. That somehow made the buildings, sights, and people look like a color movie with the sound turned off.

"Well, sir, I'm glad it's going okay," I said, trying to put some enthusiasm in my voice. "I really assumed you'd send down another major."

We pulled up in front of the VOQ, and he turned to look at me as he set the parking brake.

"I learned a long time ago not to throw something off that was going along in balance. You're not my first choice, but things are as I want them to be right now," he said, taking off his hat and wiping the sweat from the back of his neck. "Besides, you said it pretty well yourself. Your folks know what they're doing, and I sent you two young officers who'll fit right in with that. Don't get a big head from what I said. They'll all carry you."

Good. That was the Colonel Canada I had come to know. And that was some spy system he had, too. For a minute there I had been afraid I'd been acting like a lifer or something. There was a world of difference between me and guys like Canada; my entire Boy Scout troop never got beyond the second-class badge.

"Well, look, that's enough business," he said, returning to that cheery planeside mood. "Why don't you get to your room and get squared away, and I'll come back around five or so and pick you up for dinner." This guy was either ice or hot fudge, I thought. But he didn't have to be nice, that was for sure.

"Well, yes, sir, I'd like that very much," I said, getting out while the mood was good. I got my B-4 bag out of the back seat and walked around to the driver's side. I bent down and, realizing I wanted to say something, he rolled down the window. "My dad was an enlisted guy in the Army, sir. I just wanted you to know that he's going to forgive half of Pershing's officers their sins when he finds out a full colonel met his kid at the airplane today."

That took him a few seconds to digest. Then he said, "You tell him there are a lot of sergeants down on Tolsan-Do who would have come looking for me if I hadn't, Appo. I'll see you at five." Then he drove off, a smile on his face. He was Colonel Virgil E. Canada. I liked him an awful lot.

Dinner that night was at Canada's quarters on hill 180, overlooking Osan. That hill had been the site of one of the fiercest battles of the Korean War, he told me on the way over. A lot of Americans had died getting the allies to the top of it. So now there was a group of VIP quarters up there with a lot of first-class meetings and dinner affairs. "Just to rub the North Koreans' nose in it a little," he said. "We 're dug in up here to stay from now on."

That dinner was an event I'll remember for a long time. I felt like an insider. When we got to this little bungalow he lived in, we were met by a houseboy who took our hats. "Everyone else here, sore," he said to Canada as we walked in the door.

It turned out that the colonel had invited two others besides me. I shook hands with Lieutenant Colonel Bill Adams, his operations officer, and an army artillery officer, Lieutenant Colonel Ralph Ellers. Ellers was the army air defense missile representative to the radar ops Canada ran in Osan. Ellers also had a Ranger patch on his uniform. That meant he could "kick your ass with class," as his fellow Rangers would tell you.

We started the evening sitting in the colonel's little living room, the sliding doors wide open, giving us a view of the base below. Nothing but the night air and the view came through the screens. You could watch the lights out on the long runway, parallel strings of blue, with white streaks made by planes taking off and landing in between. The tower light rotated like a lighthouse beacon, and the lights of the base itself added to the total effect. It was beautiful. Up above was a starlit sky. The surrounding mountains were dark, but peppered here and there with tiny pinpoints of light.

The houseboy brought out any drink you wanted. We just sat there, sipping scotches and bourbons, making small talk. The two LCs asked me how I liked Tolsan-Do, and I told them I honestly did. The Army officer told me the island had been a big prisoner-of-war camp during the Korean War. Ellers said that our base there had been much larger during those days. "You guys actually had goons of your own then, believe it or not," he said. I told them it was fascinating to walk around the old Japanese operation. "Lots and lots of history there," said Canada.

The scotch, the easy talk, and the view all made me feel comfortable. And I didn't feel like these three were shoving their rank down my throat either. Canada's relaxed, good-natured side was his asset. He made you feel welcome.

Finally, a little middle-aged lady came out and gave us a cute little bow. "You come now to eat," she said. Her voice was high and sing-song, and she was very charming.

"When Peggy says get up, gentlemen, she means right now," Canada said. We all followed him into the dining room. What a table Peggy had set for us.

We sat at a Western-style table, in high-backed chairs, but everything else about the table was pure Korean feast. "This is a *you kuksa*," Peggy said, pointing to the big steaming crock of soup. It was noodles, chopped pork, and eggs. The eggs sort of floated around, cooked up like scrambled. "And this *shin-sull-lo*; this *mandu*; this *chopvhae*; this *kim*; and this *you pab*." *Pab* was rice.

"On Tolsan we have much *kim*," I said.

"Yes much *kim* on Tolsan-Do," she said smiling at me. *Kim* was dried seaweed. All the others were great meat and vegetable dishes. We helped ourselves to a little of everything.

"Colonel Judd tells me you took him to a great place to eat down on Tolsan, Norm."

Christ, I thought, now I was Norm. "Yes, sir, in Soopoo, a little rustic, but good." I paused and then looked at Peggy, standing at the ready near the head of the table. "But not so good as Peggy makes." That was met with toasts and statements of agreement by all. She winked at me.

Dinner was talk mostly of food and things to see in Seoul. "When I really want to get away from it all," Ellers said, "I check into the Bando for a day or two and just relax. The food right there is great, you know."

"It is, and that reminds me that you, Norm, are going to have to get up to Yong Dong Po for a check-in with the AFAG people up there."

I remembered Dubbs telling me about the two hats he wore. Well, I had inherited them.

"See Colonel Belford up there when you do."

"Forrest Belford, sir?"

"Yes."

"Wasn't he General Pitts' exec?"

"Yes, he got promoted and took a big job there."

It was beginning to be a small Asian Theatre, I thought. The old boy network pretty well had things under control.

More small talk and lots of food, and then dinner was over. We moved back into the living room for green tea. Peggy put the beautiful ceramic teapot on the coffee table and excused herself. Canada seemed to be putting on his business face.

"Gentlemen," he said, clearing his throat and moving on the edge of the couch, "I thought we might break bread tonight and then get a little work out of the way."

Everyone mumbled an enthusiastic "Yes, sir," in unison.

"We're planning to increase the sorties down in the Tolsan area, give those controllers down there more experience. I'd say I'm talking about as many missions as we can fly on the good weather days." He took a sip of tea. "You think they're a pretty good bunch, don't you, Norm?"

"Yes, sir, I do. They don't get a lot of intercepts, but it's a good group of controllers." Everyone was looking at me.

Canada nodded. "Well, I'm going to give them the practice, and I've sent you a couple of good young instructors."

"Yes, sir, they seem fine. Is there some special reason for all of this, sir?" I asked.

"You never know what the hell the future holds. You guys are as far south as we can get here. Out of the way. And it's the best place to beef up without putting up signals." He looked at the other two. I had the feeling they had heard this before.

"I just want you to push the training and get your counterparts in good form. Korean controllers need more intercepts. Tolsan gets it now."

A day later, I was sitting in a blue staff car, headed for Seoul. I was scheduled for my AFAG brief and the South Eastern Asia orientation at the AFAG headquarters, located just outside of Seoul, in a place called Yong Dong Po. I felt like I was in way over my head. When I talked to Colonel Belford on the phone, he had pretended to take a long pause when I told him who was calling. "Oh, you mean the Appo Kid? Yes, we're expecting the Appo Kid."

After I checked into the VOQ, it was indeed Forrest Belford who I saluted at AFAG headquarters, only this time he was wearing eagles. "General Pitts gave Canada an outstanding report on you, Appo, and God knows you came through when your buddy got his balls cut off," he said, after I expressed my doubts about either of the hats I was wearing.

"Old Virgil's just keeping you on edge. He's got things for you to do." But when I tried to press him for more specifics, he only told me to "train the shit out of 'em down there and send me the bills." We talked a little more about procedures, what I could and couldn't legally do, and that about wrapped up the whole trip to see him. "Good thing now is you have an Air Force Advisory Group badge to wear, and the Korean cops won't touch you."

I now held a purse string. Even though the status-of-forces agreement had put all U.S. military people under civil jurisdiction while they were walking around Korea, the guys with AFAG badges had immunity. "That's going to help a fuck-up like you," he said with his hearty laugh. "And speaking of that, let's go fuck-up together tonight."

We did. I had never been in the big city before, and Seoul turned out to be a swinging place. Everywhere, it catered to the American out on the town. On the Yong Dong Po complex alone, there were scores of great clubs and restaurants, but the city was filled with even more. There were clubs everywhere, and we hit them all.

There were uniforms everywhere. You had to be in uniform. So sergeants and colonels and petty officers and captains and corporals all bellied up to the bars and sat in the smoke-filled nightclubs. Slitted skirt was everywhere. This was old Hubert A. Hoddington's slide spectacular come to life. With Belford I could tie on that long awaited buzz and forget the nightmare I had been through. And I was as horny as hell. Christ, there was cunt everywhere.

In the Double O Seven Club, Belford introduced me to the owner, Mr. Chae, who said, "You from Tolsan-Do? I born dere." And he joined us for a slug of his cold OB. The place was great. I was getting snockered. His floor show, "All Girl Review," was nothing but hair, ass, and leg, with plenty of red and blue spotlights. When we left there, Mr. Chae and I were blood brothers. "Rock, women, and storm," we said as we shook hands for about the hundredth time. "Tolsan is rock, women, and storm."

In the A Frame Club, Belford ran into some other guys from the AFAG, three LCs, and a major so drunk he couldn't talk. That place was plush, too. It had the same kind of floorshow, but after the girls danced around, this terrific broad came out and sang. She was good. She sang "Arirang," the greatest folk song known to Korea, and our table sang along. Mostly we hummed because we didn't know the words.

Belford had lost his hat by this time, and I was feeling omnipotent. The singer did "Danny Boy" at our request. Talk to anybody who's ever been to Korea, and they'll tell you that for some strange reason—known only to Buddha—"Danny Boy" is like a second national anthem. When they sing it in English, they cry. We sang along on that one, too.

Finally, old Miss what's-her-name took the mike and looked our way. "You know we hava many good singers here tonight. Over here are the best ones in place." All the other tables cheered. We tried to take a bow. The snockered major was asleep, face down on the table.

"Would this one singer come up and sing a song?" she said. I really didn't know she was pointing at me until I heard Belford yell out, "Yeah, send up the Appo Kid for a song, by damn." The others yelled, "Here's our man."

And so I was up on the little red stage, my arm around her, trying to focus on the crowd. It was all just spotlights and smoke and cheers. "Geez, at least it's a hometown crowd," I said.

"Where you from?" she said.

"I from Tolsan-Do, home of rock, women, and storm," I said.

"Do you know Tolsan island?" she asked the crowd.

They all yelled back "yeah" and "send him back" and stuff like that. But it was all just one big mess of sound and light. I had even lost track of where our table was.

"Now you gonna sing a song, Tolsan boy. Okay?"

"Sure," I said, taking the mike from her. When I did that, and said "Sure," I became aware of the great output the mike had. It also had a fine echo effect. That made me think of my Lou Gehrig schtich.

"Do you 'member when old Lou Gehrig retired from baseball?" I asked.

I got a positive response from the lights and smoke. "Do you also remember hearing it on radio . . . or seeing Gary Cooper play it in *Lou Gehrig Story*?"

More positive response.

"Well, didn't it sound like this to you?" I said, putting the mike closer. Doesn't this sound like the echoes his voice made in Yankee Stadium when he talked?" And then I went into it. "I -I -I. Feel-Feel-F eel. Like-like-like. The-the-the. Luckiest-luckiest-luckiest. Man-man-man. In the world-world-world." They liked it, or they just thought I was crazy, but anyway, they cheered me on and pelted me with cherries, swizzle sticks, ice and lemon peels, and I came back with "Oh, when those cotton fields get rotten, you can't pick very much cotton," and the singer and the band and the damn place followed along with me. And before I went back to the table, the singer put her arms around me with everybody whistling and she kissed me with everything she was worth. I staggered the wrong way and then finally found my table.

"Appo, you did us proud," Belford said.

While I had been bombing on stage, the rest of the table had picked up companions. Belford and the three guys who were still not passed out all had little dollies on their laps. Somebody had put a little paper American flag in the fist of the guy who had conked out. The staff was made from a long bar straw. He looked marvelously silly.

Then this sweet voice said, "Do you knowa me from Tolsan-Do?"

I turned around, and there was a great looking chick standing in front of me, dressed in a slinky red evening gown.

"Why, it's our Miss Ihm," I said. "The girl who speaks good English from Tolsan *kisaeng* house."

"And you Mista Appo," she said giggling.

I just sat there, wondering how in the hell she could have traveled all the way to Seoul.

"So, you want me to sit down?" she said.

"Oh, yes, please sit down, Miss Ihm." So now I had a dollie on my knee.

"We country people from Tolsan-Do must stick together, yes?" And with her gorgeous face only inches from mine, she smiled and said, "*Neh*," the Korean word for yes.

There must have been two or three more clubs that night. We all piled into *kimchi* cabs, including the girls, and made the rounds. Seoul was well lighted and everywhere alive. Traffic was heavy and crazy, that hectic mix of cars, cabs, trucks, wagons, and bikes, all hell-bent for election down the streets. And horns. Horns beep-beeped all around us.

Shops and stores and buildings were built on top of each other and jammed side by side. Neon lights and long billboards advertised the wares of Korea. Most were written in Hangul, but every once in a while you'd spy an English ad aimed at GI Joe. And though the style and artwork was obviously Asian, it mimicked Madison Avenue, the streets and the shops and the signs were a strange mix, too.

Miss Ihm felt wonderful to me. She had sat on my lap in the A Frame, and then in the crowded cab. She was firm and all there under the tight red silk. Putting my hand on her waist shot wonderful, miserable pain through my whole body. The bounce and roll of the taxi made it even more exciting.

At the last place we went to, the Crazy Aces Club, Belford grabbed me by the arm and whispered in my ear, "Appo, I'm going to leave with Dottie here in a minute or so. Then it's every man for himself, okay?"

"Yes sir, and the women be damned," I said, trying to keep my eyes in close focus.

"But, Appo," he said, pulling me back, "don't forget about the curfew now. You hear?"

Curfew? Right. They had a curfew in Seoul. On Tolsan there was no curfew. People could come and go as they pleased, but in Seoul, you were off the streets at midnight. Belford's announcement and warning came at eleven-thirty.

Not five minutes later, Belford and his dollie got up. "We'll see you later, Appo," he said, over the din of the noisy club. "Miss Ihm, you take care of this Tolsan boy, okay?" He winked at me. "It's time to go on I & I, Intoxication and Intercourse."

"Yeah, I take care," she said, squeezing my hand.

"We go now too," she said to me. Okay, I thought, but now it was almost a quarter to twelve. I'd never be able to make it back to the Yong Dong Po VOQ. "We can hurry now to my housa before get off street time."

Outside of the Craze Aces, the last three of the taxis were waiting around for last-minute fares; Miss Ihm grabbed one as soon as we hit the sidewalk. She gave directions to the driver, and we were on our way to her place. Seoul was turning off its bar and restaurant lights; the Korean government was gearing up its surveillance system that keeps an eye out for infiltrators from the North as the city sleeps. I often wondered why twelve was the witching hour. Was there an agreement between North and South that the infiltrators would only try to penetrate after the midnight curfew cleared the streets, to give the South a better chance of spotting them?

After making our way through a maze of back streets, we pulled up in front of a complex of low concrete buildings. When I got out my wallet, Miss Ihm took it and counted out the money for the driver. "I give him good tip. Korean man need money for family."

"Yes, yes," I said. "Give him whatever you like." She smiled.

He reached back in our direction and she put the money in his hand. He looked at it and said, "God bless you," in very good English.

"He very nice man," she whispered to me. "We alla help each other."

Back outside, she took my hand and led me on a short walk on a narrow, winding path that went through three or four connected courtyards. Finally, she took me onto a long wooden porch. I leaned against a wall and she took off my shoes. Once through the sliding doors, we were in a really nice little one-floor apartment. It had good furniture and even a big stereo.

The place was very neat. The décor was a little on the Kewpie Doll side, with lots of chintz and red, but it had a very comfortable feel.

It could have been the apartment of a single secretary or even schoolteacher. But it was a Korean hooker's pad. And I was sitting on a comfortable western-style couch with . . . the hooker.

It was quiet. I was quiet. It had been easy for me to sneak little handfuls of her at the clubs and in the taxi, but now my bravery retreated on the couch. It was she who broke the silence and slyly asked me that question famously known to anyone who has ever served in Asia: "Now what you gonna do, gee-eye?" You heard that all day long among the troops. Your team is hung up on making a decision? You hear it. Trying to decide what to do tonight? You hear it. Which road to take in the jeep? You hear it. Now, I got asked the question for real.

I didn't have to answer. She made it easy for me. And once I got started, I couldn't get enough of her. I had come close to going all the way a couple of times, but Miss Ihm brought me down without a fight. She was terrific.

Her body was smooth and firm and had a fragrant aroma that stirred deep feelings in me. It was that same fragrance that I smelled all over Korea. Sometimes it was too harsh, like in a crowded marketplace. It seemed to hang over Korea like an invisible smoky haze, a mix of kimchi, fish, flowers, sea air, dust, clothes, and even a hint of night soil. Here with her, it was just right.

Up close, we looked into each other's eyes. I studied her. Her long hair was straight and very black. Her almond eyes were large and brown, with slanted folds. Her cheeks bones were high, the nose flattened at the bridge. That close her skin was tan, with a copper tinge.

She was long and tall. When I unbuttoned her blouse, I found those same dark brown nipples sitting in the center of her cute little breasts. Thin waist. Well-shaped butt. Beautifully shaped legs. Pretty feet. If you're going to commit adultery, do it with a dollie like this, I thought. Do it with class.

"I nice for you?" She asked. All that, and she could talk.

"You very nice for me, Miss Ihm," I said, kissing her on the forehead. "You so easy for me to be with."

"Drinkie people no speak true," she laughed. "You forget all about me tomorrow."

But I was hardly thinking about tomorrow. My sensuous excursion around her body and her seductive responses only made me want to throw myself into the immediate moment. It was a private moment, guarded by the curfew, thousands of miles away from home and common sense.

She led me to the bedroom, and I lost my Korean cherry. I had also brought the Trojans along.

Afterward, feeling as if I had never been so relaxed in my life, I thought I heard the sound of rain on the tin roof above us. As I listened to it, I guess my eyes went to the ceiling. I liked what I heard. It sounded like rain, or maybe like tree limbs, or a drummer's brush on a brass symbol.

"You hear?" she said, looking up as well.

"Rain?" I asked, pointing up.

"Ancestors," she replied. Then she swept her hands over the cover top, her fingers imitating little fast feet. I nodded. Yes, it was the hordes of rats that came running out into the Korean night, running over the rooftops of Seoul. The sound made by thousands of little clawed feet running on tin. Well, why not. They were up there, and I was down here. "Many ancestors out tonight," I said. She smiled and passed me a cigarette. We shared it silently, listening to the ancestors.

There were no complications. No problems. No hotel guys bugging me. Not even a hard floor, because she had a western-style bed. She even turned off the light on her nightstand.

Packer came into my thoughts, for a quick moment. Like him, I was lying in bed with a Korean woman in my arms, drifting off to sleep, just as he had on his last night on earth. Balls, please be there in the morning, I prayed. And in my dreams, the ancestors spoke of the past all through the night.

The next morning it was easy to check if my balls were intact because I was naked. They were there, but she was not beside me. My watch said 0830. I felt like I had gotten the best night's sleep I'd had in a long, long time. I didn't even have a hangover. My only pressing problem was that I had to take a leak something terrible. I was one huge, bursting bladder. Quick look around the room. No honey jar.

My briefs were gone. The rest of my clothes were missing as well. I didn't have to do much searching for them with my eyes. Though the room was clean and bright, it was spare on furniture. Besides the bed and nightstand, there was only a tall two-door lacquered chest. It reflected like a decorated skyscraper on her beautifully polished linoleum floor. The walls were neatly papered with floral designs. Between me and the tin roof, the ceiling almost looked like cedar paneling. The room was nice, but I had to pee.

The room had one single bedroom window, through which came the sounds of a very busy street: cars, motorbikes, people, children, sirens. "Ica crème, ica crème, ica crème," sang a voice. But the thoughts of ica crème at 0830 made my need to piss all the more urgent.

As I got out of bed, I felt a little unsteady. Maybe my hangover diagnosis wasn't as accurate as I had first thought. Once on my feet, I wrapped the top quilt around me. Thinking my clothes must be in that dresser, I walked over to try the doors. No luck. It had the kind of giant lock on it like you'd expect to find in a medieval dungeon. Thieves were a big problem in the Republic of South Korea. Miss Ihm had pretty well covered her bets with that lock and on that massive dresser. I'd guessed you'd need large bolt cutters and a fireman's axe to steal her treasures.

I was betting that my clothes and wallet were among those treasures. I didn't think she'd be out hocking my clothes or spending my money with me standing naked back in her apartment. She was protecting my stuff. But she also had me imprisoned. I was literally trapped, me and my screaming bladder.

Maybe I could find something in the living room, I thought. But when I slid the panel open a crack, I saw five other girls sitting out there on the floor. "Gooda morning, Mista Appo," one said cheerily. They all laughed. "He not appo," another said. "He used a lubber."

"Miss Ihm here?" I said timidly.

"No, she not back," said another sweet, sing-song voice. Who in the hell were they?

"They my sister," Ihm said, coming through the front doorway on cue, as if she'd read my mind. She was carrying a black lacquer tray. "Thisa you breakfast." Behind her followed an old woman who carried in a large rectangular paper package. She quickly sat it down on the floor and left.

Miss Ihm looked great. She was conservatively dressed like any proper young woman you'd see on the streets of Seoul. Her big smile lit up the room.

"Ihm, you're wonderful," I bowed and said. "Before I eat, could I please just find the *binjo*?"

"I bring," she laughed.

She did bring a jar and insisted that she would carry it back into the bedroom. "Now you make water," she said, putting it down in the corner. I couldn't wait and relieved myself with my back to her. When I turned back, she was laying out my neatly folded clothes on the bed. The wallet was on top. As she folded up the brown paper that had held my clean clothes, she said, "I take out money for wash woman."

She took a man's robe out of the dresser and motioned for me to put my arms through the sleeves. It was clean and very comfortable. She pulled a mat from underneath the bed, I sat down, and the tray was placed in front of my crossed legs.

Dressed in my robe, I ate two poached eggs, some kind of little buns, rice cakes, and hot tea. Everything was delicious.

"You fun to watch," she said as I relished the wonderful feast in the land of the morning calm.

When I drank the last of the tea, I thought it was probably time for me to get dressed and go. But she said, "You get one more time from me afta breakfast." One more time!

The robe came off. While her "sisters" laughed and talked in the next room, Miss Ihm took me back to Shangri-La. This was a bed and breakfast like no other in the world.

As I got dressed, I reviewed the schedule ahead. It was Friday. I had already met with Belford and staff at AFAG. My choggy back down to Tolsan-Do was scheduled for Tuesday. Aside from checking in again with Belford, I pretty much had four free days to spend in Seoul. I had a great deal going for myself.

When I walked into Miss Ihm's living room, the girls saw my uniform and said, "Ah, Captain!" They were congratulating Ihm on making it with an officer. That meant she could pick up some good rice money. Well, she will, I said to myself.

"I take you back to you VOQ. You can call Mista Belford from there. Then we go see my city." It was like I had a personal secretary.

Military base quarters in Korea are always filled with Korean employees. They can either be a big help or a pain in the ass, depending on how you play it. Technically, Miss Ihm wasn't permitted access to the Q, but when we came through the front door, she spoke with the couple in charge of my floor. It looked to me like a very happy exchange. They smiled, turned back to their ironing, and we walked down to my room

When we got to my VOQ room, I got Belford on the phone. He was in a great mood: "Hell, no, I wouldn't know what the hell to do with you around here. Kid, my direct order is to go do grass roots research on this country and its people."

I did have a piece of business for him, however; though I'd be sending up Lee's requests, I wouldn't be around in November for the start of next year's hunting season. "Well, you never know, but good luck, Norm, with everything down country," he said and hung up.

That was like the last day of school before Christmas vacation. For the next four days I'd be on I & I with a gorgeous broad who screwed you after breakfast.

"You need shower?" she said, sitting on the edge of my bed, leafing through a base directory.

"Well, yes, I do," I said.

"Okay, you go, and then I take one, too. You keep this room, but you stay night with me."

Her schedule of events was right on target, but I made one small adjustment: We took the shower together.

Nobody bothered us while we fooled around on my bunk and then took a long shower. Afterward, as she meticulously dried off with a big government issued towel, she stopped to say, "I tell people who work here you will give them all good tip when you check out, okay?"

To which I saluted smartly and said, "Yes ma'am, so ordered."

Ever on task, she went through my things and put my travel kit in the bag she carried, along with some socks and underwear.

On our way off the base I stopped by the O Club, cashed a check, and bought some won. You got one hundred and thirty won for a dollar. I knew from Dutch that a good salary in Korea was the equivalent of forty bucks a month. No wonder all Americans were rich in Korea.

She had been patiently waiting in the lobby. When we got outside, I handed her fifty buck's worth of won. "I hope this will pay for breakfast tomorrow," I said.

She looked at the roll of money and said, "I had my finger crossed you would give me something on our last day. You give me now. You good gee-eye, numba one."

We started our tour of Seoul at her favorite beauty parlor, which looked to me more like a barbershop back home. It had a long row of chairs from which the hairdressers got their hooker patrons ready for another big night on the town. There were a lot of looks and giggles when I sat down in a chair along the wall to wait for her, leafing through well-worn American glamour magazines. I could tell Miss Ihm was very proud to show me off.

After her trim and wash, we did some serious sightseeing. By bus, cab, and foot, we covered almost every important landmark in Seoul: The capitol building, complete with dome; the Tower Hotel, tallest building in the city; Dukseo Palace and museum, home of artifacts and treasures from the King Gojong Dynasty; Changdok Palace, 1404 B.C. residence of King Taejong;

Changgyongwon Park, with its zoo and botanical gardens; and Namsan, where we rode a cable car to a spectacular view of the city.

From Namsan I saw the steel bridge that spans the Han River. I remember that as the bridge Colonel Lee told me he had crossed on the journey to his parents' home at midpoint in the raging Korean War. The rubble of that day was now cleared away, and I looked down at a growing, busy city. It made me happy for Colonel Lee. Happy for Korea.

Then we walked for miles along Tae-pyong-ro Street, smack in the heart of the city. I bought her a dress, some shoes, and she got the idea to get this sexy nightgown worn by a mannequin in a boutique window. My stash of won was disappearing, but it was fun to take her on a spree. I knew I was racking up points for the night ahead. To be sure, that night and the nights to follow were dynamite, as were the breakfasts. Miss Ihm was the perfect hostess.

She was also a very special person. The girls she referred to as her sisters came to the apartment every morning. I found out that she was helping those who fell down on their luck. Sometimes a girl would catch something or get pregnant. When her long-time GI would finally get transferred, times would be lean until the girl scored again. And when age finally caught up with a *yobo*, the good times would be gone forever. The brass ring was a long-time GI who didn't drink a lot and treated his girl well. "Short-time drinkie man no good. Numba ten," breakfast club member Miss Han told me one morning. When a group of girls supports each other, they could pull each other through tough times. Ihm Me was a damn good sister.

Sunday morning I got up a little earlier than my usual eight-thirty or so, and I found Miss Ihm feeding a small boy a bowl of rice and some fruit out in the living room. "He is Mista Hwang," she said. "He come here every morning for his breakfast and a little kiss, too. Justa like you."

He was about nine, but smallish for his age. His big eyes made you want to pick him up and hug him. He was a half-Korean child, whose mother had abandoned him. Now the sisters took care of him.

There were other children. Mistakes. Half white children. Half black children. All the offspring of GIs who had taken that "last choggy" for the States. That afternoon I bought another box of Trojans.

My casual fling in Miss Ihm's compound made me a witness to the other side of I & I. Survival was the real point of the high heels, stockings, and tight skirts. Miss Ihm survived by being a working girl and there were thousands of her sisters all over South Korea. The little Mista Hwangs were the unintentional, unwanted byproducts of the system. In addition to his hunger, he'd always have another strike against him in the Korean society. He had mixed blood. Now old Norm Whitman was in the game. I was helping pay a rice bill, but I was also enabling the system.

On the last night we spent together, we walked around Seoul's streets, enjoying the warm summer night. Our stop at a Korean teahouse was a real treat: Hot tea and savory rice cakes. The place was full of people. When we came in, we got some dirty looks, but one guy in particular passed by our table, looked down, and said something to her with a hiss.

"What'd he say? " I asked, watching him go out the door.

"He say nothing," she said, looking down at her cup. She tried to brush it off, but I could tell it hurt. After that, I became more aware that we were often the target of disapproving looks and comments.

Late Monday night I got a staff car to take me back down to Osan. It picked me up at the Q after Ihm Me and I had dinner at the Young Dong Po Officers' Club. She said she'd be able to get back downtown by herself. My B-4 bag was stowed in the hostess desk closet. When I retrieved it, she took my stuff out of her bag and put it in mine. "Short time over," she said. "I find long time now."

"I hope you find number one GI for long time, Miss Ihm." She had been a great companion. Hell, she was a good friend. As I stood there saying goodbye to her, the martinis I'd had with dinner were making me feel very sad about leaving her. I already knew that I'd be lonely without her. "Ihm Me, " I said, taking her in my arms, "I really like you."

She pushed me away with mock disbelief, and then gave me a big smile. "I tell you before. Drinkie people no speak true."

The car was waiting outside the club, I got in, waved at her through the window, and headed for Osan. I'd had my fling.

22

Unholy Orders

The next day it was back over the roof of Korea for the Appo Kid. Lieutenant Ko once told me the Korean peninsula was pictured in folk tales as a rabbit who sits upright in the face of China. The ears are pointed northward to Manchuria, its backbone is formed by the eastern mountain range that runs along the Sea of Japan, and two paws are made from the peninsulas that run westward into the Yellow Sea. I thought about that rabbit, below me, sniffing the wind for danger. Conquered by the Tangs, the Manchus, and the Mongols in ancient times, the rabbit had been occupied by the Japanese from 1910 to 1945, and then divided by the Russians and the Americans after World War Two. Little wonder, I thought, why it sniffed. Poor little rabbit, girdled at its middle and caught between giants.

About one hundred ninety miles out of Tolsan the pilot, Captain Fred Peters, let me sit in the right seat. The copilot moved to the nav table. I wanted to listen to Benjamin Control follow us in. My new lieutenants were okay. I listened to Carl Betts over my headphones.

"Air Force Three-Seven-Niner, starboard now one-seven-zero for Benjamin."

"Roger," Peters said, "turning one-seven."

"Roger, Three-Seven-Niner. Benjamin now three-six-zero for seven-zero-miles. Weather high thin scattered, visibility excellent, set altimeter two-niner-five-decimal-six. That's two-niner-five-decimal-six."

We rogered all of that and pretty soon zoomed over the coast. Then Peters gave his goodies report, telling Benjamin that one of the movies on board was *The Appo Kid Returns*.

"Oh, no, Three-Seven-Niner, we've seen that oldie before." It hadn't taken Goldman long to make a smartass out of Betts, I thought.

Then we got a call I'd never heard before. "Three-Seven-Niner, also be advised that Star of David has two hundred pounds cold for you to pick up."

We looked at each other and gave it palms up, shoulders up. Peters repeated, "Roger, understand two hundred cold," like the pro he was.

The island was ablaze with color. Green everywhere. We could even see the orchards where they grew Korea's orange crop. We were losing altitude for our run in, and it made it easy to pick out people, houses, and moving traffic. Horses raised their heads at the sound of us. A great ox strained his yoked head and neck to see what had made the shadow pass before him. Summer was blessing the farm folk of Tolsan-Do.

With a turn out to sea, another pitch, and another, we were lined up on the grass strip. Peters slid her in beautifully. I hardly felt us bounce.

I hadn't even unbuckled when I heard a familiar voice coming forward. "Oh, Jesus, you let him ride up front. You took a chance like that, Captain Peters? You didn't let him touch anything, I hope?"

"So glad to see you again, Goldman," I said. "I got so tired of all of those NCOs up in Osan and Seoul, with their military bearing and respect for rank."

He ignored me. "Captain Peters, I have some cold packs for you, sir. You'll probably want to tie them down.

"Don't tell me," I said. "I'll bet you're none other than Star of David, right?"

"Shalom. You win the box of Snickers," he said, shaking my hand.

"What's in the cold packs?" asked Peters.

"Sir, it's frozen lobster tails for the Osan NCO Club, sir. I cleared it with Seventh Aerial a couple of days ago."

"Oh," said Peters, deciding that was as far as he'd go with it. Goldman had a legitimate cargo form with him. It was an official food buy. It looked up-and-up.

"Oh, yeah," I said, searching Goldman's face. "I forgot. We're going to be sending a lot of that stuff back in the next couple of months. You ought to try it, Fred."

That beautiful day started a string of beautiful days for all of us on the little site. Everyone was busy, and we were getting things done. The most important part was that Tenth Fighter Wing was flying a bunch of sorties with us, and our Korean controllers were really getting sharp. Between me and the two silver bars, they could control just about any tactic. Dick and Carl pitched in with the English lessons, too. That was key. They controlled in English, and we kept pumping it into them. I'd have put them up against any control squadron anywhere in Korea. We were good.

Colonel Lee was right with us. Anytime we'd have birds under our control, he'd be there on the dais. And Moon and Park would be right there with him. "I think we very ready," he said one day. He was right. "But I think with all thisa increased visibility I must fix up my site even more."

"What did you have in mind, sir?" I asked.

"My squadron entrance is not impressive like the arches up on the mainland." He drew in a big breath of air on that, a tic most Koreans had when they were making a profound statement. "On ranger base, arch has a Latin saying that means the men there are very strong. I see that on arch all over, and when I visit America I see it on all base."

"Oh, you mean a motto, sir. Like *Semper Fidelis*?"

"Yes, exactly what I mean. Motto," he rolled it over in his mouth. "Motto," he said again, savoring the sound of it. "You must help me get a motto, Captain Widman."

"Sir," I said, trying to hold back my delight, "I will get you one very soon."

The day Lee gave me the motto request was also the day I met a sad-faced Father Paul sitting in the Q. I knew something was wrong with him the minute I came in for our before-dinner martini. "What's with you?" I said.

He was sitting in the overstuffed chair. "I got a letter from the Chief of Chaplains today. I'm being reassigned for retirement."

Paul would go back to Lackland Air Force Base, Texas, and be on the staff of the Chaplains' school there until Christmas time. Then he'd probably be assigned as the pastor of a church in the Arch Diocese of San Antonio, his original home base. He didn't want to leave the island. He didn't want to leave the Air Force. He didn't want to be a parish priest. But he'd been twice passed-over for major, and he would soon have twenty years of military service. There was nothing he—or anybody—could do.

That night, he and I and Goldman got super shit-faced. The only thing we had to cheer us was the fact that Tolsan-Do lobster tail was catching on like wildfire. Every choggy that came in would radio for Star of David to have so many pounds of cold pack to go. And one day a C-130 out of Japan radioed Benjamin to say they needed to land, check something on board, and "pick up two hundred pounds" as long as they were on the ground anyway.

In fact, Goldman had turned a shed in back of the NCO club into a processing house for the operation, and the club membership was working as hard on that enterprise as anything else on the compound. The till was growing. Prices were going down, down, down in the club as a result.

"Norm," Paul said through his beer moustache, "could you imagine what Dubbs would think if he knew you were turning this place into a fish market?"

"And that we are actually letting little, dirty Korean kids into the theater to see cartoons on Saturdays," put in Goldman.

"Aw, shit," said Paul. "I'm going to miss it all. The place's just getting fun." He had big tears in his eyes.

"Look, Paul," I said, patting him on the arm. "It's already July. Your tour is over. And I'm out of here in October, for gosh sake."

"And I'm gone in September," said Goldman. "Besides, we're tired of going to mass. You've got to give us a break."

The more we put away the more we talked about our friendship, about giving Dubbs a hard time, about old Oyster. Goldman said that one of the girls had told him that Dubbs had sent for Sue. For some reason, that made me think of Ihm Me, but I didn't mention it. That one would stay a secret forever.

Paul took us through World War Two again. We did the entire Wheeler Field thing with him, from mass with Sergeant Rimmel to the end of the attack. "You know, one of my favorite people there was Miss Sheldon, one of my night school teachers at the University of Hawaii," he said, wiping his nose. "The university was very small then, but we took courses there off duty. If I could ever find her, I'll bet she'd know what happened to old Rimmel."

Rimmel and Paul had been separated the day after the attack. Those two had laid out all of the bodies from their squadron the night of seven December, tagged them, and wrapped them in blankets. They had been close friends before the attack, but that night had been very special. "We were welded together by the sheer power of the horror of it all. We kept each other going."

"Well, maybe you'll just have to write her or something," I said.

"Tried that. Wrote everywhere. I have never found either one of them, but I'm sure she'd know about Rimmel. She and Rimmel were very good friends." He was pouring the gin down with a vengeance.

"Look," said Goldman, "let's make a pact. If any of us gets to Hawaii, try to find Miss Sheldon."

"She lived near Wheeler, in Wahiawa. But she's probably married and you'll never do it. She's probably long gone from Hawaii." He was into one of his crying jags.

"Now, look, Paul, you have this habit of laying these things on us and you're the one who's supposed to be providing us with the spiritual uplift. You're the priest, and we're your flock, man."

"So make us cheer up," said Goldman.

Paul was getting dense. "You know what you say when they call your name at ordination time?"

"You'll be sorry?"

"No, you dumb Jew, I'm serious." He blew his nose. "They say your name and you're lying there, face down, and you say '*Ad Sum.*'" He blew again. "That's right. They say, 'Paul Francis Fisher,' and you say '*Ad Sum,*' and that means 'I Am Here.' That means you're ready to serve God."

We didn't say anything for a minute.

"You know, Father Paul, you're always going to leave a little of yourself wherever you go. And I can tell you that folks are going to know you were here on this site for a long time to come."

"I haven't done anything you can even name, Norm. Not one thing."

"I can, too. You said masses, and kept us going, and you were there when only a priest could have helped old dead Oyster."

He liked all of that, bless his heart. He was listening like a little kid.

"And you know what else?"

"What?"

"You gave the Republic of South Korea Air Force, Seven-Seventy-First Radar Squadron its new motto. Every time somebody drives under the brand new arch Colonel Lee is going to build, they'll read the motto: *Ad Sum. I Am Here*. And a little piece of Father Paul Francis Fisher will be there, by God. How many other guys have left behind a legacy like that?"

Lee loved his new motto. As a matter of fact, he and I decided to have a Korean-American Day at the site. The highlight of the day would be a memorial service, and the official dedication of the new arch.

"At that time, I will also present Chaplain Fisher with a going away tribute from my compound."

So we put together a big bash. The more we planned, the more it grew. The Star of David Tolsan-Do NCO Club Fund offered to furnish refreshments for the occasion, and Sergeant Ellis and I thought it was "fairly" legal for the mess hall to contribute a big meal for all of the participants. Who would quibble with a bunch of hamburgers and hot dogs anyway? And, Colonel Lee's people were going to bring over Korean dishes. There was going to be plenty to eat and drink.

Dutch, his people, and Lee's engineering crew worked hard on the arch construction project. It took almost two weeks of constant work to build the curved wooden span and pour the two concrete and rock pillars that would hold its legs on either side of the road. Several times a day, Lee and I would check on the work. He loved seeing it take form.

At about the end of the first week, while we were watching them work on the concrete pillars, I noticed that the guard shack that would stand under the new arch looked a little worn. Hell, I thought, that just wouldn't do. "Colonel Lee," I said, looking in its direction, "could I have your permission to fix up gatehouse with maybe some new boards and paint?"

He looked at the shack very carefully, eyeing it as the Korean commander is supposed to when taking such a suggestion from a subordinate. "Permission granted," he said finally. "I give Mista Dutch more men to help with that, too."

The whole affair got so complicated I suggested we form an Arch Dedication Committee. Goldman and Ellis headed up the refreshment-entertainment division; the two lieutenants would coordinate protocol; and Mountain was put in charge of logistics. Colonel Lee put Major Moon in charge of Korean operations, and he had a bunch of subdivisions, too. We all started meeting every other day just to get everything straight. Every time we'd meet, Colonel Lee would have two or three more names to add to the guest list.

A new name or two would always come up in the same way. Lee would clear his throat a couple of times—which meant everybody be quiet because the commander is going to talk—and then he'd say: "My people also want to invite the Governor of thisa island and some school officials who also should be here."

"Yes, sir," Carl Betts would say, and Major Moon would hand him the new names, written out neatly on rice paper stationery. In fact, the enterprising Lieutenant Betts decided he'd make up a printed program, complete with all the names of invited dignitaries. But the night I almost had a heart attack was when Lee said, "I talked to my ROKAF commander in Osan and he say he will come and also bring Colonel Canada on his C-46 airplane."

Betts looked at me. I said, "Carl, be sure we have a special mention on the program for those two." Lee was all smiles.

"Sir," I said, "what a fine gesture on your part." So, Dutch got working on making the spare Q rooms and lodge rooms look extra good. I'd never know who Lee was going to ask next. I thought we'd better be prepared.

Dutch was making a reviewing stand out of a flatbed, because Lee had decided to march his troops under the arch. We were even getting a band from Tolsan City, along with a schoolgirls' chorus. I hoped Ellis had lots of hamburger meat. One August was going to be the big day. It was a fitting date, for Father Paul would leave on the next day's choggy.

"Friendship Day" finally came. The day before, Canada and Brigadier General Dai Han Baki came down on a ROKAF C-46, along with Lieutenant Colonels Adams, Ellers, and Judd. Lee threw a beautiful dinner party in a downtown restaurant in honor of their coming to the ceremony. Naturally, he had his staff there, and Paul and I got invited, too. Everybody made a speech that night. Canada was the Canada that I was beginning to like. His only private words to me that night were, "Sometime over the next couple a days we've got to talk." There was no edge to his tone, so I didn't worry about it.

The ceremony started out with a flag raising at the big poles that were erected between the American and Korean compounds. Those babies were the most imposing things on the entire site area. Concreted in an oval base, there were three thirty-five-foot poles made from spun steel. From them we flew the flag of Korea, the UN flag, and Old Glory. The idea that morning was to stand in formation and raise the three colors in tribute to all that had happened in Korea and to honor the powerful friendships that had been forged out of it. That friendship, we wrote in the program, had "made it possible for free Koreans to build a living symbol of the democratic way of life and create a mighty guardian against communism in the Far East."

The whole gang assembled at seven in the morning for the flag raising. Canada, General Dai, Colonel Lee, and I stood out in front of the two contingents of troops, decked out in our class A uniforms. Lee gave the word for the music and three Korean flag raisers stepped out, along with three flag bearers. It was impressive. The band from Tolsan City was quite good. They played the Notre Dame fight song.

Slowly, the flags ascended and we snapped to with salutes on General Dai's command of "Plee-sent alms." Everything looked good.

Then the wind came up. It was whipping all three flags around pretty hard as they made the trip up. Just as they reached the end of the climb, everyone let out a subdued groan. The Stars and Stripes tangled in the lines and caught in the swivel. It looked terrible, all wrapped around the pole and sort of pulled out of kilter. But the band played through the fight song another time, and the other two flags, at least, looked good. Once secured, the wind made two of them look like flags on postcards. All except for ours.

All of a sudden, Captain Ko came out of nowhere, kicked off his shoes and socks, put down his hat, and started up that pole. I mean he went up it fast, in the same kind of style I've seen in movies where guys climb up coconut trees. He was good.

We were still holding our salutes, but all eyes were on Ko. The band played, and it was like some daredevil circus act we were watching. Well, even better, because he got to the top and in about twenty seconds he had the U.S. star spangled banner unwrapped, pulled tight, and with a sweeping gesture he threw old glory into the wind. It painted the sky red, white, and blue. It looked great. And Ko gave it a big salute, holding on with his left hand and bare feet. Everybody said, "Ah," together. He was back on the ground in a flash. "Ord-er alms," shouted the General, and we all just broke out in applause. Not normally the procedure when you stood reveille, but highly appropriate that August morning on Tolsan-Do.

That set the tone for the rest of the day. At eleven the dignitaries were all standing on the flatbed, decorated with sheets converted into bunting by some fine Korean hands. The band played Korean marches, and the center of attraction was the beautiful new arch that spanned the entrance to the compound. Dutch had really put himself into it, not to mention the refurbished gatehouse. In Hangul and English, the first long passage on the arch read: "Welcome To The 771st Republic of Korea Air Force (ROKAF) Air Control and Waring Squadron (AC&W) Tolsan-Do." And under that, flanked by two fierce dragons, was: *AD SUM*—I Am Here. In marched troops from Lee's compound. They did a fine job. Behind them came ROKAF trucks and jeeps, with Lee's officers sitting in them. My guys came through, riding on the backs of the trucks that picked up the choggy baggage. Goldman was next in the ambulance, followed by the site fire department, both engines, and a bunch of school kids in their black uniforms and hats. The last thing through was this great float the ROKAF had put together with flowers and colored paper stuck into a chicken-wire frame. It was a garden with the UN, Korean and American flags in it, along with a couple of very pretty women, the ROKAF telephone operators, in traditional Korean dress. Everybody ate it up.

The Korean girls sang "Arirang," some very beautiful songs I'd never heard before, and—in honor of America—"Take Me Out To The Ballgame." Canada gave me a big smile, and the thumbs-up sign on that one.

Then the speeches. Most of them were in Korean, with Ko doing the translation. That made them all twice as long. The Governor spoke first, saying that he was very proud to have the site on his island. He was a big Korean, with graying hair. Very distinguished, I thought. General Dai said that Korea was free because of a strong defense, and that our site was a very important part of that. Lee talked about the arch being a symbol of two great nations working together for peace, and the motto meant that the "power of this base will always be here to serve freedom." I think Canada was a little surprised when they asked him to talk, but he came through like a trooper, saying that he was "overwhelmed by the spirit and dedication to be found on Tolsan-Do." Every speaker got a great big hand. Those who had marched or ridden through the arch had joined the crowd, making it a nice size.

Most all of the priests were there. And the very last thing on the agenda made them beam with pride. Colonel Lee presented Paul with a beautifully framed citation thanking him for his community and military service, signed by both Lee and the island Governor. Paul was touched. Lee asked him to say something, and old Paul just stepped forward a little more and said, "I see so many friends here. Could I just put a blessing on this crowd and this arch according to my own custom, and say that I hope you will share it with me in the spirit of your own?" After translation, that brought a terrific response from the crowd. When they quieted down he raised his right hand, thumb and forefinger joined in a circle, the other three fingers together and erect, and said, "May Almighty God bless you, in the name of the Father, Son, and Holy Spirit. Amen." Lee had his motto, a new arch, and a better gatehouse. Paul had a memory to last forever. And I had a lump in my throat.

Afterward, everyone came into the compound and joined in on an old-fashioned American hot dog and hamburger picnic. Ellis and a bunch of the other NCOs cooked the food on big drums, cut in half, stoked up with red-hot coals. All of the tables we had in the dining hall were lined up in a big row, covered with linen, and heaped with paper plates, ketchup, and dozens and dozens of big crocks of Korean food. At the end of the line you could have beer, Coke, or hot tea. People sat anywhere along the compound street and ate. When you were full, you could walk around and sightsee. I even had the cartoons up and running for the kids. It was the Fourth of July, Korea Day, UN Day, Armed Forces Day, the Knights of Columbus picnic, and the Moon Festival all rolled into one.

Lee introduced me to the Governor and a bunch of the important local high men. The Police Chief was there, too. He gave me a big handshake and bow. Standing there in the bright sun, laughter and good-natured sounds all around me, I was haunted by the image of a dark night with a glowing red hum. As Lee had told me, the Koreans say that in life you always have four days warm followed by three cold. I felt a chill when I thought about the future.

Late that night I had two meetings: military business with Canada, Adams, and Ellers; and a farewell with Father Paul.

The meeting with Canada took place in my office in the HQ, Dubbs' old reading room. It was a good place to meet for something serious, especially at night or on the weekend. Except for mailroom traffic, the place was deserted. You only checked the mailroom on a choggy day anyway.

So the four of us carried another cup of coffee over there after dinner and shut the door. I had my fingers crossed that he was going to tell me a major was coming to overlap me my last three months. He was starting to get that serious look about him even as we started down the street, trying not to spill our java.

"Norm," he said, and that scared me because I was Norm when he wasn't pissed at me, "did you know that the Republic of Korea has about forty-five thousand troops in Vietnam?"

Now, that direction really threw me for a loop, but I played along. "Yes, sir. I know they're involved. Some of the lieutenants have friends serving there and every once in a while they'll tell me about letters and so on."

Canada nodded and took a sip of his coffee.

Then Ellers took over. "I'm glad you knew that, Norm, because a lot of Americans are totally ignorant of the ROK involvement. Thing is, it's all Army or Marine." He sipped, too. I felt like I was in a briefing. "Just to get perspective, I'll tell you that the first ROKs in were two medic units in sixty-five, followed by the Tiger and Blue Dragon Divisions later that same year. And they've done themselves proud."

"They've opened the entire coast highway up between Qui Nohn and Pleiku," added Adams.

Canada just looked at me while they were telling me that. Now, what the fuck was this all about, I thought to myself.

"'Course, the ROKAF is a little out of the picture on this one, because the ROK Army flies its own helicopters, just like ours. And the ROK Navy's been in on the Marine support. So the ROKAF's out in the cold." And Canada said that like he was throwing Adams the next line.

"But, Norm, we couldn't very well let a squadron of ROKAF F-5s go on in there and run close-air or target missions. It might not be wise." He did have the next line.

"Norm," Canada said, leaning forward, "you can help us fill a couple'a squares in that regard, I think."

"Sir?" I said, looking to the door.

"We think a small tactical radar deployment exercise—ROKAF all the way—might satisfy the ROK Air Staff guys who feel left out. Not just a controller cross-train deal in one of our control centers, but a short shot in-country with a TAC type field exercise," said Adams.

Canada took the floor again. "President Park's made any number of commitments to Vietnam and, of course, forty-five thousand ground pounders are already raising hell over there. A quick TAC operation wouldn't be anything at all next to that, but it would be ROK Air Force."

"And damned good training for them, Norm," added Adams. Ellers just nodded in agreement.

"What would they control?" I asked.

"Our guys. On simple stuff. Hell, they're ready right here," said Canada with a half smile.

I looked down at my cold coffee. "So, you're thinking that maybe the Benjamin Team's the one to send in there?"

Canada shook his head yes.

"But they're not TAC types," I said.

"You know as well as I do that you sit at one radar on a hill or another in a trailer, and it's pretty much all the same. A controller's a controller. Right?" said Adams.

Now I knew why we had gotten the increased flying time. They wanted to give Benjamin the practice it needed to deploy to a combat situation.

"They could do it," I said, mentally going back over the month's intercept activity.

"And I think Colonel Lee's the perfect leader for a thing like this, don't you?" asked Canada.

"Absolutely, sir," I said.

Adams kept going. "Yes, it's a little on the cosmetic side, a gesture if you will. But, still, we can get Benjamin good exposure and good training."

Nobody said anything. It was awkward pause time. I wanted to get out of there and go to the movie. Paul and the Fathers were yucking it up over there without me. I had gotten rec services to send down *The Cardinal* as kind of a joke for Father Paul's last movie. They had to look all over for it and finally got it as a rental in Japan.

"How'd you like to be the advisor on it, Norm?" Bang.

My mind had wandered, but I heard it. I heard it. I came back, after a fashion, with a tried and true line. "Me, sir?"

"Affirm," said Adams.

"Well, I've only got three months left, and I'm seriously thinking about punching out," I said, grasping for I don't know what. "When would this happen?"

"Around December," said Canada, drilling me with his eyes.

"Well, see sir, there you are right there. I rotate in October."

He came right back with, "I know that, Norm. I also saw your intent to separate, but listen to what I have to say for just a few minutes."

All three of them were watching me. Geez, I thought, where's the little light that hangs down from the ceiling. Do I get a drink of water, one phone call?

"You didn't take your R and R. The Packer thing and the takeover kind of got in the way, and I really appreciate the way you didn't even bring it up. You could take that in the next couple of weeks—say to Hawaii—see Angie, and think over your decision to get out."

He knew my wife's name. Nice touch. But why would a guy extend so he could take R and R when he could end tour and have all of the R and R at home—safe—that he wants?

"And I'd offer you this package. Extend about three months; that gives you time to think. Take your R and R to Hawaii; that takes care of other things. And look over Hawaii while you're at it. If you go with the Benjamin group to Vietnam, I'll personally guarantee a four-year assignment to Hawaii at Wheeler Air Force Base as the PACAF expert on Korea radar deployments and Korean radar matters."

"But, what if I decide to punch after all?" I asked, maybe getting a little interested.

"Then you'll know that was right. I learned from personnel that you've already put in and taken out your intent two times. That doesn't sound like a guy who's sure to me. You don't even have a job lined up, do you?"

"No, sir."

"You leave Vietnam in, say, February, and we'll at least put a damn good medal on your chest. Hell, you could punch out of Hawaii in a year or so after you got there. You'd at least have bucks coming in while you're looking or whatever."

It did sound halfway good. Or was I just crazy, I thought.

"But, sir, another thing that I've got to say is that . . . well, I'm not any kind of special deal. There are any number of controllers in-country who would jump at this, and they're probably better officers in the long run."

Adams put up his hand like he was in class, asking the teacher for permission to speak. And Canada gave it to him.

"Sir, I'd just like to say that Norm should give himself credit for getting close to this group down here. At Osan there are so many advisors and so many counterparts that the close ties don't really form. At other sites, yes, but then those sites don't have Colonel Lees at them, either."

"Yes, Norm, that's really the point. We're not saying you're Jimmy Doolittle. But all of you work together damn well. Lee can handle things, but he'll need an American."

Finally, Ellers put his two cents in. "The mobile unit comes in and sets up. You don't have to get involved in any of that. And the Korean Tiger Division'll be all around you guys for protection. All you'll have to do is help coordinate air ops. It's that easy."

"And you'll only be in Vietnam a month and a half at the most," said Canada, giving me a thumbs-up sign.

"Does Colonel Lee know any of this yet?" I asked.

"He's got a hell of a good grapevine, Norm, but if he didn't have a hint, he's getting the whole story from General Dai right now. Your Friendship Day came in very handy for us all."

"Well, what do you say, Norm?"

I took a deep breath. "Okay, I guess I'll do it." I was crazy. Now I knew I was crazy.

I went right back to my room and hammered out the longest letter I'd ever written Angie, in or out of Korea. I could get it on the choggy the next day, and she'd have it in about three days. The plan was that Lee and I would go up to Osan within a week and work this whole operation with both sides of the house. The meetings would take place in Seoul as well as Osan. I'd be able to call Angie on the commercial line from there and get her response. I couldn't believe what I had done to myself. I was extending. I was going to Vietnam. I was crazy.

In the letter, I told her how much I loved her and I asked her to consider a plan. I couldn't really tell her we were deploying, so I said I was extending because they needed my help and in return I laid out the Hawaii thing. I also very honestly went back over my fear that I didn't have the best plans about what I wanted to do after we punched. Maybe it was radio, or TV even. Maybe it was law school. I didn't know. I didn't bullshit her. It was a good letter. I conceded that I'd made the decision, but I hoped she'd agree. All I could do was cross my fingers.

On the way back from the mailroom, I ran into Paul, Goldman, and most of the priests. I spotted them first and just on impulse I sang out this crazy Irish reel thing. "It was Ryan and Danny and Regis and Patty all say'n goodbye to our Paul. They came from the movie so Catholic and groovy these five priests they all had a ball," I sang and then cracked up.

"Oh, he's danc'n on the par man's grave and the karpse isn't even kald yet," said, Ryan, I think.

And I yelled back, "Aw ga won 'tis lucky we are to be rid of such a one as Paul Francis Fisher."

"See that?" Goldman said. "Give 'em command and they're all the same."

We had us a hell of a party that night. I mean we had everybody. Not only did we end up with every GI on the site, and the priests, and Lee and his bunch, but we also had our visitors from Osan. Lieutenant Colonel Bill Adams loosened up and organized the fighter pilot style drinking games; Lieutenant Colonel Ellers demonstrated paratrooper dives from the roof of the Q after half of a bottle of Beam; and none other than Colonel Virgil E. Canada turned out to be one hell of a crooner. In the words of Regis Riley, "The man sings like an angel."

After we heard Canada sing a few pieces like "I'm Gonna Take A Sentimental Journey" and "Ebb Tide," he took requests. "Irish Eyes" and "Danny Boy" were big, as I remember. On those, we all joined in and we just kept on thinking of songs. We did "I've Been Working On The Railroad," "Whiffenpoof Song," and "Show Me The Way To Go Home." But the best were his solo renditions of old fighter pilot favorites like "I Went Boom Today," "There Was Shit All Around," and of course, "There Are No Fighter Pilots Down In Hell (only Navy Aviators, Bombardiers, and Navigators!)."

When Dutch came in at about twelve-thirty in the morning, he said something to the effect that people from Holland could out eat any people on the face of the earth when it came to hot food. "I do not thinka so Mista Dutch," Major Moon was quick to say. And right then and there the First Annual Tolsan-Do Father Paul Francis Fisher Memorial International Hot Food Contest was on, with two jeeps full of allies dispatched to go and seek out the hottest food in the kingdom.

Canada and Goldman wrote the rules while the food was being rounded up. Essentially, Canada, Dutch, and Paul would match bites of food with Majors Moon, Park, and Captain Ko. Plates would be put in front of the teams all containing the same item, and they'd work their way to the next hottest dish. You could quit anytime you'd had enough. "I vill be da last one eating," vowed Dutch. Holland's reputation was on the line, by God.

When we asked for funds, everyone pitched in. I couldn't believe the amount of food that came back. "Some of us will just eat for the joy of it while the crazies go at it," said Goldman.

We let Colonel Lee start the contest. He dropped a handkerchief and with great applause, the eaters took a bite of the first dish. It was *kimchi*. They chomped. Everyone was still in.

More *kimchi*. Some of it looked pure red in color. Nothing. They all asked for the next dish and the next. "Dis is child's play," said Dutch, patting his stomach.

Then came sauces. You dipped hot stuff in hot sauces. We lost Canada on the second sauce. "I've got to think of my singing career," he said, clearing his throat and gratefully taking the glass of ice water I handed him. Dutch and Paul faced the three Koreans.

More sauce. That put Paul out, who was starting to look a little green. Moon went out, too. Dutch laughed in the faces of Ko and Park. "Two against one," he said.

That prompted Colonel Lee to raise his handkerchief. "I am the not partial ref for thisa contest. Mista Dutch only has to go against one of my officer at this time. Two is not fair now."

We decided that Dutch and Park would face each other off to the finish. They took a break and chugged down some cold Bud. Then the peppers came out. Dutch was great. We were all saying that he was at least going to tie. But there was only one problem: Koreans don't like to lose contests like that on home turf.

The Rocks were controlling what dishes came out, and I thought I saw a conference in the food area. Pretty soon, the peppers started getting smaller. "Norm," Canada whispered in my ear, "those little peppers are pure hell." But old Dutch hung in there, although I thought I saw a strange look creeping over his face.

Finally, they brought out one little green pepper, about as big as your pinkie. They cut it in two, and both men popped a half in. That was it. Dutch almost passed out. I mean, he went down. One minute he was sitting there, confident and chewing. The next, he was down on his knees. All he could do was wave his hands.

A great roar went up from the Koreans. They had won the championship. But God only knows how. That little green thing was something else. For some time after that, we speculated about it. Was it really just a pepper? Had Park really eaten his half? Was it drugged? We'd never know. Goldman had looked for it in Dutch's mouth, and on the floor. But the old boy had swallowed the evidence.

Dutch spent the rest of the night in a spare room. Goldman gave him some medicine and kept checking him. But the party went on. We ate and drank and toasted Friendship Day, Captain Ko's pole climbing, and the departure of Father Paul. Canada led us in more song. On Ellers' last jump, he just lay back down on the grass and went to sleep. I asked him if he was all right and he said, "Fuck yes, I'm a ranger." We covered him with a blanket and Goldman said, "You can say that again."

People drifted away and jeeps left, and somehow it was just Paul and me sitting out on the Q steps. There wasn't a cloud in the sky. It was one of those nights when the stars were just terrific. We were both shit-faced.

"Goin' to miss you, Norm," he slurred.

"Me, too," I said, still swigging beer.

"Don't even know what I'm goin' to do with myself when I get to San Antonio. Ya know?"

"You'll hear confessions, make communion, and do what priests do."

He was giving in to a crying jag. "What in the hell kind of a priest am I anyway, for Chrissake."

"Extraordinary."

"Do you, answer this honestly . . . do you think I 'm a drunk?"

I thought about that. I looked at the beer in my hand. "Yeah, we both are."

"What?"

"We're both drunks. If we don't quit, we're gonna die." There, I thought, I said it.

He tried to get up, but he slipped back down on his rear end. He tried again and finally made it up. It was an unsteady hold he had on the upright position, but he maintained it by weaving back and forth.

"Well that's a fine thing to say to me on the last night I'm here," he said, tucking his shirt in. "I'm not going to stay and take that." He turned and almost fell on his face going up the step. "You're no friend of mine anymore," he said, edging his way back to his room. "You're no friend to me."

"Drinkie people no speak true," I yelled back over my shoulder.

The next day Goldman and I gathered Paul and his boxes and suitcases together, put them in the ambulance, and had a great brunch at the dining hall. Carl Betts finally called there to tell me the choggy was on its way in.

"This is it, Father," I said, "your last ride to the strip." Along with Canada and the Korean General and the two Osan LCs, we put him on board. But not before he had blessed and hugged everyone on the line.

"Norman," he said to me before he went up the ladder, "Jesus would have chosen this place for His remote."

"Well He sent you down to take care of us," I said. And then that was that. When we rode back up to the site I felt homesick for him. The arch we drove under said *Ad Sum*.

23

Lessons of War

About a week later, Colonel Lee and I went to Osan on the ROKAF C-46. Most Americans wouldn't ride on the Korean planes because they were afraid they weren't maintained as well as ours. Well, it was a fine flight. In fact I thought the goon's second cousin was a little smoother. There were some differences between the 47 and the 46. The C-47 Skytrain was the military version of the old Douglas DC-3 airliner, flown by carriers like Eastern in the thirties, forties, and fifties. When she joined the Army Air Force, she was dubbed the Dakota or the Gooney Bird. We called her the Choggy, the Korean expression for back and forth. With two 1100 horsepower engines, the Goon bravely flew the Hump in World War Two. The C-46 Commando boasted two 2000 horsepower engines and twice the cargo space as its Gooney cousin.

We spent the time going to a lot of meetings, but it was vital information. We were learning just where we'd go and what we'd do. It was a good plan.

Sometime in December, we were going to fly straight into a newly built base about halfway up Vietnam. It was called Phu Cat. We'd spend just a little time there and then go to our destination, a place on the coast called Song Cau. It was a little knob on the coast, smack on the ocean thirty-five miles from Phu Cat and only about twenty miles from a city called Qui Nhon. The beauty of it was that Song Cau was big Tiger Division territory, and our mobile radar setup would come in by sea. We'd be out of the way, protected by crack Korean troops, and easily serviced from the seaport. The ROK Navy was to be our supplier. It was a Korean venture from A to Z.

December was a good time to go, too, because it was a stand-down time for both sides. The GIs were into Christmas, of course, and the Vietnamese—both North and South—went into a big lunar holiday called Tet. Nothing much happened in Vietnam from about the first of December until early

January. Unofficial Rules of Engagement, I guess. I remembered Bailey's letter to Packer mentioned that stand-down period. Yet I also remembered how Bailey had said we used it to go kick some ass.

Most of our briefs and planning took place at Osan. I met a lot of people. There were joint meetings and separate meetings. Every night Lee and I would sit in one of our Q rooms and go over what had happened that day. We'd just talk because everything was classified, and we couldn't carry written material back. Our notebooks were locked up in a safe. The code name for the whole thing was Crystal Dragon. The crystal stood for the all-seeing crystal ball of radar and we were the dragons who would use that power to do great deeds.

I had to get tactics down cold. But it sure wasn't anything old Benjamin's guys couldn't handle. It was a combination of flight-follow and join-up with tankers. I didn't think there was much of a chance that we'd control a fighter intercept on a hostile, a bogey.

There were fighters all over Vietnam: F-105 Thunderchiefs, sometimes called "Thuds"; F-4 Phantoms; F-100 Super Sabres; and even prop jobs like the A-lE. Everybody was involved in the air. The Air Force, the Marines, the Navy from carriers, and, of course, the South Vietnam Air Force, called VNAF. Benjamin's controllers studied all of the airplanes, all of the tactics. We even thumbed through pictures of the bombers and the gun ships and the reconnaissance aircraft.

On a typical fighter mission the planes would bust off, bound for targets in either South or North Vietnam, sometimes even Laos. They'd have so much ordinance hanging off them that they had to take off with minimum fuel. The procedure was to get airborne and then join up with a tanker for more gas. You need radar control for that. Likewise, they'd need refueling somewhere on the way back. They'd need flight-follow, too. That was the controller's job in Vietnam. Bailey's letters to Packer had given me my first insights into the job. Now I was getting ready to do it myself.

Crystal Dragon would do its mission from a mobile tactical control radar at Song Cau. One thing I wasn't supposed to tell the Koreans was the fact that another control site, like Monkey Mountain, would be monitoring our frequency and watching on their scopes as well. That was just in case. I had mixed feelings about it. Maybe we'd need it at first, but I was sure we'd be old hands in no time. But I kept that under my hat and decided it was okay. I just didn't want Lee and company to feel like they were being coddled. I didn't want them to know Big Brother was watching.

Crystal Dragon was clean, well thought out, and simple enough to work.

The Korean Air Force would indeed participate in Vietnam and perform a vital mission. It wasn't like flying their own F-5s in on a target, but the ROKs would at least do some controlling. Who knew, maybe the ROKAF would even fly its own missions someday. This was a start. If they did get sorties, these controllers would have the experience to control them.

Lee and I spent a lot of time together in the evenings. Once or twice we ate at Canada's place, and General Dai had a nice party for us at his quarters on Osan. We got a lot of very personal attention. But there was always some part of that day when the two of us would walk around, or just sit over a meal or drinks at the O Club. The late night sessions were the best.

The first time we had breakfast in the club together, it was full of civilian employees having a last cup of coffee before work. There were a lot of American civil servants at Osan, among them a surprising number of American women. They were secretaries, librarians, things like that. I guess I was pretty obvious about eyeing those round-eye gals because Lee whispered to me in a very confidential way: "Is it true what they say about Western women?"

But there was no going downtown or bar hopping with Lee. He was very quiet and just liked taking it easy. He loved to talk about Korea, about life. He told me about the Ying and the Um symbols on the Korean flag and how that round *T'aeguk* at its center locked those two forces—negative and positive—together as a symbol of the dualism of the universe. "Do you not think all man try to keep positive and negative in balance?" he asked me.

"North. South?" I said.

"East. West?" he said.

When I asked him what his religion was, he told me, "Most Korean man sit on three-leg stool. One leg is Buddhism. One leg is Confucianism. One leg is Shamanism. Therefore, we can cover every kind situation."

By the end of a solid week, I knew Crystal Dragon well. I knew what we'd practice. I was ready. And I also called Angie from this soundproof booth in the Osan Club. It was run by the Korean Telephone Company, and you had to schedule your call a couple of days in advance. As it was, my planning wasn't all that great because I woke her up at three in the morning her time.

But it didn't matter.

"I can't believe it's your voice," this lovely sweet, faint voice said. I had to press the receiver to my ear to pick it up.

"It's me, Angie. God, you sound good."

"You, too."

"Did you get my letter?"

"Yes. I get so few, who can miss one when it comes in."

There was a pause. The problem was that there was an echo, too. You talked and then you heard yourself. You found yourself trying to get a sort of timing down.

"I . . ."

". . . was exciting . . ." We interrupted each other.

"Go, Angie. You talk," I said.

"I said yes, I will meet you in Hawaii. Dad and Mom are going to take care of the kids, and Dad's buying my ticket.

"Wow . . ."

". . . plan is a good one. I like the plan." Talking with her was wonderful, never mind the delay and the echoes.

"Wow . . . I'm so happy you think this is okay."

". . . know what you would have done anyway. This gives us a chance to talk, and I know I'd love living in Hawaii for a couple of years."

The little man who ran the show was giving me the signal that my time was about up.

"Angie? Angie?"

"Yes, honey."

"I'm being told that my time's about shot . . . what do you think about the fifteenth of October to meet . . . on fifteen October in Honolulu?"

"Yes, on the fifteenth. I'll write you which hotel 'cause I know you're not the best organizer in this family. Okay?" She was already taking care of the details.

"Angie . . . I love you so much."

"I love you too. Please, please take care of yourself. The kids say hello Daddy."

I didn't deserve her. I had screwed Ihm and not felt guilty, but the phone call brought the full weight of Catholic guilt down on me like a ton of bricks.

I'd signed up for the ROK flight again; Lee wasn't going with me. He would stay a few days more, meet with his people in Seoul, and visit his mother. "I take you to see my city for an evening before you return Tolsan-Do."

We took a staff car back up to Seoul the next afternoon. And he checked me into the famous Bando Hotel. I'd stay there one night and then catch my flight to Tolsan-Do back at Osan. Lee would go to the home of his uncle, where his mother had been living since the father's death.

I'd seen the bright lights and attractions of the city with Belford and Miss Ihm, but with Lee I saw an entirely different Seoul. He took me to a fantastic restaurant where these dollies cooked and fed us *sukiyaki*, real Korean style. But these weren't street girls. They were high-classed women who kept their attention on serving food and tea and playing music on drums and a stringed thing that sounded like a zither to me. Their "Arirang" was played beautifully. The food delicious. This was far better than any of the places I had been. It had real class.

After the food and entertainment, we sat on the polished floor and drank tea. All around us I could hear the sounds of parties. The voices, laughter, chatter, and the clink of glasses in the other rooms was as pleasant sounding to me as the footsteps of the ancestors on Miss Ihm's tin roof. There wasn't another round eye in the room, and I didn't get any dirty looks. It felt good to be totally isolated from my culture.

"To Crystal Dragon," I said, raising my teacup.

"Yes," he said, doing the same, "and to your first time in war."

Our two companions smiled at our comradeship with approval, though they had no idea of what we had toasted to.

"Even though I go to Vietnam," I said, letting the hostess pour me more tea, "I will not have the same experience as you. I will not be watching a war in my own country."

"I wish that you neva do and that I neva do again."

"Maybe because we all fight in Vietnam, we never will face that?"

"Thisa Vietnam very complicated. No person fully understand what it mean. When I was cadet at my ROKAF Academy, as I tell you before, the war came. Everything was scatter. But we join with first unit we see, and I was with ROK Army. After everything more clear I was put with American artillery. Do you know artillery?"

"The big guns?"

"Yes," he laughed, "big guns. And me Air Force Cadet."

Lee motioned for more tea and the little server by him jumped.

I had noticed before that the Korean women reacted to their own males differently than they did to us. There was politeness there, but he was a bit abrupt, too. The ladies treated GIs like devilish little boys who needed their peckers squeezed, but Lee was treated like a father. "Because I am cadet I am with Americans. It is good time for me to study English. I remember one picture in my mind. It is the picture I have of my first time in war; my memory captured that picture. Would you like to hear?"

I nodded. You bet your ass I wanted to hear.

"I was assigned to Colonel Hanway. He was West Point man and he liked to teach me because I was cadet. He was very good to me." Lee emphasized that point with a raised finger that said make no doubt about that. "He would take me in his jeep when unit ordered to fire. We go forward to observe hits from glasses." He put his hands to his eyes in the mock shape of field glasses. I nodded that I understood.

"One day we riding forward and stop on hill road near where North Korean are said to be. Colonel Hanway take glasses and search hills from our position." Lee searched with his hands still formed in two circles, miming the moves of that long ago moment. He was Colonel Hanway. Then he stopped his smooth movements from right to left, left to right, and leaned forward as if to concentrate on something he had spotted.

"Ah, ha," he said, with a crafty smile. "Lee, look here, I find something." The glasses went down and he pretended to take them from Hanway. "Then I look through glasses," he said, adjusting an imaginary focus, "and I see what he find. It is North Korean soldier, sitting on side of hill. He is far away. He does not see us. He is resting on the hill with rifle down by side, and he is eating from tin can. He is eating his rice for the day I think."

He's Hanway again, poking his companion in the ribs. "Lee, we have something for that son-of-a-bitch," he says with a big smile. And then he's himself, lowering the glasses, and looking toward the imaginary Hanway. The girls don't understand him, but they silently nod approval at his artful mime.

"Hanway gets on radio and I put glasses up to look while he makes call. I watch thisa Korean man eat rice and I hear Colonel Hanway say coordinates. He is Korean man sitting on a hill eating rice, but he is also so many degree latitude and so many degree longitude." All the while Lee holds his imaginary glasses tensely to his eyes.

Again, the Hanway pose for an instant. "You just keep watching, Lee." The imaginary glass went back up. "I hear him say, 'Fire at will' and pretty soon shells sing over us and everything is flying dirt in the glasses, and then there is nothing but a hole. And for long time still I watch that spot. Like you swat a fly he is gone."

He finishes with the Hanway pose, looking over at the person sitting next to him, the person still looking through the glasses. "Lee, thisa is the sport of kings!"

When we left the restaurant we walked the streets a while, working our way through the crowds. I still wasn't used to the way you were bumped around by passersby. They had no precious bubble around them, and they didn't respect your Western bubble, either. It was just the way you went down a street, knocking shoulders.

Without warning, everything suddenly came to a halt on the street. The first thing I noticed was that traffic had stopped and all of the cars, bikes, and trucks were pulled over to the curb. Everywhere there were policeman and rifle-toting soldiers pushing the streetwalkers onto the sidewalks. Everyone was lining up as you would for a parade.

Sure enough, some military trucks, loaded with watchful soldiers and military police, did come down the street. Then this fast moving motorcade came rushing by, sirens blasting, motorcycles and black limos mixed together. "This one is President Park coming by," Lee told me. We both saluted as the long limo passed. They didn't mess around when they moved their guy through the streets, I thought. Sometimes the fun and the food and the everyday routine made you forget that Korea was a no-nonsense place. They were playing for serious.

24

Aloha

The next day I was on my way back over the roof of Korea, strapped into the best seat this old ROKAF C-46 had. I was the only GI on board, of course. Just me and the Korean crew. Nobody spoke English.

When we came up on the island, two Korean crew members pulled up some of the metal floor sections, exposing a couple of lines under there. They left and came back rolling a drum over the floor. My God, I thought. It said "Hydraulic Fluid" on the barrel. They connected that up with the largest line, and started cranking this wheel on top of the drum. I was concentrating on the operation.

One of them, a Technical Sergeant, looked over at me and said, "Landing gear down. Landing gear down." They were pumping the landing gear down by hand. Crank. Crank. Crank. We were coming in on Tolsan-Do.

I spent the next few weeks working hard on intercept training. I wanted to simulate refueling intercepts. Over and over again, I had the Benjamin controllers run the F-5s in on the stern of target F-5s. Dick Fife and Carl Betts did the same. I had the ROK instructors teach refueling procedures during the skull sessions. To the best of my knowledge, only Lee and I knew what this was all about. I sure hadn't told my two lieutenants.

The Star-of-David Fund was in the lobster business in a big way by this time. The NCO Club was rolling in bucks. Planes were coming in from all over Southwest Asia, finding an excuse, like a maintenance check, to stop and take on hundreds of pounds of good frozen Tolsan-Do tail. A radio request for so many hundred pounds cold became routine for Benjamin Control. That was a request you wouldn't find in the USAF standard publication on radio-telephone terms.

Goldman had even hired three Koreans to process the things, and fishermen downtown were killing each other to sell the big crayfish to the crazy Americans. Everybody was happy.

Carl Betts had made an interesting discovery. There was a strange looking bunch of radio gear in the same room we kept our radio set, the one we could sometimes contact Osan on when things were just so. It was a single side band job.

Carl had asked about that gear, because it had a huge tape deck attached to it. "Man," he said to Sergeant Mountain one day, "that sure looks like a station rig to me."

"It is, Lieutenant," Mountain said. "There used to be a little broadcast station here years ago. They played Armed Forces Radio programs over it."

"Does it still work?"

"Probably, sir."

That's how Radio Tolsan was born, with Hot Carl as its number one DJ. Mountain and the two communications sergeants had that little station putting out five watts in no time; we could be found at "twelve-twenty-seven on your dial." Locals didn't have to search for weak Japanese stations anymore, because we had our own. Just about everyone on site had his own program.

In places like Tolsan, there's not a lot to do, so one of the big hobbies is to tape great music on your big Japanese tape deck. All the GIs bought them, and the library system kept the albums coming in by the score. My guys would spend hours taping music. You took it all back home and you had enough taped music to last you a lifetime.

When Radio Tolsan came on the scene, the guys now had an outlet for their tapes. Everyone made programs in their rooms and then loaded them up on the station deck. Your program—made up of each person's selection and even chatter—went out all over the island. It was very popular in no time. Why not? You could hear the latest album by everyone from the Beatles to Johnny Cash. The kids got English lessons along with it.

My major contribution was not only the permission to do it, but also the unique sign-on tape that started each day's broadcast. It consisted of me saying, "This is Radio Tolsan." After a two-second pause for the sound of a baseball bat hitting a large metal drum, I'd say, "with studios located six thousand seven hundred feet below the summit of Mount Tolsan." We'd sign off with both the American and Korean national anthems.

The whole thing was illegal as hell. The Armed Forces Network was a very carefully run organization, made up of an exact number of stations all over the world. They didn't know it, but there was one more station on the air.

Of course, only English was spoken over those legitimate stations. On Radio Tolsan it was only a matter of time until Captain Ko introduced the Hanguk Hour, a program for and about Korea in Korean. Ko even had guests from around the island. With that kind of programming, we were absolutely number one in the market. No commercials, of course.

Ko and I would occasionally do this man-in-the-street thing. We'd take a portable tape recorder downtown and go interview shop owners, school teachers, politicians, people like that. We even went out on a fishing boat once. It, too, was all in Korean.

The only time we ever got bad review was when we'd run out of programs and one would play over and over for days. Because of an automatic feature on the station deck, you could do that. Lee's switchboard would be swamped when we'd leave one on too long. "Please changa program," he'd tell me. And if we were out of new productions, we'd kill our signal for a day or two.

Goldman's folks sent him tapes instead of letters. Once when we were in such a situation, he presented "The Goldman Family" for a full three hours. The Koreans downtown probably didn't get much out of that, but those of us who tuned in did get quite a kick out of Tolsan's only Jewish soap opera. Would Uncle Murray save his wholesale suit business? Would Martin, the son in the Air Force, return to pharmacy school? Would cousin David marry the girl from Chicago? Goldman had spent a lot of time editing them and adding commentary. He even had fake commercials for things like "Glow in the Dark Bagels" and "Chutzpa Pills."

Between radio Tolsan and plenty of intercept training, it wasn't any time at all before I was packed and taking a real plane ride: C-141 Starlifter from Osan to Tokyo, Tokyo to Honolulu.

We only stopped in Japan long enough for fuel and some more cargo. It was a great flight, mostly guys going from all over for R and R, Rest and Relaxation. We picked up the Vietnam types on the refueling stop. They couldn't wait to get on board. We were all looking forward to the same thing.

A C-141 is a big plane. There are no windows, just a big cargo hold. It's a super jet, with four Pratt and Whitney turbofan engines. More than a hundred and fifty feet long, you can get about a hundred and fifty people in it or sixty-four thousand pounds of freight. That day, there must have been about a hundred of us, all sitting in rows, in a big metallic tube. Crew sergeants even served us box lunches.

I ended up sitting with a group of pilots from Nha Trang. We were all captains. We were all half preoccupied with fantasies of our wives, who seemed to us as beautiful as any *Playboy* centerfold. You just couldn't imagine how you'd let any one night go without making love. Honolulu would make up for that.

I couldn't get much out of them about Vietnam, and I couldn't tell them why I wanted to hear about it. I could read the frustration they had about it by the way they acted about the war.

"We're really not supposed to win the damn thing," this guy Al Robbins said.

"Between the fuck'n peacenik hippie college kids and the fuck'n press, what we are doing right doesn't mean a shit anyway." That was about the only thing the guy next to me had to say the whole trip. His nametag said "Peck."

"You know the only thing I'm never going to forget about the whole thing is this stream that runs smack through Nha Trang," said Robbins, leaning over his seat at me. "There's a morgue smack on that stream. They let their embalming machines empty into it every day. You have to walk over a bridge to get from the Q to the mess hall. For at least six trips a day, before and after you eat, you gotta look down at that bloody water."

"It's Army blood," Peck said.

"Some consolation," said Robbins.

Angie was right there to meet me. She was beautiful. It's always something of a shock to see someone you're so close to after so many months of separation. She looked so beautiful. There she was, with a big smile and a Hawaiian lei to put around my neck. The other wives were so equipped, too, but she was the best.

When I took her in my arms, I almost blew my load right there in my pants. It was like instant passion. It was just like in junior high school, when you started getting hardons. I had to position it so that spectators wouldn't see me walking alongside her in the airport with a hard-on poking at my pants. I couldn't wait to be alone with her.

About all I did was grin at her. I did that all the way through getting my bags, riding in the taxi, and checking in at the Halekulani hotel. My God, I was on Waikiki Beach with a beautiful brunette with great legs.

"You look good," she said to me after we properly christened our bed.

"Well, you're not so bad yourself," I said, looking her body over for all of the little secret things I knew about it. It was beautifully warm and easy to lie there in the altogether in each other's arms.

"I love you," she said. "I just wish you'd write more."

I felt so dumb. She was such a prize, and I hadn't made any attempt to really write. "Letters seem so futile," I said, pulling her to me.

"Well, letters aren't what I came to Hawaii for," she said, kissing me. We both did more of what we had come for. Afterward, I told her about everything and everyone, save two items: Crystal Dragon and Miss Ihm. It was a complete, but unclassified briefing.

Everything was perfect: us, the hotel, Hawaii itself. The Halekulani had this great buffet breakfast you ate on its stone patio, right on the Waikiki Beach walk. There was just a little patio wall between your table and the long busy beach. It seemed like the whole world walked by there and sooner or later you'd spot someone you knew.

We could have stayed at the military hotel, Fort Derussy, but Angie's father had sprung for this one. We did go to the great Hawaiian show the Derussy O Club had, complete with hula dancers and fire eaters. That place had been packed with American warriors, all on R and R with their wives, whooping it up before daddy had to climb back into a fighter, patrol some jungle river, or lead a bunch of riflemen into combat with "Charlie," an enemy who wore black pajamas and sometimes worked on your civil engineering crew or cut your hair in the PX barbershop by day.

The terrible truth was that some of those who were taken by the hand and led up on the stage to dance with the hula girls wouldn't ever see these wives after this R and R. Some of them would be plain dead, while others would check into another hotel, the Hanoi Hilton. While Angie and I whispered to each other, I reminded myself that I had bought myself a little ticket in those sweepstakes, too.

We ran into both the Robbins and the Pecks at the show. Everybody was a little high and feeling great, and we hung together the rest of the night. We ended up out on the terrace of the Royal Hawaiian, under the old banyan tree that had presided over the 1940s radio show "Hawaii Calls." I had listened to that as a kid, and now there I was.

Al Robbins had been a minor league baseball player before he had joined the Air Force and gotten his pilot's wings. He kept us in stitches with stories of the minors. The best one was about this catcher who was playing past his prime. One day his teammates played a trick on him. Half dressed for the game, he was called to the manager's office. While he was away, they nailed his playing shoes to the wooden floor of the locker room. But they didn't know that at that very moment he was being fired.

"When he came down, he sat on the bench and reached down for his shoes. They didn't budge. 'You fuck'n guys,' he said, 'they canned me and now you've gone and nailed my fuck'n shoes to the floor.' He just got up and walked out. We left those goddamn shoes there all season, nailed to the floor. For the whole season, we never touched them"

"Are they still there?" Angie asked, always so interested in details.

"Probably not, Angie," Robbins said. "That was the locker room for the now defunct Denver Bears. I was one of their pitchers, twenty-three years old, getting nowhere. Right at the end of the season I got myself a hammer and nails, and I nailed my own shoes right next to his because I saw myself in that old guy. Only I decided I'd nail my own down before somebody else did."

He paused to take a drag from his cigarette. Its tip glowed brightly as he did. "I walked away from there on my own and finished school." Silence.

Peck finally broke the silence with, "You know, you'd swear you were back in Nam, there are so many slopes around here."

"Sam," his wife Gail said, punching him on the arm. "He's terrible, I swear."

"At least they speak English," Robbins said.

"Norm's been teaching the Koreans English, haven't you," Angie said proudly.

"They any good?" asked Robbins.

"I think they're terrific," I said.

"I was in Korea once," Peck said. "Some kid pulled my wristwatch off my arm as I passed a crowd in a jeep and damn near tore my hand off. They'll steal you blind."

"I got my wallet picked right out of my pocket once in Evanston, Illinois. What do you think, Sam? Right in America, for God's sake," I said. Nobody said anything for a long time.

"What do you teach 'em," Al said, relieving the tension a little.

"Not the kind of thing you get on the language records. I help them with practical English so they can control better."

"Yeah, I've tried using these damn Vietnamese-made-easy books in Nam. They don't work."

"You read these advertisements in *Popular Mechanics* for books and records like that," I said, and then went into my radio announcer's voice. "You'll be speaking like a native in no time at all. You'll learn such phrases as 'Where might I buy a garden hose?' 'Are these pitted olives?' and 'Do you have any of your grandmother's underpants handy?'"

Everyone laughed. Angie said, "Norm!"

We were drinking Mai Tais. I'd never had them before. They were good. Angie liked them because they were fruity. I liked them because they got results.

We sat there, enjoying the place, the drinks, the company. I liked Robbins a lot, but Peck was a bit sour. Both of their wives were great. It was so neat having Angie there next to me, telling everyone about the kids and how we might be coming to Hawaii. That made me think a little about the dues I'd have to pay to get us there.

It was probably around two in the morning when we all finally gave it up. As we got up to say goodnight, Peck raised his glass and said, "To every Goddamnbody back at Phu Cat."

I hadn't asked him where he was assigned. It hit me right in the skull. "To Phu Cat," I said, looking at the stars through the old banyan tree. "And to all of us."

We didn't waste a moment of Hawaii. If we weren't in the sack making love, Angie and I were out looking the place over. We walked the entire length of both Waikiki beach and the Ala Moana Canal. We went to Pearl Harbor. We saw the Arizona Memorial. We drove our rental car up to the center of the island and found our way through the main gate at Wheeler Air Force Base.

"Angie," I said, somewhat overwhelmed by history, "this is where Father Paul was during the attack. My God, can you imagine we're right there?"

I even found the Base Information Office where a captain showed me how to get to the old Pursuit Squadron HQ building. It had a communications outfit in it, but the building was still pretty much as it had been when Paul was there. The guys in it showed me where the walls had been blown in. I found myself standing in what I was sure had been Paul's room. It was the Executive Officer's digs now.

Outside was the walk where he and Rimmel had carefully lined up the bodies of their buddies. It was a beautiful day, and the air was full of the perfume of Wheeler's flowers and shrubs. War couldn't have been further away. Just across the street was the Base Chapel. Most everything was the same.

"Angie," I said, "Paul always wanted to find out what happened to Sergeant Rimmel."

"They didn't see each other again?"

"No. Paul went off to fight in the Philippines. He never saw Rimmel again," I said, looking up at the pink building that haunted my friend's mind. "But he thinks if he could find this teacher, Miss Sheldon, then he might find out about Rimmel. I think she and Rimmel were lovers."

"Sounds romantic," Angie said, smiling. "Let's try to find her."

"Where the hell would we start?" I said.

"In the phone book. Where else?"

"Under Sheldon?"

"Under Sheldon in the 1941 directory."

We didn't find that directory, but Angie can be persistent. Over the remaining days of our Hawaiian R and R, she'd devote a little time each day to the project of locating Miss Sheldon. She finally hit pay dirt at the University of Hawaii.

"Voila," she said one afternoon after hanging up the phone. "Miss Sheldon, who taught a composition course popular with off-duty servicemen, married Professor Pabish in the chemistry department."

"And?" I said.

"And she still teaches at the university and lives in a place called Hawaii Kai right at this very moment." With that announcement, she grabbed the room phone book and started thumbing through the Ps.

"Pab . . . Pab . . . Pabish. George R. Pabish . . . 922-5811."

"I'll be damned," I said.

"Okay. Detective work's done. You make the call."

I hate the phone. I've always hated the phone. Mindless, rude intruder upon showers, dinners, solitude, and lovers, it can call the nation's highest executives from important meetings and conversations to hear the babblings of any idiot who can dial.

"Angie, I don't know," I said. "It's been a lot of years. She's married to somebody now."

"I know," she said, handing me the damn thing. She sprawled out on the bed. "Make the call, and I'll be nice to you."

So I dialed.

Five rings and a middle-aged voice said hello.

"Mrs. Pabish, my name's Norman Whitman. I'm a Captain in the Air Force. It may be we have a mutual friend." I felt like some kind of a phone salesman. I wanted to get to the point before she thought I was a nut. "Do you remember a young soldier named Paul Fisher? He was stationed at Wheeler Field around the time of the Japanese attack."

She was silent for a moment. "Oh, my . . . yes. I haven't . . . have you seen him recently?"

"Yes, I was stationed with him in Korea. It's kind of complicated, but he's trying to put some pieces together from that time." Silence. "Listen, Mrs.

Pabish, I 'm sorry if I've bothered you. I feel silly that I called you now that I think about it."

"No, no. I'm glad you called, Captain. It's just been so many years. What is Paul doing? He's still in the Army?"

"No, he's in the Air Force."

There was silence again, "Is he well?"

"Yes he is. It's nothing like that."

"After the attack he left so suddenly, I had no idea of what had happened to him. It was all very hard on him."

"Yes. That's really why I thought I'd try to call you."

"I'm glad you did."

"Mrs. Pabish, you probably remember Paul's buddy, Sergeant Rimmel."

"Oh, yes, Henry Rimmel. You don't have to tell me that Paul's still bothered by that. I know. Paul couldn't accept the fact that he wasn't on post when the attack came." She paused for a few seconds and my reaction was to sit down on the bed. "He was on a pass. He was with me. I was fixing him breakfast when the planes came over." She was getting that out fast and firmly, with a resolve that said, Don't judge it, just listen. "We went outside, and you could see the smoke and the planes making their dives right from where we were in Wahiawa." She paused again. "I gather he didn't tell you the details, did he?"

"I guess the thing I'd like to know about is Sergeant Rimmel."

"He had agreed to cover for Paul while he was on pass. Paul had the only private room in the barracks, and Henry liked to stand in for him because he'd get to sleep in Paul's room as part of the deal. Henry couldn't stand the noise in the barracks and that was how it was that poor Henry was killed there in Paul's room." She wanted a response.

"Yes, Mrs. Pabish, I'm sure Paul somehow blames himself."

"Poor Paul just ran so fast to the base. He had his uniform on. He got there after it was all over, and I know he worked for the rest of the day taking care of what had happened. After that, he was just lost."

I had opened up a place I shouldn't have, I thought. She was a very nice lady. I had called her, out of the blue, on a bright day in Hawaii, like so many she'd had since the times I had reminded her of. She was married to some guy by the name of George Pabish, That was how things were, and I was playing around with something I had no business getting into. I knew I had to end it as soon as I could.

"Will you see him?" Her voice startled me.

"Yes I will," I lied.

"But he is all right?"

"Yes, ma'am, he is. Still bothered by things, I guess."

"And he has good friends," she said helping me end it.

"He has us all," I said. I put some firmness in my voice. "Mrs. Pabish, I want to thank you so much for talking to me, for sharing some painful memories with a voice over the phone. I might have known Paul would have known someone like you."

"Thank you. I'm glad you called."

You can tell when somebody's listening hard over the other end of a phone. It has something to do with the depth of the silence, the intensity of it. There are no background noises, no rustlings, no hints and diversion. We hung up together.

Angie and I just sat on the bed for a while, holding hands and letting the Hawaiian breeze wash over us as it blew through our hotel window. Outside, down below on busy Waikiki, the surf rolled in and countless R and Rs were in various stages of beginning, happening, and ending. "Angie," I said, "I think if I thought about not drinking I could do a better job for us."

The rest of the trip was as wonderful as the start, yet richer. We drove around the entire island, stopping to swim at all of the famous beaches: Waimea Bay, the Pipeline, Laie. We did that on a Sunday, and by chance we found a little Catholic church in a town called Waialua that was just starting mass. Saint Michael's was smack in the middle of sugar plantation country. We sat there with the congregation, everyone an islander with Hawaiian, Polynesian, Asian, or Portuguese ancestry saying the prayers of the mass and loving the closeness we felt for each other.

The night before it was all over, we sat out under that old banyan tree again and reviewed our options. I could get out of the Air Force, or be right there in Hawaii in just a few months. I mumbled something about law school, too.

"Norm, I'll go along with whatever you decide," Angie said, holding my hand, searching my eyes for a reaction to her words. "The Air Force is fine. Law school's fine. I think I'm more excited about some of the other things you've said, though. You'll do a good job at whatever you do. I just want us to be happy." She was never more understanding and beautiful.

25

Goddespeed

Angie went out on United, and I hitched a ride out of Hickam on a 141. I went back into Yokota where I put my name on a standby list for Korea. I was on leave status, so guys in my category had to wait for an empty seat. The lists were huge, the terminal overflowing with troops going to Vietnam, families going PCS, and standbys like myself.

In fact, there was so much traffic, Uncle actually contracted commercial airlines to carry troops. World Airways was doing a thriving business. You crossed your fingers for a seat. It was much easier to go from Korea on a standby than it was to get back. I also learned that a lot of the 141s heading for California were full of those lightweight caskets, the kind that Packer went home in. No waiting. All aboard.

I didn't dare leave the terminal, so I amused myself watching the people. Funny how the sailors acted and looked like sailors, the airmen like airmen, and the grunts like grunts. Marines always looked sharp and somehow a little naïve. A goodly number of the dependent wives were attractive, especially the ones dressed up to travel. Watching them made me horny for Angie.

I watched one of the TVs they had scattered around the terminal. The Japanese wives pretty well had those tuned to Tokyo stations, so I sat and watched Japanese commercials. It was easy to guess what they were selling in some, and then again some were plain bizarre. The Japanese language seemed to have a lot of loud grunts in it, and that came out in the zeal the characters expressed for the product. The little tunes they played for the crackers, medicines, and weird cartoons were Asian upbeat and crazy, too. Between commercials I watched parts of *Bonanza*, with voices dubbed in. The best part was to watch old Hoss say his lines in Japanese.

Finally, I ran out of things to do. Just before I started to scream with boredom, I got an inspiration: General Pitts and his boys—save for Belford—were headquartered here. Old Clinton Davis was here, I thought. Since it was three in the afternoon, I looked up Pitts' office number. The directory I had still had Belford down as the executive Officer. Damn. I didn't want to talk to a stranger. So I tried to find Clint. Nothing.

After losing my nerve five times, I finally dialed Pitts' office. "General Pitts' office, Colonel Yates speaking," said the voice. It was Bud Yates.

"Sir," I said, "This is Captain Norm Whitman from Tolsan. Do you remember me?"

There was a pause. "You mean the Appo Kid, don't you?" he laughed.

"Yes, sir, one and the same."

"Hey. Where are you?" he said, making me feel at ease and not stupid for calling.

"Sir, I'm in the terminal waiting to see if I can get a standby for Kimpo."

"You know, I was going to try to get ahold of you, wait a minute." I could hear muffled conversation while he put his hand over the receiver.

"I'm sending a car over for you, Appo. Look for a blue staff car out front in about ten minutes."

"But, sir," I objected, "I may miss my chance for a seat."

"Christ, Norm, we can get you to Korea. Get your ass out front."

When I got to the office, Yates took me right in to see the general. I guessed he wanted to talk about Crystal Dragon.

"Gee, Bud," he said to Yates, "wait till the Japanese find out that Appo's here. We'd better get him back over to Korea fast." We shook hands.

"I'll see what I can find, Norm," Yates said, shutting the door on us.

"I'm glad I thought to call you, sir," I said.

"Listen, Appo, so am I. I got a big one for you to do in November."

We were going to Vietnam a month earlier than I'd planned?

The general got very serious, sat forward in his chair, and talked in a very confidential tone. "Keep this close under your hat, but we're goin' to host the First International Hunting Meet at your place."

I just looked at him blankly. "Sir?"

"What I want to do is invite a team from each of the Major Far East and Pacific allies to come on over to Tolsan and shoot birds for a couple of days in competition. Most birds killed wins."

We planned out the First International Hunting meet. He would invite teams from Japan, Australia, the Philippines, Taiwan, Vietnam, England, and, of course, the U.S. and Korea. In reality, most of these folks would be foreign embassy folks, like Brigadier Rushworth representing the UK. "But the idea is to build a little international camaraderie and have a hell of a good time."

I'd help Clint get the lodge ready, fix the permits with the island hunting office, and arrange the logistics for the meet. The general would get the teams there and see to it that things were paid for.

Just as I was going out the door, he motioned me back in for a moment. "You took the Vietnam thing?"

"Yes, sir, I did. That's why I'll be there in November."

"Look, that's a political gesture more than anything else. Just get them in there, run a few refueling missions for a month or so, and then pull out. That place is owned by the ROKs. The cover's excellent. We just want them to be able to say they did it." Then he patted me on the shoulder.

"Thank you, sir," I said, feeling good about the Vietnam venture. Political gesture made it sound harmless.

"You got him a flight, Bud?" he asked Yates.

"He's wheels up on a World Airways in thirty minutes, boss." That had to be one of the smartest phone calls I'd ever made, I thought. The hunting meet was going to be a pain in the ass, but the flight back and the soft words about Crystal Dragon were outstanding.

When I got back to Tolsan, everything was smooth. My two lieutenants met me at the choggy and had nothing but good news. The weather had been great and Benjamin had logged well over a hundred intercepts for the two weeks I was gone. Colonel Lee had been in place for almost every one. The control English was superb, Carl told me.

As I was loading the jeep with my bags, old Star-of-David came walking up to me, popping me an overdone salute. "Well, did she know you?"

"She did, but we spent the whole time trying to think of who she could get to marry you."

"Well, whatever she finds better like Colorado," he said, waiting for me to pick up on that.

"You got orders, then?"

"Air Force Academy. I'm going to the cadet dispensary."

It turned out that the only person on the whole site that had a problem was the fire chief, Mr. Paek. When we all got back from the flight strip, he wanted to see me right away. I invited him to come over to the Q living room, where I could pour him an orange drink and make him feel important. Old Paek and his boys really kept those engines shining and running smoothly. They were there at the strip for every flight, rain or shine, because of the ever-present danger that one of the flights would smack in. Paek and company were always ready.

In fact, they loved to zoom out of the fire station when they got the word to meet the choggy. It was quite a show. Sirens and lights blazing full bore, they loved to show off as they went through the village to the flight line. It was about time I paid him and the department some attention.

After we settled into the overstuffed chairs, orange drinks in hand, I said, "Mr. Paek, what can I do for you today?"

He was proud to be there talking with me, but his face became very serious. "We still do not fight fire downtown. Now it is dry again, and people of this Tolsan-Do say we neva come if housa burn."

Their fellow Koreans knew they were good, but the firemen had always taken a lot of flak because our rules wouldn't let them fight a local fire. For years, they had been badmouthed. "Now my men very unhappy," he said. "They want to help fellow Korean, but neva can. We all lose face."

I could well understand how they felt. We came trespassing through the town all the time, chasing airplanes that never crashed while their houses really did burn down. We had the good stuff, but never helped.

"Maja Dubb neva give me chance," he said.

"Okay, Chief," I said, "The next time there is a fire, you come and tell me and I think maybe we can do."

His face lighted up. I'm sure he knew I was going to say yes.

"I go tell my men now," he said, standing up. Giving me a big salute, he said, "You do good for Korean people." He practically ran out of the Q. He'd really be a big man downtown now, the first fire chief to break the no-fight-local-fires barrier.

It wasn't more than three days later that he came running up to Goldman and me just as we were going in the NCO Club. Goldman knew what I had promised. "Look at him run. All of Tolsan must be on fire, sir."

"Sore, sore. Big fire now burns down Korean building. They only need our truck to save it, sore."

He looked like a little child, standing there begging to go.

"Okay, Chief, let 'er rip," I said. No sooner did I say that than he turned and signaled with his hand. The number one engine came roaring out of the firehouse, loaded down with Korean firemen. He ran to it, hopped into the cab, and the whole crew went thundering out of the compound.

"Goldman," I said, "let's follow them in the jeep."

It didn't take too long for us to spot the cloud of dust that was the chief and number one engine. I let the jeep out and Goldman and I gave it a couple of "Ya-Hoos." But they didn't take the turn to the town. Instead, they made a right and the dust cloud headed toward the sea road. "Where the hell'er they going?" I yelled over the jeep noise.

"Stay with 'em," Goldman replied with a forward-ho motion of the right hand.

So we followed our engine down the dusty sea road. Finally, Goldman pointed ahead to a rising column of smoke and said, "There it is." I pressed the accelerator down so we'd be there for that glorious moment when the fire was put out by our guys.

Sure enough, I could make out the engine as we got closer. The chief had violated my rule by going so far away, but I decided I wouldn't say too much. This was a large village, on the way to the priests' pig farm. The fire seemed to be out, and the engine was in front of a pretty well ruined building. I had wanted to see our guys in action, but everything appeared to be over.

When we finally pulled up on the scene, I saw our engine and the damaged building all right. There was no fire here at all. Our engine had gone too fast, couldn't make a sharp turn, and plowed right into the building. It was stuck halfway into the building as a matter of fact.

Chickens were walking on the rear of the fire engine, people were forming into a large crowd, and I spotted my fire chief in the middle of a group of very angry Koreans. The other firemen were standing around, looking ashamed. As if on cue, as I pulled up, the chief turned and pointed at me. All eyes looked in my direction. I could tell I was in charge of something again. In the background, about a mile up the road, I could see a building burning to the ground.

Once we got to translating, I found out that this was, or had been, the newest building in the village. We all went inside the local "office," and I talked to several men in police uniforms, some village officials, and other assorted high people. Finally, I signed my life away on some pieces of paper and we left. I told the chief I'd send the motor pool for him and the engine, if they could haul it out of there.

When I got back, I phoned Colonel Lee. I told him the story, and he said: "Your driver very stupid to go into the building." I agreed. I needed help, too. He agreed. He told me he'd have to call the head policeman on the island. Once again, Lee was trying to save my bacon with the local cops.

The accident happened on a Saturday. It only took Colonel Lee a few hours after my call to set up a meeting with the head Chief on Sunday afternoon. What a convention that one was. Jeeps came from everywhere. The Q living room filled up with our firemen, people I had seen at the disaster site, and lots of other officials came because the big man would be there. Come he did, in a five-police-jeep caravan about an hour after things were set to happen. This same Chief had been with us at Oyster's hooch and at the dedication of the ROKAF arch. He was as pleased as ever with my salute as he got out of his jeep. We went into the Q, and he and I and Lee sat in front of the gathering.

The story was told and retold out on the living room floor. My chief told the big Chief what had happened, complete with engine sounds and crashing noises. In tears, the owner of the building told his side. The translation, for my benefit, was pretty good. I especially liked the part where my chief pleaded for his driver's driving privileges and his own, since it was me—after all—who had ordered them to go to the fire.

Not only was the building a disaster, but the fire engine looked grim as hell. It wouldn't be fighting any fires until the banged-in front and cracked radiator were fixed. That was what I didn't want them to find out about up in Osan. God help me if there really would be an aircraft crash. I had managed to put our big fire engine out of commission.

After all the storytelling, the big Chief told Lee he'd like just the three of us to go to another room. I took them down to my room, and when we closed the door he became all smiles, bowed, and had Lee tell me he was delighted to see me again.

"He says you are one of his good friends here," the colonel told me. "Now pour three of us some whiskey and serve him first," he said.

The Chief beamed at the drinks, sat down in Dubbs' old easy chair, and began to talk. Lee translated.

"He feels so bad for you. He knows you feel bad," Lee said.

"Yes, sir," I said at the Chief, bowing in my chair.

As the Chief continued, so did Lee. "But this is not all so bad, says this police chief. He says your firemans and civil engineers can, ah, build the building back up and help make it good again. He says he can make a rule that the people did build it too close to road in the first place. They did a stupid thing not to let enough road for important firefighting trucks to pass."

"Yes, sir."

"Now also, he know a man who does metal work so good you cannot tell, and he knows your own motor pool can fix the bad radiator."

Lee looked at me and said, "He and I talk of these things long time last night. Korean good at fixing broken things up. We can make the building look like new, the truck look like new. Your motor pool can make the inside good. My people checked."

Sergeant Camp had in fact told me that the only thing he couldn't do was the bodywork, and if I could get him to Japan he'd be able to get the parts he'd need to get the radiator going.

Lee continued with, "These village people and your people will work on this together."

"Sirs," I said, looking at them both, "what can I do as a way to make up for the stupid thing my people did?" I said it calmly but I held onto the arms of my chair. The big Chief had me right where he wanted.

Lee and the Police Chief talked in Korean for a few minutes, and then Lee gave me the bill. "This police head man says there is now coming to the island a big holiday. On this day he must give people like the Governor of the island just the right kind of gift. He thinks he must give good whiskey to these people on that day."

"Ah, sir, should I give him some bottles, or what?" I said.

"No," he said. "He will pay for it. He says he needs around twenty cases of good all kinds whiskey."

"Done," I said.

Everything did work out. The firemen and Dutch's engineers worked on the building and there was even a ribbon-cutting ceremony, with me as one of the guests of honor. Sergeant Camp had flown, illegally, to Japan on a flight that had dropped in for some lobster and brought back a new radiator. Along with the violation of sending an NCO to Japan without orders and passport, I had also sold a foreign national twenty-two cases of assorted whiskey at below cost. I threw in one extra case on the house. The truck was hammered out, painted, received a new radiator, and looked like the day it rolled off the Detroit assembly line. We even made it to local fires after that, and put them out. Everybody was happy.

The time to say goodbye to Goldman followed on the heels of our firefighting adventures. In my mind, it was a milestone event. Of all the GIs I knew on my crazy Korean tour, this Jewish staff sergeant had meant the most to me. Father Paul had been wonderful, and old Oyster had been part of the good times, too. But Goldman was the steady, wisecracking pundit who kept you humble and made you want to stay with it. He was always there when you needed him.

His going away party was a big one. All of the NCOs, most of the priests, and Koreans from everywhere came to toast Goldman's reassignment and watch this godawful skin show he'd brought in from Tolsan City. These dollies took it all off and danced around in front of the fireplace to the tune of the "Stripper," played by a Korean trio made up of an accordion, trumpet, and drums. It was so gross, it was good. The priests excused themselves to the dining area during the entertainment.

I had a few beers, but I was trying to keep the booze under control. So far I had done very well. I hadn't been blitzed since before Hawaii. I was trying.

Around midnight, Goldman came around to my corner of the bar. Regis Riley and I were sharing letters we had gotten from Paul. They were brief, but warm. He was in place in the Chaplains' school, hating every minute of it.

"Father, I need the commander for a minute," he said, and motioned me to follow. He had two glasses and a paper bag.

"What's up," I asked.

"Just follow the doctor. It's a ritual, sir."

So we walked out of the club, and Goldman motioned me into the club wagon. "We gotta take a drive," he said. "This is my last night, and I'm in charge."

Out the gate, under the arch, and down the town road. I held the paper bag and the two glasses. There was a cold bottle in the bag; I could feel it through the wet brown paper. He kept his eyes forward until we came up on the icehouse. I nodded my head.

Our old friend, Mr. Min, let us in after a rap or two and Goldman handed him some won. "You let us go back room, okay, Min?"

"Yeah, sure, Mista Goldie," he said, pointing his finger. It was chilly. I remembered the first time I'd been there.

Goldman and I walked to a room I'd never been in before. It, too, was full of ice, something of a storeroom. You could see that people were renting space there, keeping high value perishables there during the summer. Of course, I knew in my mind's eye what else this room had held.

He handed me a glass and pulled a bottle of champagne out of the bag. Pop went the plastic cork, and he poured the bubbly into our glasses.

"Father Paul wanted this to be the going away toast for all of us--for him, me, you, and Oyster. He wanted me to say that the best part of us was our humanness and that we should drink to that and the friendship we had known together. Let me say that Paul was a priest who could say 'Shit,' Oyster was a man who could love dogs, I was an enlisted man who could tolerate some officers, and you were a man who could love the three of us." He put his glass up in the air. "To rock, women, and storm," he said.

"To the high skies and fat horses beyond," I said, clinking his glass.

We smiled at each other. "I was supposed to give you this from Paul, but he says it's from us all to you." He brought out a little piece of tissue paper, wrapped over itself, tied with string. It was light, but something was in it. I fumbled with it and brought out a very worn gold Saint Christopher medal on a chain. On the back side it said: Henry W. Rimmel, USA. "Put it on," said Goldman. I did so with tears freely streaming down my cheeks.

Next day, Goldman got on the choggy and headed for leave with his folks and then the Air Force Academy, Oyster's alma mater.

26

Chopper

The last event of the summer arrived one Saturday afternoon. I had just taken a steam bath and a shower, and midway through the shave I got a call to come up on the hill because "airplane calls for gee-eye controller." It was Lieutenant Ko, who was certain it was a choggy flight. I didn't think it was, and a quick check of my notepad confirmed it. I was okay. There were no scheduled choggies from Osan.

It was a real pain in the ass to have to climb the hill. I was getting ready to go to a big party hosted by the island Governor. Colonel Lee had said he'd be by to pick me up around 1900, so I had allowed myself time for a steamer, shave, and a couple of good belts before he came. Now I'd have just enough time to dash up there and see who the hell was inbound. I decided to put on my dress blues so I'd be ready for Lee in case I got delayed.

Up I went and sure enough my query was answered, "Roger Benjamin, this is Army 33574, inbound, heading one-seven-five, angles 2, estimate your strip two-five past the hour."

I sat down at the scope, swept out to seventy-five miles or so and then spotted a big blip at about forty miles out. I couldn't figure why the Army was coming in. "Army 33574, say why landing Tolsan and say what kind aircraft, over."

"Roger, R and R Chinook flight out of Camp Carroll. We're going to stay at your site and tour Tolsan-Do."

I hadn't got any word about any R and Rs. Who in the hell authorized that, I thought to myself. I didn't need this shit. I had to get to that party. "Who cleared you for seaflight, 33574?" I asked with a cut in my voice. Helicopters weren't supposed to fly between Tolsan and the mainland unless we knew about it, and the hard-fast rule was that they had to fly in pairs. You didn't just drop in on us.

"Just meet us at the strip, Benjamin."

"Maybe you better turn your ass around, Army 33574, since you're not cleared Tolsan."

"Negative, Benjamin, and watch your language on frequency!" he said in a tone I didn't much like. He added, "We've plans made and need turnaround anyway." Turnaround! I had him there; I didn't have any gas. We didn't refuel. We couldn't give him turnaround.

"Roger, Army 33574, understand you can't return due to fuel. You're declaring emergency. And fuck you, I say again, F-U-C-K you. You're now bearing one-eight-zero Tolsan strip, look for the weather tower, wait landing until you see fire engines signal with red flasher. I'm in blue jeep. See me." Don't you tell me not to swear on the air, you grunt, I thought.

I handed the flight-follow-over to Captain Ko and told him this was an unauthorized landing and to log it into the control book that way. Ko was saying, "He saysa he is no emergency," at me as I headed for the jeep and the strip. I didn't much like grunts, never did.

Ko's crew had notified the firehouse, and I saw the trucks pulling out below as I climbed into the jeep. I could also see a dot approaching from the sea, and that had to be Army 33 whatever-the-hell.

It was a Chinook. She came thunderassing in, whirling and bam-bamming, bigassed green Army eggbeater. There were heads peering out from every window. Geez, I thought, even one of the co-pilot's got civvies on. What the hell kind of a deal was this anyway?

They all got out, about thirty people, dressed like tourists, carrying bags, cameras, and even golf bags. Hell, I'd have to call the motor pool for a bus to get them all up to the site. After the engines were shut down, up walks this Army major—the only guy in uniform—like he was MacArthur landing at Wake Island.

"I'm Major Macalister, are you the person I talked to?"

"Yeah," I said. "I'm the American commander here. I don't understand what the hell this is all about."

"Hell," he said, "it's really not all that complicated. I'm bringing these troops down here for a well-deserved vacation, just for a few days and then home. You don't have anything against taking care of the troops, do you?"

He was a real smart ass. His black hair was just right and his flight suit was very neat. Looked like he might be a West Point bastard.

"No, I don't. If you had told us you were coming, I'd have been delighted. Now I'm going to have to really scramble to find enough clean beds and linen because our big lodge is closed until the season opens. Our extra help is laid off till then. Even that would have been okay, if you'd just asked. I'll bend rules anytime to accommodate this kinda thing," I said looking into his fixed, smart assed, self-assured eyes.

"Just do the best you can. Let me say I understand."

"You bet I will. You think you're some kinda hero, bringing them down. They're going to have a hell of a good time. I'll sleep 'em in the lodge and our NCO club'll be delighted to have the business. I'll even ride their asses up to Tolsan City tomorrow, and all over the fuck'n island for pictures or whatever."

"Fine," he said, without even being a little grateful or civil.

"But I've got my bone to pick with you. You didn't let us know. I'll tell you what else. You didn't file a flight plan, and you didn't fly with another chopper, and you weren't cleared for Tolsan-Do."

"Look," he said trying to dismiss me, "in the field you bend rules a little for the common good. Don't give me all this flak."

"One more thing," I continued, as if he hadn't interrupted. "You didn't read the flips very well, either. You've got just one more problem. I'm not a turnaround facility here. I don't have a single drop of gas. I can't get your Army ass out of here. If your people think you're somewhere else, they're soon going to know where you are, 'cause you're going to have to ask for fuel to be flown in. Boy, you think *I* threw rules at you. Just wait till you see how big this one is going to be."

Now I had his attention. I could tell his ass was in a pucker.

"You're going to run up a hell of a bill for this gas stop, Army. It's going to take days for them to figure out how to do it."

"Hey, listen," he pleaded, "don't call anybody yet. I gotta have time to think."

I just left him standing there and put in the call for the bus. He stood there for a while, talking to the other pilot. They were really sweating it out. Finally, the bus carne and took their troops to the site. They both came over to talk some more.

"Can you do anything at all?" the co-pilot said.

"I've got to get to an important function right now," I said, motioning them toward the jeep. "I'll take you to the Q and we'll talk tomorrow."

The ride to the BOQ was silent, with me really kicking up dust. I didn't want to have Lee waiting around for me and when we pulled up he was, in fact, sitting in his jeep. I parked, hopped out, and left them sitting there. "There's the Q. Use rooms 22 and 23. I gotta go." And we drove off.

On the way, I told Colonel Lee who the Army officers were. "I wonder why this helicopter makes a landing on my strip."

He laughed at my anger and said, "You sometimes get too worried about little problems. This helicopter just makes a good surprise for us both."

He seemed happy about the whole thing. At least I hadn't brought in any unexpected visitors without clearing with him. I didn't like to leave him in the dark about anything.

The party was a honey. Typical of these affairs, I was the only GI there, and, typically, I was treated royally. It didn't take too many passes of the *chung jung* pot to get me buzzed. We all sat at a long table, legs folded, and ate good food. Though I only could talk English to a very few, somehow I understood everyone. It was hard to stick with the booze moderation experiment when I went to a Korean party. They won't take no for an answer when it comes to passing the *chung jung*.

The strange thing about being there with those people was that through facial expressions, zany movements, and a line translated here and there, I always felt we communicated very well. But the rice wine didn't hurt a bit, either.

Colonel Lee was seated next to me, and next to him was the Governor. After the party had been in full swing for a while, he turned his attention to me and we exchanged a few glasses.

"Your helicopter pilot has big problem that I told to the Governor," he said, putting down a slug of wine.

"Yes, sir, he does," I said.

Lee moved his hand in a calming motion. "Maybe he does not need to be in trouble. But I must first tell you a story that I think you will understand. Will you understand a story about a Korean man?" he said, getting very serious.

"Yes, sir."

"Long time ago when the Korean War is going, my ancestor commander here on Tolsan was colonel like me. He have more to worry about than me. There was much to do. He even had airplanes of his own for the trip to Osan base. He even have gas for these planes. Your own people have gas, too, for their planes that stayed in this base."

We were interrupted for several minutes as the group was led in impromptu song. The more rice wine I put down, the more I remembered the words to "Arirang."

"That Korean commander very smart man," Colonel Lee continued. "He find out that Americans decide not to keep gas at this base after the war.

Now, he thought this was bad thing. If a new war came and Koreans after that needed gas, there would be none. Can you see why he is worried about that?"

"Yes, sir."

"He order that some of this gas to be put in safe place in case of the emergency. He have another fuel dump built, but he did not tell his American counterparts about that. But do you think he steal this gas?"

"I think he exercised damn good command judgment," I said, toasting with my wine glass.

"I must also tell you that I said this thing to the Governor, and he also said it was bad that the Army helicopter pilot will get into trouble. I want to offer some of this gas to him. My engineers say it will run this kind helicopter."

"Colonel, this guy doesn't deserve it, but that's a fabulous thing for you to do."

Lee smiled. It was that smile that told me he had yet to give me part two of his speech. "The Governor say that the parents of his wife, and even his own father, have never see Tolsan from the air. Many high government officials never see Tolsan from the air."

The beauty of the Korean brand of you-scratch-my-back-I'll-scratch-yours was its simplicity of line. "Colonel Lee, I think you and the Governor have made some good plans."

"Yes, we think there might be chance for all these people to see the island in this helicopter. I have enough gas to do this, and it will cost nothing to American Army. We use gas for good community relations. Pilot will want to pay back. He can do this thing by taking these people on air tour of island."

I couldn't wait to get back to the Q.

When I came through the front door, the Army guys were sitting in the living room. It looked like they hadn't moved for hours. They were the picture of glum.

"Hi, gents," I said, as I walked behind the bar for a beer.

"Did you find the rooms?"

"Yeah. Hey, listen. I can't get out on your phones," the major said.

"Yeah, the comm only works about once a month down here. We could be at war, and I'd never know it."

"Damn!"

"You could use the long range radio setup, but the only problem is that everyone in Korea can listen in. It comes out over a loudspeaker up in the Osan and Seoul command posts."

"Boy, you're really enjoying this, aren't you?" the co-pilot said.

I put my beer down hard on the bar. "Okay, look. You two guys come in here like you own the place, act like snobs on the radio, and then I find out you didn't even cover your asses the right way. You did a dumb thing, not to mention the fact that it really was a pretty stupid move from the standpoint of safety. Christ, do you always fly into places where there's no fuel?"

They just looked at each other, trying to hold back the urge to slug me. I knew they'd love to break a chair over my head.

"I'm all for taking care of the troops, but you guys need wet nurses just to keep you out of trouble. You don't do this to a commander. You really put me on the spot."

That did soften them, just a little. I took a swig of Bud and leaned forward. "But I can get you out of it. The Korean CO here has fuel stashed away. He's gonna let you fill 'er up."

"That's damn decent."

"Yeah, but it has a price tag on it," I said as I put down the last of my beer. I walked to the fridge, opened the door, and got down to get another one. I spoke to them with my back turned, saying the words into the open, cold fridge. As I talked, I made puffs of winter breath. "You guys are going to be tour guides tomorrow. Colonel Lee will fill you up 'even this night,' and after the tour tomorrow, you get your tank for home."

"Shit," the pilot said, "I can't do something like that without approval from God, for Christ's sake. I'd be taking a hell of a chance."

I looked at his buddy and popped my next beer. "Is he a friend of yours?"

The guy nodded.

"Well, then tell him, explain to him again what he's already done. I can't believe he's worried about that, after he's just broken every goddamn rule in the flight manual. Are you crazy, or what?"

"He's got us by the short ones, Rich," Co said to Left Seat.

"Man, I'll tell you, Whitman, you and your Koreans are the biggest bastards I've run into anywhere out here."

"Say one more thing about Colonel Lee, and you'll get gas drop zilch."

"Okay, you shit, we'll have to do it."

"Good," I said. "A Major Moon will be over here in the next hour or so. One of you will have to go down to the strip with him and show his boys the fine points of filling up your bird. Get some sleep. Tours start at zero nine hundred tomorrow morning sharp."

With that, I tossed away my last drink of the day and headed for my room. How sweet it was.

The next day was glorious. At eight or so all these Koreans started showing up on the strip. God, was it colorful. I loved it. The women were dressed in traditional full dresses and the men had on their best suits. The old men wore these great, broad-brimmed hair hats. That was a sign of grand old age, wisdom, position, and, mostly, survival.

Many brought along crazy-wonderful things, like pet goats. The goats had ribbons on them, too. The ladies carried parasols. They all spread out mats and broke open baskets filled with dried weeds and fishes and all sorts of rice cakes, treats, and fruits. It was one of the happiest, most colorful scenes I'd ever been a part of.

There were lots of little children, too. They were all decked out in their school uniforms and they were having a ball running around the chopper. Lee had set up a tent affair for the Governor and his party. When I arrived, everyone was all smiles. The rice wine was plentiful.

The Army was sitting inside the ops shack, looking at a map I'd given them of the island. Lee had given it to me.

He and the Governor had marked all the places they wanted to fly over. To tell you the truth, I was impressed with the pilot's concern for mapping out the flight plan so he'd fly it all.

When they were just about ready, the pilot said to me, "Do you know how they fueled me?" Without waiting for any reply on my part, he said, "They did it by goddamn hand. Those little bastards had a hand pump and put it in drum by drum. Can you believe that shit?"

"Yes, I can. Don't forget, they're inscrutable."

At nine hundred on the dot, the Governor, his father, wife, mother-in-law, kids, and other friends took off on the first pass. There was an intercom on board, and I had driven just one more stake into the Army's hide by asking that Captain Ko use it to announce the tour's high points to the people on board. That was a nice touch, because it really did turn the chopper into a tour bus.

So it went, for more than five hours. They even took the goats on board. Everyone loved it. And I really have to give the Army credit. They did a great job. It was indeed a great day for American-Korean relations.

I got drunk and ended up going off to a follow-up party in Tolsan City that night. It was on the Governor. Lee and I and all the Korean officers piled in jeeps and six-packs and headed north. I didn't have to spend the evening on the site. I did tell Mountain to see to it that the Army officers got a good dinner and anything else they might need. As for their troops, they had a great time. The NCOs treated them to everything you'd want on the island, including that bus ride and night in Tolsan City.

Hung over, I made it back to the Q just in time to see the bus leave for the strip. Mountain was taking the two pilots in his jeep. They stopped parallel to Colonel Lee's and with engines running, he told me everything was in good shape. The fuel crew had worked all night to get the chopper filled up again.

The major was sitting next to Mountain, and when my briefing was over, he leaned over to say, "You son-of-a-bitch, I'll never forget what you did to us. If I ever get the chance, I'll shit all over you, you fucker."

"Glad you dropped in," I said. We drove off.

Lee let me out in front of the Q and said, "Sometimes a man is too close to a thing to see good in it."

We spent the fall putting the finishing touches on our intercept techniques, and even had five actual refueling operations out over the East China Sea. General Pitts sent some F-4s over to Osan for a week, and a SAC tanker accommodated us out of Guam.

After the week's training was over, Lee said, "Benjamin did very good on this thing." He was proud that his Korean controllers had been able to cover those missions so well, with American pilots at the stick. It was the exact mission we'd perform in Vietnam.

The weather started to shift as we went into the fall. My old tour completion date came and went. We were getting closer. Lee and I and his staffers poured over the ops orders, maps, and photographs they sent us from Osan and Seoul. It was all very well planned out. Our firm departure date for Seoul was 1 December 1967.

As a crew, we all worked well together. Lee would be commander, of course. I was counterpart. Major Moon would perform his operations officer's duties, with Major Park heading up communications and maintenance liaison. The mobile radar unit would have its own technicians. Our chief controller would be Captain Ko, with Lieutenants Kwon, Han, Yi, and Pae on crew as our meat and potatoes controllers. Though Lee was expected to be aloof, Ko and I and the rest did more and more traveling around together. We'd have beers in the Q, sit together in the movies, and even drink tea downtown in some of the little places. Carl and Dick wouldn't be going, and I suspected one of them would take over the helm once I'd departed. Betts was about due to pin on his captain's bars.

27

The Contest

I was going to throw Clinton Davis that line about the swallows coming back to Capistrano when he got off the choggy, but I thought better of it. "Clint," I said instead, "every pheasant on the island just took cover."

"Well they'd better, sur, because we's gonna have us a real shoot 'em up come here in a coupala weeks." He gave me a big salute and that huge ham of his to shake. That always left an impression of the Maynard College seal on the side of the knuckle next to my ring finger.

We were in the hunting lodge business again, but only as an interlude before the deployment. I decided to let Carl Betts be the lodge coordinator, but I'd do the lion's share of the work on the big hunting meet. Even old Dolly was back with us, looking everywhere, everyday, smelling for the scent of her lost buddy.

I had Dutch build a big scoreboard for the meet. That would show the daily total of birds killed for each team. True to my promise, I drove to Tolsan City with Ko to talk over the license procedure with the Ministry of Agriculture and Forestry head. Ko did the talking; all they took were the lists of people General Pitts had sent with Clint. "He say government of Korea take care of rest."

On the way back, we had lunch with Fathers Pat Flaherty and T.P. Sullivan at Corpus Christi. I hadn't seen old T.P. for a long time. His legs were getting worse, so they weren't bringing him down island much by that time. I handed him a fifth of Irish Whiskey when we came in. "At least there's one young beye here on this island that has respect for age," he said, looking in Pat's direction.

"Aw, go on, if he'd come empty handed you'd be turn'n him away without food," Pat laughed, giving me a wink.

But the old man was already too busy getting down to the logistics of having the house girl bring glasses. "Won't ya have a drop, Narm?" he finally said.

The three of us visited over the whiskey before lunch.

The conversation got around to Goldman, and the two priests both expressed their admiration for him. I told them the new medic, Sergeant Kitch, was a nice young fellow, "But there could never be another Goldman."

We drank to that.

Talk of Paul. A real surprise. "Narman, did you know Paul has petitioned to come hare?" old T.P. asked me with a twinkle in his old red eyes.

"Here? Tolsan?"

"Yas, he's try'n to work a thing so he's do'n God's work here as a missionary."

"Can he do that?" I asked, feeling a surge of excitement.

"It's going to be hard, hard, Narm," Pat said. "But our old goat here has some chips at the Vatican he's never cashed in."

T.P. raised his glass and nodded.

"I can't think of anything better, more perfect for Paul," I said.

We had lunch and the conversation alternated between English and Korean. They made Ko feel very welcome. It would be fun, I thought, to understand my Korean pals talking in their own tongue. The whole visit was very nice. The news of Paul's venture was terrific; he hadn't mentioned it to me, but I guessed that was because he wanted to announce it as a *fait accompli*. Good thing I had spies.

As we walked out the door, old T.P. hobbled next to me and put his hand on my arm. "Now, Narman," he said, looking up into my face very seriously, "you and the rest be wary of your dragons. Here in the East there are some that are good and others that 'er bad. You'll have to watch for the difference very carefully, and Almighty God will help you with that."

"How did you know?" I asked, putting out my hand.

"The bamboo telegraph is a wily thing, son. A thing that works two ways, too, ya mind."

"I'll be careful, Father. We all will." Ko and I looked back from the jeep and waved at them, framed in the doorway of the rectory. T.P. made the Sign of the Cross.

Six November would be day one of the First International Hunting Meet. Our guests started to come in the Friday before it. Sunday the fifth would be the big kick-off banquet in the NCO Club. I really wanted things to go well, and I was damn grateful to have Clint with me. I had experienced almost a complete turnover of GIs since August. I had a new First Sergeant, Lyle Trapp, and the NCO club was being run by our new motor pool guy, Staff Sergeant Mike Quinn. New faces everywhere. But Tolsan lobster still sustained the club. Paul had put a motto on the arch; Goldman put cash in the register. Legacy.

The lodge and the Q were overflowing. Brigadier Rushworth and three British Embassy guys comprised the UK team; General Dai, Colonel Lee, and two ministers from President Park's cabinet were Korea's; the U.S. team was Pitts, Canada, Yates, and Belford; and the Australian Ambassador, Sir Henry Peterjohn, with three military aides, made up the quartet. The teams from Japan, Thailand, the Philippines, and Taiwan sort of blended with each other. I really didn't get all of the names, except that the Japanese team chief was named Tojo. That had been a big name in World War Two, but it wasn't the same guy. I did go over the names of the delicate little fellows from Vietnam: General Xinh, Colonel Dzu, and Majors Giac and Giam. Their names reminded me of something Ray Bradbury would make up. Or perhaps they rolled for their names on dice that had only Xs, Dx, Zs, and letters like that on their faces.

We all had a grand time at the banquet. It was a Tower of Babel. General Pitts was assumed to be the host, so he made introductions and said some words. Only about half of the group really caught everything. Clint had spent days getting headquarters in Japan to have the rules run off in every language; for a guy who couldn't read he was a savvy communicator. That really saved the day.

It was funny to see how the Korean and Japanese teams put as much distance between themselves as they could. Bad blood there.

The hunt would be three days. To win it was simple: kill the most birds. Teams would be put in different areas, transported back and forth in the bird wagons. Breakfast and dinner on compound, lunch in the field. The whole site was involved. Lee and I had every jeep, truck, and wagon tied up. All the NCOs had jobs, too. Some were field safety, some hunt administration, and some spent the time driving from team to team for pickups and deliveries. Everyone loved it; I would have excused any guy who didn't want to help. Dick and Carl ran the hill. Clint and I were general coordinators.

We were pretty much tied together by mobile radio, and radio Tolsan served as an announcement point. Every hour or so it would give an update on where the teams were hunting and sometimes even how the bird count was going. Carl had programmed a lot of good music for the thing, including a tape of "Turkey in the Straw," the theme song. That played just before one of the updates or an unscheduled announcement.

Everything was planned for. Clint had done a great job of seeing to it that each team would get the opportunity to hunt in each of the designated areas. You had a shot, so to speak, at every area and the same amount of time in each one as well.

Pitts and Canada were overjoyed about all of this, saying that the planning was superb. To tell you the truth, it was that sort of magnificent planning that had me just a little uneasy as Pitts was making his opening remarks. That uneasiness came from the superb advance planning Colonel Lee had done in regard to one strategic detail.

As the guides were introduced and stood at the front of the room, pointing out the areas on these big beautiful maps Dutch had made up, I sat with Clint and worried over Lee's strategic planning. In a nutshell, the reality of the situation was, in Lee's own words, that, "Korea does not lose any contest on Korea soil." He had said that to me the night he had several of his men carry a bunch of boxes of freshly killed pheasants into our big walk-in freezer in the mess hall.

"Just in case our Korea team has a bad day, we can now make the odds smile for us," he said, watching with approval as the still warm birds were put down on the freezer floor. "But you do not worry, the Uniteda States will come in second. I have enough bird for us both."

The voice of the guide went on in broken English, translated into Thai, Japanese, Chinese, and Vietnamese, when a team member needed to help another with a word or two; and I prayed that nobody would know about our "birds in the hand," as Clint had called them when I shared the plan with him on pain of death. No need to unnecessarily worry either Canada or Pitts we had agreed.

After the speeches; the briefings; the distribution of licenses, schedules, and special arm bands; the dinner, desert, and hot drinks, General Pitts stood and said, "Captain Whitman, have you a toast?"

"Yes, sir," I said on cue. "I have seven, to be exact. Gentlemen, rise if you will, and drink to the greatness and continued prosperity of the Republics of Korea, Japan, the Philippines, Taiwan, Vietnam. To the United Kingdom and the United States of America."

"Here, here," the room full of allies shouted, and I heard each shout the name of his own homeland as well.

"So, with that, gentlemen," Pitts said, "we'll all retire until we meet the challenge of the morning."

As they all filed out, some bowing and smiling my way, I thought about the Republic of Korea's frozen birds across the street in the mess hall. I wondered who would win third place.

The hunt itself was just as much fun as I had thought it would be. We all had a ball running around in the wagons checking on things and delivering lunches. Clint would get up at dawn with them, but not me. I'd wait until about eight and catch him just as he was finishing up last minute details. I'd grab a roll and coffee and hop in with him. Our new medic, Sergeant Kitch, was taking his responsibilities very seriously; once I rode around with him in the morning. He was no Goldman.

I scratched out a letter to Angie while I bounced around with him. Though I had increased the alcohol intake a little, I had managed to send no less than two letters a choggy. Hers to me were joyous about that. She was sad because I was going to miss another Christmas.

"Just hold it, and I'll be home to collect on everything I've missed," I wrote. I still hadn't decided just what I'd do after the "gesture" in Vietnam.

I visited with the American team some during lunches, but Pitts and Canada were downright intense. They were worried about their bird count. The first day it was: USA, 17 kills; Japan, 16 kills; Korea 16 kills; Vietnam, 15 kills; Australia, Taiwan, Philippines, and the UK, 14. Because I had toasted the United Kingdom the night of the banquet, Japan had asked the next day if Australia and the British team would throw together. The answer was no, they'd be separate teams in competition. Rushworth told them the title "United Kingdom creates confusion everywhere." After that, I felt better about Lee's plan. The Japs had cast a suspicious eye on the wrong alliance, because those figures started to turn in a certain direction the second day.

The big scoreboard in the club said: Korea, 37 kills; Japan, 35 kills; UK, 34 kills; Australia, 30 kills; USA, 29 kills; Taiwan, Philippines, 25 kills; Vietnam, 23 kills. Canada and Pitts were fretting. Colonel Lee winked at me when I said to Pitts, "Sir, you have one more full day."

They did. Everyone had a great day. All eight teams shot the hell out of Tolsan's pheasants. You could hear shotguns going off everywhere for miles and miles all over the southern part of the island. Over Radio Tolsan, Hot Carl announced that the "Japanese team has shot an incredible twenty-three birds so far, with a full afternoon of hunt to go before the end of the meet." He played a minute of "Turkey in the Straw" for emphasis.

It wasn't long before Hot Carl broke in with more theme and the word that, "The Korean team just passed Japan, reporting in twenty-six, yes, twenty-six kills this morning. That keeps Korea out ahead with a total of sixty-three birds for the hunt and Japan close behind with fifty-eight. No word from any others yet, but stay tuned." He played fifteen seconds of "Turkey" and then came back with, "America, where are you?"

Well, America was hunting like crazy in area number five, out on the seaward road. Not doing badly, either. They had twenty birds to turn in. That meant they had a total of forty-nine birds. If you went by Hot Carl's report, that would put them only nine birds behind the reported second placers, the Japanese. Without an accurate picture of the entire field, it was hard to tell.

I walked along with Canada and Pitts at noon, munching on a sandwich. They decided to hunt straight through. So they all ate and stalked birds, dogs and guides doing the flushing, as it was with every team.

"God damn, Virgil," Pitts said, "I don't want the Japs to beat us."

"No, sir," He said through his ham and Swiss.

"Norm, you should have a better update system, dammit," he said, eating and walking hard.

"Sir, I know, but the wardens have a tough time counting and collecting at the same time," I said, wanting to kick him in the ass for taking this so seriously. My God, they had these special hunting togs on, with red hats and all kinds of strings and leather gizmos. I wanted to tell them how the Koreans on the island snared the birds, setting and harvesting little string traps in beat-up pants, thongs on their feet. They got more birds than all of these pussies with shotguns, dogs, and guides.

The birds could only be collected by Republic of Korea wardens, driving through the areas. This was to insure a fair hunt. They gave you a receipt for your kills, and then threw them in their wagons. The hunt would get enough for their big celebration dinner, but the rest would go to the poor. In Korea things always went to some mysterious "poor." There were so many poor, you wondered how they picked out any particular group for such donations. Before that happened, though, there was a final count of each day's total kill back at the compound, with a representative of each team there to watch. That number had to equal the total of all of the bird kills on the wardens' receipts.

The Americans were also weary of carrying their quarry. They hadn't gotten a pickup all day. "Hell's fire," Pitts yelled, "they had a count on the Nips hours ago, and we haven't even gotten a pickup. Norm, get on a radio and demand a pickup."

"Yes, sir."

"Tell 'em it's almost fuck'n time to quit."

I was saved by the sight of a khaki Land Rover coming over the hill in front of us. Two wardens were headed our way. "Christ, now they've scared all the birds ahead of us," yelled Belford.

The mood changed to one of dismay and temptation when the wardens took the birds and then handed the general a receipt for not twenty fowl, but thirty-four. Pitts looked at the receipt and then showed it to Belford.

"Kid, they speakie English?" Belford asked me.

"No, you saw. They just hand communicate with you," I said, and then I went over to their Land Rover. "English? You English?"

"*Aniyo. Aniyo*. Eeenglish, *aniyo*," one of them said.

"He can't count worth a shit, either," laughed Belford.

"Well, sir," I said, "we can get some help . . ."

"No, shit. Leave it be. It's too damn confusing now. We'll get it straight or whatever later," the general said.

"Yeah, and I'll bet these guys fuck the whole thing up today anyway," Belford said.

Canada was just silent, looking out to the sea.

Meanwhile, the wardens bowed from their seats, put the Rover in reverse, and made their way out of our area. They smiled and nodded their heads until they were turned around and bouncing back down toward the site.

"So long, Einstein," waved Belford.

I saw a hand wave from the jeep. Ah, corruption, I thought. Yes, old *aniyo* Albert was dumb all right. He sure as hell knew that twenty fresh birds plus fourteen frozen ones totaled up to thirty-four kills.

Later on, that was just enough to get the Red, White, and Blue into a final position of second place. Pitts' team totaled out to 63 birds. The Korean overall victory was achieved through a total of 70. Japan came in third with 61. The rest of the field looked like this: UK, 55; Australia, 50; the Philippines, 44; Taiwan, 41; and Vietnam, 35.

At the grand count I watched Pitts' face when the total came out perfectly. All members from each team were in on that last count. One little card table of wardens totaled the chits over and over again, while the guys counting birds did it a careful five times as well. Mr. Ku, County Headman and representative of the island Governor, took whispers from the wardens and then stepped forward. "Korea winner," he said to a great outburst of applause. "Uniteda State second," he continued, with us adding cab hailing whistles to the applause.

"Japan thurda." More, polite applause for the guys who really gave it a go. Hell, I thought, in this contest, third place was nothing to sneeze at.

There was a great deal of handshaking going on after that. Very polite gestures on the part of everyone. Korea's team was elated. Pitts was proud of his second place.

"Everything okay, sir?" I asked, putting out my hand, maybe raising my eyebrows a little.

"Oh, well . . . hell . . . that other thing. There's no use bringing a thing like that up. We'd just create an unnecessary incident." He patted me on the back. "Good job on the whole thing, Kid. I'm proud we did so well."

"Don't forget to shake hands with all of the wardens, sir," I said, winking. "They really did a great job, too. You know, that was all gratis. The Korean government donated their time and services."

"I'll do that right now, Norm. I'll do that right now," he said, walking off to extend his thanks.

I felt a hand on my shoulder. It was Canada. "You ever hear the old saying, 'never get into a pissing contest with a skunk,' Norm?"

"Well, yes, sir, but Colonel Lee's been teaching me the Korean proverbs."

"Do you have an appropriate one now?"

"How about, 'The road to perfection is sometimes roundabout'?"

"You mean 'crooked,' don't you?"

"Yes, sir."

All around us, the club lobster preparation building was buzzing with handshakes, hunters, shotguns, guides, and good fellowship. I just stood by Canada enjoying it all, thinking about the proverbs. I felt Dolly put her cold, wet nose in my palm.

We had the end-of-hunt banquet, ate pheasant, and watched the big trophy cups go to the first three teams. For just participating, you also got a great drinking mug, with "First International Hunt" printed on it. The food was great, but you had to watch out for the little lead shot pellets in the meat.

About the time the banquet was winding down, I got a chance to talk with one of the Vietnamese, Colonel Dzu. He had been standing by the bar by himself, sipping on a drink.

"Sir, I am so happy you could come to Tolsan-Do," I said, putting out my hand. He was a delicate little guy, with eyebrows that looked painted. His features were tiny and sharp.

"Yez, yez, I am so happy," he said, giving me a big smile. His voice was like a child's.

"Do you return to your country now?"

"I not ah go now. We see this country first, and ten we go to see other country."

I was so used to the Koreans, their robustness, that he seemed like a cheap Asian doll.

"I understand things are going well in Vietnam now?" I said. I don't know why I said it that way, but I wanted to see what this guy thought about his war.

"Yez. We will win against the communist soon. We make the big push right now called Success Offensive."

That night, Canada and Lee and I and Pitts sat in the Q living room by ourselves. It was a good meeting, because we were really talking about the deployment, not hunting meets and dead birds. The general was a little shit-faced, but with it nonetheless.

"I'd just like to wish all of you the very best on your venture, on Crystal Dragon," he said, giving it that concerned look you want from a three-star general.

"My government is proud to do this service for Vietnam. Maybe Tiger Division does a good job for war. Now our Crystal Dragon team will in small way demonstrate Korean Air Force power." He was most serious. Lee wanted this mission. It did in fact mean a great deal to him to represent ROKAF in a sensitive, important role. It would have pissed him off to hear it called a "gesture." On that night we were only about three weeks away from show time.

I was beginning to get that feeling in my bowels, the one I got before I had to fight bullies. "You know," I said, "I like the name Tiger Division."

Lee cleared his throat in the way he did when he wanted to have the floor for a point. "There is a Korean saying that goes 'Where there are no tigers, the hyenas become self-important.'"

"And a dragon or two doesn't hurt a thing either," I said.

We got rid of our guests over the next two days. A choggy took a group north, and a C-130 from Japan picked up the general and those going back to Yokota. From there, the rest would head for Clark, Taipei, and Tan Son Nhut. Now I had time to pack and write a last letter or two. It was like a hush had come over the site. I thought about dragons and tigers.

28

The Dragon

On the evening of 25 November, everyone going on the mission attended a party at the best teahouse in Moklepo, the next town up on the north road. It was a Saturday night. That morning I had attended the mass for the Feast of Saint Catherine, as I had the year before with Paul, Goldman, and Pitts' hunting party. At the breakfast afterward, Ryan O'Donnell told me old Saint Katie had been tortured on the wheel and decapitated at Alexandria for converting the pagans to Christianity. I told him it couldn't have been her who had appeared at the rectory window only a year before, since that specter was reported as whole in body. "Ah, God love you, Narm, a good point. Right before my eyes all the time. It's further proof of what I believe in my heart," he said, smacking me on the back. I was glad I helped him.

Thoughts of Saint Catherine disappeared with each sip of *chung jung* that night. We were all kind of mellow, I guess you'd say. Though girls served us the food, they didn't join in. It was stag, with Colonel Lee sitting at the head of the long low table. There were nine of us.

We had trained for the intercept missions. We had studied the maps and plans. We even knew a little about what the place looked like, this Song Cau on the coast of Vietnam. We were ready.

I can't remember what we said or every toast we made. I know we sang "Arirang" and shook hands a lot, wishing our mission great success. But one thing really stands out about that evening. It was a great moment in my life.

Colonel Lee stood up, and Major Park, in a very serious voice, said, "Captain Norman Widman, you now come here by the commander."

I looked around at everyone, and then I dutifully got up and made my way toward Lee.

He cleared his throat. "We are all the Crystal Dragon team. You are counterpart, but more."

I heard approving clapping and noise behind me.

"So, you cannot wear your hat on thisa mission," he said, taking a box from Park. "You will be in Tiger country there and you will be with this Crystal Dragon team from Republic of Korea. So you will wear this hat. "

He handed me the box. "I open?"

"Yes," everyone said.

So I took off the lid, and inside there was the standard black field hat of the Korean Air Force. They were really like black baseball hats. I took it out, and it had three diamonds on the front, the rank of Korean captain. On the side it said "Whitman." And on the back there were Korean Hangul characters.

"Sir," I said, putting it on. "I'm so proud to have this." Then I turned around, saluted, and everyone applauded.

"The words on the back say that you belong to this team and that Korean soldier should follow you . . . help you," Lee said.

I turned back and saluted him. He returned it. Counterpart hell. I was a Korean.

On Tuesday, 28 November 1967, the Crystal Dragon cadre assembled at the Tolsan flight strip at 0700 in the morning. It was cold, but clear. All of the fire company was there, and the ambulance, and a couple of baggage trucks, but I had given the order that we wanted only essential personnel there. Dick worked the hill, but Carl Betts drove me to the strip. He was the site honcho now; I told Canada he would be a good one. He had pinned on his captain's bars on 1 November.

We all had neatly pressed fatigues on. Theirs were different from mine. But our black baseball hats were identical.

It seemed strange to leave the island. I left about half of my stuff in one of Dutch's special crates, all nailed up. Only my name was on it; I told Carl I'd send an address. I'd probably get back to Osan or Seoul after our "gesture," but I doubted I'd ever return to the rock. So, when the big C-130 landed and our stuff was put on board (along with two hundred pounds of frozen Tolsan Tail), I shook hands with Captain Carl Betts for good.

"Take good care of old Benjamin Control. She's all yours, partner," I said.

Then we rolled down the strip and out to sea. I thought just for a minute about my first glimpse of the island. It had been fall, late harvest. Oxen had still been in the fields working. Now our takeoff gave us a view of winter. Black and white film would have been just fine for the pictures.

For some strange reason, the burial mounds of the island seemed to stick out. Over every grave in Korea there's a round mound of earth. "Happy mountains" they called them. On Tolsan they're surrounded by a little square stonewall. They were easy to see on the bare winter earth floor. I saw thousands of them. Beware the wicked dragons, I thought.

We spent Wednesday and Thursday in Seoul, at Yong Dong Po. There was a BOQ set apart from the others that did very nicely for us. It wasn't idle time we spent there. We got shots and routine physicals—done by both ROK and American doctors—and the supply guys gave us these neat boots with green cloth necks. "Jungle boots" the sarge who fitted us called them.

We got a pretty good briefing by an Army Major who had several tours in Vietnam under his belt. He talked in that military briefing monologue style, very proper and with an air that suggested our mission was very important. It wasn't a bad show. I liked Lee to get that kind of treatment.

"Gentlemen," he said, standing with his hands in parade rest fashion behind his back, "the South of Vietnam has a monsoon climate with rather consistent temperatures of between seventy-seven and eighty-six degrees on the Fahrenheit scale. Two seasons exist. The wet and the dry."

I wondered what the hell could be in between.

"Now, you gentlemen are getting there at a time in the year when it's dry." He went over to the map. "Okay, your destination is the Qui Nhon area, Binhdinh province here, and that will pretty well be in a dry period. I understand you'll move over to the coast itself—here in the Song Cau area— and you'll find that has the characteristic seaport climate. Typhoon season is about over. But you'll still get showers. Expect bugs, look for large rodents, and be wary of snakes, as Vietnam has about twenty poisonous varieties. Are there any questions so far?"

"Colonel?" I said, offering to let Lee field a question. He shook his head no, so I got mine off. "Maj, what about enemy activity in that area now?"

"Viet Cong influence is a fact of life anywhere in country, Captain, but at this period in time, the North has suffered heavy setbacks in battle, supply lines, and in the gut by way of bombing above the seventeenth parallel. There's just been a big drive. I know you're well aware of the Tiger Division's influence in your destination area. I'll be surprised if you see Charlie at all. Of course, you're gett'n there during Christmas time and, more importantly, it will be Tet—Nguyen Dan—or the Vietnamese New Year, a big time both North and South. Things will be very quiet while you and the enemy celebrate. In fact, there's going to be a thirty-six-hour cease fire at Tet."

Lee leaned over and whispered in my ear. "My contacts tell me there might be a building of troops anyway . . . even though the Tet come."

"Colonel?" the major said, looking at Lee.

"Nothing to ask," he said.

The major went on about customs peculiar to the Vietnamese. You shouldn't pat them on the head he told us, and every Korean in the room nodded approval because any good Asian knew that. Then our major told us about other strange customs as well, all of them common to the Korean and Vietnamese cultures. He should have stuck to weather.

Canada popped in one day, and we met a gang of Korean generals, too. It was a time to chat and act excited and feel important about what we were doing. Most of the Korean big shots spoke English, but these visits were all about their talking with the Korean Crystal Dragons, not their American tagalong. So I hung in the background.

Before Canada left, he motioned me into an empty Q office and closed the door. "Whitman," he said, "I'm counting on you to keep your nose clean over there."

"Yes, sir," I said.

"I'd keep the partying to a minimum, for one thing."

I didn't know what to say, and I didn't want to go on record with a flat-out agreement on that one. I was cutting down; but I wasn't going to take the pledge, either.

"I think you'll like finding your tongue and your courage from someplace in your gut, rather than from a snort. You use both methods now. This might be a good time to play it straight."

"I'm going to give this all I have," I said, trying to ease his concern.

"What did you decide about staying in?" he asked, not acknowledging my response.

"Don't know yet. I'll write you for sure, sir. I need a little more time," I said.

"You're doing well with the Air Force. You just have to decide if that's gonna make you happy to be a lifer. So, I hope you get a sign that'll help you decide."

"I'm going to think about it real hard," I said, reaching out to shake his hand. .

Then we walked out and down the hall where he said goodbye to each of the Koreans. They paused long enough to shake his hand and then went back to their own visitors.

Out at his car, Canada opened the door and then said to me, "You'll do fine, Norm. Did you know you'll get combat pay, too?"

"Seems like a waste of taxpayers' money, sir."

He gave me the thumbs-up sign from inside the car. He pointed to his head. He meant my baseball cap. I laughed and nodded. He drove off. I also had my Saint Christopher medal on.

It was our own C-141 out of Kimpo, do not stop at Saigon, go directly to Phu Cat Air Base, Republic of Vietnam. We couldn't see a thing, because there were no windows, of course. Everyone applauded on touchdown. When the cargo hold went down, hot air rushed in on us. It smelled of grass.

An Air Force major, security policeman, came on board right away.

"Gentlemen, welcome to Phu Cat Air Base, please folla me out to the terminal where we'll process you in as quickly as possible. No smoking in the terminal induction area, please."

It was quick and painless. All they wanted was to collect these green cards each Korean had. A look at my orders and ID was all they wanted from me.

"This bus will take you to your temporary area. Your bags will folla," he said, and that was that.

We saw Phu Cat from the bus windows.

It was a brand new base. Neat. The buildings were two-story wooden jobs, painted Army green. We were given one to ourselves. There was an O club, a small one, just down the street, but we were also allowed to eat in a little dining hall in the other direction. We got all of that from Lieutenant Colonel Al Lloyd who was waiting for us at the BOQ. He was efficient, but stiff. It was because we were a classified mission, and that meant you told us what we were supposed to know and then you left us alone. I'm sure that was more out of a fear that you'd fuck up if you talked to us too much or something like that.

"Now you can go just about anywhere you want, Captain Whitman, but going off base is not encouraged. The Koreans must stay on, though, until they clear in with the Tiger Division people. Once they make that move, then you'll all be on your own down coast."

"Is there anybody here now who wants to meet with us?"

"No. But I understand you'll be picked up later this week. We're just your holding area until then. I'd kind of get used to Vietnam here while you can and relax."

Our bags came. I put some stuff away. After that I sort of had that "Well here-we-are-now-what-the-hell-do-we-do" feeling you got when you'd hurry to get someplace and then there would be nothing to do. Colonel Lee said he wanted to take a nap, but the two majors and most of the lieutenants headed straight for the BX. They were authorized any purchase in any American BX in Vietnam, and they couldn't wait to do it. They would also make the same pay as their equivalent U.S. counterparts as long as they were in Vietnam. The money was burning holes in their fatigue pockets.

Ko stuck with me, and we decided to walk around the base a little before we did anything else. It was really a nice facility. You almost got the feeling it was put together by city planners; everything was neat and new. It had been totally constructed before any GIs came through the gates. Called "Turn Key" base construction, it was done by a combination of Red Horse Army Engineers and civilian contractors in early 1967.

The place was surrounded by barbed wire fence and coils of wire. The ground was flat, and when I looked over the fence and beyond, I was reminded of one place: Hawaii. To the west loomed up this mountain range that looked just like the Koolava range on Oahu. They looked like big rock formations covered with moss. It was trees, of course, but you imagined that some giant could scrape that moss stuff off with his front teeth. Beyond those mountains were the central highlands of Vietnam.

To the north was rolling terrain. To the south it was flat.

"I think this is a very beautiful place if we could walk there over the fence," Ko said.

"Yes," I said, "maybe Korean and American men make it so we can someday soon, but right now we find BX and have something cool to drink."

When we found the BX, we met up with the rest of the team. They were walking around with their shopping carts, filling them to the brim. Some had two. They were buying three and four sets of Noritake China, not to mention Akai and Panasonic stereos. At last they were in the land of the big BX. At one point, Ko wandered off for a minute, and I stopped to buy two cold six-packs of Coke.

An Air Force major was standing in the aisle, watching my crew wheel their carts around. He looked at me and said, "They say that the way we'll win this war is to tell the Koreans they've just opened up a big new BX in Hanoi. Then get the hell out of the way and let 'em push through to it."

I just smiled and said, "So they're Koreans, huh?"

"Yeah," he said, watching Lieutenant Kwon turn up an aisle, "and if the truth be known, they're probably the best damn soldiers in the whole goddamn place."

As we walked back on the new sidewalk, I suddenly had a thought.

"Ko," I said, "I tell you a silly thing, but I think I am homesick for Tolsan."

"I know," he said, looking down as he walked. Hours and hours in a closed C-141 hold, hot afternoon, new smells, strange looking countryside, and new sounds. Maybe it was just the jetlag. But it was all coming down on me. I was reassured that Ko felt it, too. Lee was smart; he sacked out. I went back, drank my coke, and did the same. I dreamed of a cool, crisp, clear Korean day on Tolsan. I dreamed about Angie.

A knock on my door woke me up. I was soaked from sweat. I had that stale Coke taste in my mouth.

"Captain Widman?" It was Lee.

When I opened the door, he was standing there with another Korean, but this was an Army LC wearing fatigues. On his left shoulder there was a large patch; it had the head of a roaring tiger on it, mouth open, teeth showing. There were crossed rifles over his right pocket. He was grinning from ear to ear.

"This is an old friend of mine, Captain Widman," Lee said. "This one is Lieutena Colonel O."

29

P.J.

I don't know how, but there was no doubt in my mind that Lee knew this guy was going to turn up at the Q a few hours after we landed. He had walked right out of the jungle to make contact with us. That's sometimes called bamboo telegraph, but I thought it was a hell of a lot more sophisticated than that. After he got off that airplane, Lee took a nap because he knew he'd be going to work soon after. He hadn't asked any questions at any of the briefings the GIs gave him; he hardly paid Lieutenant Colonel Lloyd any mind at all. He knew he was on schedule. His.

Lee gathered me and Park and Moon up for a meeting with O in a little dayroom on the top floor of our Q. The others knew this was high-level stuff, so they gave us plenty of room and made no noise at all. I brought up the rest of my Cokes. There we were, sitting on the couches and chairs, sipping on Cokes, me and my buddies from Korea.

"Colonel Lee and I are friend since we are both small boy in Seoul city," O said. "He tells me you are a good man for Korea."

"Thank you, sir. I'm proud to be with this mission." I was damn glad to establish my allegiances with this guy right from the start. He was every inch of him a soldier. His fatigues were creased just right, but had that well worn look. He was also a big boy for an Asian: at least six-two, and very well filled out. I wanted him to know I was very definitely on his team. My ROKAF baseball hat was on my head.

In a very polite way, he nodded to me and then began to speak in Korean to Lee. Moon and Park just sat there, listening. Every once in a while, somebody would look at me and smile; they were telling me it was business time, I was okay, and I'd know what I was supposed to know when I should know. That was just fine by me. I sipped my Coke and thought about what

Angie, or my dad, or the kids I'd known in Pittsburgh would say if they could see this. It was cool, man.

Maps were brought out. We all gathered around one that was spread out on the coffee table. More Korean was spoken. O was putting a lot of body language and steam in his presentation. I knew this guy was going to take care of us.

"Captain Widman?" he finally said to me. "This is where my Tiger unit lands in the October, nineteen sixty-five. Here." He had his finger on Qui Nhon.

"Yes, sir," I said.

"Blue Dragon Division lands here at Cam Ranh and march to Tuy Hoa."

That was another dot about a hundred and fifty miles to the south of the Tiger landing.

"Since that time we have cleared all this land from Viet Cong with hundreds of battle."

He was looking at my reaction to all of this.

"Sir, I'm very proud to sit with a hero of Korea who fights with Tiger." I hit the target with that.

"Do you see this road number nineteen?"

"Yes, sir."

"We haba make all clear, so even in two days Crystal Dragon will be taken down that road by my people."

"Colonel O also tells me that a ship from our navy has even already unload our radar equipment."

Some advisor I was. I didn't have a clue about how, or when, that would be done. The where I knew: Song Cau.

Everyone from our team ate with O in the little officer's club at Phu Cat. The employees were Vietnamese, the first I'd really seen other than the guys on the hunting team. The standard model still seemed to prevail: smaller and more delicate and more childlike. They had great smiles. We asked for a big table and got it. I could tell they had a healthy respect for their brothers from the Land of the Morning Calm. We got very, very good service.

We got to the O club fairly early. There were only a few GIs walking around, but as the meal went on, the bar and dining room filled up. We were getting plenty of attention. The crowd was a mix of pilots and support types. I had to take a leak, so I got up to hit the john and went by a group of them at the bar.

"Hey, Whitman," somebody yelled. I looked down the line of drinkers. It was Peck, the guy from R and R in Hawaii.

"Aloha," I said, walking up to him.

"What the hell are you doing here?" he asked.

"I came over for a tour. Your good words about Phu Cat made me want to see the place in the worst way," I said.

He looked at me for a second or two. "You're with the bunch in the dining room?"

"Yes."

"Koreans, right?"

"Yes. But how are you doing?"

"About four months to go, man, and this will be behind me," he said. He looked strained.

"Well, look, maybe I'll see you around, huh?" I said, thinking I'd better go to the john and get back to the table.

"That's tough company you're keeping there, Norm. We don't see a lot of the Rocks. They have a piece of the southern part of this air patch, but they don't come up here often."

"Do they have a headquarters there or what?"

"Yeah, I guess. It's kind of a weird part of the place, and I stay the hell away from it."

"Just watch out for the Ton Ton Club over there," this other guy laughed, helping himself to our conversation.

"What's that?" I asked.

"It's a club right outside the south gate. The Koreans hang there and some of our FACs and a lot of characters I couldn't even begin to place in any particular category." The Forward Air Controllers, or FACs, were some of the gutsiest guys in the Air Force. I hoped I'd get a chance to meet some of them.

"Okay, I'll be careful, Sam," I said. "I gotta get going. Maybe we can get together."

He grabbed my arm. "But what are you doing, anyway?"

"To be truthful, I'm trying to get away so I don't say anything I can't, okay?"

For just an instant, our eyes met in one of those lock-ons that comes with personality conflict, put down, or who knows what. He let go of my sleeve and I said, "See ya, Sam." I felt eyeballs in my back all the way to the john. I went back to the table the long way around.

We had a pleasant dinner. They all got bowls of rice and some good Vietnamese dishes. We had this soup called *pho*. The main dish was fish, with hot sauce. O ordered that for them. He could speak Vietnamese, and I think our waitress was accommodating his special needs because the menu didn't really show that much native food. We got good service. Why not? This Korean spoke Vietnamese and knew the turf. He also spoke English. Good thing for us, I thought, that he and his Tigers were with us.

"Tomorrow night, Captain Widman, I take you and Colonel Lee to my Officer Club. We haba small Korean installation here on thisa place."

"I'm looking forward to it, sir," I said, feeling the gaze of Sam Peck and the bar crowd behind me. I'll bet they never got an invitation, I thought.

As Phu Cat had been quiet that day, it was all activity that night. After I got in bed, I lay there in the heat, listening to the booming of 40 mm pom-pom guns being fired by an Army field artillery unit on the north side of the base. I think automatic weapon fire was coming in on us. It kept up all night. Yes, I was in Viet-fucking-Nam.

When I woke up, I was looking at the ceiling. I've always been a ceiling studier. In my room as a kid, I had old friends and wicked enemies whose faces were engraved in the ceiling plaster. There were whole scenes there: battles, a circus, even copulation, which I didn't know was there until I was fourteen. On this ceiling I saw Asian faces. They were smiling down on me, but I knew some were not friends.

At home, the draft was up, and thousands of college guys were on their way to Canada. I was studying the ceiling in a VOQ in Vietnam. Norm Whitman, warmonger. Baby killer.

I had a back room. When I finally got up, I looked out the window to see those beautiful mountains. I wanted to see if some giant hadn't scraped off that luscious moss yet. No, still there. Maybe San Sin, the mountain spirit, kept him at bay.

I looked down and spotted Lee out on the back patio, dressed in a loose black kimono, slowly, slowly waving and swiping a large sword around and around. He was barefooted. It looked like slow motion. He'd twist and turn and throw that sword around. It was all coordinated, very graceful. It was also a very private moment. If that had been someone from my hometown, somebody out back of my fraternity house, I'd have tapped on the pane or pulled up the sash and yelled something like, "Looks good" or "All right, what's the deal?" But I didn't dare. In fact I pulled the Venetian blind cord, making it shut tight. Though it was not hard to watch, I didn't want to. There was a lot about Lee I didn't know.

Ko came and got me for breakfast. The mess hall was terrific. You could have almost anything you wanted: fruit, juices, bacon, any style eggs or omelet, rolls, and drinks.

That mess hall was a mixed bag of officers, enlisted, and a few Vietnamese. Our team didn't really get any hard stares, but we did draw a passing look or two. The major I had seen in the BX was just a little behind us in the line, and when we found a table I could see him heading for Ko and me and the rest.

"Hi, I'm P.J. Ellsworth. Can I join ya?"

He was in his flight suit, like the day before, a little short guy, wiry build, thinning hair. He even wore glasses. An unlikely warrior, I thought. But he had a manner about him you liked right off. He was very much at ease with both himself and you. Not pretentious.

"I know a lot of the Tigers," he said, "but I don't often run into Korean Air Force types."

"We here to tour area and watch Korean soldier in field," Ko said.

"Well, you came to a good place, Captain. Your Tigers have this place in order, believe me." He had a bit of a drawl, and always a big smile. I liked him.

"How do you, ah, come into contact with the Tigers, Maj?" I asked.

"I'm a FAC, so I'm always working with them on close air support, or whatever it takes to keep them alive."

"Oh, I see," I said, concentrating on my two over easy. The FAC, or Forward Air Controller, was the meat-and-potatoes man in this war. He usually flew around in a little light airplane, flying low and slow, spotting targets, talking with friendly ground troops, and then telling the fighters where and when to drop their bombs. FACs marked the targets with smoke rockets and they really stuck their asses out for the enemy to shoot at when they did that. They were some kind of sierra hotel, hot-shit guys.

He got along very well with us and had the good sense not to ask us anything more about what we were doing there. We talked about the war and how it was going. He had the best picture I had gotten yet about what it was like, the no-bullshit story.

Besides telling us how well the Koreans were doing, he also talked about the B-52 strikes.

"But I've always heard that the VC find out when they're going to get hit and then get outta there before the strikes," I said.

"Probably, but the point is that they had to move," he said in his easy-going, low-key way.

"So?" I said.

"It keeps pressure on them. They have to keep moving. In a war like this you don't only think kill. You think control, pressure, confusion. Never let 'em dig in."

We were on our third cup of coffee, tea for the Koreans, of course.

P.J.'s bottom line was, "I really think we've got 'em down on their knees. Word out of the North is the bombing's not only scaring hell out of them, but literally destroying their supply capability." He paused for a sip. "I think we'll see a cease fire. I'm serious."

"Boy," I said, "that doesn't jive with what I read in the stateside papers."

"Well, the media don't understand this thing, that's all. I have the best job over here. I fly low and slow, and I talk to the guys slugging it out. I drink with 'em at night. I see results, and I trust the ground pounders I talk to."

FACs had three radios in their planes: VHF, FM, and UHF. They could talk to their own control point at Phu Cat on the VHF; they got assignments to fly to such and such an area from that. But once in the area, they could talk to the troops on the ground directly over the FM radio; often in the middle of a hot battle, the grunts could ask a FAC for close-air support. After he and those troops worked out marking the target with smoke, the FAC could call in fast moving fighters on the UHF radio. That's when the action started, when he directed them to fire on his smoke marks.

"Some of the fighter jocks get to know the troops on the ground if they make an effort, but I know the voices I'm talking to when I'm working. The fast movers never hear them. It kind of separates them, you know."

"Do you talk with my Korean mans?" asked Lieutenant Yi.

"Oh, yes. Heavens yes. Everyday. Everyday. I 'm assigned to Tiger support."

He filled us in on so much that morning. We got the scoop on Phu Cat, too. It was pretty far inland and on flat ground. Thus, it was both vulnerable and difficult to protect. The Air Force security police who made up the perimeter guard were flown out to their observation towers by helicopter, mostly Chinooks. "They're out there pretty far," P.J. said. "They're a little jumpy about that, too, but I understand their job has fringe benefits."

"What?" I asked.

"We're so remote up here there's not a nightlife like they have down in Saigon. Somehow, the ladies of the night found a good thing by entertaining the troops in the towers." He laughed and shook his head.

"Where do they come from?" I couldn't believe it.

"From the little town over here. You think that's something, they have to walk through mine fields to get to the towers. Not one of 'em blown up yet." Always the dollies, I thought. God, how the women of Asia took care of our guys. "So you do see Eurasian kids along the roads up here. Accidents."

One thing led to another, and P.J. finally ended up taking us down to the flight line. Somehow, all six of us got into his jeep. Filling up VWs in the fifties would have been a snap for my Crystal Dragon lieutenants.

Just as we pulled up, a flight of F-100s went busting off the end of the runway, a single, 10,000-foot job, with a Southeast/ Northwest Asian theater orientation. They were probably going out for close-air somewhere. All of the birds at Phu Cat were camouflaged. A couple more F-100s took off while we watched. There were four squadrons of them at Phu Cat. We also saw some C-7 Caribou transports, and there were our old choggy birds all dressed up for war as AC-47 "Spookies." P.J. proudly took us on a walk around inspection of his O-1E "Bird Dog."

"Hell, no, I never know what I'm going to get when I call for air. It can be our guys or the VNAF," he said, opening the door of the little O-1E. He lowered his voice a little and said, "You know, I don't think you realize it, but the VNAF are probably better egg droppers than the GIs. They're okay."

Ko and the lieutenants were wide-eyed at everything.

"We hang eight two-point-seven five-inch rockets on her, and that's how I lay my smoke." He laughed and pointed into the cockpit. "My bomb sight is the second screw on the windscreen divider here. Nothing but sophistication." P.J. loved his plane; he loved his job. A blonde dollie adorned the nose of the plane, "Pretty Patty" printed under her reclining pose.

We stood there on the ramp, and we flew vicarious missions just by listening to his stories.

"You worry about what we call a short round: too close to our own troops, short of the line I mark. So when old lead comes on my mark, I and the ground work 'em to where we want the pickle." It reminded me of Lee and his artillery adventure.

Sometimes it wasn't even air support. "I work artillery all the time, too. That's accurate. You just keep having them adjust the big guns until you're on the mark. You can hit that spot all day."

We all got a chance to sit in the cockpit. The little single engine Bird Dog seemed like a toy alongside the big jets we saw roaring down the runway. That close to the flight line, the noise of their engines made your ribcage vibrate.

He called those swept wing F-100s "the fast movers." In fact, there were even F-100F models out there on the ramp that performed a high speed FAC mission in Vietnam called "Misty FAC." These guys would fly a specific area day in and day out, becoming fiercely familiar with it. After a while they'd be able to pick out targets of opportunity, or note strange new developments out there. Once they did, they could start blasting away and send for more fighters to help them. But that wasn't P.J.'s style.

"I fly low and slow and I use glasses," he said, handing Lieutenant Kwon a pair of field glasses. He pointed over his shoulder with his thumb at a flight of F-100s coming back and landing. "I see and hear what they can't. I 'm really in contact with this crazy war." There were patches on the skin of his Bird Dog, places where ground fire had shot through it. "You can bet they don't fire at me when I'm just look'n around. They know better. I fly with these windows open," he said, showing us how the side ones gave him plenty of open air. "Ground fire sounds just like popcorn. If I hear that, I'm going to rain fire down on 'em. So, the only time they open up on me is when I'm marking smoke or bringing something in on target."

I told him a story my father loved to tell. He was in World War One, proud that he was on five fronts. He'd seen the early airplanes flying over the lines. Once in the Argonne, some crazy guy had fired at a German plane that had flown over, and it wasn't long after until their unit took the worst artillery barrage they'd ever gotten. "The old Dutchman had given the guns our position," Pop would say.

P.J. liked that. "Things haven't changed a bit have they?"

When our flight line tour was over, P.J. dropped us off at the Q. He wasn't going to fly for the next couple of days since he had some down time coming. We agreed we'd get together sometime for a drink. He was the only GI on Phu Cat we really knew.

"They'll have you over to the Ton Ton Club very soon I'm sure," he laughed. "I'll bet I see you there."

Yes, the Ton Ton Club. That was the place just outside the southern part of the base, near the Korean compound. Ton Ton was also the call sign of the FACs who flew Bird Dogs out of Phu Cat. Our new friend P.J. had a big piece of the war.

We just hung around the VOQ. All of the newly purchased stereo sets were plugged in and playing away. There were about six of them going at once, no two records were the same. It was really sound city, mixed in with the takeoffs and landings out on the busy flight line. But Lee and his two majors weren't there to enjoy the BX purchases of their young officers. A note on my door told me they were out with Lieutenant Colonel O and for all of us to wait around for them to return. O and some of his Tigers wanted to tour the Phu Cat area and then go to a party. I had a feeling we'd soon be seeing the action at Ton Ton.

In the meantime, I retreated to my room to read. I had bought a *Playboy* at the BX the day before. Fantasy time.

30

Ton-Ton Madness

About four in the afternoon, an old bus pulled up in front of the Q. It looked like a school bus, but it was painted camouflage instead of the familiar rural route yellow. We were off for a tour.

Colonel Lee and I sat in the front of the bus, with Lieutenant Colonel O in the seat ahead of ours. With him were Majors Choe, Son, and Hong. They all wore the Tiger patch; they all spoke English.

I saw even more of Phu Cat from the bus window. We rode through the flight line area again. P.J. had taken good care of that area. To the Korean area of the base. Though it had the same architecture, the insides of the buildings reminded me of Lee's office areas. But these were ROK army troops, not ROKAF. Nonetheless the teapots were chugging away, despite the hot, dry weather. The Republic of Korea colors proudly flew in front of the HQ building.

Inside, we were briefed on the Song Cau area by several ROK Army captains. To my surprise, they even had a detailed engineer's drawing of our little mobile radar compound, plus a set of photographs. They showed a tiny site, with the mobile radar already in place. The rest of the control post was located in three trailers, and I could see we'd also carry on a lot of business in heavy tents.

Most of the briefing was in Korean. Just like old times, Ko translated for me. Again like old times, the briefer would occasionally throw in something in English for me, just so I'd have face. "A person from the Monkey Mountain control will join you sometime thisa month, Captain Widman. They will contact you." That was a good piece of info, I thought. At least I knew somebody was thinking about what we were doing. The guidance at Phu Cat had been zilch.

After tea and a lot of handshaking, we got back on the bus and drove right out of the gate. For the first time we were really in Vietnam. My first impressions were mixed: it was both a beautiful and a sad place. The village outside the gate was filthy. It was a thrown-together affair of shacks and shops, with a wide dirt road running through it. Like so many places I'd seen in Korea, the street and side streets had that same hustle and bustle of bikes, motorcycles, and small trucks. It was third world panorama I'd gotten used to, but this place looked shabbier. There weren't many cars. Traffic was mostly military.

The people wore outfits that looked like pajamas; I'd been expecting that. Lots of the women wore the conical straw hats. Some of the women carried bundles of sticks or soda cans on their shoulders. Kids were everywhere. These were a poor, poor people. They looked so native. There were people in the Asian squatting position everywhere, eating out of bowls or just watching the traffic go by. They looked pathetic.

Once in a while, you'd see someone a bit better off. Pretty girls were sprinkled in with all of the peasant looking characters. They wore these form fitting pants outfits called *ao dai*, with long black hair falling down their backs. Ko mumbled something to the others every time he saw one of them walking down the side of the road or peddling her bicycle. I was relieved to see them; they were like a ray of hope, a piece of color and life, in the middle of impoverished confusion.

There were monks, too. They wore these bright orange robes and walked together in pairs and threes. Bald as billiard cues, they gave the mass of humanity some color and character. For the most part it was a passive poor humanity I saw, walking with a load of sticks or squatting in the dirt. Some of the glances they gave us weren't the friendliest I'd ever seen either.

We rode out of the town and hit the countryside. I saw beautiful rice paddies on either side of the road, and that picked up my spirits a little. We passed a lot of ROK Army traffic. Two trucks passed us with a whoosh; I thought I actually saw guys tied to the front bumpers and grilles.

"Colonel O, sir," I said, "was man on front of those trucks?"

He laughed and nodded. "They are the vee cee our people capture. Maybe they will help other vee cee to know that Tiger will keep this area clear."

I saw that a few more times. I couldn't tell if the men tied to the bumpers were alive or not.

O was studying my face. "Sometime I take you to village where the vee cee hava tied women and children upside down and cut their gut out to hang. In Tiger area vee cee are treated the same."

I know that sight would make an impression on my mind. Those trucks would soon pass through the village back there, I thought. No wonder we got some strange stares, as well as extra good service at the O club!

The high point of the tour was an ancient stone tower standing alone out in the countryside, just on the edge of some thick jungle. We all piled out and walked to it, enjoying the chance to stretch.

"Colonel O wanted us to see because this one is very old observation place put here to warn about enemy," Lee said. "Like our Crystal Dragon, they build to see for distance, and transmit by fire and sign the message of what they see." These towers were built every so many miles a thousand years or so before our bus ever came pulling up. Made of precisely cut stone, they were very tall. I thought about the people we had seen in the village, about their makeshift shack town. It seemed to me that the quality of Vietnamese life had deteriorated since their long ago ancestor warriors had put those towers up. Yet one thing had remained constant: war dominated the scene.

We all climbed the ancient stone steps and took a turn at the same view a long ago warrior had on his turn at watch. Looking out across the countryside, you could see for miles. You could see the next tower up the line. All around was the green of this exotic place and the beautiful mountains in the distance. Somewhere in those mountains was a thing called the Oregon Trail, a famous VC infiltration route. Even as I looked out on the expanse of bush and mountain, I knew that there could well be a hostile force there, perhaps looking back at the roundeye standing in the tower. I turned quickly to the east, to see if I could make out the ocean. The Koreans were still staring west, snapping pictures with their new Japanese cameras from the American BX in Vietnam.

Then we had a picnic at the foot of the tower. O's bus driver broke out boxes of American canned drinks, canned fruit, dried fish, rice crackers, and even fresh oranges. I ate everything except the fish. We sat there on the grass, Army and ROK trucks passing by us out on the road, talking in little groups.

"When Lieutena Colonel O and I are small boy in Seoul city, we always say we will travel," Colonel Lee said to me, slugging down his Coke.

"Well you made it," I said, and they all laughed.

When we pulled back onto the road, you knew it was time to go. It wasn't dark yet by any means, but you could feel the night coming. You wouldn't want to be out by that tower at night. Whatever the sunlight pushed back into the recesses of green surely came back with the dark. All day long I had heard an occasional thud and bang; it was starting to get louder, closer as we left. I was in a war zone; I was in Viet-fucking-Nam.

We came back to the village, but we turned in the opposite direction of the Phu Cat south gate. The side street we did take took us a little way until we pulled up in front of a building made from everything you could imagine: mostly it was cement, wood, and tin. It said "Ton Ton Club" over the doorway, and the loud music coming from it told you that it was already crowded and jumping.

"Thisa is my Officer Club," O said.

"You don't worry about this place because we are friends of the Tiger Division," Lee whispered to me. I thought about the old joke that has Tonto reassuring the Lone Ranger as they walk into a Comanche powwow.

I had been a fan of the comic strip "Terry and the Pirates" all of my life. As soon as I walked into the Ton Ton, I thought I had walked right into the Sunday funnies. There were strange characters going in and coming out. You stopped first in a long hallway, not to take off your shoes, but to take off your fatigue shirt or whatever you were wearing that showed your military rank. There were hundreds of hooks and hanging posts. On them were assorted Korean, American, and Vietnamese officer tops, plus some outfits I couldn't begin to identify. The point was that you went in there with only a T-shirt on, passing under a sign that said, "Leave your rank and your problems at the door," in English and Hangul characters.

When you went through the door, you were hit with the smell of smoke and booze. It was a big place, long bar on one side and actual turning fans up on the ceiling. Everywhere were men in T-shirts, a lot of them green. Hats, strangely enough, seemed to be okay, though the only ones you saw were either the fatigue or go-to-hell jungle cowboy brand. There were round tables to sit at, lots of them, and a dance floor in front of a stage area. A local Vietnamese hard rock band was playing a strange version of what seemed like "Foxy Lady" up there, and a couple of local go-go girls were bumping and grinding, with only white boots on.

It was crowded as hell. You had to turn sideways to get in and move toward the bar. I followed Lee and O; folks did open a bit of a path for them. It closed rather quickly as I tried to dash through its tail. We finally made it to an empty table; I was surprised to see one available. O was seating Lee and the two majors and very politely put me down in a chair, too. Ko and the lieutenants didn't follow. I saw them disappear into the bar crowd.

The music was loud; the talk was loud. The languages were mixed. I knew Lee and the rest were talking in Korean, but there was such a din that I didn't think I could hear them if I tried. The place was just so fascinating that all I really wanted to do was look.

There were Vietnamese dollies everywhere. They wore black or red high heels and wonderfully sexy slit skirts. They were sitting on bar stools, showing it all, or sitting on laps. Customers could put their hands right up skirts without fear of public censure. Crotch rubbing was an okay thing. Out on the dance floor, pelvises locked and rubbed in time with the beat. The place made me want to smoke, drink, dance, and fuck all at the same time.

O was saying something to me, but I couldn't hear him. I put my hand to my ear. "He say, what do you think of his club?" Lee relayed.

"Tell him . . . tell him," I literally yelled, "I think this is where the action is."

O nodded and laughed at the message. I really didn't want to talk; I wanted to watch and maybe even get involved.

A three-ring circus, there was literally an act going on in every part of the Ton Ton. In most cases, the patrons were as fascinating as the girls and the band put together. I let my eyes scan back and forth, taking it all in. They watered from the smoke, which also contributed to an eerie fog-like atmosphere. The smoke caught light, softened it, and made the whole place seem like an old film noir movie or a night at the seashore in the fog.

Above the bar there was a huge homemade display. Central to it was a large photograph. You could tell it was an enlargement, probably done in a military photo shop. The reconnaissance boys had that kind of equipment. This photo was of an Asian man standing in front of two microphones; it was a shot of some sort of press presentation. One mike said KBS, and I knew that was Korean Broadcasting System; the other said MBS, for the Mutual Broadcasting System that had been one of my speech teachers when I was very young. But the guy in front of the mike wasn't a happy broadcaster; his hands were obviously tied behind his back. He wore beat-up army clothing and his face was strained.

That big photo was pasted on large white poster board, the kind you used for briefings. Above the photo was printed:

4 Oct 1966—Tiger Division, 9th Company, Chae Koo Battalion. Conquer the fortress. Attack jungle zone north of Mt. Phu Khat. 35 Vietcong killed & 14 Soviet-made rifle captured.

Then, under the photograph it said:

Interesting statement by prisoner Quing Dien: "When the Tiger division, far more effective than American or Vietnam forces, come to attack, we are ordered to escape:"

Over to the right was a little scoreboard affair:

Number of battles	120 (We come Oct. 22, 1965)
Enemy Killed (confirmed)	2,839
Enemy Killed (presumed)	1,000
POW (Captured)	683
POW (Surrendered)	125
Total Contacts	4,767

Not a bad record, I thought. They had fought guys who carried Soviet-made weapons before.

The whole thing was framed in bamboo. Under it the bartenders poured drinks and the three groups of soldiers drank, enjoyed camaraderie together, and fondled the tits and cunts of Vietnam's little daughters.

"Well, I knew you'd turn up," a voice and a firm hand on my shoulder said together. It was P.J., wearing a white T-shirt that said "Fuck communism" on it.

I introduced P.J. all around, but he and O needed no introduction. Through the maddening noise, O yelled in my ear, "P.J. is a very good man for Tigers. He brings in good air fire for us."

We put down lots of beer. They had cold OB and Crown, as well as most American brands. There was any kind of hard stuff, too. But I stuck with suds.

With a "Come on, I'll introduce you to some people," P.J. took me out of my chair and brought me to the bar, right under the scoreboard and the blank eyes of prisoner Dien's photograph. There I met more Ton Ton FACs: Danny Shoup from Columbus, Al Green from Boston, and Don Pitts, a black guy, from Atlanta. There was also this big guy, Carl Rowan, an F-100 misty pilot from Detroit, who wore a T-shirt that said "I am the God of Hell Fire." When he introduced me, P.J. yelled, "He has that on his helmet, too."

Ko and Yi were standing by them. More introductions. They thanked P.J. for the tour of the flight line and sprung for beers. Ko was already so smashed he couldn't get his wad of MPC out of his pocket. These guys were now wealthy because of their raised salaries, at least while they were in Vietnam. I was glad they were enjoying it.

I met some VNAF F-5 pilots, who were TDY to Phu Cat. P.J. brought me over to them and said, "I want you to meet Norm Whitman, call sign the Appo Kid." That startled me. "Don't look so surprised," he said, laughing. "A good reputation stays with a guy. Your handle always follows you on the next flight in."

Captains Nam, Manh, and Kha were weaving back and forth under the weight of many rounds of gin and tonic. That made their little high voices sound like one of those water bird whistles you got as a kid. They told me I had just missed seeing Nguyen Cao Ky, the hotshot fighter pilot Vice President of Vietnam; he had just left the place, leaving them with a fistful of MPC to buy drinks with. Now I had a beer in one hand and a gin and tonic in the other.

The Vietnamese guys were okay. Their English wasn't as good as the Korean lieutenants, but all of us communicated very well. The booze helped. They were dedicated to retaking the North. In fact, Manh was from a northern province. He had hundreds of missions under his belt. Each of them shared his zeal for uniting Vietnam. These guys didn't look at all like they came from the same country as the poor bastards out on the street, squatting and staring at the passing traffic. There were two kinds of Vietnamese: very poor and very rich. The guys who drank in the Ton Ton ran the country.

P.J. had gotten a black marking pen from somewhere and made me stand at attention while he wrote on my T-shirt. There were a number of spur-of-the-moment, hand-printed T-shirts around the place. When he was done, I looked down and read it as best as I could, my eyes not being able to focus too well on sloppy upside-down printing. It said: The Appo Kid.

I got smashed and talked about how great Korea was and how happy I was to be getting smashed in the Ton Ton. When I get in that state, time seems to evaporate. Night and day don't exist. Temperature and lighting remain constant. Ton Ton was eternal. Drinks went down like water.

They cranked up the band's speakers several decibels louder, now making conversation even more impossible. "P.J., is this place always this hectic," I asked at the top of my voice.

"Yeah, this group ought to audition for the sixth PsyOp."

"What's that?"

"It's the psycho warfare boys. They make these tapes that the choppers play out over the jungle at night. It's loud and creepy. My favorite is one called 'The Wandering Soul.' Scares the be-Jesus out of 'em." Then he turned and went to talk with his flying buddies who were now gathered at the end of the long bar.

I was tone deaf and oblivious to most everything around me, but there was one guy a couple of bar stools away from me that seemed to want my attention. When I focused, he was staring right at me. I tried to ignore him, but when I'd check my three o'clock position, he'd held his position, giving me a steady evil eye. Finally, when I met his stare for more than a glance, he said, "Fuck'n clown," with a menacing grin. "Fuck'n clown," he taunted.

Then I was distracted from the opposite direction. At my nine o'clock a little long-haired dollie in a red slip dress snuggled up close and wrapped herself around my left arm. "Hey, Joe," she smiled. "You wanna buy me a drink?"

The legs get me every time, the legs and the high heels. "Sure," I said. "What's your name?"

"Me Dottie," she said. "Give me MPC. I buy." So I just reached in my pocket and handed her a bunch of disorganized military bucks. She turned to the bartender, got a fancy cocktail glass of whatever. She didn't hand me back any change.

"You likie Don Don?" she asked.

"Yes," I said, running my hands all over her crossed legs. "Nice people here."

"You tink Dottie nice?"

"You've got great legs, Dottie," I said.

"You wanna rub your dick on my leg?"

She didn't waste any time. No long conversations. No shared life histories or Zodiac signs.

"I suck youa ball for you. You cana fuck me. Do anyting," she said, resting her hand on my crotch.

"Hey!" she said. "Whatcha wanna do?"

I slid my hand further up her mini skirt.

"Not for free. You sposed to do that in my house. You *So Moui*," she said, giving me the Vietnamese rating that was equivalent to the Korean numbah ten.

Christ, I had to keep her from making a scene. I put my finger to my lips. "Shoosh. It's all okay. Be calm, Dottie. Look. Money, money, money here for more drinks," I said, pulling it out of my wallet.

That instantly calmed her down. She did an emotional one eighty.

Christ, I thought, how embarrassing. I looked around again to see if they were preparing to turn a spotlight on our little act. No, too much noise, too much confusion. Not a soul had noticed our little domestic scene, not even the asshole who'd been pulling my chain.

Counting the money, she said, "You let me keep all?"

"Yes, please, you keep."

"I get you sex excited, yes?" she asked with a tinge of pride in her voice. She put her hand back on my crotch. "Hey, little mista one eye, you there?" she said, talking to and rubbing my crotch.

Bringing her hand back up, she rubbed her finger and thumb together. "Come on my house. I give you one free fuck from me."

She reached on the bar and got a pack of cigarettes. She got one going with a Zippo lighter that had a 7th Cavalry insignia on it.

All of a sudden P.J. was back. "Found a friend, huh?" he said.

"I make him tall," she said, putting the butt out in an ashtray that looked like a skull.

"Boy, she knows how to keep a secret," he said. Like it was nothing at all, he added, "Spend enough time in here and you build up your tolerance to their, ah, come-on tactics."

"He come wid me now," she said to P.J.

"No, no, he go with me. You say bye, bye."

"Dottie, It was great to talk with you," I said, pushing off the barstool.

"I get you next time. You get one free. You not *So Moui*." Then Dottie disappeared into the crowd like she was never there.

P.J. took my arm. "Look, Colonel Lee and some of the others left. I promised Lee and Colonel O I'd get you and the lieutenants rounded up and back in one piece."

"But let's have just one more beer before we go," I said, hoisting an imaginary glass in the air.

"I'll drink to that," he said with a wink.

The two of us bellied up and ordered OBs. My eyes once more went up to the photo of prisoner Dien. The score hadn't changed.

"Fuck'n clown." I couldn't believe it, but there was that mocking voice again. P.J. heard it, but didn't turn around. He just gave me a sidelong glance.

"Fuck'n chicken shit clown."

"P.J.," I said, "do you know where the lieutenants are now?"

"Yeah," he said, pointing over to a table.

"Well, let's get them and get out of here. I don't want any problems."

"Hey, clown." I ignored it. "Ho, clown. You clown," the voice said. So I turned around to look at my taunter. When I did, he smiled and toasted me with his glass. Red-faced guy with pockmarks all over his cheeks.

"That's right, clownie. Let me see your clown face."

Some of the other bar standers were interested by now. That created a small quiet zone where we were. I started shaking just a little.

"Do I know you?" I said.

"No, I just remember watching you on Super Circus. You're the clown who blew the ringmaster. You ate the elephant shit."

I'd never seen the guy before. He was a total stranger. But he had singled me out, and he had decided I'd be the target of his dumb-assed comments. That was the part I hated. The guy was silly. No, he was evil. Here he was, sitting in a bar at Phu Cat, saying stupid things to me. There were thousands of VC in the country, and he was giving me a hard time.

"Yes, clownie. He's a mad clown now."

I had to size this up quickly. I was drunk; he was drunk. I thought I had him in size by a little, but that wouldn't matter a damn bit if he were some kind of a ranger or infantryman. His pants looked Air Force, though. But I couldn't tell. This T-shirt thing hampered the sizing-up process.

"The clown is an A-P-P-O Kid." He said, spelling out P.J.'s designer T-shirt artwork.

My advantage was right now, I thought. I was on my feet; he was on the barstool. He wasn't going to let me alone. So, I decided I'd kick his ass. I decided to do it because he was a bully. I prayed he wasn't a kung fu expert. In the Ton Ton, the chances were he might be. But I gambled.

In my neighborhood I had learned one great lesson: take advantage of the element of surprise. No reason why it wasn't a good principle here, too. I pulled out my wallet, but dropped it on the floor.

"Awkward clownie," he said. He was watching me like a hawk. But he didn't move.

I picked up the wallet with my left hand and grabbed the leg of his chrome barstool with my right. Then I pulled that stool toward me with everything I had. Bam. He tumbled down on his back, smacking his head once on the bar and again on this step that ran underneath it. Somehow the stool landed on top of him and while he struggled to get it off of him, his overturned glass ran a stream of beer on him. He was like a June bug turned over on his back.

"Man down here," I yelled, and made a beeline for the door. Out in the hall I grabbed my fatigue top, and it wasn't long before P.J., Kwon, Yi, and Ko followed.

"Is this everybody?"

"Yes," Ko said.

"Then let's haul ass."

We piled into P.J.'s jeep and went back through the south gate of Phu Cat. It had been quite a day. That would be enough of the Ton Ton, I thought.

31

Operational

The next time I saw the school bus we were loading everything we had on it. In went our suitcases, the stereos, and the china, along with lots of other booty. We were on our way to Song Cau. Crystal Dragon was for real now.

P.J. was there to see us off.

Colonel Lloyd, too. He gave me a big yellow envelope. "This will fill in the gaps," he said. "It came in from MAAG down in Saigon."

P.J. motioned me aside. He handed me a brown paper bag. "This is an extra I got ahold of. You're a fast man with a barstool, but this might help out better down country," he said grinning. Inside the bag was a beautiful .45 and holster set. "This belonged to one hell of a great guy who didn't make it back from a mission. Don't shoot yourself in the leg," he said, as I got on the bus.

"Don't worry," I said. "I'll never put any bullets in it."

Our bus joined up with a regular convoy out on the highway. We'd take the famous Route 19 to Qui Nhon and then Highway One to Song Cau. Lee and I sat side by side. Lieutenant Colonel O was in a jeep in front of the bus. We all applauded when we rode out the south gate.

"I hear that you uphold Tiger tradition in the Ton Ton club," Lee said with a smile.

"Yes, sir, it turns out I knocked down a big bad finance officer who decided to sleep once he hit the bar floor," I said, laughing. "So the first dragon I meet here was just a paper one."

P.J. had heard that the dumb ass had chipped his elbow when he hit the hard floor. Though he had passed out from the fall and the booze, the word was he was looking for the guy who had pulled the stool out from under him. He was going to have a lot of looking to keep him busy.

"Well," said Lee, still thinking about what I'd said, "at least you face your dragons. Some man never do."

Maybe, I thought. The ones on barstools. But I still had dragons in myself that needed slaying, and those I was still too afraid to meet head-on. They were the ones that gave me the bad dreams in the middle of the night and the shakes early in the morning. I thought about what Canada had said, and then on that road headed for Song Cau I promised myself that I wouldn't drink anything for as long as I would stay in Vietnam. I knew I wanted to make it forever.

The ride down to Qui Nhon was beautiful. As we traveled, the sea got closer. It didn't take long because it was only twenty miles out of Phu Cat. We came to it from high ground, and it was a beautiful sight. There were established houses, and you could identify the French influence. It was a seaport. There were big oil storage tanks, supplied from tankers. The fuel was then pumped inland via a big pipeline. We fed the war from ports like Qui Nhon.

We didn't have time to look around. I was sorry, too, because there seemed to be a lot to explore. The people, the houses, and the shops looked better. There were passenger cars and the walkers along the streets looked more like businessmen and folks with a purpose. There were poor among them. But this town was happier. It seemed more alive.

We turned out on Number One and followed the coast southward. That was a slower going, thirty-five mile ride. We passed a lot of military traffic, and there were also actual marching troops out on the road. Most were Koreans, or ARVN, but once I spotted a group of American army types. I waved at them as we went by, and a sergeant gave me a thumbs-up sign. His lieutenant looked at me as if I was crazy.

Out in the ocean I saw a lot of ships. They were bringing in supplies and putting the larger vehicles of war on the Vietnamese roads. I guessed they were ours, or under contract to the U.S. war effort. "Some of those ships are ROE Navy," Lee reminded me. Yes, they had brought our radar to us. It was waiting just down the road.

It wasn't long before we drove through a small village. There was a ROK Army checkpoint there. We had passed through several of those on both roads. It was a barbed wire affair with a gatehouse. The guard in the shack stopped us and then put the gate up. There were plenty of soldiers there with rifles to stop those not so recognizable. But we always got a snappy salute and wave through for our six-vehicle convoy. We, too, had a couple of trucks filled with Tiger riflemen, just in case we met resistance.

"Here is my squadron," Lee said when we got to the end of a dirt road.

I saw the radar sail, smaller than Tolsan's, and the three trailers. There was even an arch over the road. It said "Det #1, 771 ROKAF A C & W Squadron. *Ad Sum.*" If only Paul could have seen it. Maybe I'd get Ko to take a picture with his new BX camera and send it. I still hadn't bothered to buy one. Getting there, just like that, out of our temporary Phu Cat BOQ was another mind-blowing experience. Everything was set up. When we got off the bus, we only had to walk to our positions. It was Crystal Dragon Control ready to go.

There were three Americans already there to greet us. They were the Air Force Communications Service team that would stay with us, put us on the air, and maintain the equipment. Captain Al Cobb was the honcho. He had three staff sergeant maintenance troops with him: Ray Ellsworth, comm; Don Hammer, radar; and Dick Butcher, generator and scope repair. They were all volunteers, left behind to keep things running. The installation team had already gone.

Cobb took us through the vans, and we covered every inch of the equipment. The radarscopes, UPA 48s, were just a tad different from our Tolsan UPA 35s, but I could tell the team felt comfortable with them anyway. They couldn't wait to start controlling for real. Everyone took a turn sitting at the scopes. There were four scope positions: two in the control van and another two in the communications van. A third van housed the radar gear. Each trailer van was about fourteen feet long and seven feet high. Our radar sail, the antenna, was just to the right of the trailer cluster. It sat on a four-legged pedestal. Everything was powered by a diesel generator. Compact and portable, you could set up one of these mobile radars anywhere.

The Tigers would be our perimeter guard and security. We'd have about a dozen or so with us all the time. We were going to have Korean Army cooks, too. Our mess hall was a sturdy tent with a wooden floor and sides. You could raise the canvas walls, but there was still a mosquito net there to protect us.

We'd sleep in tents just like it, but they were partitioned off into rooms for the senior guys. I'd have my own little room, as did Lee, Park, and Moon. Ko and the lieutenants would bunk in one big tent.

There was a headquarters tent, too. The installation team had put down flagstone walks that connected all of the tents and trailers. Everything looked very neat and in very good condition. It was the typical Tactical Air Command forward airmobile radar control post. I had studied about that at radar school at Tyndall Air Force Base, though I never thought I'd be living on one in Song Cau, Vietnam. It was like a super Boy Scout camp; for two months or so it would be home base.

Cobb was a great guy. He was a tall blonde fellow from Salt Lake City, Utah. I invited him to come over and talk while I unpacked. He filled me in on how it was to live in a tent at Song Cau. I couldn't get over the dressers and big closets they had in my room. There was electricity and even one of those mildew bulbs in the big wooden closet.

"Every once in a while the bugs get heavy, so you'll want to check your netting," he said, rubbing his hand gently alongside the heavy cheesecloth stuff. "But when the wind blows, you'll batten down the hatches." We were right on the West China Sea; Song Cau was, in fact, a little knob that stuck out into the ocean.

My counterparts wasted no time moving in. Cobb and I smiled when we heard a stereo go on. It was the Beatles.

"What are they like?" he asked.

"There's not a loser in the bunch. The Colonel's a gem."

"Well, he's going to like his radar. The thing works really good, Norm. They gave us the best kit they had on hand."

It did work well. The next day we turned everything on, and Crystal Dragon had eyes. We could see out a good two hundred miles or so, just enough to fuel any planes that were in our area. As a matter of fact, it turned out that we'd work with the U.S. Navy, too. The big envelope I had gotten from Colonel Lloyd told me that the F-18 Hornets flying off carriers would contact us on the way out and back. And, of course, we'd also work with the F-100s out of Phu Cat. Since they took off with minimum fuel, we'd help with the fill-ups prior to target runs. There would be plenty of business for us. But we'd start with single flight-follow.

I also had a "U.S. Personnel Eyes Only" document that told me we'd be monitored on frequency in the event we fucked up. But I didn't think we'd screw the pooch.

As the days passed, we checked everything out. We started putting a crew on every day. In the ops van we had two control scopes, so we'd put two lieutenants on duty in the morning and two in the afternoon. If Ko and I and Moon wanted to bring up a senior director scope, we could fire up the two positions in the comm van. Lee would sit in the ops van.

Cobb served as Major Park's counterpart. They had both attended the same radar maintenance officer school at Kessler Air Force Base in Mississippi, so there was instant rapport there. The team/counterpart concept was working out beautifully.

On 20 December 1967 we made contact with our first fighter. It was one of the F-100s from Phu Cat, assigned to us for two hours. Lieutenant Kwon was the controller given the honor of controlling the first flight-follow. It was quite an event when we heard this voice say, "Hello, Crystal Dragon Control, this is Dora zero-three." Ko tooled him all over the sky, testing out the radio frequencies, radar, and the IFF paint. We even had a height-finder radar that gave us the altitude of anything flying in the area. Everything worked.

In fact, Cobb said, "This has got to be a first. Nothing goes this good."

From then on we got into a routine and worked our way up, gradually adding more responsibilities. Lee was always there anytime we were performing live operations, and we kept our radar on and stayed on guard frequency when we weren't. More and more, the Navy threw flight-follow from ship-to-land at us. They were coded Neptune missions. All we really did was watch and record the progress of the birds as they left the carrier for the target, but it was damn important for those guys that someone was watching. Every once in a while, fewer birds would come back than we had followed inland. That, and the constant thud and boom off in the distance, reminded us that this was not practice.

On 23 December we were buzzed by an O-1E. It wasn't long before we got a call on guard. "Hello, Crystal Dragon, this is Ton Ton zero-niner."

"Ah, roger, zero-niner," Ko answered. "Go ahead."

"Roger. Relay message to Appo Kid that P.J. will be down with Christmas dinner tomorrow along with Santa Claus. Over."

I wrote out a response for Ko to relay on notepad paper. "Roger. He say 'Ba Humbugs' but you come anyway."

Early Christmas morning three U.S. vehicles descended upon us, escorted, of course, by a Tiger contingency. It was old P.J., all right, but Colonel Canada and the Korean Air Force brass were with him. That, I guessed, was the Santa part. Good, soft way to pull inspection on us, I thought. Do it in the name of the birth of the Messiah. But we looked good, anyway, though the big stand-down had really taken hold. Nothing was flying. Both sides were getting ready for their holidays.

"Merry Christmas, Norm," Canada said, handing me a bunch of letters from Angie. They had all gone to Tolsan-Do. P.J. gave me two boxes. I hadn't escaped the Yule Tide depression. Home had found me on the coast of Vietnam.

Lee was really proud to see General Dai. We all walked around as a group, getting comments like "most impressive" from Canada when Lee would brief our progress.

"Thanks, pal, for letting me know," I whispered to P.J. while the others took a look at our radar.

"Come on, Kid, this made it all painless," he laughed. It turned out that P.J. and Canada were good friends; the old boy network never escaped you.

The real surprise package was none other than Lieutenant Bailey from Monkey Mountain, Oyster's classmate. "You only have the refueling missions to get under your belt, Colonel Lee," Canada had said. "So they sent down the Lieutenant here to help you cut your teeth." That was fine, but because of who Bailey was, I felt just a little weird. Oyster was something I didn't want to think of while I was where I was.

They did literally bring down Christmas dinner. It had been prepared up in Phu Cat, put in coolers and boxes and tins, and our Korean mess boys only had to heat it up and reconstitute it a bit. The cooking instructions were in Korean Hangul. So we had us a real feast, mixing traditional Western Yule plates with fancy Korean holiday rice cakes and soup. I knew Angie would send a tree, so I opened up the box I guessed it was in, and we had a three-foot, honest-to-God American Christmas tree on the table. She never forgot.

Though there was wine, I passed. I saw Canada give me a raised eyebrow look when I passed it by. "Trying to lose weight," I said to him.

"Good, get good and lean," he said, raising his glass.

Once the tables were cleared away, we somehow got into impromptu speeches. Then Ko led "Arirang." After that, the GIs all sang a couple of Christmas carols.

Bailey was a little quiet. He really didn't know the crowd. We were cronies; that was evident. So I changed seats.

"Chuck, I was a good friend of Andy Packer's," I said.

"Yes, sir, I thought you were. He wrote me about you. I was going to tell you that he really put a lot of stock in you and the chaplain . . ."

"Yes, Father Fisher."

"Yes, sir, that was the one he said."

We just kind of sat for a moment, not knowing what to say next. I tried to think of something, but I rejected every lead because he'd know I'd read the letters. That was legal, of course. But I didn't want to use that info. It didn't seem right.

"Sir, you know Oyster wasn't really cut out for the Academy or any of this. He only came because of his dad. Did you know about his dad?"

"No," I said, concentrating on his words over the noise of "God Rest You Merry Gentlemen."

"Well, his dad lost a leg in a B-66 pile-up in the fifties. He was forced to retire and work in the fishing industry there in Virginia. He wanted Oyster to finish what he started."

"He really tried then, didn't he?"

"That made him finish the zoo. But Andy always said that he and his father should have traded. His dad would come out to the Academy and talk about flying, about the Air Force, and Andy would talk about fishing."

He was a good kid. Later he got up and recited "The Night Before Christmas." Oyster would have loved it; it had funny verses, a parody of the original.

Our guests left early and planned to stay the night up in Qui Nhon. Bailey would be ours for several weeks. He would give our guys some chalk and blackboard training first, and then we'd get into the refueling business as the stand-down wrapped up. Everybody was happy.

When Canada left, he had one of his famous parting shots for me: "Norm, I hope the finance officer up in Phu Cat with his arm in a cast never finds out who the Appo Kid is. You'll never get paid again."

"Let's not tell him, sir," I said, saluting.

"Just stay lean," he said. "Think thin, as they say."

In early January, Lieutenant Colonel O got Lee and me and took us up to the town of Song Cau. It was just a little place, but there was good shopping for local souvenirs. We couldn't really travel without a Tiger escort, and I didn't much want to anyway. But Tet, the big Nguyen Dan New Year's was almost upon us, and VC activity was drying up. The big thing was to buy these glazed pottery elephants in Vietnam, and there was a factory in Song Cau that turned them out.

There was a lot of port activity up there, too. I almost didn't believe my eyes when I found a U.S. Navy Lieutenant Commander and a Navy Chief Petty Officer assigned there on a permanent basis. The commander was the advisor to the harbormaster, and between them they coordinated thousands of tons of shipping a month. I was all excited to see him, but he turned out to be a big shit.

Lee and O dropped me off at his little office while they went off to arrange something. He grudgingly let me sit down for a cup of real coffee. "You with the bunch down at Song Cau, huh, captain?"

"Yes, sir," I said.

"Well, they're managing to get enough U.S. Government property out of here, too, the fucking crooks." He was looking out on the harbor.

"Hey, wait a minute, Commander," I said, putting down the coffee. "What are you talking about?"

"Come on, mister," he said.

"What are you talking about?" I said again. Louder.

"Look, every single week the ROK Navy pulls up out there, and the Tigers and every other Korean outfit in this place send truckload after truckload of air-conditioners, refrigerators, freezers, car parts, furniture, and machines out to those ships."

He looked back out on the ocean.

"That's not even to mention everything they can buy and steal and cart off from every BX in the country. Christ, they're sending everything to Korea as fast as we can bring it in."

I thought about it. I thought about what it meant. "How can you prove a thing like that?"

"God, the one guy you're with is the biggest offender in this area. He operates an elephant factory here. Sends out all kinds of crap for sale back in Seoul."

I stood up. "Thanks for the coffee," I said.

"Tell your friends I don't much like crooks," he said. "Don't worry about it. I have a hunch our guys think it's a cheap enough price to pay for fifty-thousand Korean soldiers."

"Boy, I can see why they picked you."

"You know what they always tell me?"

"What?"

"Write your Congressman, swab."

I shut the door and walked away fast.

On the way to the jeep I picked up a gang of little boys. "Hey, Joe," they'd say. "You got gum? You got candy?" God, I thought, that was a line out of World War Two. It was the "Joe" thing that made it sound that way. The kids in Korea would say, "Hello. Hello. You got candy?" You heard that in Seoul.

This older kid came up and said, "You want good fuck book, Joe? You want picture of fucks?" That was new maybe. Maybe not.

Anyway, I said, "Where candy store. Where buy candy?"

When O and Lee found me, I had just finished passing out my second purchase of all sorts of weird Vietnamese goodies. We had to practically fight my way to the jeep. "Now they will know you," O laughed. It was all very sad.

Further down the road they asked how I enjoyed visiting with the Navy

Commander. "He is a good man, but I think he is too close to this thing to see good in it." Lee turned around and nodded. They always gave me the backseat, the place of honor.

Being sober at Song Cau did strange things to me. I was shaky the first couple of days, and then my system got screwed up. I had trouble sleeping. When I did, I'd wake up in a sweat. It was hot, but I think it was from the cold turkey.

By late January I was really feeling good, but I'd get strange dreams. The one that stayed with me for days was not so much a dream with a sequence, but a look at a picture. It was a picture in a book, a big book. In it there was a guy who was posing in a room, sitting on this animal, for lack of a better word. He was sitting on this big thing, and it was standing on an old-fashioned rug in an old-fashioned room. If I had to pick a time period, I'd say the nineteen-twenties.

There was even an old-fashioned lamp in the room. One of those high ones, with a shade that had tassel around it. There were pictures on the walls, too. Old castles and farm scenes. Just what you'd expect to find in a good sitting room, or hotel room in the nineteen-twenties.

It was all in black and white. It had that smoky quality about it. Whitish near the edges.

The guy looked sick. He had circles under his eyes; he was skinny and pale. He had sort of a cowboy outfit on and even a cowboy hat. But it was like a kid's cowboy hat, with a chin string that hung down. The whole outfit was like the kind they used to bring around neighborhoods, taking pictures of children on a pony for a price. There was a quickie cowboy outfit to put on for the picture.

But even though he looked so worn, this guy had a wild look about him. He was happy to pose. Proud of the thing he rode. He looked as if he'd been traveling around on it for years. He looked right into the lens, a bit embarrassed, but proud. Like a guy going upstairs with a beautiful hooker. He knew you saw him, but he wasn't going to come back down on account of that.

This thing he rode. It was furry, but in places the stuffing was falling out. There were bare patches on it. Like an old couch has, or an old stuffed deer head. It had a face, too. It was a human sort of face, with a moustache. It had weird eyes. It had a big smile. The strangest thing was that it had its front leg up in a rakish way, like a burlesque dancer.

Together they looked into the lens, posing for that picture of long ago.

Under the photo it said: "His horse of one thousand delights." When I awoke I was wet with perspiration. It took days to shake off the weird feeling it gave me.

On 23 January the *USS Pueblo* was captured off the coast of North Korea by four patrol boats. I thought about the mission Lee and his countrymen had run the year before when the North tried to take those South Korean fishing boats. This time though, with the *Pueblo*, it was an English language mission. No Korean controllers. No F-5s out of Suwon. Lee could have made the comparison but he didn't. His only comment was, "I am very sorry this happen. It comes at bad time."

Crystal Dragon went on. Not much business because of the stand-down, yet Bailey taught them a lot about control and what they'd do with tanker hitch-ups. It was a review, but good.

O would come down to see us often, filling us in on the war. He and the other Tigers all over the country were confident about sending the North into an armistice position. But he was also worried about the political climate in America. "You people are not fully understand. I think tired of far-off war."

O said that he thought the North was in bad shape. "We keep push, and it will happen. But cannot let up."

"Look for vee cee to give big fight before they fall back into the cave," Lee said.

That night I read and re-read Angie's letters and looked again at all of the crayon pictures I had gotten. The only bad news was that little Mike had knocked out his front tooth riding a bike down a board they had put on the front porch steps. Angie was still saying that whatever I decided would be okay. I had at least decided that I was going to stay off the booze. I set one February as my day to either tell Canada I was going to Hawaii or have my separation orders cut. I knew I was scheduled to leave Vietnam in March. Talk was that maybe they'd replace us all with another Korean crew and keep on doing that. It was still a little half-assed. We had yet to do refuels anyway. All I knew was that I had come a long way since I'd put down on Tolsan-Do for the first time. Outside of being in on something different, the Vietnam gesture was getting boring.

32

Heroes

At 1200 hours on 30 January 1968 I was thinking about Joe E. Brown in the old movie classic, *Showboat*. In that he played this steamboat captain who went around yelling "Happy New Year." He put great emphasis on the "Hap" and then he'd let out "EE" slowly and loudly. I yelled out, "Hap-EE-New Year," just like Joe E. Brown.

Chuck Bailey and I planned out this New Year party for the whole site. Last year on Tolsan-Do, Lee and company had helped me celebrate the Western New Year, so now I thought we'd all celebrate the Vietnamese New Year. Everyone was for it. Celebrate Tet.

We decorated the mess tent, and I bought a bunch of Vietnamese party food up in Song Cau. We had a stereo in there playing away, and Cobb had even wired a TV up earlier for the evening's entertainment. Qui Nhon had American TV shows. Thanks to Cobbs' guys we now could get TV, and Colonel O had supplied the set. Well, at least it wasn't leaving the country. It had been great to see "Bonanza." We were bringing in the Year of the Monkey in style.

Colonel Lee was telling me how the term "Gook" got started. "In the Japanese Army they always sent Korean in first. They fight very hard, like the American Marine. But when islands are captured, they decide maybe to not die for Japanese cause," he said.

Bailey and Cobb were taking this all in as well. Lee was in good form. "So they decide to give up to American." He put his arms up in surrender fashion. "They not know English, but they know word for American in Korean language. It is *mee-gook*."

He stood up for the punch line. "Korean is *han-gook*. American is *mee-gook*."

He went to the far side of the tent and then came running back to us with his hands up.

"They say, '*mee-gook, mee-gook, mee-gook*' to the American soldiers."

We started laughing. His re-creation was the best part. "Then the gee-eye say, 'So you are, gook.'"

He said that at 1245 hours. That was when Ko came running up to the tent from the communications trailer. He shouted something to Lee, and the Colonel went out of there on the run.

"What?" said Bailey.

"Let's get to the trailer," Cobb said, and we all moved out.

Sergeant Ellsworth was working the radio feverishly. We always kept on line with the U.S. Army net out of Qui Nhon. They relayed our fighter instructions, takeoffs, and landings. They could also patch us into Phu Cat directly. Lee was allowed to talk to Tiger on it, too.

"Captain Cobb, sir, it's an alert on the net; the VC just shot up Nha Trang."

We listened to the net as it became more and more active. There was movement reported everywhere. At 0135 Ban Me Thout was attacked in the Central Highlands. "That's not too far away, really," Bailey said.

All around us, the Tiger guard was on alert. Lee was getting reports from their lieutenant every fifteen minutes or so. He told us we'd have their protection, but that everything else in the area was headed for the protection of Qui Nhon. "Happy New Year," Cobb said.

Around 0300 we got a direct call from Phu Cat. The word was that things were happening. We were supposed to put on a crew and monitor the emergency guard channel. We told them we had done that. We had all four scopes up. Lee was in place, too.

Inside the ops trailer we could listen to the radio and monitor guard. Everything was confusion. I suddenly found our political gesture turning sour. I was sleepy, too. "There's coffee in the mess tent," Cobb said. "Yours truly made it for the after-party blues."

"Well, the party's sure as hell over," I said. "I'll bring the pot and some cups."

It was a little weird walking over to the mess tent, but the paths were lighted. The Tiger guards were standing around the compound. When I got there, I poured myself a cup of coffee and sipped it as I tried to figure out how I'd carry the other cups and the pot over there. I was looking for at a tray when I heard Cobb yell, "Norm, they're hitting Qui Nhon . . ." He was yelling from inside the comm trailer. He had the door open, and I could see the reds and glows coming from inside.

Then somebody took a big flash picture of him. It was too much flash because it made everything white. Click. He was captured in the doorway on film. The red inside was drowned out by the light. Firecrackers brought in the Year of the Monkey. I thought maybe our guard was setting them off. My ears were ringing from it all.

Somebody pushed me down. Probably the guy on the barstool. It was a hell of a party.

When it was over, I stood looking at the ops van, turned on its side, spilling out wire and smoke. It had taken a direct hit, right where Colonel Lee had sat. It had blasted him all over the inside walls. Captain Ko, who could climb flagpoles with such beautiful agility, had been crushed into his radarscope. Everyone in the ops van was dead, and the comm van had been blown so far that it was in pieces. It looked like a train wreck. Bailey, Cobb—everyone was dead.

Lieutenant Kwon was sitting next to me on the ground. He was crying and holding his sides. I think he had pushed me down when the whole thing started. Charlie had been so close that they had been able to take direct, deliberate aim on everything. It must have been satchel charges. Charlie knew we would all be in the vans. Only the trip for coffee had taken me away, and the call of nature had saved but one Korean son of Crystal Dragon. He was now crying next to me at first light and holding himself where little chunks of metal had hit him. I had them, too, in an arm and on my legs. My ears weren't working well, either.

The Tigers were walking around, nodding to me. But none of the guards spoke English. We had lost a few of them, too. But I had no way of talking with them. O was surely with the main forces.

I sat down and held Kwon while he cried. I held him for a long time. He was a *han-gook*, and I was a *me-gook*. He was barely conscious, but he gathered up his strength to sit up and say, "I ashamed I not died like my colonel and my friends."

There wasn't anything I could do about any of it. But finally I said, "They are very proud of you. Now you must tell the story of their bravery. You will tell their story in Korea . . . and I will tell the story in America."

Sometime around noon I heard that waffling noise a chopper makes. This Tiger came running to me saying, "Geey-eye. Gee-eye. Gee-eye," and he was pointing out on the road. It was a chopper, a U.S. Army Chinook, painted green. My legs hurt, but I pulled Kwon up and I made him walk over there with me.

When I got to it, pushing Kwon along, the rotors were tearing up the place. Those things make a hell of a wind. Inside was the Navy Commander from Song Cau and a couple of other people strapped in. They were all shouting at me. They were all teeth and shout and they were waving me in. I pointed to Kwon. Somebody shouted, "Korean."

I shouted back, "So he is."

"Okay, hurry up," they yelled. In he went.

I was standing there in that wind, looking around, soldiers looking at me. I was just about ready to get in, and from out of nowhere this young girl handed me a baby. A baby. In all the rotor wind.

She was crying and trying to push it in my arms. Everyone inside was yelling at me. The baby had dirty blonde hair.

I saw the pilot, who was screaming. I made out his words. "Get in now, you dumb shit. We got to get out of here."

It was more lip reading than anything else. I recognized him. Somehow it was my Tolsan chopper jock. It was our guy from the no-gas-on-the island affair. The guy who flew the tours. He sure as hell recognized me.

She was still pressing the baby. She knew the VC would kill it. Hordes of people were coming down the road. The Tigers were good and started to form a circle. One came to pull her back. They wanted to keep the locals away from the chopper so I could get on. Not a thought about themselves.

"You get on. You." I said to her. She didn't understand. There was so much blowing dirt and confusion. I took her by the arm.

Inside the chopper, my Army man was going wild. He wanted out before the crowd caught up with us. The Navy Commander was yelling, too.

I was making her hold her baby tight, and I pointed into the chopper. "You," I said pointing. Then an impulse. I brought the Saint Christopher medal up over my head and put it around the baby's tiny neck. Rimmel's medal. Paul's medal.

That made her understand somehow.

"One seat left," yelled the guy next to the pilot.

"She takes it. She holds the baby," I yelled into the cockpit.

"No."

So I pulled the .45 P.J. gave me and stuck it right up where he could see down the barrel. "I'll shoot, Army. Put her on or else nobody goes."

Pilot looked at that. At me. Then he smiled. "Okay, fuck. Okay. "

As he gave the order, the others helped her and the baby in. "We all saw it. You did this yourself, you dumb fucking bastard."

I still held the gun.

Then she was on and they pulled out of there so fast I closed my eyes to keep them from being sand-blasted away. But I caught a glimpse of pilot through the Plexiglas, laughing and giving me the finger.

I was left standing there with the Tigers. After two tries, I got the damn pistol back into the holster. No bullets anyway.

Highway One could take me to Qui Nhon. O was out on that road somewhere. Truckloads of air-conditioners and freezers would soon be coming by, too. Old P.J. Ton Ton's bound to be airborne.

"I'll just walk out," I heard myself yell.

The Appo Kid was going home. Lean and clean.

Readers Guide

1. Why did the author include scenes like the drugstore "Musical Comedy" in the novel?
2. Why did Norman have such a hard time getting himself to write letters home?
3. Did Major Dubbs have any redeeming qualities?
4. Which senior military officer, either American or Korean, do you think was the best example of a good leader?
5. Explain Adja's relationship with Oyster. Predator? Victim? Prostitute?
6. What did Oyster hope for in his relationship with Adja?
7. Overall, how would you describe the spiritual side of the Catholic missionaries?
8. What, if any, would you point to as Norman's chief strengths as a leader?
9. As a person?
10. Based on the observed behavior of the characters in this novel, how do you think the Koreans who came into contact with them would describe what they saw?
11. Do you think the lobster operation put together by the Tolsan-Do crew was the proper activity for an American military unit?
12. Should there have been a U. S. military-sponsored hunting operation on the island?
13. Was Colonel Lee a hero or a calculating opportunist?
14. Did the characters in this story take advantage of the Korean women they knew? Or did they somehow make life easier for them? Symbiotic?
15. Was Norman prepared for tragedy? Leadership?
16. Was the joint American/Korean military mission on Tolsan-Do critical to the defense of South Korea?

17. How do you think the final scene in Viet Nam will change Norman Whitman?
18. How was Norman shaped by his experiences growing up in Pittsburgh? By college? By Angie?
19. Was being in the military the right choice for Norman?
20. What do the concluding lines—"Lean and clean"—suggest about Norman's future?

www.ingramcontent.com/pod-product-compliance
Lightning Source LLC
Chambersburg PA
CBHW020420030726
47495CB00006B/1598